The explosive —————————————————— hailed as "honestly fabu——————————————————— Cussler, creator of the b——————————————— eries, returns with an a——————————————— rigue featuring the enig——————— ——— action hero Juan Cabrillo . . .

In the remote wastes of Greenland, a young scientist has unearthed an artifact hidden in a cave for a millennium: a 50,000-year-old meteorite known as the Sacred Stone, which possesses potentially catastrophic radioactive power. But the astounding find places him in the crosshairs of two opposing terrorist groups who seek the stone for themselves.

One is a group of Muslim extremists who have stolen a nuclear device. With the power of the meteorite, they could vaporize any city in the West. The other group is led by a megalomaniacal industrialist who seeks to carry out the utter annihilation of Islam itself.

Caught between two militant factions bent on wholesale slaughter, Juan Cabrillo and his ship of high-tech mercenaries known as the Corporation must fight to protect the scientist and the Sacred Stone—and prevent the outbreak of World War III . . .

conti—

DIRK PITT® ADVENTURES BY CLIVE CUSSLER

Trojan Odyssey
Valhalla Rising
Atlantis Found
Flood Tide
Shock Wave
Inca Gold
Sahara
Dragon
Treasure
Cyclops
Deep Six
Pacific Vortex
Night Probe
Vixen 03
Raise the <u>Titanic</u>!
Iceberg
The Mediterranean Caper

FICTION BY CLIVE CUSSLER WITH PAUL KEMPRECOS

Lost City
White Death
Fire Ice
Serpent
Blue Gold

FICTION BY CLIVE CUSSLER AND CRAIG DIRGO

Sacred Stone
Golden Buddha

NONFICTION BY CLIVE CUSSLER AND CRAIG DIRGO

The Sea Hunters II
The Sea Hunters
Clive Cussler and Dirk Pitt Revealed

SACRED STONE

CLIVE CUSSLER

and CRAIG DIRGO

BERKLEY BOOKS, NEW YORK

THE BERKLEY PUBLISHING GROUP
Published by the Penguin Group
Penguin Group (USA) Inc.
375 Hudson Street, New York, New York 10014, USA
Penguin Group (Canada), 10 Alcorn Avenue, Toronto, Ontario M4V 3B2, Canada
(a division of Pearson Penguin Canada Inc.)
Penguin Books Ltd., 80 Strand, London WC2R 0RL, England
Penguin Group Ireland, 25 St. Stephen's Green, Dublin 2, Ireland (a division of Penguin Books Ltd.)
Penguin Group (Australia), 250 Camberwell Road, Camberwell, Victoria 3124, Australia
(a division of Pearson Australia Group Pty. Ltd.)
Penguin Books India Pvt. Ltd., 11 Community Centre, Panchsheel Park, New Delhi—110 017, India
Penguin Group (NZ), Cnr. Airborne and Rosedale Roads, Albany, Auckland 1310, New Zealand
(a division of Pearson New Zealand Ltd.)
Penguin Books (South Africa) (Pty.) Ltd., 24 Sturdee Avenue, Rosebank, Johannesburg 2196,
South Africa

Penguin Books Ltd., Registered Offices: 80 Strand, London WC2R 0RL, England

This is a work of fiction. Names, characters, places, and incidents either are the product of the author's imagination or are used fictitiously, and any resemblance to actual persons, living or dead, business establishments, events, or locales is entirely coincidental. The publisher does not have any control over and does not assume any responsibility for author or third-party websites or their content.

SACRED STONE

A Berkley Book / published by arrangement with Sandecker, RLLLP

PRINTING HISTORY
Berkley trade paperback edition / October 2004
Berkley international edition / July 2005

Copyright © 2004 by Sandecker, RLLLP.
Cover illustration by Edwin Herder.
Cover design by Rich Hasselberger.
Interior text design by Julie Rogers.

ISBN: 0-425-20365-4

BERKLEY®
Berkley Books are published by The Berkley Publishing Group,
a division of Penguin Group (USA) Inc.,
375 Hudson Street, New York, New York 10014.
BERKLEY is a registered trademark of Penguin Group (USA) Inc.
The "B" design is a trademark belonging to Penguin Group (USA) Inc.

PRINTED IN THE UNITED STATES OF AMERICA

10   9   8   7   6   5   4   3   2   1

CAST OF CHARACTERS

JUAN CABRILLO: Chairman of the Corporation

MAX HANLEY: President of the Corporation

RICHARD TRUITT: Vice President of the Corporation

THE CORPORATION TEAM (OPERATIVES)
(in alphabetic order)

GEORGE ADAMS: Helicopter Pilot

RICK BARRETT: Assistant Chef

MONICA CRABTREE: Supply and Logistics Coordinator

CARL GANNON: General Operations

CHUCK "TINY" GUNDERSON: Chief Pilot Fixed-Wing

MICHAEL HALPERT: Finance and Accounting

CLIFF HORNSBY: General Operations

JULIA HUXLEY: Medical Officer

PETE JONES: General Operations

HALI KASIM: General Operations

LARRY KING: Sniper

FRANKLIN LINCOLN: General Operations

BOB MEADOWS: General Operations

JUDY MICHAELS: Pilot

MARK MURPHY: General Operations

KEVIN NIXON: Magic Shop Specialist

TRACY PILSTON: Pilot

SAM PRYOR: Propulsion Engineer

GUNTHER REINHOLT: Propulsion Engineer

TOM REYES: General Operations

LINDA ROSS: Security and Surveillance/General
    Operations

EDDIE SENG: Director of Shore Operations/General
    Operations

ERIC STONE: Control Room Operator/General
    Operations

THE OTHERS

LANGSTON OVERHOLT IV: CIA officer who hires the
    Corporation

HALIFAX HICKMAN: Billionaire industrialist

CHRIS HUNT: U.S. Army officer killed in Afghanistan

MICHELLE HUNT: Mother of Chris

ERIC THE RED: Legendary explorer

THE EMIR OF QATAR: Leader of the country of Qatar

JOHN ACKERMAN: Archaeologist who locates the meteorite in Greenland

CLAY HUGHES: Assassin hired to recover the Greenland meteorite

PIETER VANDERWALD: South African death merchant

MIKE NEILSEN: Pilot hired to fly Hughes to Mount Forel

WOODY CAMPBELL: Drunk in Greenland who rents Cabrillo a snowcat

ALEIMEIN AL-KHALIFA: Terrorist planning to bomb London

SCOTT THOMPSON: Leader of the team on the *Free Enterprise*

THOMAS "TD" DWYER: CIA scientist who discovers the meteorite's danger

MIKO "MIKE" NASUKI: NOAA astronomer who assists Dwyer

SAUD AL-SHEIK: Saudi procurement official for the hajj

JAMES BENNETT: Pilot who transports the meteorite from the Faeroe Islands to England

NEBILE LABABITI: Terrorist for London operation

MILOS COUSTAS: Captain of the *Larissa*, the ship that delivers the bomb to England

BILLY JOE SHEA: Owner of a 1947 MG TC Cabrillo borrows to chase the bomb

ROGER LASSITER: Disgraced CIA agent who delivers the meteorite to Maidenhead

ELTON JOHN: Legendary musician

AMAD: Young Yemeni who will deliver the bomb

DEREK GOODLIN: Whorehouse owner in London

JOHN FLEMING: Head of MI5

DR. JACK BERG: CIA doctor who forces Thompson to talk

WILLIAM SKUTTER: Air Force captain who leads the team in Medina

PATRICK COLGAN: Army warrant officer heading the team to recover prayer rugs in Riyadh

PROLOGUE

FIFTY THOUSAND YEARS ago, and millions of miles from Earth, a planet was twitching convulsively to herald her destruction. The planet was ancient but her eventual demise had been cast from the start. She was an unstable orb with poles that constantly shifted polarity.

The planet consisted of rock and magma with a metal core. Over the countless eons since it had formed and cooled, an atmosphere was born. The gaseous layers were comprised of argon, helium and some hydrogen. Life was born on the surface of the planet—a low, base form of microbe.

The planet never really had a chance to develop complicated life forms. The microbes consumed oxygen molecules to multiply, keeping the surface and atmosphere barren of cells that could evolve. The planet's surface rock turned into superheated liquid mush as each revolution around its sun drew it closer toward the fiery furnace. The planet revolved not in a spin around her axis like Earth, but rather in an ever-increasing barrel roll as the poles shifted, and the melted rock surface began to spread like lava from a volcano.

Each hour, each minute, each second brought her closer

to her sun, and she gradually shed her skin as if the hand of
God were scraping her surface with a wire brush.

The stellar dandruff that was cast into the atmosphere
reached the edge of the gaseous envelope and was turned
white-hot by the sun, bursting with the force of a thousand
nuclear bombs. Sucked back to the surface by gravity, the
reentering projectiles ripped more of the fragile crust
away. More and more of the crust dissolved.

The doomed planet had only a short time to live.

As the protective covering was lost to space, the inner
metal core temperature continued to rise and the orb inside
began to spin. Large cracks in the surface spread and frac-
tures formed, releasing larger and larger chunks of molten
rock into space. And all the while the planet's metal core
grew with incredible intensity. Then, all at once, it happened. A massive slab of rock on the side closest to the sun
gave way. The poles shifted one last time and the planet began spinning wildly.

Then she exploded.

Millions of metal orbs flew into space, their molecules
rearranging themselves as they melted like solder under a
flame. A lucky few made it past the gravitational field of
the sun. Then they headed on a long journey into the deep
reaches of space.

TENS OF THOUSANDS of years had passed since the unknown planet exploded, scattering its remains into the uni-
verse. From a great distance the approaching debris
appeared blue. One piece became a finely detailed orb.
Many fragments had been sucked toward the surfaces of
other planets in space, but this one traveled farther than the
rest and eventually came to rain down on a planet called
Earth.

The single metal orb entered Earth's atmosphere on a
low trajectory from west to east. She split in the ionosphere
and calved off a smaller spherical orb of pure metal. The
mother meteor came in along thirty-five degrees latitude.
At this latitude, it was dry and arid. The baby, lighter and
smaller, was pulled farther northwest, heading toward the

sixty-second-degree latitude, where the surface was covered with a layer of ice and snow.

Two different environments of the same planet brought two different results.

The mother and her molten metal reformed into a glowing orb after spitting out her young. She came over a coastline then streaked across a barren desert in a decaying trajectory. Blasting high above the sand, rocks, and cactus, the one-hundred-yard diameter, 63,000-ton nickel-iron projectile slammed into the earth, carving a one-mile-diameter crater in the dry soil. Clouds of dust headed skyward, then began encircling Earth. Months would pass before all the fallout filtered back to the earth.

The baby was pure and silver-gray. The action of the initial explosion and the molecular rearrangement while traveling through space had formed a perfect sphere that appeared like twin halves of geodesic domes locked together. Traversing farther along the planet, she slipped through space quietly, her smooth surface meeting little resistance from Earth's atmosphere, with none of the anger and rage her mother had contained. She dropped lower and lower, like a golf ball with a topspin.

Soaring over the shoreline of an island capped with ice, it was as if she was being pulled to the earth by a magnet. Her diameter was but eighteen inches, her weight a hundred pounds. Drifting lower until she was only ten feet over the snow and ice, she lost her forward speed as gravity brought her down. Her heated metal surface melted a track in the snow and ice similar to a ball rolled by a child to make a snowman.

Energy expended, her heat dissipated, she came to rest at the base of an ice-covered mountain.

"WHAT HATH HELL wrought?" the man asked in Icelandic as he poked an object with a staff.

The man was short but formed of layers of muscle that signaled years of hard work and labor. The hair on his head and the thick beard that grew from his cheeks was a brilliant red like the fires of Hades. Thick white furs covered

his torso, while his leggings were constructed of sealskin
lined with sheep's wool. The man was prone to fits of rage,
and truth be told, he was not far removed from a barbarian.
Banished from Iceland for murder in the year 982, he had
led a group across the cold sea to the ice-shrouded island
where they now resided. During the past eighteen years he
had built a settlement on the rocky coast and his colony
had survived by hunting and fishing. In time he had grown
bored. The man, Eric the Red, began longing to explore, to
lead, to conquer new lands.

In the year A.D. 1000 he set out to see what lay inland to
the west.

Eleven men accompanied him at the start, but some five
months into the expedition, with spring coming, there were
but five remaining. Two had slipped into crevasses in the
ice, their screams still coming to Eric as he slept. One had
slipped on ice and bashed his head on a rocky outcropping.
He had twitched in tormented pain for days, unable to see
or speak until he blissfully died one night. One had been
taken by a large white ursine when he ventured away from
a campfire one evening in search of a freshwater stream he
swore he'd heard nearby.

Two had been taken by disease, suffering racking
coughs and fevers that convinced the remaining survivors
that evil forces were lurking nearby and stalking. As the expedition party thinned, the mood greatly changed. The ela-
tion and sense of wonder that compelled the men at the
start had faded, replaced with a sense of doom and fatalism.

It was as if the expedition was cursed and the men were
paying.

"Hoist the ball," Eric ordered the youngest man in the
expedition, the only one to have been born on island soil.

The teenager, Olaf the Fin, son of Olaf the Fisherman,
was apprehensive. The strange gray orb rested on a rocky
outcropping as if placed there by the hand of God. He had
no way of knowing that the object had descended from the
sky some forty-eight thousand years before. Olaf approached the orb cautiously. Everyone in the party knew of
Eric's penchant for violence; in fact, everyone on the icy
island knew his legend. Eric was not asking—he was de-

manding—so Olaf did not attempt to disagree or argue. He merely swallowed hard and bent down.

Olaf's hands touched the object and he found the surface cold and smooth. For the briefest of instants he felt his heart miss a beat—but he continued on. He attempted to lift the orb but found it too heavy for his expedition-weary arms.

"I'll need help," Olaf said.

"You," Eric said, motioning to another man with his staff.

Gro the Slayer, a taller man with light yellow hair and pale blue eyes, took three steps forward and grabbed one side of the orb. Both men used their back muscles and lifted the orb to hip level, then stared at Eric.

"Make a sling from the tusked one's skin," Eric pronounced. "We will take it back to the cave and build a shrine."

Without another word, Eric set off across the snow, leaving the others to tend to the discovery. Two hours later the orb was safely inside the cave. Eric immediately began planning an elaborate enclosure for the object he now believed had come directly from the gods in the heavens above.

ERIC LEFT OLAF and Gro to guard the heavenly body while he returned to the settlement on the coast for more men and material. Once there, he learned that a son had been born to his wife in his absence. He named him Leif in honor of the spring season, then left him with his mother to raise. With eighty more men and tools to excavate the cavern where the orb was hidden, he set off north toward the distant mountain. Summer was near and the sun was visible around the clock.

GRO THE SLAYER turned on his pelt bed then spat some loose fur from his mouth.

Rubbing his hand across the bearskin, he watched in surprise as the fur balled up in his palm. Then he stared at the orb in the dancing light of a torch placed in the wall.

"Olaf," he said to the teenager sleeping a short distance away, "it is time to rise and face the day."

Olaf rolled over and stared toward Gro. His eyes were red and bloodshot and his skin blotchy and flaking. He coughed lightly, sat upright and stared at Gro through the dim light. Gro's hair had been shedding and his color was all wrong.

"Gro," Olaf said, "your nose."

Gro raised the back of his hand to his nose and saw the red of blood. More and more often he had found himself with a bloody nose. He reached down and tugged on a painful tooth. It came out in his fingers. He tossed it aside and rose to his feet.

"I'll cook the berries," he said.

Stirring the fire, he added a few sticks from their dwindling supply then retrieved a sealskin bag containing the red berries they boiled to make a bitter morning drink. Walking outside the cave, he filled a dented iron pot with water from the stream of a nearby melting glacier, then stared at the marks scratched on the wall outside the cave.

Two or three more marks and Eric the Red was due to return.

By the time Gro returned inside the cave, Olaf was standing, dressed in his lightweight leather pants with his shirt laid on a rock nearby. He was scratching his back with a stick, and the skin was flickering to the ground like the first light snow of a new winter season. Once the itching had subsided he slid his leather shirt over his head.

"Something is amiss," Olaf said. "Both of us are becoming sicker as each day passes."

"Maybe it is the foul air inside this cave," Gro said quietly, placing the pot on the fire.

"I think it is *that*," Olaf said, pointing to the orb. "I think it is possessed."

"We could move outside the cave," Gro said, "and erect a tent for living."

"Eric ordered us to stay inside the cave. I fear if he returns and finds us outside we will feel his wrath."

"I looked at the marks," Gro said. "He is due to return in three sleeps—no more."

"We could take turns watching for his return," Olaf said quietly, "then hurry back inside before he catches us."

Gro stirred the berries in the boiling water. "Sudden death or slow sickness—I think it best we avoid what we know will happen for what might or might not."

"A few more days," Olaf said.

"A few more days," Gro said as he placed an iron dipper into the pot. He filled a pair of iron bowls with the berry liquid and handed one to Olaf.

FOUR MARKS ON the entrance of the cave later, Eric the Red returned.

"You have the racking cough," he said as soon as he saw the condition of the men. "I do not want you to infect the others. Return to the settlement but take up residence in the log house to the north."

Olaf and Gro set off to the south the following morning—but they never reached home.

Olaf went first, his weakened heart simply giving out three days after the start of the journey. Gro didn't fare much better, and when he could walk no more he made camp. The furry beasts came soon after. What wasn't consumed immediately was spread about by the carnivores until it was as if Gro had never existed at all.

AFTER WATCHING HIS two men disappear into the distance, Eric gathered the miners, engineers and laborers he had brought from the settlement. He cleared a spot in the dust on the floor of the cave and began sketching his plans with a stick.

The plans were ambitious, but a gift from heaven should not be treated lightly.

That day the first parties began to map out the cave. In time it would be learned that the cave stretched nearly a mile into the mountain and the temperature increased as the cavern ran downward. A large pool with freshwater was located deep inside, with stalactites descending from the ceiling and stalagmites rising from the floor.

Groups were sent to the coast to locate long poles of driftwood to construct a series of ladders up and down the passages, while others carved steps into the rock. Intricate doors were fashioned from slabs of rock that pivoted on balanced hinges to hide the object from others who might seek her power. Runic carvings and statues were hewn from the rock, and light was reflected from the few openings where fresh air entered the cave. Eric supervised the work from the settlement on the coast. He visited the site rarely, letting the vision in his mind be his guide.

Men came, worked, became sick and died, only to be replaced by others.

By the time the cavern was finished, Eric the Red had decimated his population base and the settlement would never recover. Only once did his son, Leif, see the glorious monument.

Eric ordered the entrance sealed, and the object was left for those yet to come.

PART ONE

1

LIEUTENANT CHRIS HUNT rarely talked about his past, but the men he served with had gathered a few clues from his demeanor. The first was that Hunt had not grown up in some backwoods hillbilly haven and used the army to see the world. He was from Southern California. And, if pressed, Hunt would volunteer he was raised in the *Los Angeles area,* not wanting to disclose that he grew up in Beverly Hills. The second thing the men noticed was that Hunt was a natural leader—he was neither patronizing nor put on an air of superiority, but neither did he try to hide the fact that he was competent and smart.

The third thing the men found out today.

A chill wind was blowing down from the mountains into the Afghanistan valley where the platoon under Hunt's command was breaking camp. Hunt and three other soldiers were wrestling with a tent they were folding for storage. While the men were bringing the ends together longways, Sergeant Tom Agnes decided to ask about the rumor he had heard. Hunt handed him the side of the tent so Agnes could fold it into halves.

"Sir," Agnes said, "rumor has it you graduated from Yale University—that true?"

All the men were wearing tinted ski goggles but Agnes was close enough to see Hunt's eyes. A flicker of surprise, followed by resignation, flashed quickly. Then Hunt smiled.

"Ah," he said quietly, "you've found out my terrible secret."

Agnes nodded and folded the tent in half. "Not exactly a hotbed for military recruiting."

"George Bush went there," Hunt said. "He was a navy pilot."

"I thought he was in the National Guard," Specialist Jesus Herrara, who was taking the tent from Agnes, said.

"George Bush Senior," Hunt said. "Our president also graduated from Yale, and yes, he was a National Guard jet pilot."

"Yale," Agnes said. "If you don't mind me asking, how did you end up here?"

Hunt brushed some snow from his gloves. "I volunteered," he said, "just like you."

Agnes nodded.

"Now let's finish breaking down this camp," Hunt said, pointing to the mountain nearby, "and head up there and find that bastard who attacked the United States."

"Yes, sir," the men said in unison.

Ten minutes later, with fifty-pound packs on their backs, they started up the mountain.

IN A TOWN where beautiful women abound, at age forty-nine Michelle Hunt still caused men to turn their heads. Tall, with hazel hair and blue-green eyes, she was blessed with a figure that required neither constant dieting nor endless exercise to appear trim. Her lips were full and her teeth straight, but it was her doelike eyes and flawless skin that gave the strongest visual impression. And while she was a beautiful woman, that was as common in Southern California as sunshine and earthquakes.

What drew people closer to Michelle was something that cannot be created by a surgeon's knife, honed through dress or manicure, or developed through ambition or change. Michelle had that thing that made both men and women like her and want to be around her—she was happy, content and positive. Michelle Hunt was herself. And people flocked to her like bees to a flower in bloom.

"Sam," she said to the painter who had just finished the walls in her art gallery, "you do such nice work."

Sam was thirty-eight years old and he blushed.

"Only my best for you, Ms. Hunt," he said.

Sam had painted her gallery when it had opened five years before, her Beverly Hills house, her condo in Lake Tahoe and now this remodel. And every time she made him feel appreciated and talented.

"You want a bottle of water or a Coke or something?" she asked.

"I'm okay, thanks."

Just then an assistant called from the front of the gallery that she had a telephone call, and she smiled, waved and began to walk away.

"That's a lady," Sam said under his breath, "a lady."

Walking to the front of the gallery, where her desk faced out onto Rodeo Drive, Michelle noticed that one of the artists she represented was coming through the front door. Here her amiability had also paid off in spades—artists are a fickle and temperamental lot, but Michelle's artists adored her and rarely changed galleries. That and the fact that she had started her business fully funded had contributed greatly to her years of success.

"I knew today was going to be good," she said to the bearded man. "I just didn't know it would be because my favorite artist would be paying me a visit."

The man smiled.

"Just let me take this telephone call," she said, "and we'll talk."

Her aide corralled the artist toward an area with couches and a wet bar off to one side. As Michelle slid into her desk chair and reached for the telephone, the aide took the artist's drink order and a few seconds later began packing ground espresso into the machine to draw him a cappuccino.

"Michelle Hunt."

"It's me," a gravelly voice said.

The voice was one that needed no introduction. He had swept her off her feet when she was a young woman of twenty-one, freshly arrived from Minnesota, seeking a new life of fun and sun in 1980s Southern California. After an on-again, off-again relationship, necessitated both by his inability to be bound to a relationship, as well as his frequent absences for business, she had borne his son at age twenty-four. And though his name never appeared on the birth certificate—nor had Michelle and he actually lived together before or since—the pair had remained close. At least as close as the man allowed anyone ever to come.

"How are you?" she asked.

"I've been okay."

"Where are you?"

It was the standard question she asked him to break the ice. Over the years the answers had ranged from Osaka to Peru to Paris to Tahiti.

"Hang on," the man said easily. He stared at a moving map on a forward wall near the cockpit of his jet. "Six hundred and eighty-seven miles from Honolulu on the way to Vancouver, British Columbia."

"Going skiing?" she asked. The sport was something they had enjoyed together.

"Building a skyscraper," he answered.

"You're always up to something."

"True," he noted. "Michelle, I called because I heard our boy has been sent to Afghanistan," he said quietly.

Michelle had been unaware—the deployment was still secret and Chris had not been able to disclose his destination when he'd been dispatched.

"Oh my," she blurted, "that's not good."

"That's what I thought you'd say."

"How'd you find out?" Michelle asked. "I'm always amazed by your ability to ferret out information."

"It's not magic," the man said. "I have so many senators and other politicians in my pocket I've had to buy larger pants."

"Any word on how it's going?"

"I guess the mission is proving harder than the president envisioned," he said. "Chris is apparently leading a hunter-killer squad to locate the bad guys. Limited contact so far—but my sources claim it is cold and dirty work. If he doesn't contact you for a while, don't be surprised."

"I'm afraid for him," Michelle said slowly.

"Do you want me to put in a fix?" the man asked. "Have him pulled out and sent stateside?"

"I thought he made you agree never to do that."

"He did," the man admitted.

"Then don't."

"I'll call you when I know more."

"Are you going to be down this way soon?" Michelle asked.

"I'll call you if I am," the man said. "Now I'd better go—I'm starting to get static on the satellite line. Must be sunspots."

"Pray our boy is safe," she said.

"I might do more than that," the man said as the call ended.

Michelle replaced the receiver in its cradle and sat back. Her ex-beau was not one to show worry or fear. Still, his concern for his son had been palpable and personal. She could only hope his worry was misplaced, and that Chris would come home soon.

Rising from the desk, she walked toward the artist. "Tell me you have something good," she said easily.

"Outside in the van," the artist said, "and I think you'll like it."

FOUR HOURS AFTER sunrise, one thousand feet higher up the ridge from the camp where they had spent the night, Hunt's platoon met a determined enemy. The fire came from a series of caves just above and to the east. And it came all at once. Rifle fire, rocket-propelled grenades, mortars, handgun fire rained down. The enemy dynamited the mountain to create rock slides, pelting the ground below, and they had mined the ground where Hunt's troops sought refuge.

The enemy's goal was to wipe out Hunt's team all at once—and they would come close.

Hunt had taken refuge behind a series of boulders. Bullets were ricocheting off the rocks to all sides, sending chips flying through the air and striking his men. There was nowhere to hide, no way to advance, and their retreat had been cut off by a rock slide.

"Radio," Hunt shouted.

Half his team was twenty yards ahead, another quarter ahead and to the left. Luckily, his radio operator had stayed close to the lieutenant. The man edged toward Hunt on his back to protect the radio. For his effort he received a wound to his kneecap when a bullet grazed his raised knee as the man pushed himself closer. Hunt dragged him the rest of the way.

"Antencio," Hunt shouted to a man a few feet away, "take care of Lassiter's wound."

Antencio scurried over and began cutting away the radio operator's pants. He found the opening was not deep and began to wrap a bandage around the knee as Hunt flicked on the radio and adjusted the dial.

"You're going to be okay, Lassiter," he said to the radio operator. "I'm going to get us some help in here posthaste. Then we'll have you medevaced."

The fear in the soldiers' faces was obvious. For most of them, as for Hunt, this was their first time in battle. As their leader, he needed to take control and form a plan.

"Control, Control, Advance Three," Hunt yelled into the microphone, "need positive support, grid three zero one eight. Taking heavy fire."

"Advance Three," a voice said immediately, "report situation."

"We're pinned down," Hunt said, "and they have the high ground. Situation critical."

Hunt glanced up as he was talking. A dozen bearded men in flowing robes were starting down the hill. "Get some fire up there, men," he screamed to the forward half of his team. A second later a volley of shots rang out.

"Advance Three, we have a Spectre two minutes out and inbound. Four whirlies—two carriers and two gunships—

will be off the ground in three. It'll take them another ten minutes to reach your site."

Hunt could hear the whine of the massive propeller-driven gunship racing up the canyon miles below them. He peeked over the rock to see eight of the enemy still advancing down the hill. Raising himself, he shot off a rocket-propelled grenade. A whoosh then a thump as the charge flew through the air and ignited. He followed up with a volley of automatic weapon fire.

"Advance Three, acknowledge."

"Advance Three, affirmative," Hunt yelled into the microphone.

Where there had been eight there were now just four. They were only twenty yards from his forward team. Hunt swiveled his bayonet and locked it in place. The forward team seemed paralyzed. They were young, unseasoned and about to be overrun. A mortar landed close to the boulders and exploded. The area was showered with powdered rock and dust. From higher up the mountain another group of the enemy started down the hill. Hunt stood up and started firing. He sprinted the twenty yards ahead to his men and met the advancing enemy head-on.

Three's a charm, and that's how many Hunt shot dead in the gut. The last one he bayoneted, as his clip was empty. Taking his sidearm from his holster, he finished the man off, then slid to the ground, replaced his clip and rose and started firing again.

"Back it up, men," he shouted, "behind the boulders."

Two by two his men retreated to the relative safety of the boulders to the rear, while the men remaining kept fire on an advancing enemy. The enemy was high on distilled poppy, misplaced religious zeal and the narcotic khat leaves they were chewing. The slope was red with the blood of their fallen comrades but still they advanced.

"Advance Three," the radio squawked.

Antencio reached for the radio. "This is Advance Three," he said. "Our C.O. is away from the radio, this is Specialist 367."

"We've located a B-52 at another target," the voice said. "We've diverted her to assist."

"Affirm—I'll tell the lieutenant."

But Antencio would never have a chance to relay the message.

Only Hunt and a grizzled old sergeant were left at the forward site when the AC-130 arrived on station. A second later a wall of lead began pouring from the 25-, 40- and 105-millimeter guns that poked from her sides.

The sergeant had seen a Spectre live-fire before and he wasted no time. "Let's back it up, sir," he shouted to Hunt, "we have a few seconds of cover."

"Go, go, go," Hunt said, yanking the sergeant upright and pushing him toward safety. "I'm right behind you."

The Spectre crabbed sideways from the recoil of her firing guns. A few seconds later the pilot pulled her up and out to turn and make another pass through the narrow canyon. As the gunship ended her turn and lined up for her second run, seven of the enemy still advanced. Hunt covered his sergeant's retreat.

He killed five of the enemy with a combination of a rocket-propelled grenade and a concentrated field of fire. But two made it close to Hunt's position. One shot him in the shoulder as he turned to retreat.

The second one slit his throat with a wicked-looking curved knife.

Starting down in the dive for the fire run, the pilot of the AC-130 saw Hunt being killed and radioed it to the other aircraft. Hunt's troops saw it as well—and the sight removed their fear and replaced it with rage. As the AC-130 lined up for the pass, the troops rose and charged another wave that had just left the cave and was advancing downhill. Pushing forward as a team, they reached their fallen leader and erected a protective circle around his body. They waited for the enemy to advance, but as if by magic, or sensing the fury of the American troops, the enemy began to turn and retreat.

TWENTY THOUSAND FEET above them and less than ten minutes from the target, the pilot of the B-52 flicked off the microphone and replaced it in its cradle.

"Did you all hear that?" he said quietly on the intercom to his crew.

The plane was silent save for the drone from the eight engines. The pilot didn't need an answer—he knew they'd all heard what he had heard.

"We're going to turn this mountain into dust," he said. "When the enemy comes for the bodies, I want them to need to collect them with a sponge."

FOUR MINUTES LATER the helicopters came for Advance Three. Hunt's body and the wounded were loaded in the first Blackhawk. The rest of the soldiers, heads hung down, climbed into the second. Then the helicopter gunships and the AC-130 began raking the hillside with a fury of lead and explosives. Soon after that the B-52 came calling. The blood flowed down the hill and the enemy was obliterated. But the show of force came too late for Lieutenant Hunt.

In time, only the need for revenge would remain to mark his passing.

And it would be years before that played out.

2

THE *OREGON* SAT alongside a pier in Reykjavik, Iceland, tied fast to the bollards. The vessels in port were a mishmash of both workboats and pleasure crafts, fishing boats and factory trawlers, smaller cruisers and—unusual for Iceland—a few large yachts. The fishing boats supported Iceland's largest industry; the yachts were here because the Arab Peace Summit was currently in session.

The *Oregon* would never win any beauty contests. The five-hundred-plus-foot-long cargo steamer appeared to be held together mostly by rust. Her upper decks were littered with junk, her upper and lower hull were a cacophony of mismatched paint, and the derrick amidships looked as if it might tumble into the water at any moment.

But the *Oregon*'s appearance was all an illusion.

The rust was carefully applied radar-absorbing paint that allowed her to slip off radar screens like a wraith, the junk on the decks only props. The derricks worked fine; a couple operated as intended, a few were communication antenna, and the rest flipped away to reveal missile-firing pods. Belowdecks her accommodations rivaled the finest yachts. Opulent staterooms, a state-of-the-art communications and command center, a helicopter, shore boats, and a complete fabrication shop were inside. Her dining room rivaled the finest restaurants. Her sick bay was more akin to an expensive hospital suite. Powered by a pair of magneto-hydrodynamic propulsion units, the ship could run like a cheetah and turn like a bumper car. The ship was nothing like her outside appearance indicated.

The *Oregon* was an armed, high-tech intelligence platform staffed by highly trained people.

The Corporation, who owned and operated the *Oregon,* was comprised of ex-military and intelligence operatives who hired themselves out to countries and individuals needing specialized services. They were a private army of mercenaries with a conscience. Often secretly tasked by the U.S. government to perform missions because they were outside the scope of congressional oversight, they existed in a shadowy world without diplomatic protection or governmental acknowledgment.

The Corporation was a force for hire—but they accepted clients carefully.

For the past week they had been in Iceland providing security for the emir of Qatar, who was attending the summit. Iceland had been selected for the meetings for a variety of reasons. The country was small, Reykjavik's population was only around 100,000, and that helped with the security concerns. The population was homogeneous, and that made outsiders stand out like sore thumbs, which added to the ability to detect terrorists intent on disturbing the peace process. And lastly, Iceland claimed to have the world's oldest elected parliament. The country had been involved in the democratic process from centuries past.

The agenda for the weeklong meetings included the occupation of Iraq, the situation in Israel and Palestine and the spread of fundamentalist terrorism. And while the summit was not sanctioned by the United Nations or any other world governing body, the leaders in attendance realized that policy would be formed and courses of action decided.

Russia, France, Germany, Egypt, Jordan, and a host of

other Middle Eastern countries were attending. Israel, Syria and Iran had declined. The United States, Great Britain and Poland, as the allied liberators of Iraq, were there, as well as a host of smaller countries. Nearly two dozen nations and their ambassadors, security, intelligence operatives and handlers had descended on Iceland's capital city like a swarm of mosquitoes in the night. With the city's small population, the numerous spies and security people were as obvious to the citizens of Reykjavik as if they had been wearing bikinis in the freezing cold weather. Icelanders were fair of skin, blond of hair and blue-eyed— a hard combination to fake if you are trying to blend in with the locals.

Reykjavik was a city of low buildings and brightly painted houses that stood out against the snow-covered terrain like ornaments on a Christmas tree. The tallest building, Hallgrimskirkja Church, was but a few stories high, and the plumes of steam from the geothermal springs in the area that warmed the houses and buildings gave the landscape a surreal appearance. The smell of hydrogen sulfide from the springs tainted the air with a slight rotten-egg odor.

Reykjavik was clustered around the year-round ice-free port that housed the fishing fleet, the mainstay of Iceland's economy. And, in contrast to the country's name, the winter temperature in the city was actually milder than New York City's. The citizens of Iceland are both extremely healthy and seemingly happy. The happiness can be traced to a positive state of mind; the health, to the abundance of local hot springs pools.

The Arab summit meetings were taking place at the Hofoi, the large house now used for city functions that had also been the site of a 1986 meeting between Mikhail Gorbachev and Ronald Reagan. Hofoi was less than a mile from where the *Oregon* was docked, a convenience that made security an easier affair.

Qatar had used the Corporation in the past—and they enjoyed a mutual relationship of high regard.

*   *   *

OUT OF RESPECT for the Christian participants of the summit, no meetings had been scheduled for Christmas day, so belowdecks in the galley of the *Oregon* a trio of chefs was putting the finishing touches on the coming feast. The main course was in the oven—twelve large turduckens. The turduckens were a treat to the crew—they were small deboned chickens stuffed with cornmeal and sage stuffing, inserted into deboned ducks with a thinner layer of spice bread stuffing, which were then stuffed inside large deboned turkeys that had been lined with an oyster and chestnut stuffing. When the carcasses were carved, the slices would reveal a trio of meats.

Relish trays were already on the tables: iced carrots, celery, scallions, radishes and julienne zucchini. There were bowls of nuts, fruits, and cheese and crackers. Trays of crab claws, raw oysters and lobster chunks. Three kinds of soup; Waldorf, green and gelatin salads; a fish course; a cheese course; mince, pumpkin, apple and berry pies; wine; port; liqueurs and Jamaican Blue Mountain coffee.

None of the crew would leave hungry.

In his opulent stateroom Juan Cabrillo toweled his wet hair, then shaved and splashed his cheeks with bay rum aftershave. His blond crew cut required little maintenance, but in the last few weeks he had grown a goatee, which he now carefully trimmed with a set of stainless steel scissors. Satisfied with his work, he stared in the mirror and smiled. He looked good—rested, healthy, and content.

Walking into the main cabin he selected a starched white shirt, a finely woven lightweight gray wool suit tailored in London, a silk rep tie, soft gray wool socks and a pair of black, polished Cole Haan tassel loafers. After laying them out, he began to dress.

While knotting the red-and-blue-striped tie he did a last check, then opened the door and walked down the passageway toward the elevator. A few hours ago his team had learned of a threat to the emir. A plan was now in place that, if successful, would kill two birds with one stone.

Now if they could only locate the stray nuclear bomb that was missing halfway across the globe, the year could end on a positive note. Cabrillo had no way of knowing that within twenty-four hours he would be traveling across a frozen wasteland to the east—or that the fate of a city by a river would hang in the balance.

3

IN CONTRAST TO the warmth and conviviality aboard the *Oregon,* the scene at the remote camp near Mount Forel just north of the Arctic Circle in Greenland was more subdued. Outside the cave the wind howled and the temperature was ten degrees below zero without accounting for the windchill factor. This was the ninety-first day of the expedition, and the thrill and excitement had long since worn off. John Ackerman was tired, discouraged and all alone with his bitter thoughts of defeat.

Ackerman was working toward his doctorate in anthropology from the University of Nevada, Las Vegas, and his current surroundings were as far removed from his familiar desert as an underwater seamount to a parrot. The three helpers from the university had gone home as soon as the semester had ended and replacements were not due to arrive for another two weeks. Truth be told, Ackerman should have taken a break himself, but he was a man possessed by a dream.

Ever since that first moment when he had located the obscure reference to the Cave of the Gods when writing his doctoral thesis about Eric the Red, he had been compelled to find the caves before anyone else. Maybe the entire affair was just a myth, Ackerman thought, but if it existed he wanted his name and not some usurper's to be associated with the find.

He stirred the can of beans on the metal stove that sat under the tent he had erected near the mouth of the cave. He was sure from the description he had translated that this was the cave Eric the Red had mentioned on his deathbed, but despite months of effort he had yet to get farther than the seemingly solid wall twenty feet to the rear. He and the others had examined every inch of the walls and floor of the cavern but they had found nothing. The cave itself appeared man-made, and yet Ackerman was not sure.

Seeing the beans were warming properly, he peeked outside to make sure the antenna for his satellite telephone had not been blown over in the wind. Finding it secure, he returned inside and checked his e-mail. Ackerman had forgotten today was Christmas, but the holiday greetings from friends and family reminded him. As he answered the messages, the sadness inside him grew. Here it was a festive day, when most Americans would be with family and friends, and he was in the middle of nowhere, alone and chasing a dream he no longer truly believed existed.

Slowly, the sadness turned to anger. Forgetting about the beans, he grabbed a Coleman lantern from the table and walked to the far end of the cave. There he stood, fuming and cursing under his breath at the course of actions that had led him to a distant and cold wasteland on this the holiest of nights. All his microscopic examinations and careful dusting with paintbrushes had yielded nothing.

There was nothing here—it was all a wash. Tomorrow he'd start packing up the camp, put the tent and supplies on the sled behind the snowmobile, then as soon as the weather cleared enough he'd make the run for the nearest town, Angmagssalik, some one hundred miles away.

The Cave of the Gods would remain a myth.

Seized by a growing anger, he shouted a curse and swung the fuel-filled lantern in an arc, then let go of the handle when it was pointed at the ceiling. The lantern flew through the air and smashed into the rock roof of the cave.

The glass bulb shattered and burning liquid gas spilled onto the ceiling and down. Then suddenly, as if by magic, the flames reversed as they were sucked into the cracks overhead. The remaining burning fuel was drawn inside four cracks that formed a square.

The roof of the cave, Ackerman thought, we never searched the roof of the cave.

Trotting back to the front of the cave, he opened a wooden crate and removed the thin aluminum tubes they had used to lay out a grid on the floor of the cave for the detailed archaeological examination. Disassembled now, they were each four feet long. Rooting around in a nylon supply bag, Ackerman found some duct tape and wrapped it around the tubes until he had a staff twelve feet in length. Grasping the tube like a javelin, he quickly walked back into the cave.

The broken lantern was lying on the floor still burning, the metal body dented and the glass globe missing, but it was still spewing light. He stared up at the roof and saw that the smoke from the now-burned-out fuel had left a barely visible outline of a square.

Lining the pole up on one side, Ackerman slowly pushed.

The thin stone covering that formed the hatch had been constructed with angled sides. As soon as Ackerman applied pressure, it slid on ancient wooden dowels until it opened like a greased shutter on a finely crafted window.

Then, once the hatch was opened, a walrus-skin-woven ladder dropped down.

Ackerman stood still in amazement. Then he extinguished the still-burning Coleman, walked back to the front of the tent and noticed the beans boiling over. He removed them from the stove, then found a flashlight, basic supplies in case he became stuck, a rope and a digital camera. He walked back to the ladder to climb toward his destiny.

Once through the opening, it was like Ackerman had climbed into an attic. Here was the true cave. The one he and the students had examined so closely was merely a carefully constructed ruse. Shining the light, Ackerman walked in the same direction as the opening in the cave below. At about the same distance as where the one underneath led out, Ackerman found a pile of rocks arranged to appear as if it were a natural landslide. Later he could clear the rocks away and peer out over the frozen wasteland, but for now, and for the last several centuries, the rock slide had protected the secrets.

The ruse had tricked Ackerman, just as it was designed to do.

Turning away from the rock slide, Ackerman carefully bypassed the hole in the floor, then stopped and dropped one end of the rope to the floor. Carefully playing out the line, he headed down the corridor carrying the flashlight above his head.

The walls were adorned with pictographs of men hunting, beasts slain and ships on journeys to faraway lands. It was obvious to Ackerman that many men for many years had toiled inside the cavern. The cave widened and the light caught openings where, well preserved by the cold, furs and hides lay upon sleeping pallets stacked one atop the other. They had been hacked from the rock and dirt as ancient bunk beds for miners. He followed a passage alongside the sleeping area that featured several short offshoots from the main cave toward an area darkened by cooking fires. Long, rough-hewn tables, brought into the cave in pieces and assembled on site, filled a dining hall with high ceilings. Sweeping the light, Ackerman could see whale-oil reservoirs with wicks built into the walls for light.

There was easily seating for a hundred men.

Ackerman sniffed the air and found it fresh. In fact, there was the slightest of breezes. He began to theorize that Eric the Red's men must have figured out how to bore vent holes and create a flow-through system to rid the cave of bad air and odors. Farther past the dining hall was a small room with angled rock troughs against the walls. The troughs were filled with steaming water. Knowing these were crude toilets but figuring over a thousand years had passed, Ackerman dipped his finger into the water. The temperature was hot. They must have located a geothermal stream and diverted it, Ackerman thought. A few feet farther ahead, just past the crude toilets, a large pool sat elevated and spilled down into the troughs. The baths.

Past the baths, Ackerman headed down a narrow passage whose walls had been smoothed and adorned with geometric designs etched into the rock and dyed red and yellow and green. Ahead was an opening framed by carefully selected decorative stones.

Ackerman walked through the opening into a large chamber.

From what he could see the walls were round and smooth. The floor of the chamber was fitted with flat rocks to form an almost perfectly level floor. Geodes and crystals hung from the ceiling like chandeliers. Ackerman reached down and adjusted his flashlight. Then he stood up, raised the light over his head and gasped in awe.

Flowing up from the center of the room was a platform where a gray orb sat on display.

The geodes and crystals hanging from the ceiling scattered light from the flashlight into thousands of rainbows that spilled around the room like a spinning disco ball. Ackerman exhaled and the sound was magnified.

Stepping up to the chest-high platform, he stared at the orb.

"Meteorite," he said aloud.

Then he removed the digital camera and began to document the scene.

After climbing back down the ladder, he retrieved a Geiger counter and a book on metal analysis and tried to determine the orb's composition. He soon figured it out.

AN HOUR LATER, back down from the upper cave, Ackerman assembled the digital images and readings from the Geiger counter into an e-mail package. After spending another hour composing a glowing press release about himself and including that in the message, he sent the e-mail to his benefactor for approval.

Then he sat back to bask in his glory and await a reply.

AT THE ECHELON monitoring station outside London near Chatham, most of the world's communications were

34 CLIVE CUSSLER

recorded. A joint English–United States operation, Echelon had received a fair share of scrutiny from the press on both sides of the pond. Quite simply Echelon was nothing more or less than a massive eavesdropping apparatus that snagged worldwide communications and ran them through a computer for review. Certain words were flagged so that if they appeared, it triggered the message to be spit out for review by a human. Then the flagged message passed up a chain of command until it was forwarded to the proper intelligence service or ignored as unimportant.

Ackerman's e-mail from Greenland passed up to a satellite before being relayed back to the United States. On its way back to earth, Echelon snagged the message and ran it through its computer. There was a word in the message that triggered a review.

In time the message would pass along the chain of command from England across the ocean on a secure line to the National Security Agency in Maryland, then on to the Central Intelligence Agency in Langley, Virginia.

But there was a traitor inside Echelon, so the review went to more than one location.

Inside the cave on Mount Forel, John Ackerman was living a fantasy life in his mind. He'd already pictured himself on the covers of most of the archaeology magazines; now he was formulating an acceptance speech for what, in his mind at least, was something akin to the Academy Awards of archaeology.

This find was huge, like the modern-day opening of a pyramid, like finding an untouched, perfectly preserved shipwreck. Magazine articles, books, television shows loomed. If Ackerman played his cards right, he could ride this find into a lifelong career. He could become the acknowledged grandmaster of archaeology, the man the media always called for comment. He could become a celebrity—and nowadays that was a career in and of itself. With just a little manipulation, the name John Ackerman would be synonymous with great discovery.

Then his computer chirped to report an incoming message.

The message was succinct.

*Don't tell anyone yet. We need more proof before the
announcement. I'm sending a man up there to check
it out. He will arrive in a day or two. Just continue
documenting the find. Super work, John. But mum's
the word.*

At first reading Ackerman was irritated by the message.
Then he reflected and was able to convince himself that his
benefactor was probably taking the time to build a media
storm for the find. Maybe he was planning to give one of
the major networks an exclusive and needed time to set up
the interview. Maybe he was planning a simultaneous blitz
of magazines, newspapers and television.

Soon Ackerman was awash with these thoughts and his
ego started to run wild.

The larger the shower of publicity, the greater his future
fame.

For Ackerman, ego tinged with self-aggrandizing would
prove a deadly combination.

4

SOMETIMES IT IS better to be lucky than smart. High atop a hotel in a city know for risk takers, a middle-aged man named Halifax Hickman stared at the digital pictures on the computer and smiled. Reading a separate report he had printed out a few hours before, he did a few calculations on a pad of paper then stared at the images again. Unbelievable. The solution to his problem had arrived—and it had come with a tax write-off for the donation.

It was as if he had slid a quarter in a slot machine and hit a million-dollar jackpot.

Hickman started laughing—but it was not a laugh of happiness. The laugh was evil and came from a place without joy. Tinged in revenge and shaded by hatred, it rose from a recess deep in the man's soul.

When the laugh had subsided, he reached for the telephone and dialed.

CLAY HUGHES LIVED in the mountains north of Missoula, Montana, in a cabin he'd built himself, on a plot of land 160 acres in size that he owned free and clear. A hot springs on his property provided heat for the cabin as well as for the series of greenhouses that supplied most of his food. Solar and wind energy provided electricity. Cellular and satellite telephone communications kept him in voice contact with the rest of the world. Hughes had a bank account in Missoula with a six-figure balance, an address at a pack-and-ship office to send and receive his mail, plus three passports, four social security numbers and driver's licenses with different names and addresses.

Hughes liked his privacy—not uncommon among assassins who enjoy keeping low profiles.

"I have some work for you," Hickman said.

"How much?" Hughes asked, cutting to the chase.

"Maybe five days, for fifty thousand dollars. And I supply the transportation."

"I take it someone is going to have a bad day," Hughes said. "What else?"

"I'll need an object delivered somewhere when it's done," Hickman told him.

"Does it help the cause?" Hughes asked.

"Yes."

"Then the delivery will be free," Hughes said magnanimously.

"My jet will be there in an hour," Hickman said. "Dress warm."

"I want gold," Hughes said.

"Gold it is," Hickman said as he disconnected.

AN HOUR LATER a Raytheon Hawker 800XP touched down at the Missoula airport. Hughes shut off the engine of his restored 1972 International Scout. Reaching into the rear, he unzipped a bag and checked his firearms once again. Satisfied all was in order, he zipped the bag closed and lifted it out onto the ground. Then he closed the rear gate, bent down and armed the explosive device that he used as a burglar alarm.

If anyone messed with his vehicle while he was gone, the Scout would explode, hiding any evidence of his ownership as well as his personal papers. Hughes was nothing if not paranoid. He hoisted the bag onto his shoulder and made his way toward the jet.

Forty-seven minutes later the jet crossed into Canada on a north-northeast course.

5

THE DAY AFTER the e-mail from Greenland was intercepted, Langston Overholt IV was sitting in his office at CIA headquarters in Virginia, staring at a picture of the meteorite. He glanced at a report on iridium, then stared at his list of agents. As usual he was shorthanded. Reaching into a bowl on his desk, he removed a tennis ball and methodically began bouncing it against his wall and catching it when it returned. The repetition relaxed him.

Was this worth pulling agents off another assignment? It was always risk versus reward. Overholt was awaiting a report from the CIA scientists that might shed more light on the possible threat, but for right now it looked pretty straightforward. He needed someone to travel to Greenland and secure the meteorite. Once that was done, the risk was minimal. Since his agents were tied up, he decided to call an old friend.

"Two five two four."

"This is Overholt. How's Iceland?"

"If I eat another piece of herring," Cabrillo said, "I could swim to Ireland."

"Rumor has it you're working for the commies," Overholt said.

"I'm sure you know about it," Cabrillo said. "Security breach in the Ukraine."

"Yeah," Overholt said, "we're working it as well."

Cabrillo and Overholt had been partners years before. A bad deal in Nicaragua had cost Cabrillo his job with the CIA, but he'd kept Overholt out of the mess. Overholt had never forgotten the favor and over the years he'd funneled Cabrillo and the Corporation as much work as oversight would allow.

"All this terrorism," Cabrillo noted, "has been a boon for business."

"Got time for a little side deal?"

"How many people will it require?" Cabrillo asked, thinking about the jobs they were already contracted for.

"Just one," Overholt said.

"Full fees?"

"As always," Overholt said, "my employer is not cheap."

"Not cheap, just quick to fire."

Cabrillo had never gotten over being hung out to dry, and with good reason. Congress had raked him over the coals, and his boss at the time had done nothing to cool the fire. He had about as much compassion for politicians and bureaucrats as he did for dental drills.

"I just need someone to run over to Greenland and pick something up," Overholt told him. "Take a day or two."

"You picked a prime time," Cabrillo said. "It's freezing cold and twenty-four-hour darkness this time of year."

"I hear the Northern Lights are pretty," Overholt offered.

"Why not have one of your CIA drones handle this?"

"As usual, none are available. I'd rather just pay your crew and wrap it up with a minimum of hassle."

"We still have a few days' worth of work here," Cabrillo said, "before we're free."

"Juan," Overholt said easily, "I'm pretty sure this is a one-man job. If you could just send one of your men over there and retrieve what we need, he'd be back before the end of the summit."

Cabrillo thought about it for a minute. The rest of his

team was handling security for the emir. For the last few days, Cabrillo had been staying aboard the *Oregon* and tending to corporate business. He was bored and felt like a racehorse in a stall.

"I'll take the job," Cabrillo said. "My people have this end controlled."

"Whatever floats your boat," Overholt said.

"I only need to fly over and pick something up, right?"

"That's the drill."

"What is it?"

"A meteorite," Overholt said slowly.

"Why in the world does the CIA want a meteorite?" Cabrillo asked.

"Because we think it might be made of iridium, and iridium can be used to construct a 'dirty bomb.'"

"What else?" Cabrillo asked, now becoming wary.

"You need to steal it from the archaeologist who found it," Overholt said, "preferably without him knowing."

Cabrillo paused for a second. "Have you looked in your den lately?"

"What den?" Overholt said, taking the bait.

"The den of vipers where you live," Cabrillo said.

"So you'll take the job?"

"Send me the details," Cabrillo said. "I'll leave in a few hours."

"Don't worry—this should be the easiest money the Corporation has made all year. Like a Christmas gift from an old friend."

"Beware of friends bearing gifts," Cabrillo said before disconnecting.

AN HOUR LATER, Juan Cabrillo was finishing his last-minute arrangements.

Kevin Nixon wiped his hands on a rag, then tossed it onto a bench in the Magic Shop. The Magic Shop was the department aboard the *Oregon* that handled mission fabrications, equipment storage, specialized electronics, disguises and costumes. Nixon was the shop overseer as well as creative inventor.

"Without accurate measurement," Nixon noted, "that's the best I can do."

"Looks great, Kevin," Cabrillo said, taking the object and placing it in a box that he sealed with tape.

"Take these and these," Nixon said, handing packets to Cabrillo.

Cabrillo slid the packets into the backpack.

"Okay," Nixon said, "you have cold-weather clothes, communications gear, survival food and whatever else I thought you might need. Good luck."

"Thanks," Cabrillo said. "Now I need to head topside and talk to Hanley."

Less than an hour later, after making sure Max Hanley, Cabrillo's second in command, had the operation in Reykjavik progressing properly, Cabrillo caught a ride to the airport for his flight to Greenland. What seemed like a simple matter would grow increasingly complex.

By the time it was over, a nation would be threatened, and people would die.

6

PIETER VANDERWALD WAS a merchant of death. As the former head of South Africa's EWP, or Experimental Weapons Program, under apartheid, Vanderwald had been overseer of such horrific experiments as human chemical sterilization through food additives, the spread of toxic air-borne plagues and biological weapons in public areas, and the introduction of chemical weapons into the population in liquid form.

Nuclear, chemical, biological, auditory, electrical—if it could be used to kill, Vanderwald and his team built it, bought it or designed it themselves. Their classified trials showed that a combination of agents, judiciously applied, could be used to sicken or kill thousands of the black South African population within thirty-six hours. Further studies detailed that, within a week, 99 percent of the unprotected population from the Tropic of Capricorn south, or half the entire tip of Africa, would eventually perish.

For his work Vanderwald received an award and a cash bonus of two months' salary.

Without long-range delivery systems such as ICBMs or SCUD, and with only a limited air force to call upon, Vanderwald and his team had perfected methods of introducing the death agents into the population, then had them spread by the victims themselves. The name of the game had been seeding the water supplies, allowing the wind to carry the plague, or using tank trucks or artillery shells for dispersal.

EWP had been masters at the game, but as soon as apartheid ended they were quickly and secretly disbanded, and Vanderwald and the other scientists were left to fend for themselves.

Many of them took their payoffs and retired, but a few like Vanderwald offered their specialized skills and knowledge on the open market, where an increasingly violent world was interested in their unique talents. Countries in the Middle East, Asia and South America had sought his counsel and expertise. Vanderwald had only one rule—he didn't work for free.

"YOU GOT A piece of that one," Vanderwald said easily.

A light breeze was blowing from the tee box toward the hole. The temperature was an even eighty degrees. The air was as dry as a bag of flour and as clear as a pane of glass.

"The breeze helped," Halifax Hickman said as he walked back to the cart and slid his club into the bag, then walked to the front and climbed into the driver's seat.

There were no caddies on the course, nor any other golfers. There was just a team of security men that drifted in and out of the trees and brush, a couple of ducks in the lake and a skinny, dusty red fox that had scampered across the fairway earlier. It was strangely quiet, with the air holding memories of the year nearly passed.

"So," Vanderwald said, "you must really hate these people."

Hickman stepped on the accelerator and the cart lurched forward down the fairway to their distant balls. "I'm paying you for your knowledge, not for psychoanalysis."

Vanderwald nodded and stared down at the photograph again. "If that's what you think it is," he said quietly, "you have a gem. The radioactivity is very high and it is extremely dangerous in solid or powdered form. You have a variety of options."

Hickman pressed on the brakes as the cart approached Vanderwald's ball. Once the cart had stopped, the South African climbed from his seat, walked around to the rear and removed a club from his bag, then approached his ball and lined up to take a shot. After a pair of practice swings, he stopped and concentrated, then made a smooth arcing swing at the ball. The ball blasted from the clubhead, gaining altitude as it traveled. A little over a hundred yards distant, it dropped to the grass less than ten yards from the green, just missing the sand trap.

"So a powdered form introduced from the air would do the trick?" Hickman asked as Vanderwald climbed back into his seat.

"Provided you could get a plane anywhere near the site."

"Do you have a better idea?" Hickman said as he accelerated away toward his ball.

"Yes," Vanderwald said, "striking at the heart of your enemies. But it will cost you."

"Do you think," Hickman asked, "that money is a problem?"

7

SOMETIMES TEMPERATURE IS as much a state of mind as a condition. See waves of heat rising from the asphalt and chances are that you will think it is hotter outside than if you see the same road lined with snow. Juan Cabrillo had no illusions as to what he was seeing. The view out the window of the turboprop as it made its way across the Denmark Strait from Iceland to Greenland was one that could chill a man's heart and make him rub his hands together in pity. The eastern shore of Greenland was lined with mountains, and it was a desolate and barren sight. In all of the thousands of square miles that comprised eastern Greenland, there was a population of less than five thousand.

The sky was deep blue-black and roiling with clouds that held snow. One did not need to touch the white-capped waters far below to know the water temperature was below freezing and the tossing torrent was in liquid form only because of the salt content. The thin rime of ice on the wings and the edging of frost on the windshield added to the image, but the thick ice cap that covered Greenland, barely visible through the windshield ahead, lent it the most chilling and ominous feel.

Cabrillo made an involuntary shiver and stared out the side window.

"We're ten minutes out," the pilot noted. "The report advises wind of only ten to fifteen. It should be a cakewalk landing."

"Okay," Cabrillo said loudly over the noise from the engines.

The men flew along in silence as the rocky outline loomed larger.

A few minutes later Cabrillo heard and felt the turboprop slow as it neared the outer edge of the airport's pattern. The pilot steered the plane from his crosswind leg onto the downwind leg that would take them parallel to the runway. They flew for a short distance and Cabrillo watched the pilot adjust the flight controls. A minute later the pilot turned on his base leg, then flew for a short distance and turned again onto his final approach.

"Hold on," the pilot said, "we'll be on the ground shortly."

Cabrillo stared down at the frozen wasteland. The lights lining the runway cast a pale glow against the afternoon gloom. The markings on the runway came into and out of view in the blowing snow. Cabrillo caught sight of the slightly extended wind sock through the haze and growing darkness.

The airport at Kulusuk, where they were landing, served the tiny population of four hundred and was little more than a gravel runway tucked behind a mountain ridge along with a couple of small buildings. The nearest other town—Angmagssalik, or Tasiilaq, by its Inuit name—was a ten-minute helicopter ride away and had three times the population of Kulusuk.

When the turboprop was just above the runway, the pilot gave it rudder and straightened it out against the wind. A second later he kissed the runway as light as a feather. Rolling across the snow-packed gravel, he slowed in front of a metal building. Quickly running through the postflight checklist, he shut down the engine then pointed to the building.

"I've got to fuel up," he said. "You might as well head inside."

8

AT THE SAME instant Cabrillo was landing at Kulusuk, the pilot of the Hawker 800XP was just shutting down his engines at the airport at Kangerlussuaq International Airport on the west coast of Greenland. Kangerlussuaq featured a six-thousand-foot-long paved runway that could handle large jets and was often used as a refueling station for cargo flights bound for Europe and beyond. The airport was nearly four hundred miles from Mount Forel but was the closest facility with a runway long enough to take the Hawker.

Clay Hughes waited while the copilot unlatched the door, then he rose from his seat. "What are your orders?" Hughes asked.

"We are to wait here until you return," the copilot said, "or receive a call from the boss telling us to leave."

"How do I reach you?"

The copilot handed Hughes a business card. "Here's the number for the satellite phone the pilot carries. Just call us and give us a half hour or so to prepare."

"Were you told how I'm supposed to get from here to where I'm going?"

The pilot poked his head out of the cockpit. "There's a man approaching the front of the plane," he said, motioning toward the windshield. "My guess is he's here for you."

Hughes placed the business card in the pocket of his parka. "All right, then."

An icy wind was blowing across the runway, scattering the dry powdered snow like confetti on a parade route. As Hughes climbed down the stairway from the Hawker, his eyes immediately began to tear.

"You must be the party I was hired to fly out to Mount Forel," the man said, extending his hand. "My name is Mike Neilsen."

Hughes gave Neilsen a fake name, then stared overhead. "Are you ready to leave?"

"We can't leave until morning," Neilsen said. "Two rooms were arranged at the hotel for you and the pilots. We can leave at first light—provided the weather breaks."

The men started walking toward the terminal. "Do you have enough range to fly directly to Mount Forel from here?" Hughes asked.

"I have a range of six hundred miles in still air," Neilsen told him. "However, for safety I think we should refuel in Tasiilaq before we attempt the mountain."

They reached the terminal building, and Neilsen opened the door then motioned for Hughes to enter. Neilsen steered Hughes toward a desk where a lone Inuit sat at an ordinary-looking metal desk. His mukluks were atop the desk, and he was sleeping.

"Isnik," Neilsen said to the dozing man, "time to work."

The man opened his eyes and stared at the two men in front of him. "Hey, Mike," he said easily. "Passport, please," he said to Hughes.

Hughes handed the official a U.S. passport bearing a false name but his actual picture. Isnik barely glanced at the document then stamped the entry.

"Purpose of visit?" he asked.

"Scientific research," Hughes answered.

"I guess no one comes here for the weather, right?" Isnik said as he made a notation on a slip of paper on a clipboard on his desk.

"Can you ask the pilots to walk over to the hotel after they are cleared?" Neilsen asked Isnik.

"You got it," Isnik said, sliding his boots back atop the desk.

Neilsen started leading Hughes to the door out of the terminal. "This is an old U.S. Air Force base," he said. "The hotel was base housing. It's actually quite nice. It has the only indoor pool in Greenland and even a six-lane bowling alley. For this country, it's the closest thing to four-star lodging."

The men covered the short distance across the parking lot to the hotel and Hughes received his key. Two hours later, after a meal of musk ox steaks and French fries, he settled in for the night. It was still only early afternoon, but tomorrow he had a lot of work to do and he wanted to be thoroughly rested.

9

JUAN CABRILLO BREEZED through customs at the tiny terminal at Kulusuk then stared at a map on the wall near the door leading out. In the brief months of summer, Kulusuk Island was ringed by water. As soon as fall arrived and the temperatures dropped, the seawater froze into thick sheets of ice. And while the ice never reached a thickness that could support the weight of a locomotive, for example, cars, trucks or snow vehicles had no trouble venturing across to the mainland.

In winter, Kulusuk was an island no more. It was attached to Greenland by ice.

From where Cabrillo stood, it was slightly over sixty miles north to the latitude that marked the actual Arctic Circle, and from there it was a dozen or so more to Mount Forel. Winter solstice, December 22, was only a few days past. That day, at the exact location of the Arctic Circle, was the only single day of total darkness each year.

North of the circle, depending on how far one went, the blackness was constant. The farther north, the longer that condition remained. At the exact spot of the Arctic Circle and to the south of it, December 22 marked a turning point.

As winter progressed toward spring, the daylight grew longer by minutes each day. By the time summer came, the midnight sun would rise and in the area north of the Circle, the sun would not set for some time.

It was a cycle that had repeated itself for countless eons.

Outside, a howling wind raked hard pellets of frozen snow against the windows in the terminal. The weather looked as appealing as the interior of a meat locker. Cabrillo stared and felt a shiver. Though still indoors, he tugged at the zipper to his parka.

Since Kulusuk was just south of the Arctic Circle, there would be a few minutes of light today. By contrast, Mount Forel was still in total darkness. The next few days and weeks would see the top of the mountain begin to catch the first rays of light. Then, as the months passed, the sunlight would begin to drip down the sides of the mountain like yellow paint poured atop a pyramid.

But looking outside one would never guess the sun had been, or was, anywhere near.

Right now, however, Cabrillo was less concerned with the darkness than he was with transportation. Walking off to the side of the terminal, he removed a satellite telephone and hit the speed dial.

"WHAT HAVE YOU found out?" he asked when Hanley answered.

Because of Overholt's urgency, Cabrillo had left the *Oregon* without a clear plan on how he was to travel to Mount Forel. Hanley had assured him that by the time he was on the ground there would be a plan in place.

"There are some dogsled teams available for charter," Hanley noted, "but you'd need a guide as a musher—and I didn't figure you wanted a witness, so I ruled that out. The helicopters that service Kulusuk have regularly scheduled routes, from Tasiilaq and back, but they don't hire out and the current weather has them grounded."

"Not walking weather," Cabrillo said, staring outside.

"Or skiing," Hanley added, "though I know you pride yourself on your skiing ability."

"So what is it?"

"I had the computer pull vehicle registrations from the area—it didn't take long, as there are only four hundred or so people in Kulusuk. I discounted snowmobiles because you'd be exposed to the snow and cold, plus their tendency to break down. That leaves us with snowcats. They are slow and burn a lot of fuel, but they have heaters and plenty of room for storage of supplies. I think that's our best bet."

"Sounds reasonable," Cabrillo said. "Where's the rental place located?"

"There isn't one," Hanley said, "but I pulled up the names and addresses of private owners from the Greenland registry and made a few calls. None of the people that own them have home telephone numbers, but I reached the pastor of the local church. He said there is one man that might agree to a rental—the rest are in use."

"What's the address?" Cabrillo asked, removing a pencil and small pad of paper from his parka for notes.

"The address is the sixth house past the church, red walls with yellow trim."

"No street addresses this far north, huh?"

"Everybody knows everyone else, I guess," Hanley said.

"Sounds like the natives are friendly."

"I'm not too sure about that," Hanley told him. "The pastor mentioned the owner drinks quite a bit during the winter. He also said almost everyone in town carries firearms to ward off bears."

Cabrillo nodded. "So basically, I just need to convince an armed drunken native to rent me his snowcat and I'm on my way," Cabrillo said, patting the packets of one-hundred-dollar bills in his parka pocket. "Sounds simple enough."

"Well, there's one more thing—he's not a native. He grew up in Arvada, Colorado, and was drafted into the army during the Vietnam War. From what I've been able to piece together from the databases, once he returned he spent a few years in and out of VA hospitals. Then he left the country with the idea of getting as far away from the U.S. as possible."

Cabrillo stared out the window again. "It looks like he reached his goal."

"I'm sorry, Juan," Hanley said. "In two more days, when the summit wraps up, we could reposition the *Oregon* and Adams could fly you up in the helicopter. Right now, however, this is all we've got."

"No sweat," Cabrillo said, staring at his notes. "Sixth house from the church."

"Red walls," Hanley said, "and yellow-painted trim."

"Well then, let me go meet a madman."

He disconnected and walked through the door leading outside.

CABRILLO LEFT HIS boxes of supplies at the airport and approached a snowmobile taxi with an Inuit teenager standing alongside. The boy raised his eyebrows when Cabrillo gave the address but he said nothing. He seemed more concerned with the fee, which he quoted in Danish currency.

"How much in U.S. dollars?" Cabrillo asked.

"Twenty," the boy said without hesitation.

"Done," Cabrillo said, handing the boy a bill.

The boy climbed onto the snowmobile and reached for the starter button. "You know Garth Brooks?" the boy asked, assuming everyone in the United States must know everyone else, just like in his village.

"No," Cabrillo said, "but I played golf with Willie Nelson once."

"Cool. Is he any good?"

"Wicked slice," Cabrillo said as the boy hit the starter and the engine roared to life.

"Get on," the boy shouted.

Once Cabrillo was seated, the boy raced away from the airport. The snowmobile's headlight barely cut through the darkness and blowing snow. Kulusuk was little more than a cluster of homes a mile or so from the airport. The sides of the houses were partially covered by snowdrifts. Trails of smoke and steam came from inside. Teams of dogs were clustered near houses, along with many snowmobiles; skis were propped up into the snow, tips aloft; snowshoes hung on nails near the doors.

Life in Kulusuk looked hard and grim.

North of town, the expanse of ice leading across to the mainland was barely visible as a dim outline. The surface of ice was black and slick as wind blew the snow and piled it into small drifts that ceaselessly formed and reformed. The hills across the frozen ice were only visible as an outline, a different color gray against a backdrop of nothingness. The scene looked about as inviting as a tour of a crematorium. Cabrillo felt the snowmobile slow then stop.

He climbed from the back and stood on the semipacked snow.

"Later," the teenager said with a quick wave of his hand.

Then the boy turned the yoke hard to the left, spun around on the snow-packed street and raced away. Cabrillo was left alone in the cold and darkness. He stared at the half-buried house for a second. Then he started walking through the drifts toward the front door. He paused on the stoop before knocking.

10

HICKMAN STARED AT the records from the Saudi Arabian Office of Procurement that his hackers had lifted from a database. The records had been translated from Arabic into English but the translation was far from perfect. Scanning the lists, he made notes alongside the columns. One entry stood out. It was for woven wool kneeling pads and the supplier was located in Maidenhead, England. Reaching for his intercom, he buzzed his secretary.

"There's a Mr. Whalid that works for me at the Nevada hotel. I think he's an assistant food and beverage director."

"Yes, sir," the secretary said.

"Have him call me at once," Hickman said. "I have a question for him."

A few minutes later his telephone rang.

"This is Abdul Whalid," the voice said. "I was told to call you."

"Yes," Hickman said. "Call this company in England for me"—he rattled off the telephone number—"pretend you're a Saudi Arabian official or something. They have a multimillion-dollar order for woven wool kneeling pads,

and I want to know what exactly that means, *woven wool
kneeling pads.*"

"Can I ask you why, sir?"

"I own mills," Hickman lied. "I'd like to know what
these items are, because if we can make them, I'd like to
know why my guys didn't bid on the job."

That made sense to Whalid. "Very good, sir. I'll call
them and call you right back."

"Excellent." Hickman returned to staring at the picture
of the meteorite. Ten minutes later, Whalid phoned again.

"Sir," Whalid said, "they are prayer rugs. The order is so
large because the country is replacing the entire inventory
used at Mecca. Apparently they do this every ten years or
thereabouts."

"Hmm, so we missed an opportunity that won't be
around again for a while. That's not good."

"I'm sorry, sir," Whalid said. "I don't know if you are
aware that I ran a mill in my own country before the overthrow. I'd be very interested—"

Hickman cut him off rudely. His mind was racing.
"Send me a résumé, Whalid," he said, "and I'll see it goes
to the proper person."

"I understand, sir," Whalid said meekly.

Hickman hung up the telephone without as much as a
good-bye.

PIETER VANDERWALD ANSWERED his cellular telephone as he was driving down the road just outside of Palm
Springs, California.

"It's me," the voice said.

"This is not a secure line," Vanderwald said, "so speak
in generalities and let's keep the call to less than three
minutes."

"The substance we spoke about," the man said, "can it
be applied in an aerosol form?"

"That's one way it could be used. It would then transfer
by air or get distributed along a human chain by touch or
coughing."

"Would the substance then transfer from person to person if it was on their clothing?"

Vanderwald stared at the digital clock on the radio of his rental car. Half the allotted time was gone. "Yes, it would transfer from clothing and skin, even through the air."

"How long would it take for someone to die from exposure?"

The digital clock on the dash flipped over a number. "Within a week—maybe less. I'll be at my land line tonight if you want to talk more."

The line went dead and the man sat back in his chair. Then he smiled.

"JUST OVER TWO million seems a steep price, considering last year's revenue," the lawyer said over the telephone. "Once they fill the contracts they have, their books are a little bare going ahead."

"Just do the deal," Hickman said quietly. "I'll write off any losses against the gains on my Docklands property."

"You're the boss," the lawyer said.

"You got that right."

"Where do you want the funds to come from?"

Hickman scrolled through a screen on his computer. "Use the Paris account," he said, "but I want to close the transaction tomorrow and take possession of the company within seventy-two hours at the latest."

"You think there'll be a shortage of British mills for sale in the next couple of days?" the lawyer said. "Or do you know something I don't?"

"I know a lot you don't," Hickman said, "but if you keep talking you'll only have seventy-one hours to put this together. You just do what you're paid to do—I'll take care of planning."

"I'm on it, sir," the lawyer said before disconnecting.

Sitting back in his chair, Hickman relaxed for a moment. Then he picked up a magnifying glass on his desk and stared at the aerial photograph in front of him. Placing the magnifying glass down, he examined a map. Lastly he

opened a file folder and flipped through the photographs
inside.

The photographs were of victims of the Hiroshima and
Nagasaki nuclear bombings at the end of World War II.
And although the photographs were graphic and disturb-
ing, the man smiled. Vengeance is mine, he thought.

THAT EVENING HE called Vanderwald on his land line.

"I found something better," Vanderwald said. "It's an
airborne plague that affects the lungs. Very toxic, it should
kill eighty percent of the population of the country."

"How much?" Hickman asked.

"The amount you need will be six hundred thousand
dollars."

"Have it delivered," Hickman said, "along with as much
C-6 as you can find."

"How big is the structure you're intending to demol-
ish?" Vanderwald asked.

"The size of the Pentagon."

"That much will be a million two."

"Cashier's check?" Hickman asked.

"Gold," Vanderwald said.

11

CABRILLO STARED AT the musk ox horns on the door, then reached over and lifted a fish-shaped iron door knocker and let it slam against the heavy planked door. He heard the sound of heavy footsteps from within, then it grew quiet. Suddenly a small hatch in the door the size of a loaf of bread opened and a face peered out. The man had shallow cheeks, a tobacco-stained gray beard, a mustache and bloodshot eyes. His teeth were stained and grimy.

"Slide it through the hole."

"Slide what through the hole?" Cabrillo asked.

"The Jack," the man said, "the bottle of Jack."

"I'm here to speak to you about renting your snowcat."

"You're not from the trading post?" the man said with more than a hint of disappointment and despair.

"No," Cabrillo said, "but if you let me in to talk, I'll go down and get you a bottle afterward."

"You're talking Jack Daniel's," the man asked, "not the cheap stuff, right?"

Cabrillo was cold and growing colder by the minute. "Yes, made in Lynchburg, Tennessee, black label—I know what you mean. Now open the door."

The peephole closed and the man unlocked the door. Cabrillo walked into a living room decorated in squalor and disarray. Dust from last summer coated the tables and upper edges of the picture frames. The smell was a mixture of old fish and foot odor. A pair of lamps on two side tables cast pools of yellow light into the otherwise dark room.

"Pardon the mess," the man said. "My cleaning lady quit a few years ago."

Cabrillo remained near the door—he had no desire to enter farther into the room.

"Like I said, I'm interested in renting your snowcat."

The man sat down in a battered recliner. A liter bottle of whiskey sat on the table at his side. It was almost empty, with barely an inch left in the bottom. Then, as if on cue, the man poured the last of the bottle into a chipped coffee mug and took a drink.

"Where are you planning on going?" the man asked.

Before Cabrillo could answer, the man had a coughing fit. Cabrillo waited for the end.

"Mount Forel."

"You with those archaeologists?"

"Yes," Cabrillo lied.

"You an American?"

"Yep."

The man nodded. "Pardon my manners. I'm Woody Campbell. Everyone in town calls me Woodman."

Cabrillo walked over and extended his gloved hand to Campbell. "Juan Cabrillo."

They shook hands, then Campbell motioned to a chair nearby. Cabrillo sat down and Campbell stared at him without speaking. The silence sat in the room like a brick on a potato chip. Finally, Campbell spoke.

"You don't look like an academic to me," he said at last.

"What's an archaeologist supposed to look like?"

"Not like someone who has been in battle," Campbell said, "like someone who has had to take another man's life."

"You're drunk," Cabrillo said.

"Maintenance drinking," Campbell said, "but I don't hear you denying anything."

Cabrillo said nothing.

"Army?" Campbell said, staying on the topic.

"CIA, but it was a while ago."

"I knew you weren't an archaeologist."

"The CIA has archaeologists," Cabrillo noted.

At that moment there was a knock at the door. Cabrillo motioned for Campbell to remain seated and walked over to the door. An Inuit dressed in a one-piece snowsuit stood with a sack in his hand.

"That the whiskey?" Cabrillo asked.

The man nodded. Cabrillo reached in his pocket and retrieved a money clip. Peeling off a hundred-dollar bill, he handed it to the man, who handed over the bottle.

"I don't have change," the Inuit said.

"Is that enough to pay for this and another to be delivered," Cabrillo asked, "and some extra for your trouble?"

"Yes," the Inuit said, "but the owner will only allow me to deliver Woodman one bottle per day."

"Bring the other tomorrow and keep the change," Cabrillo said.

The Inuit nodded and Cabrillo closed the door. Carrying the sack with the whiskey inside, he walked over to Campbell and handed it to him. Campbell took the bottle out of the sack, wadded up the paper and tossed it toward a trash can and missed, then cracked the seal and filled his cup.

"Appreciate it," he said.

"You shouldn't," Cabrillo told him. "You should give it up."

"I can't," Campbell said, eyeing the bottle. "I've tried."

"Bullshit. I've worked with guys with a worse problem than yours—they're straight today."

Campbell sat quietly. "Well, Mr. CIA," he said at last, "you figure a way to dry me out and the snowcat is yours. I haven't used it in months—I can't leave the house."

"You served in the army," Cabrillo said.

"Who the hell are you?" Campbell said. "No one in Greenland knows that."

"I run a specialized company that does intelligence and security work—a private corporation. We can find out anything."

"No shit?"

"No shit," Cabrillo said. "What was your job in the service? I didn't bother to ask my people that."

"Green Berets, then the Phoenix Project."

"So you worked for the Company, too?"

"Indirectly," Campbell admitted, "but they turned their back on me. They trained me, brained me, and cast me away. I came home with nothing but a heroin problem I managed to kick on my own and a host of bad memories."

"I hear you," Cabrillo said. "Now where is the snowcat?"

"Out back," Campbell said, pointing to a door leading out the rear of the house.

"I'm going to check it out," Cabrillo said, starting for the door. "You sit here and figure out if you really want to quit. If you do, and the snowcat checks out, then I have an idea we can discuss. If not, then we can discuss me paying you enough money to keep you in Jack until your liver fails. Fair enough?"

Campbell nodded as Cabrillo walked out.

Surprisingly enough, the snowcat was in perfect shape. A 1970 Thiokol model 1202B-4 wide-track Spryte. Powered by a Ford 200-cubic-inch six-cylinder with a four-speed transmission, it was bodied like a pickup truck with a flatbed on the rear. A light bar was mounted on the roof, an extra fuel tank on the rear bed, and the treads looked almost new. Cabrillo opened the door. Inside was a metal hump between the seats where the strangely angled gearshift resided, as well as a pair of levers in front of the driver's seat that controlled the tanklike steering. Cabrillo knew that with a flick of the levers the Thiokol could spin on its treads in a circle. The dashboard was metal, with a cluster of gauges in front of the driver and heater vents down lower. Mounted behind the seat, hung on racks on each side of the rear window, was a large-caliber rifle. There were emergency flares, a tool kit with spares, and detailed waterproof maps.

Everything was freshly painted, oiled and maintained.

Cabrillo finished his inspection and walked back inside. He stopped just inside the door and knocked the snow off his boots, then walked back into the living room.

"What's the range?" he asked Campbell.

"With the extra fuel tank and some jerry cans, it'll get you to Mount Forel and back, with an extra hundred miles or so in case of trouble or snow slides," Campbell said. "I wouldn't hesitate to make a trip anywhere in her—she's never let me down."

Cabrillo walked over near a fuel-oil stove. "Ball's in your court."

Campbell was silent. He stared at the bottle, looked up at the ceiling, then looked down at the floor and thought for a moment. At this pace, he had maybe one more summer. Then his body would start shutting down—or he'd make a drunken mistake in a land where mistakes are not forgiven. He was fifty-seven years old and he felt like he was a hundred. He had reached his end.

"I'm done," Campbell said.

"It's not that easy," Cabrillo said. "You have a tough battle ahead."

"I'm ready to try," Campbell said.

"We'll get you out of here and into detox in return for the snowcat. Do you have any living family?"

"Two brothers and a sister in Colorado," Campbell admitted, "but I haven't spoken to them in years."

"You have a choice," Cabrillo said, "either go home for treatment—or die here."

For the first time in years, Campbell smiled. "I think I'll try home."

"You've got to hold it together for the next few days," Cabrillo said. "First I need you to show me the route through the mountains here on the maps and help me prepare. Then I'm going to leave you with my spare satellite telephone so I can call you if I run into trouble. Do you think you'll be able to handle that?"

"I won't be able to stop cold turkey," Campbell said honestly. "I'd shake myself to death or go into convulsions."

"I don't want or expect you to," Cabrillo said. "You need medical care. I just want you sober enough to be able to answer the telephone and give me advice if any problems arise I can't handle."

"That I can do."

"Then hold on," Cabrillo said as he removed his satellite phone and dialed the *Oregon,* "and let me set it up."

CAMPBELL SNIFFED AT the wind and stared to the north. The Thiokol was idling smoothly a few feet away. The flatbed was loaded with extra jerry cans of fuel and the boxes of supplies Cabrillo had retrieved from the airport. Cabrillo was placing other boxes with food and items he didn't want to freeze on top of and below the passenger seat. The door was open and the hot air from the heater was creating clouds of steam.

"There's a storm coming," Campbell noted, "but I'd guess it won't be here until tomorrow afternoon or night at the earliest."

"Good," Cabrillo said, finished now and standing upright. "You remember how to use the satellite telephone?"

"I'm a drunk," Campbell said, "not an idiot."

Cabrillo stared into the darkness. "How long did you figure the trip will take?"

"You'll be there by morning," Campbell said, "*if* you follow the route I laid out."

"I have a handheld GPS and I have the compass in the 'cat and the maps you marked. I think I'm set to navigate."

"Whatever you do," Campbell said, "you follow that route. You're going to be skirting the ice cap a lot of the way, but then you'll need to go up on top. It's rough up there and constantly changing. If you get into trouble or overturn the 'cat, help will take a long time to reach you— maybe too long."

Cabrillo nodded then took a step forward and shook hands with Campbell. "You take care of yourself," he said over the increasing roar of the wind, "and watch the booze until we can get you to a treatment facility."

"I'm not going to let you down, Mr. Cabrillo," Campbell said, "and thanks for making the arrangements—for the first time in a long time I feel like there is light at the end of the tunnel. Hope, maybe."

Cabrillo nodded and then climbed into the cab of the Thiokol. Once inside he closed the door and removed his parka. Revving up the engine, he let it settle back into an idle. Then he engaged the clutch, shifted the gear lever into first and slowly pulled away from the house. The treads of the Thiokol threw snow into the air as he passed.

Campbell waited under the eave of the rear door until the lights from the snowcat faded into the darkness. Then he walked back inside and poured himself a carefully measured ounce of whiskey. He needed to calm the demons that were beginning to show their true colors.

Cabrillo felt the lap belt tug at his waist as the Thiokol started down the hill toward the expanse of ice leading to the mainland. When the snowcat had leveled out and was crossing the last few feet of snow-covered dirt before the frozen fjord, he felt a tightening in his crotch. Beneath the ice only a few feet away was a thousand feet of thirty-two-degree water and then a rocky bottom.

If the Thiokol hit a thin spot and he went in, he'd have only seconds to live.

Banishing the thought, Cabrillo stepped on the gas.

The tracks of the snowcat touched the edge of the ice then went out onto the frozen wasteland. The lights on the roof illuminated the blowing snow as the Thiokol headed across the ice. But the blowing wind made the snowflakes dance and their reflection was distorted, making distance ebb and flow.

Cabrillo was lost in a world without time or dimension.

A lesser man might have been scared.

12

IN REYKJAVIK, MAX Hanley was hard at work aboard the *Oregon*. The Arab Peace Summit was winding down and once tomorrow's meetings concluded, the emir would board his 737 and his security concerns would pass to his staff.

So far the operation had gone perfectly. The emir had been able to move freely about Iceland with an almost invisible security presence. The teams from the Corporation were masters at blending into the background. Today, after the meetings concluded, the emir had wanted to visit Blue Hole, a nearby natural hot springs pool that had been created when a new geothermal plant had been constructed. There, rich, mineral-laden water flowed among acres of volcanic rocks to form an outdoor oasis from the cold. Steam from the naturally heated waters swirled in the air, forming clouds like in a steam bath. People in the water appeared and disappeared like ghosts in a misty cemetery.

Six of the Corporation team had been nearby in the water while the emir soaked.

A few minutes ago, Hanley had received word that the emir was in the locker rooms dressing. Now, Hanley was coordinating the two separate convoys that would return the people back to the emir's hotel.

"Did you trip the switch?" Hanley asked Seng over the satellite phone.

"One in," he said, "one out. No one could see a thing."

"That should throw off the opposition," Hanley said.

"Slick as a baby's behind," Seng agreed.

"Make sure you time the two caravans to arrive a few minutes apart," Hanley said, "and go in through the back doors."

"You got it," Seng said before disconnecting.

"YOU HAVE ALL the arrangements made?" Hanley asked Medical Officer Julia Huxley as she walked into the control room.

"The detox facility is in Estes Park, Colorado," Huxley said. "I hired an Icelandic nurse who speaks excellent English to accompany him on the flight to New York and then on to Denver. A van from the facility will pick him up in Denver. All he has to do is make the flight from Kulusuk to Reykjavik alone. I've alerted the pilot and had a few Librium pills dropped at the airport for the pilot to hand-carry to him. That should calm him and help fight convulsions until the nurse here can take over."

"Good job," Hanley said. "We'll go ahead as soon as the chairman gives the okay."

"On the second matter," she said, "the boss needs to be concerned about radiation exposure when he retrieves the meteorite. I have some potassium iodine on board that we can give him when we meet up again, but the farther away he keeps the object, the better."

"His plan is to wrap it in plastic and an old blanket and carry it to the rear of the snowcat inside a metal toolbox."

"That should be fine," Huxley said. "It's the possibility of inhaled dust that should concern him the most."

"We estimate there will be no dust—in the photograph it looks like a giant ball bearing. Any dust should have burned off on reentry. So unless Cabrillo has prolonged, close contact with the orb, exposing him to the radiation, he should be okay."

"That's the score," Huxley agreed.

Huxley turned to leave but then stopped at the door. "Chief?" she said to Hanley.

"Yes, Julia?"

"I don't know if you've ever seen radiation exposure cases," she said quietly. "They aren't pretty. Tell the boss to keep the meteorite as far away from himself as possible."

"I'll relay the message," Hanley said.

13

ALEIMEIN AL-KHALIFA READ the fax once more then slipped the sheets of paper into a plastic sleeve to protect the image. The cost to the Hammadi Group for this information had been the equivalent of one million British pounds in gold. The greed and avarice shown by Man continued to amaze Al-Khalifa—for the right price most men would sell out their country, their future livelihood, even their God. The insider at Echelon had been no different. A host of gambling debts and poor financial stewardship had placed him in a position to be exploited. A slow seduction and increasingly larger payments for his treason had put him firmly within the Hammadi Group's control.

And now, after two years, the man had come through with a jackpot.

The problem was that Al-Khalifa had his plate rather full right now. Turning to the other man in the cabin of the yacht, he spoke.

"Allah blesses all that believe."

Salmain Esky smiled and nodded. "It seems to be an answered prayer," he agreed, "though it comes at an already bountiful time."

Al-Khalifa stared at him. Esky was small, a shade over five feet in height and as thin as a willow. A native of Yemen, he had dark, dusty skin, a receding chin line, and a mouthful of tiny pointed teeth stained yellow and brown. Esky was a follower, not particularly smart, but extremely loyal to the cause. All movements needed men like him. They were the pawns to be played. The fodder for the cannon.

By contrast, Al-Khalifa was tall, handsome, and moved with a grace that generations of leadership had instilled in his soul. For hundreds of years his ancestors had ruled as tribal leaders on the dusty Arabian Peninsula. It had only been in the last twenty years, since Al-Khalifa's father had fallen from grace with the Qatari royal family, that his bloodline had been reduced to ordinary status. Al-Khalifa was planning to rectify that situation soon.

Then he would follow through with his planned strike for Islam.

"Allah has blessed us with the funds to do both," Al-Khalifa said, "and we shall."

"So you want the captain to plot a course northeast to the site?" Esky asked.

"Yes," Al-Khalifa said quietly. "I'll bring the passenger aboard later."

FLAGGED IN BAHRAIN and registered as being owned by the Arab Investment and Trading Consortium, the three-hundred-and-three-foot-long *Akbar* was one of the largest privately owned yachts in the world. Few outsiders had ever been aboard the yacht, but those few had spoken of the plush salon, the large hot tubs on the rear deck, and the host of smaller boats, personal watercrafts, and helicopter that she carried.

From the outside, the *Akbar* appeared to be a floating palace owned by someone ultrarich. Almost no one would guess that she housed a terrorist cell. Along with the leader, Al-Khalifa, and the follower, Esky—both now on shore—were six more men. Two were Kuwaitis, two were Saudis, and there was one Libyan and one Egyptian. All of the men were infused with fundamentalist Muslim rhetoric. And all were ready to die for their cause.

"We're cleared to leave port," the captain said into a handheld radio.

"Once you're free of the outer harbor, begin steaming at full speed," Al-Khalifa ordered from shore. "I'll rendezvous with you in an hour and a half."

"Yes, sir," the captain answered.

Al-Khalifa slid the small telephone back into his front pocket and then stared at the electrical panel in the basement of the hotel again. "Place the charges there," he said to Esky, pointing to the main trunk line. "After the alarm sounds and it goes dark, meet me at the lower stairwell as we planned."

Esky nodded and began molding the C-6 explosive around the aluminum pipe. He was reaching into his pocket for the firing wires and triggers as Al-Khalifa walked away. Crossing through the underground parking garage, Al-Khalifa stopped, opened the rear of a van, looked inside, and then closed it up and walked across the lot again.

Opening the door to the emergency stairwell, he began climbing up flights of stairs.

Once he'd reached the floor directly under the Qatari emir's suite of rooms, he used his card key to enter a room that had been rented by his shell company. Al-Khalifa glanced at the bed he had flipped up against the wall earlier that day. Then he examined the strange-looking red-painted machine sitting on the area of the floor where the bed had formerly resided. Up near the ceiling was a four-foot-diameter diamond-tipped circular saw blade that looked like a giant version of what a woodworker would use to bore a hole in the side of a birdhouse. The blade was attached to a stainless steel shaft powered by hydraulic rams. Below the shaft was a rectangular metal box that housed the diesel engine that was used to power the boring unit. Under the engine box was an axle and automotive-sized wheels that allowed the unit to be towed where it was needed. A portable hand-control panel with a twenty-foot cable allowed the machine to be remotely operated.

When he lowered the blade, there were six feet of clearance between it and the ceiling. There was a square piece of plywood and a ladder placed alongside the machine. The entire affair had been brought to the room in parts over a period of weeks and then assembled. Maids had been kept out by giving the front desk strict orders to not have anyone enter the room.

The unit was used on construction sites to bore through concrete in order to lay cables.

Al-Khalifa figured it would go through a floor just fine.

THE EMIR OF Qatar was sleeping peacefully on the floor above. Security teams from the Corporation were passing the night on duty in rooms across the hall and adjacent to the emir's suite. They were sure the snatch would go down tonight. In the room across the hall, Jones and Meadows carefully watched the remote cameras. To the left of the emir's suite, Monica Crabtree made notes while Cliff Hornsby cleaned a handgun. In the room on the right side of the suite, Hali Kasim and Franklin Lincoln were picking at a platter of sandwiches as they waited.

There was nothing to indicate what was about to happen.

ONE FLOOR BELOW, Al-Khalifa placed a pair of night-vision goggles over his eyes, then fingered the remote control and stared at his watch. The seconds ticked past until the hand swept across 3 A.M. Then Al-Khalifa felt a rumble through the floors of the building and the lights went dead.

Al-Khalifa pushed the starter and the boring machine roared to life. Pressing the button to raise the ram, he watched as the shaft and spinning blade headed toward the ceiling. As soon as the blade made contact with the ceiling, it tore into the drywall and wooden supports, spewing wood slivers and dust into the room. The blade was through the ceiling in less than ten seconds, and fresh air from above filtered down. Lowering the ram, Al-Khalifa tossed the plywood sheet across the sharp prongs of the blade, then grabbed the control box again, climbed onto the plywood, and raised the ram with the power to the blade shut off. A second later he was up in the emir's room and stepped onto the floor.

Through the night-vision goggles, Al-Khalifa could see someone sitting in bed, rubbing his eyes. Sprinting across the suite, he grabbed a chair and jammed it under the door-knob, then raced back to the emir's bed.

Bending over, he taped the man's mouth and eyes shut, then pulled him from the bed and over to the hole. Once they were both on the plywood, he used the remote to lower the shaft and then pulled the man onto the floor and dragged him toward the door. Opening the door, he pulled the man down the hallway to the fire escape stairs and down.

Less than two minutes had passed since Al-Khalifa had started his plan.

A few minutes more and he'd be on the road.

"GOT IT," JONES said.

The Corporation teams were outfitted with small, powerful flashlights that clipped onto their belts. Eight thin beams of light flickered in the hall outside the emir's suite.

"The light went green," Meadows shouted after slipping an extra card key through the slot outside the emir's suite, "but the door won't open."

"Hali," Jones shouted, "you and Lincoln go down to the garage and block the exit."

The pair of men raced off.

"Crabtree, Hornsby," he added, "guard the lobby exit."

"Bob, back away," Jones said. "I'm going to blow the door."

Pulling a round metallic disk from his pocket, Jones removed a piece of paper protecting the high-strength tape, slapped it on the door, and flicked a small switch on the side.

"Sir," he shouted at the door, "back away from the door, we're coming in."

Jones and Meadows moved a short distance down the hall and waited for the charge to explode. As soon as it had gone off, Jones raced over and pushed through the shattered remains of the door. Racing toward the bedroom, he panned the flashlight across the bed. It was empty. Scanning the room with the thin beam of light, he came across the hole cut in the floor. Then he reached for his portable radio and called the *Oregon*.

"Code Red," he said, "the principal has been taken."

As he waited for a reply, Jones surveyed the bedroom. "Bob, see what's down there."

Meadows climbed through the hole.

"What's happening there?" Hanley asked when he came on the line.

"They grabbed our player," Jones said quickly.

"Now that," Hanley said slowly, "was *not* part of the plan."

"THIS IS THE bottom of the stairs," Al-Khalifa said to his blindfolded abductee.

Al-Khalifa was still wearing the night-vision goggles, but from what he could see, His Excellency did not seem overly frightened. He was just following along with Al-Khalifa, as if his security forces had taught him not to resist.

"Come this way," Al-Khalifa said, opening the door to the garage and dragging the emir by the arm.

Esky appeared in the goggles at the same moment that Al-Khalifa heard footsteps from above.

"Open the door of the van and remove the motorcycle," he shouted.

Esky raced over to the van, opened the rear door, and slid a ramp down to the pavement. Then he climbed inside the van and pushed the bike down the ramp. The metal ice studs embedded in the motorcycle's tires clicked like locusts on the metal ramp. Al-Khalifa had managed to pull the emir over to the van. He reached inside and removed an AK-47 assault rifle from the van's floor. Holding the emir's shirt with one hand, he swiveled around and pointed the rifle toward the door. He opened fire as soon as Kasim, followed by Lincoln, exited the stairway and came through the door. At the same instant Esky pushed the starter button. The BMW 650 with sidecar roared to life.

* * *

KASIM WAS HIT in the arm by a round but he managed to flop on his stomach and roll under a car. Lincoln escaped injury, and he crouched alongside his partner and withdrew his sidearm. He sighted down the barrel but the emir was in his field of fire.

"Cover my escape," Al-Khalifa said, handing Esky the rifle.

Esky took the AK-47 and started spraying the area near the stairwell with controlled bursts. Al-Khalifa pushed the emir into the sidecar and climbed aboard the motorcycle. Reaching for the clutch lever, he clicked the BMW into gear then goosed the throttle and pulled away from the van. Esky increased his fire.

Al-Khalifa steered to the ramp leading out of the underground facility and started to drive up to ground level.

Lincoln reached for the microphone on his lapel and called the *Oregon*.

"The principal is aboard a BMW motorcycle," he shouted.

Kasim balanced his handgun in his good arm. Carefully taking aim, he squeezed off a trio of rounds that struck Esky in the groin, heart and throat. He dropped to the ground like a sack of potatoes and the AK-47 fell to the concrete floor. Lincoln raced across the distance to the van, slid the rifle farther away, and stood guard over the dying man. The sound from the BMW grew faint in the distance.

HITTING THE TOP of the ramp at ground level, the BMW's front wheel pawed at the air. Al-Khalifa threw his weight forward to bring the wheel down and exited the parking structure onto the road in front of the hotel. He turned right, down Steintun Road, and traveled a few blocks to where it intersected with Saebraut before turning east and racing along the harbor. The road led out of town and there was no traffic.

Al-Khalifa stared at the emir in the sidecar—the man seemed strangely unafraid.

* * *

AFTER RACING ACROSS the lobby and bursting through
the hotel's front door, Crabtree and Hornsby caught sight
of the retreating motorcycle. They raced for their black
SUV parked in front of the hotel.

"Okay, everyone," Hanley said over the radio from the
Oregon's control room, "our principal is aboard a BMW
motorcycle."

Hornsby hit the key to unlock the doors of the SUV and
climbed into the driver's seat. Crabtree reached for her radio as she sat down.

"They turned east and are driving along the harbor," she
said. "We're giving chase."

AL-KHALIFA TWISTED THE throttle and took the
BMW to seventy miles an hour on the snow-covered road.
Passing three turnoffs, they crossed over a hill and were out
of sight of Reykjavik. Watching the side of the road carefully, he located a trail where he had packed down the snow
yesterday with a rented snowmobile. He turned onto the
narrow strip of packed snow and drove over another small
hill. A fjord with a thin crust of ice extended almost to the
base of the hill. Suddenly, civilization seemed far away.

There, on a pad of packed snow, a Kawasaki helicopter
was waiting.

HORNSBY SLOWED THE SUV as they passed the first
turnoff and glanced at the snow for tracks. Finding none,
he stepped on the gas and checked the next. Slowing to
check the side roads was killing time, but Hornsby and
Crabtree had no other choice.

The BMW motorcycle was nowhere to be seen.

AL-KHALIFA PLACED THE blindfolded emir in the passenger seat of the Kawasaki then locked the door from the
outside with a key. He had removed the inside latch from

the passenger side and now the emir had no way out. Walking around to the front of the helicopter, he climbed into the pilot's seat and slid the key into the ignition. As he waited while the igniters warmed, he stared over at his prisoner.

"Do you know who I am?" he asked.

The emir, still blindfolded with mouth taped shut, simply nodded.

"Good," Al-Khalifa said, "then it's time to take a little trip."

Twisting the key, he waited until the turbines had reached proper thrust. Then he pulled up on the collective and lifted the Kawasaki from the snow. Once the helicopter was ten feet off the ground he eased the cyclic forward. The Kawasaki moved forward, passed through ground effect as it rose in the air, then headed out to sea. Keeping the helicopter low over the terrain to blend in with the mountains, Al-Khalifa looked backward toward Reykjavik.

"THE TRACKS END here," Hornsby said, staring down at the snow through the open door of the SUV.

Crabtree was glancing out the side window.

"There," she said, pointing. "There's a packed trail."

Hornsby stared at the thin trail. "The snow's too soft. We'll just get stuck."

After calling the *Oregon*, who quickly dispatched George Adams in the Corporation's Robinson helicopter, Hornsby and Crabtree started hiking along the packed trail. They found the BMW motorcycle ten minutes later. By the time Adams flew overhead they had figured out what had happened. They called him on the radio.

"We have a blast patch from a rotor blast," Hornsby reported.

"I'll keep an eye out for another chopper," Adams said.

Adams flew as far from Reykjavik as he could before fuel ran low, but he saw no other helicopters. The emir had simply vanished, as if plucked from the earth by a giant hand.

14

CABRILLO DROVE THROUGH the darkness with the lights atop the Thiokol cutting a dim path through the sea of white. Five hours and fifty miles north of Kulusuk, he was finally settling into a groove. The sounds from the snowcat, which at first seemed chaotic and indistinctive, were now taking form. He could feel the pulses from the engine, the roar from the treads, and the groaning from the chassis, and he used the noises to gauge his progress. The sound and the vibrations signaled to him when the snowcat was climbing. The squeal from the treads indicated the type of surface he was crossing.

Cabrillo was becoming one with the machine.

Twenty minutes earlier, Cabrillo had first steered onto the massive ice cap that covered most of Greenland. Now, by using Campbell's maps and detailed notes, he was guiding the Thiokol through a series of ice-covered valleys. If all continued according to plan, he would reach Mount Forel at about breakfast time in Iceland. Then he'd snatch the meteorite, load it aboard the snowcat, then cruise back to Kulusuk and have the *Oregon*'s helicopter pick him and the orb up. In a few days they'd have their fee and it would all be over and done with.

At least that was the plan—in and out and home.

CABRILLO FELT THE front end lighten and jammed the levers in reverse just in time. The Thiokol stopped dead in her tracks then quickly roared backward. Since leaving Kulusuk, the trip had gone smoothly. Still, the unforgiving wilderness rarely allowed such easy passage and, had Cabrillo not stopped and backed up, in a few more seconds he and the Thiokol would have been at the bottom of a wide crevasse in the ice.

Once he had reversed a safe distance away, Cabrillo slipped on his parka and climbed from the cab. Reaching up and adjusting the lights, he walked forward and stared into the abyss. The thick wall of the glacier glowed blue and green in the lights.

Staring across the rift, he estimated the gap at twelve feet. There was no way to estimate how far down the crack went before it narrowed and closed. He tightened the hood of his parka against the howling wind. A few feet more and the snowcat would have tipped into the crevasse and downward until the crack narrowed and it was pinned facedown. Even if Cabrillo had survived the fall, there was a good chance he would have been trapped in the cab with no way out. He would have frozen to death before anyone could have found him, much less mount a rescue.

Shuddering from the realization, Cabrillo walked back and climbed into the cab of the Thiokol and stared at the clock. The time was now 5 A.M., but it was still as dark as it had been all evening. He glanced at the map, then took his divider and measured the distance to Mount Forel. Thirty miles and three hours of travel time left. Reaching for the satellite phone, he dialed Campbell. Surprisingly the phone rang only once.

"Yep," Campbell said in a clear voice.

"I just about ran into a crevasse."

"Give me your GPS numbers," Campbell said.

Cabrillo read them off and waited while Campbell consulted his map in Kulusuk.

"Looks like you took a wrong turn about a mile back," Campbell told him, "and went left instead of right. You're up against Nunuk Glacier. Backtrack and skirt the edge of the glacier. That will take you over a small rise and down into the lowland. From there you could see Forel if it was clear and not pitch-black outside."

"You sure?" Cabrillo asked.

"Positive. I've been up the canyon you're in before—it's a dead end."

"Back about a mile and turn left," Cabrillo reiterated.

"That would be a right turn to you," Campbell said quickly, "you've changed directions."

"Then I follow the edge of the glacier?"

"Yes, but right now, while you're stopped, I want you to climb out and adjust the light on the driver's side sideways. That way, once you reach the edge of the glacier, the light will illuminate the edge. The reflection will look like jade or sapphires—just glance occasionally to the side to check your progress. Once the edge of the glacier recedes you'll crest a ridge and start down again. That will signal that you're free of Nunuk Glacier. Then you'll have a straight shot up the side of Mount Forel. It's steep but the old Thiokol can make it—I've done it before."

"Thanks," Cabrillo said. "Are you going to be able to make it a few hours more if I need you? Keeping it on the straight and narrow?"

"I'm just sipping enough to get by," Campbell said. "I'll be here if you need me."

"Good," Cabrillo said as he shut the telephone off.

Climbing from the cab again, he reached up to the roof of the Thiokol and adjusted the light to the side. Then he climbed back in, shifted into first, and spun the snowcat 180 degrees on her tracks. Driving slowly, he found the edge of the glacier a few yards away and started following along.

Mount Forel was not far away, but in the snow and darkness it was still hidden.

Cabrillo needed to reach the mountain and retrieve her

secret. But there was someone else with the same plan—
and he didn't follow the same rules for fair play as the Corporation. The two of them were bound to collide.

THE EMIR FELT the helicopter slow as Al-Khalifa lined
the Kawasaki up over the fantail of the *Akbar,* and then
carefully set her down on the landing pad. Once deckhands
had chained down the skids and the rotor blade was secured, Al-Khalifa walked around, unlocked the door and
dragged him into the main salon. The emir's eyes were still
taped but he could hear what sounded like a half dozen
Arab voices. The air in the salon smelled of gunpowder,
oil, and a strange, sweet almond odor.

Hustled down a set of steps to a lower deck, the emir
was unceremoniously tossed on a bed and had his hands
and feet bound together with thick tape. He lay on his back
like a trussed chicken. The emir heard Al-Khalifa order a
guard posted outside. Then he was left alone to ponder an
unknown fate.

Other than the fact that the skin on his face had started
sweating from the heat in the cabin, the man was not overly
concerned. If Al-Khalifa was going to kill him he would
have done it already. That, and he knew his friends at the
Corporation would seek him out soon. If only he could
scratch his nose under the plastic—then he'd feel better.

"ATTACH THE WEAPONS pod," Al-Khalifa said as he
walked back into the main salon. "I need to fly to the
mountain as soon as possible."

Four of the men walked outside and started the process.
The installation went slow—wind, rain and snow were raking the *Akbar*'s deck, but the men were trained and unre-
lenting. Twenty-seven minutes later their leader walked
back in, wiping snow off his gloves.

"The pod is installed," he said to Al-Khalifa.

"Have the men come inside and gather around the
table."

The teams of terrorists slid into chairs at the long ornate

table. The gathering was a confederacy of killers, a party of thugs. They stared up at Al-Khalifa and waited.

"Allah has blessed us again," Al-Khalifa began. "As you witnessed, I captured the pro-Western emir that rules my country and have taken him prisoner. Soon I will ascend to the throne. On the second matter, a Western traitor has alerted me to the location of an orb of iridium we can use in conjunction with the bomb that is destined for London. If I can retrieve this iridium, it will magnify the destruction in London at least a hundredfold."

"Praise be to Allah," the group shouted spontaneously.

"Right now the *Akbar* is heading for the east coast of Greenland," Al-Khalifa said grandly. "In a few hours, when we arrive, I'll fly the helicopter over and recover the iridium. As soon as I return, we'll set a course for England and the conclusion of the mission."

"There is but one, and that one is Allah," the group shouted.

"For those of you that have your duties finished, I want you to rest up," Al-Khalifa said. "We will need everyone on their toes once we reach England. Soon those that oppose Allah will feel our wrath."

"Allah is great," the group shouted.

The meeting broke up and Al-Khalifa walked from the room and down to his cabin. He would grab a few hours' sleep. He had no way of knowing that this sleep would be his last until the big one.

15

AT HOTEL KANGERLUSSUAQ, thirteen hundred miles away, Clay Hughes was finishing a breakfast of bacon, eggs, hash browns and toast washed down with a pot of steaming coffee. Michael Neilsen approached his table.

"You ready to go?" Hughes asked, standing up.

"The weather has not improved much," Neilsen said, "but I'm willing to try if you want. What's your verdict?"

"We go," Hughes said.

"If I were you," Neilsen said, "I'd have the hotel pack some food for the trip—if we go down out there, it'll be some time before help can arrive."

"I'll order a platter of sandwiches and a couple thermoses of coffee," Hughes said. "Anything else you can think of we might need?"

"Just some luck," Neilsen said, glancing outside.

"I'll get the food and meet you at the helicopter."

"I'll be ready," Neilsen said, walking away.

Fifteen minutes later the EC-130B4 lifted from the snow-packed runway and started flying east. A slight tinge of yellow infused the clouds as the scant sunlight tried to penetrate the gloom. Mostly it was dark and dreary, like an omen carried on an evil wind.

The hours passed as the Eurocopter flew high above the snowy terrain.

THE THIOKOL STOPPED and Cabrillo stared at the map. He estimated that he was within an hour of reaching the cave on Mount Forel. Once he had started away from the glacier, he noticed his satellite telephone was receiving signals again. He hit the speed dial and called the *Oregon*.

"We've been trying to reach you," Hanley said as soon as he answered. "The emir was kidnapped last night."

"Kidnapped," Cabrillo said quickly, "I thought we were on top of that situation."

"They grabbed our guy," Hanley said, "and we have had no communication with either party since."

"Do you have an idea where they've taken him?"

"We're working on it."

"You get our man back," Cabrillo said.

"Will do."

"I'm almost at the site," Cabrillo said. "I'll wrap this up and get out of here. Meanwhile, you locate me some faster mode of transportation home."

"Yes, sir," Hanley said.

Cabrillo disconnected and tossed the telephone on the passenger seat.

AT THE SAME time Cabrillo started up Mount Forel, an attendant at Reykjavik International Airport was sweeping snow from the bottom of a ramp leading up to a privately owned 737. Auxiliary power units were supplying the plane with heat and electricity from both sides. The inside of the jet was lit up like a billboard and it spilled out of the windows into the dim light outside.

Peering from the cockpit window, the pilot watched as a black limousine wheeled onto the runway and pulled up alongside the ramp. He watched as four people filed out from the rear. Two of them quickly climbed the steps as the other two scanned the airport grounds to see if anyone was watching. Finding it clear, they quickly climbed up the ramp and closed the door to the jet.

The attendant unhooked the APUs, then backed the ramp away and stood quietly while the pilot started the engines. After calling the tower for clearance, he taxied out to the runway and lined up for takeoff. With a refueling stop in Spain, they'd reach their destination fourteen hours from now.

As soon as the 737 left the runway, the attendant bent down and spoke into a microphone clipped onto his parka near the hood.

"They're away," was all he said.

"Acknowledged," Hanley answered.

SINCE HIS CONVERSATION with Hanley, Cabrillo had been steering the Thiokol uphill for nearly an hour. He stopped, fastened his parka tight, and climbed out. Adjusting the lights so he could scan the mountain, he walked around to the front to knock ice from the grille. He was just about ready to climb back inside when he heard a thumping sound in the distance. Reaching into the cab, he twisted the key and shut the Thiokol's engine off. Then he listened again.

The noise floated on the wind, ebbing and flowing like the tide. Finally, Cabrillo identified the sound, and he climbed back inside the snowcat and reached for the telephone.

"Max," he said quickly, "I hear a helicopter approaching. Did you send someone out?"

"No, boss," Hanley said. "We're still working on that."

"Can you find out what's going on?"

"I'll try to link onto a DOD satellite and figure out who it is, but it might take fifteen to twenty minutes."

"I'd like to know who's crashing my party," Cabrillo said.

"One thing we found out is that there's an unmanned U.S. Air Force radar site nearby," Hanley said. "Maybe the antennas are still being used and the Air Force is flying someone there for repairs or whatever."

"You find out for me," Cabrillo said as he twisted the key and started the engine. "I think I'm almost at the cave."

"Will do," Hanley said.

USING A SLED to pack down the snow and a dozen packets of Kool-Aid, Ackerman had managed to create a nice landing spot marked with an X on a small mesa only seventy yards from the lower opening of the cave. He stared at the spot with pride. The helicopter should be able to land without the rotor blade striking the mountain. It was precarious, but it was the best he could do on the side of a mountain.

He retreated back into the mouth of the cave and waited as the helicopter approached the landing pad then hovered and set down. The rotor blade slowed, then stopped, and a man climbed from the passenger side.

CABRILLO HEARD THE helicopter land through his open window, but through the snow and darkness he had not been able to see it touch down. He was close—he could sense that. He attached nylon gaiters around his down-filled pants and removed a pair of snowshoes from the rear bed. Sliding his boots into the bindings, he fastened them tight. Then he reached in back and removed the cardboard box holding the decoy that Nixon had made.

Now all he had to do was slip into the cave undetected and make the switch.

"THE BOSS SENT me," Hughes said to Ackerman after climbing up the hill to the mouth of the cave, "to check out your find."

Ackerman smiled proudly. "She's a peach," he said, "possibly the most important archaeological find of this century."

"So I hear," Hughes said, edging farther into the cave. "And he sent me to make sure you get what you deserve."

Ackerman grabbed an already lit lantern and started to lead Hughes down the passage.

"So you're in public relations?"

"That and other duties," Hughes said, stopping at the opening in the ceiling. A few days ago Ackerman had brought a wooden ladder from inside the upper cave and dropped it down the hole. It made going between the two shafts a lot easier.

"We'll climb up and I'll give you the grand tour," Ackerman said.

The two men climbed the ladder into the upper cave.

Hughes played along as Ackerman rattled off what he had found, but truly there was only one thing he'd come for. And as soon as he had that, he was leaving.

CABRILLO TRAIPSED AROUND the side of the mountain until he came upon a spot of melted snow. Bending over, he could see that there was a small opening in the mountainside marked by rocks laying in the snow, as if they had been tossed out from inside the mountain. Warm air from inside the mountain was filtering out, melting the snow around the opening. Clearing away enough of the debris so that he could climb inside, he slid through the opening into the upper cave, then dragged the cardboard box inside.

Once he was through the opening, he found he could stand.

He walked down the shaft to see where it went.

EVEN WITH A heart of stone, Hughes was finding the cave and its inner sanctum impressive. Ackerman was standing alongside the meteorite on its altar with his arm outstretched like a prize lady on a game show.

"Beautiful, isn't it?" Ackerman gushed.

Hughes nodded then removed a portable Geiger counter from his pocket. Flicking it on, he scanned the meteorite. The readings were off the scale. A couple of hours of exposure and he'd quickly start to suffer from radiation poisoning. He realized he'd need to shield it carefully for the trip back to Kangerlussuaq.

"You spent much time close to this?" Hughes asked Ackerman.

"I've examined it from every angle," Ackerman told him.

"Have you been feeling poorly? Noticed any physical changes in yourself lately?"

"I've been having nosebleeds," Ackerman said. "I figured it was just the dry air."

"I think you have radiation sickness," Hughes said. "I'm going to need to go back to the helicopter and get something to shield this."

CABRILLO HURRIED DOWN the shaft toward the sound of the voices. Hiding behind a rock, he listened to the two men.

"I'm going to need to go back to the helicopter and get something to shield this," one said. He listened as the two men walked off and the cavern grew dark. He waited to see what would happen next.

"WAIT HERE," HUGHES said when they reached the mouth of the lower cave.

Ackerman watched as Hughes walked down the hill, approached the helicopter, and opened the rear door.

"I'll be back in a few minutes," he said to Neilsen as he removed a box from the rear, "then we can go."

"Sounds good," Neilsen said, staring out at the weather.

Hughes started back up the hill with the box. When he entered the cave he looked at Ackerman. "I brought something that will ease your suffering," he said. "I'll give it to you in a few minutes."

CABRILLO WAITED A minute until he was sure he was alone, then reached into his pocket and removed a plastic bag and ripped off the top. Removing the chemical light bar inside, he bent it in half like he was trying to break a bread stick and the tube started glowing green. Using the light to illuminate his way, he started to walk toward the meteorite. He was just approaching the altar when he heard a shot ring out.

Quickly reaching into his pocket, he removed a foil packet, tore off the top with his teeth and sprinkled the contents onto the meteorite. Then, with the sounds of footsteps quickly approaching, he slid off to the side behind some rocks and placed the green light in his pocket.

A tall man carrying a lantern walked over to the altar, scooped up the meteorite and placed it in a box. Cabrillo had left the rifle in the Thiokol, so there was little he could do right now. Cabrillo would need to intercept the meteorite farther down into the cave.

Gripping the metal hoop from the lantern in his mouth, the man carried the box out.

Cabrillo waited, until the light from the lantern petered out, then slowly walked down the cave with his chemical light held in front. He figured the men would be examining the meteorite somewhere else, and when he found them he'd make his move.

Then he bumped into the ladder and nearly fell down the hole.

Listening carefully to see if they'd heard the noise, Cabrillo waited and, when nothing happened, climbed down the ladder. At the bottom he stepped on Ackerman's body.

16

AS SOON AS Hanley received confirmation that no Icelandic civilian or military helicopters had been in the air at the time of the emir's abduction, it was child's play to coordinate this information with the port records to see what ships had come and gone close to the time.

It didn't take him long to settle on the *Akbar* as their primary target.

Accessing satellite records, he determined that the *Akbar* was steaming up the Denmark Strait between Iceland and Greenland. Immediately leaving port, he ordered the magnetohydrodynamic drives engaged as soon as they were clear of land. The *Oregon* was cruising at thirty knots and weaved through the icebergs like a slalom skier down an icy slope. He tried Cabrillo's telephone again but there was no answer.

At that moment, Michael Halpert entered the control room. "They dummied up the chain of ownership," he said, "that's why we missed the threat."

"Who is the true owner?" Hanley asked.

"The Hammadi Group."

"Al-Khalifa," Hanley said. "We knew he was planning a

move on the emir, but if we'd known he had a yacht under his control it might have gone a lot different."

Eric Stone swiveled around in his seat. "Chief," he said, "I have the link you requested established. The helicopter ident is on the screen. The make is a Eurocopter and the model an EC-130B4. I'm running the registration right now."

Hanley glanced over at the screen. "Why are there two blips?"

Stone stared at the image then enlarged the screen. "That second return just appeared," he said. "Just guessing, I'd say another helicopter is in the area."

CABRILLO HELD OUT his green light, reached down, and placed his fingers on Ackerman's neck. He felt a faint beat. Then the archaeologist stirred and opened his eyes. His eyes were watery, his skin a ghastly gray, and his lips barely moved.

"You're not . . . ," he whispered.

"No," Cabrillo said, "I'm not the man who shot you."

Pushing Ackerman's coat aside, Cabrillo took a knife from his pocket and cut away Ackerman's shirt. The wound was bad, and arterial blood was pumping out of the opening like a fountain with too large a pump.

"Do you have a first-aid kit?" Cabrillo asked.

Ackerman motioned to a nylon bag near a folding table a short distance away. Cabrillo ran over, unzipped the bag and removed the kit. Opening the plastic case, he removed some gauze pads and surgical tape. He tore open the packets as he walked back toward Ackerman, then pressed a wad of pads over the wound and taped it in place. Then he reached over and placed Ackerman's hand over the wound.

"Keep your hand here," Cabrillo said, "I'll be right back."

"The Ghost," Ackerman whispered, *"the Ghost* did this."

Turning on his heels, Cabrillo sprinted toward the entrance to the cave. As he peered out into the gloom he could hear the turbine of the Eurocopter winding up and see the outline of the flashing lights on its fuselage.

Then a second set of blinking lights appeared in the distance.

AL-KHALIFA WAS AN excellent helicopter pilot. A falsified student visa and $100,000 in fees, as well as a year at the South Florida flight school he had attended, ensured that. Looking through the windshield, he carefully scanned the terrain on Mount Forel. He had just caught sight of an orange snowcat off to the side of the mountain when the other helicopter came into view.

Fate is funny—five minutes later and he would have missed his chance.

A second later, Al-Khalifa had assessed the situation and formed his plan.

CABRILLO SLID CAREFULLY out of the cave and then flopped down behind a rocky outcropping. He needed to make it to the Thiokol and recover his rifle, but the second helicopter was facing him directly. Sliding the satellite telephone from his pocket, he glanced at the readout. Now that he was outside the cave he was receiving a signal again. He hit the speed dial and waited until Hanley answered.

"It looks like the fall of Saigon up here," Cabrillo said. "I arrived to find a helicopter on site, and now another one has just arrived. Who are these people?"

"Stony just identified one," Hanley answered. "It's a charter from western Greenland owned by a Michael Neilsen. We ran the owner for ties to any organizations but no hits yet, so I'd guess he's just a pilot for hire."

"What about the second one?"

Stone had been furiously typing on the keyboard. "It's a Bell Jet Ranger leased by a Canadian mineral company."

"The second one's a Bell Jet Rang—" Hanley started to say.

"I'm staring at it right now," Cabrillo said. "It's not a Jet Ranger, it looks more like a McDonnell Douglas 500 series."

Stone typed in some more commands and a second later

a picture of a wrecked helicopter filled the monitor. "Someone has stolen the registration and ident to avoid detection. Can Mr. Cabrillo see any tail numbers?"

"Stone says we have a stolen registration," Hanley noted. "Can you see any tail numbers?"

Cabrillo removed a pair of small binoculars from his pocket and stared through the darkness. "Two things," he said slowly. "The first is that there's a weapons pod hung under the fuselage. The second is that the tail numbers aren't visible, but I can make out letters painted on the side. There is an A, followed by a K, followed by a B. Then the rest are covered in ice. The next is maybe an A, I can't be sure."

Hanley related to Cabrillo what they had uncovered about the yacht named *Akbar*.

"It's that son of a bitch Al-Khalifa?" Cabrillo blurted. "Who's in the other helicopter? Al Capone?"

NEILSEN HAD THE rotor blade up to speed and he pulled up on the collective, taking the Eurocopter into a hover just as the other helicopter appeared in the windshield.

"Look there," he said through the headset to Hughes.

"Take off, now," Hughes shouted.

"I think we'd better set down and see what's up," Neilsen said.

With a lightning-fast move, Hughes pulled a pistol from his pocket and pointed it at Neilsen's head. "I said take off."

One look at Hughes and the pistol was enough; Neilsen moved the cyclic and the Eurocopter lurched forward. At that instant a flame erupted from the bottom of the other helicopter and a missile streaked toward where they had been hovering. The missile went wide and veered out into the frozen wasteland.

STONE BROUGHT UP an image on the monitor in the *Oregon*'s control room. "This is a DOD satellite shot one hour ago," he said quickly. "Helicopter number two came from a location offshore of eastern Greenland on a straight course for Mount Forel."

Just then Adams walked into the control room. "Our helicopter is armed and ready."

"Do you have enough range to make it from here and back?" Hanley asked.

"No," Adams admitted, "we'll be thirty to forty gallons short on the return."

"What kind of fuel do you burn?"

"One hundred octane low-lead."

"Mr. Chairman," Hanley said over the satellite phone, "we have Adams ready to go, but we're short fuel for the return trip. Do you have extra fuel on the snowcat?"

"I have a hundred gallons or so left," Cabrillo said.

Hanley looked up at Adams, who had listened to the transmission carefully.

"If I take along some liquid octane booster, we can bump the gas up so it might work. One way or another, I want to get over there and help the boss."

"I'll call the mechanical shop and have the booster delivered to the flight deck," Hanley said quickly. "You do your preflight and take off as soon as possible."

Adams nodded and raced for the door.

"I'm sending in the cavalry, Juan," Hanley said into the telephone. "He'll be there in a couple of hours."

Cabrillo watched as the second helicopter lined up on the Eurocopter to take another shot. "That's good," Cabrillo said, "because the helicopter with the fake registration just fired a missile at the chartered ship."

"You've got to be kidding," Hanley said in amazement.

"That's not all, my friend," Cabrillo said. "I haven't had a chance to deliver the really bad news yet."

"What could be worse?"

"The meteorite is inside the chartered helicopter," Cabrillo said. "They grabbed it before me."

INSIDE THE EUROCOPTER, Hughes was holding the pistol to Neilsen's head with one hand and a satellite telephone in the other.

"Fly west toward the coast," he said, "there's been a change in plans."

Neilsen nodded and made the adjustment.

At the same time, Hughes pressed a button on the speed dial of the phone and waited.

"Sir," he said as Neilsen sped up and raced over the snowy terrain, "I've recovered the object and fired the caretaker, but now there's a snag."

"What's the problem?" the man said.

"We're under attack from an unidentified helicopter."

"You're headed for the coast, right?"

"Yes, sir, just like we planned."

"The team is there and waiting," the man said. "If the helicopter follows you out to sea, they can deal with the problem nicely."

Before Hughes could answer, a second missile struck the tail of the Eurocopter and severed a blade on the tail rotor. Neilsen fought with the controls but the Eurocopter started into a death spiral toward the ground.

"We're going down," Hughes managed to shout before the centrifugal force of the spinning Eurocopter flung his hand against the side window, cracking the glass and breaking the phone.

AS THE HELICOPTERS had retreated into the distance, Cabrillo had made his way to the spot on the mountain above where he'd left his snowshoes. He was attaching them to his feet when the sound of the missile striking the Eurocopter caused him to look up. It was dark and he had a hard time making anything out for a second. Then, a few seconds later, a bright pulsing light appeared on the ground in the distance. It danced on the ground like an evil Northern Light, and then started to fade.

Cabrillo finished attaching the snowshoes then made his way over to the Thiokol and drove it in the direction of the light. Ten minutes later, when he arrived at the site, the fires were still smoldering. The helicopter itself was lying on her side like a broken pinwheel. Cabrillo climbed out and forced the jammed door on top of the wreckage open.

Both the pilot and the passenger were dead. Removing what identification he could find from the bodies and the helicopter, he searched the wreckage for the box containing the meteorite.

But he found nothing. Only a set of footprints from parties unknown.

AFTER THE LINK to Hughes had gone dead and could not be reestablished, Hughes's employer called another number.

"We've had a hitch," he said. After he explained the situation, the other party answered.

"Not to worry, sir," he said confidently, "we're trained for contingencies."

17

AS SOON AS the snow and cold had started to extinguish
the fire from the ruptured fuel tank, Al-Khalifa had pried
open the door of the Eurocopter. A quick check of the bodies had revealed open, sightless eyes that seemed to indicate death had come quickly. Al-Khalifa had not bothered
to try to identify the men—quite frankly he did not care
who they were. They were Westerners and they were dead,
and that was enough.

His main concern was the recovery of the meteorite,
and for that he'd needed to climb through the rear door to
where the box had wedged itself against a seat. Removing
the box and climbing out of the helicopter, he'd opened the
latch and flipped open the top.

The meteorite was inside, lying on foam and shielded
by lead panels inside the box.

Closing the box again, he made his way through the
snow to the Kawasaki HK-500D, placed the box on the
passenger seat and secured it in place with the seat belt.
Then he climbed into the pilot's seat, started the engine
and lifted off. As he flew out over the snow-covered terrain, the box sat on the seat like an honored guest, not a

deadly sphere of poison destined to sicken an unknowing populace.

Reaching for the radio, Al-Khalifa alerted the crew of the *Akbar* he would soon be back on board. Once he reached the vessel, they could make their way to London and complete the mission. The wrath of the righteous would soon find flight.

After that he could deal with the emir and the overthrow of the Qatari government.

"GIVE ME SOME good news," Cabrillo said as he turned his back to the increasingly strong winds.

"We located the *Akbar* on the radar," Hanley said. "We're a couple hours away. I'm planning an assault now to get our man back."

Cabrillo was watching the signal strength on the telephone. He moved to receive a stronger connection. "I'm at the site where the Eurocopter went down," he said. "It was shot out of the sky by the mystery chopper. The pilot and passenger are dead—and the meteorite is nowhere to be seen."

"Are you sure?" Hanley asked.

"Positive. There's a single set of tracks coming from a distance away. I followed them until I came to indentations in the snow from the other helicopter. Whoever shot down the Eurocopter now has the meteorite."

"I'll have Stone try to track the course of the helicopter on radar," Hanley said. "He couldn't have gone far. If it's an MD helicopter, we're looking at a range of three hundred fifty miles in total. Since he couldn't refuel, he's somewhere within a one-hundred-seventy-five-mile radius of where you are."

"Tell Stone to try something else as well," Cabrillo said. "I managed to sand the meteorite before it was stolen."

Sand was the slang name the Corporation used for the microscopic homing bugs Cabrillo had sprinkled on the orb in the darkness. They looked like dust to the untrained eye, but they emitted a signal that could be read by the electronics on the *Oregon*.

"Damn, you're good," Hanley said.

"Not good enough, someone else has our prize."

"We'll track it down," Hanley said.

"Call me when you know something."

After disconnecting, Cabrillo started trudging back to the cave through the snow.

EIGHTY MILES DISTANT and undetectable on the *Akbar*'s radar scope, the scene aboard the motor yacht *Free Enterprise* was more subdued. The men on board were infused with a fervor that rivaled the Muslims on the *Akbar*—they were simply more highly trained and not accustomed to grand shows of emotions. Each man was white, over six feet in height, and in excellent shape. Each had served in the U.S. military in one capacity or another. All of them had personal reasons for accepting this assignment. Each of them was ready to die for the cause.

Scott Thompson, the leader of the team on the *Free Enterprise*, was in the wheelhouse awaiting a call. As soon he received it, they would launch the assault. West and East were about to collide in an affair conducted in secret.

The *Free Enterprise* was racing south through a thick fog. In the past hour the ship had come alongside a trio of icebergs, the tops of which had covered at least an acre. Smaller floes were too numerous to count, and they bobbed on the seas like ice cubes in a highball glass. It was bitterly cold outside and the wind was increasing.

"Active engaged," said the captain.

High up on the *Free Enterprise*'s superstructure an electronics package began capturing radar signals from other vessels. Then it broadcast the signals back at varying speeds. Without a consistent signal return, the other ships' radars could not paint the *Free Enterprise*.

The ship had become an unseen wraith on the black, tossing seas.

A tall man with a crew cut entered the pilothouse.

"I just finished running all the data," he said. "Our best guess is that Hughes is gone."

"Then there's a good chance that whoever was hunting Hughes recovered the meteorite," the captain noted.

"The big man is tracking the helicopter at one of his space companies in Las Vegas."

"And where is the helicopter headed?" the captain asked.

"That's the good part," the man said, "right to our intended target."

"Sounds like we can kill two birds with one stone," the captain said.

"Exactly."

ADAMS WAS AN excellent pilot, but the growing darkness and wind were making his hands sweat. He'd been flying only on instruments since leaving the *Oregon*. Wiping his palms on his flight suit, he turned the cockpit heater down and studied the navigation screen. At his current speed he was due to pass over the coastline in two minutes. Increasing his altitude to clear the start of the mountain range, he scanned the instruments again.

The lack of visibility made it like walking around with a paper bag over your head.

CABRILLO WASN'T SURE if Ackerman was dead or alive.

From time to time Cabrillo would feel what seemed like a faint pulse, but the wound was no longer bleeding—and that was a bad sign. Ackerman had not moved a muscle since Cabrillo had returned to the cave. His eyes were closed and the lids were motionless. Cabrillo propped him up so the wound was below his heart and then covered him with a sleeping bag. There was not much else he could do for him.

Then his telephone rang.

"The signal from the meteorite is leading right to the *Akbar*," Hanley said.

"Al-Khalifa," Cabrillo spat out. "I wonder how he found out about the meteorite."

"I alerted Overholt that Echelon has a leak," Hanley said, "that's the only way."

"So the Hammadi Group is trying to produce a dirty bomb," Cabrillo said, "but that doesn't explain who the first people that grabbed it were."

"We haven't been able to find out any information on the passenger," Hanley said, "but my guess is that it was someone working with Al-Khalifa and they had a falling out."

Cabrillo thought for a minute. It was a plausible explanation—maybe the only one that made sense—still, he had an uneasy feeling. "I guess we'll know when we recover the meteorite and liberate the emir."

"That's the plan," Hanley agreed.

"Then this will be over," Cabrillo said.

"Neat as a pin."

Neither Cabrillo nor Hanley could foresee that the outcome was still days away.

Nor did they know it would be anything but neat.

"Have Huxley call me," Cabrillo said. "I need some medical advice."

"You got it," Hanley said as he rang off.

ON BOARD THE *Akbar,* high-powered landing lights were flicked on to light the landing pad.

Off to the side, a pair of Arabs watched as Al-Khalifa lined up over the fantail then eased forward and touched down. As soon as the helicopter's skids touched the deck, the two men raced under the spinning rotor blade and secured the skids to the deck.

The blade slowed as Al-Khalifa pulled on the rotor brake, and once it was stopped he climbed out and walked around to the passenger side. Taking the box in his hands, he walked to the door to the main salon and waited until it was opened.

He walked inside and approached the long table and sat the box on the top.

As he unfastened the clasp and flipped the lid open, the terrorists gathered around and stared at the orb in silence.

Then Al-Khalifa reached down and lifted the heavy sphere and held it over his head.

"A million more infidels dead," he said grandly, "and London in ruins."

"Praise be to Allah," the terrorists shouted.

"ONE MILE DEAD ahead," the captain of the *Free Enterprise* said, "moving at fifteen knots."

A total of nine men dressed in black waterproof uniforms were clustered in the pilothouse. The men were armed with rifles on slings, handguns, and grenades.

The *Free Enterprise* was dead in the water. Outside on her rear deck, a large black bulletproof inflatable boat was being lowered over the side. Fifty-millimeter machine guns were mounted on the bow and stern of the inflatable. Mounted to the rigid fiberglass floor of the vessel was a high-performance gasoline engine.

The boat disappeared over the side and splashed into the water.

"We go in at the stern," the leader said, "neutralize the targets, retrieve the meteorite, and then get out again. I want us back on board in five minutes tops."

"Will there be any friendlies?" one of the men asked.

"One," the leader said, handing out a photograph.

"What do we do with him?"

"Protect him if you can," the leader said, "but not if it means your own life."

"Leave him on board?"

"He's of no use to us," the leader said, "now let's go."

The men filed out of the pilothouse and onto the rear deck. They walked in single file down a set of steps built along the hull to a small platform where the inflatable was docked and idling. As soon as the men were all aboard, one of them took up position behind the wheel, engaged the drive and steered away from the *Free Enterprise*.

At a speed of fifty-five knots it did not take long for the inflatable to reach the *Akbar*.

Once they reached the rear of the yacht, the man operat-

ing the inflatable held his vessel against the rear swim platform of the steaming *Akbar* with a judicious application of
power. The men stepped onto the platform and the captain
of the inflatable backed away a short distance and kept
pace with the yacht. Slowly the eight men made their way
topside.

THE PRISONER IN the cabin on the *Akbar* had managed
to free his hands but not his legs. Hobbling over to the toilet, he drained his bladder and then sat back on the bed and
refastened his hands. If someone didn't show up soon to
rescue him, he'd have to take matters into his own hands.
He was hungry, and when he got hungry he got mad.

ONE DECK ABOVE, the only sound that could be heard
was a light thumping of boots covered by felt liners as the
men from the *Free Enterprise* spread out throughout the
Akbar. In a few seconds, the sounds of light popping like
lazy popcorn filtered through the ship. That was followed
by the sound of bodies hitting the deck.

A few seconds later the door to the prisoner's cabin was
flung open and a man in a black hood shined a light in his
face. The man in the hood looked at him again, consulted a
photograph in his hand and then closed the door. The prisoner began to tug at the coating covering his face.

The *Akbar* began to slow, then stopped.

Moving rapidly, four of the men weighed down the terrorists' bodies, starting with their leader, and dumped them
over the side while the other half of the team cleaned up
the blood. Four minutes and forty seconds after first standing on the deck of the *Akbar,* they were filing down to the
swim platform once again.

The leader of the team from the *Free Enterprise* carefully placed a box in the rear of the inflatable and the men
filed back aboard. The driver engaged the throttles and the
black boat skimmed quickly across the water toward her
mother ship.

A frozen pizza would have taken longer to cook than the assault on the *Akbar*.

Once the team was back on board and the inflatable was stowed on deck, the captain of the *Free Enterprise* pulled alongside the *Akbar*. The fog had cleared a little and the *Akbar*'s lights glinted off the black water of the ocean. The yacht was bobbing in place like a boat anchored over a reef. The difference was that here the water was too cold to dive—plus there was no one left aboard, save one, who could come out to play.

The *Free Enterprise* steamed past, then the captain gradually increased its speed.

18

ADAMS HOVERED THE Robinson helicopter above Mount Forel, then used the remote speaker to send out the sound of an air horn. He waited a few minutes then caught sight of a green glowing light from below. Flying a short distance toward the light, he sounded the air horn again to give Cabrillo warning to move away from the landing pad, then he set the helicopter down on the snow. Once the rotor blade had stopped spinning, he climbed out.

"Mr. Chairman," he said as Cabrillo walked over, "I'm glad I found you. It's as black as a sack of licorice out here."

"Everyone get out of Iceland safely?"

"It all went according to plan," Adams said.

"That's one bright spot," Cabrillo said. "Now, how are we for weight?"

"With the two of us aboard and fuel, we still have a few hundred pounds left over. Why do you ask?"

"We have another passenger," Cabrillo said.

"Who?"

"A civilian who was shot," Cabrillo told him. "I think it

was just a case of being in the wrong place at the wrong time."

"Is he dead or alive?"

"I'm not sure, but it doesn't look good," Cabrillo said, pointing toward the entrance to the cave. "Go into the cave, then carry him out to the helicopter. I'll move the snowcat over and begin refueling."

Adams nodded and started walking up the hill. At the entrance he stopped and stared north. Along the horizon blue and green lights flickered and danced like wispy sheets of fabric illuminated by dancing light. The plasma that comprised the Northern Lights was putting on a show, and Adams felt a chill from the unnatural scene.

Turning on his heels, he entered the cave.

CABRILLO CLIMBED INTO the snowcat and drove it over to the helicopter. He began to transfer the fuel using a hand-cranked pump on the top of the spare tank. He was just finishing filling the Robinson's second tank when Adams appeared through the darkness carrying Ackerman, who was still inside the sleeping bag. Carefully placing the archaeologist into the rear seat, he attached a seat belt then walked around to Cabrillo.

"I've got some bottles of octane booster that need to be added," he said.

"Give them to me and I'll put them in. I want you to get Huxley on the radio and ask her if there is anything we can do for our passenger. Explain that he has a serious bullet wound and he's lost a lot of blood."

Adams nodded then reached into a storage compartment and removed the two bottles of octane booster and handed them to Cabrillo. Then he climbed into the pilot's seat and turned on the radio. He climbed back out once he had completed the call, then reached back into the storage compartment and retrieved a collapsible snow shovel. As Cabrillo finished the refueling, Adams began shoveling snow into Ackerman's sleeping bag.

"She said to ice him down and slow his heartbeat,"

Adams said as Cabrillo walked over, "to induce hypother-
mia and put him into a suspended state."

"How long until we reach the *Oregon*?" Cabrillo asked.

"They were steaming at full speed when I took off,"
Adams noted, "so that will shave some time off the return
trip. If I had to guess, I'd estimate about an hour."

Cabrillo nodded and brushed some snow from his eyebrows. "I'll move the snowcat," he said, "you fire this up
and get everything to operating temperatures."

"Got it."

Four minutes later, Cabrillo climbed into the passenger
seat of the idling helicopter. A few seconds more and
Adams engaged the clutch and set the rotor blades spinning, and a minute after that he lifted the helicopter from
the snow.

ABOARD THE *OREGON*, Hanley was working on the
plan for the assault on the *Akbar*. Off to one side of the
control room, Eddie Seng was sketching out notes on a yellow pad. Eric Stone walked over to where Hanley was
seated and pointed at the large monitor on the wall. The
image showed Greenland's coastline, the location of the
Akbar, and the course the *Oregon* was steaming.

"Sir," he said, pointing, "the *Akbar* has not moved in fifteen minutes. The same, however, cannot be said for the
meteorite. If the signal from the sand is correct, it's moving farther away."

"That doesn't make any sense," Hanley noted. "Could
we be receiving a false reading?"

Stone nodded affirmatively. "With the Northern Lights
acting up and the curvature of the earth this far north, we
could be getting a skip in signals off the ionosphere."

"How long until we reach the *Akbar*?" Hanley asked.

"We were about an hour away," Stone said. "Now that
she's stopped, it shaves ten minutes or so off that estimate."

"Eddie," Hanley asked, "can you have your men ready
earlier?"

"Sure," Seng said, "the first man aboard does most of

the work. Once he sprays the paralytic agent into the air duct and the bad guys go to sleep, the rest is just mopping up and securing the ship."

Stone had walked back to his chair. He was studying a radio frequency graph that showed signal strengths on the various bands. "We're picking up something down low," he said.

"See if you can tune it in," Hanley ordered.

Stone fiddled with a dial then pushed a button on the console to boost the receiving strength. Then he flicked on the speaker.

"Portland, Salem, Bend," a voice said, "okay to transmit."

ON THE *AKBAR,* the prisoner had managed to free his hands again and his legs. Listening at the door of his cabin he'd heard nothing, so he'd cracked the door and peered out. There was no one in the hall. He'd slowly searched the ship from stem to stern and found it empty.

Then he had tugged off his latex mask.

He'd made his way to the pilothouse and had reached for the radio.

"Portland, Salem, Bend," he repeated, "okay to transmit."

ON THE *OREGON,* Hanley reached for the microphone to answer. "This is *Oregon,* identify."

"Six, eleven, fifty-nine."

"Murph," Hanley asked, "what are you doing on the radio?"

"THAT WAS A bold plan," Adams said as he flew the helicopter through the black sky, "using a double for the emir of Qatar."

"We've known Al-Khalifa was planning a move on the emir for some time," Cabrillo said, "and the emir went along with our little operation. He wants Al-Khalifa out of the picture as much as we do."

"You eaten lately?" Adams asked. "I brought some

sandwiches and cookies plus some milk. They're in a bag on the rear seat."

Cabrillo nodded and reached back onto the seat next to Ackerman. He opened a padded cooler bag and removed a sandwich. "Do you have any coffee?"

"A pilot without coffee?" Adams said lightly. "That's like a fisherman without worms. There's a thermos on the floor back there. It's my special Italian roast blend."

Cabrillo retrieved the thermos and poured a cup. He took a couple sips then placed the cup on the floor by his feet and took a bite of the sandwich.

"So it was planned all along to have the fake emir kidnapped?" Adams asked.

"Nope," Cabrillo said, "we figured we could grab Al-Khalifa before he made his move. The one bright spot is that we're certain Al-Khalifa has no plans to kill the emir—he just wants him to abdicate the throne in favor of the Al-Khalifa clan. Our man should be as safe as a cow at a vegetarian's conference as long as he's not found out as a fake."

Cabrillo ate another third of the sandwich.

"Sir," Adams said, "can I ask you something?"

"Sure," Cabrillo said, taking the last bite of sandwich and reaching for the coffee.

"What the hell were you doing in Greenland, and who exactly is that guy that's near death in the back of my helicopter?"

"AL-KHALIFA AND HIS men took off," Murphy said. "I'm the only one left on board as far as I can tell."

"That doesn't make any sense," Hanley said. "Is the helicopter still on board?"

"I saw it sitting on the rear deck," Murphy said.

"And you walked the entire yacht?"

"Yep. It's as if they never existed."

"Hold on," Hanley said, turning to Stone.

"Thirty-eight minutes, sir," Stone said to the unasked question.

"Murph," Hanley said, "we'll be there in a half hour. See what you can dig up before we arrive."

"Will do," Murphy said.

"We'll be there soon," Hanley said, "and then we can figure this all out."

"I RECEIVED A call from our contact at the CIA," Cabrillo said. "When we were in Reykjavik, Echelon intercepted an e-mail pertaining to a meteorite comprised of iridium. The CIA was concerned about it falling into the wrong hands, so they asked me to fly over and secure it. That gentleman," he said, motioning to the rear, "is the man that discovered it."

"He dug it out of the cave?"

"Not exactly," Cabrillo said. "You didn't have a chance to take the tour. There's a large shrine that was built on a shaft above the one you were in—very elaborate. Someone long ago must have unearthed the meteorite and fancied it as a religious or spiritual artifact. The guy in back is an archaeologist who somehow found a clue and tracked down the site."

Adams adjusted his flight controls then spoke into his headset. "*Oregon,* this is air one. We're twenty minutes out."

After receiving a reply from Stone in the control room, he continued. "The whole thing seems odd. Even if the meteorite has historical value, I don't see rival archaeologists killing each other over a find. They probably dream about doing that, but I've never heard about an instance."

"Right now," Cabrillo said, "it looks like Al-Khalifa and the Hammadi Group intercepted the e-mail and recovered the meteorite for the iridium. They must want to construct a dirty bomb with the material."

"If that's the case," Adams said, "then they must already have a working bomb of some sort to use as the catalyst. Otherwise they have a fuel and no fire."

"My thoughts exactly."

"Then after our team recovers the meteorite, we still need to locate the mother bomb."

"Once we have Al-Khalifa," Cabrillo said, "we'll make

him give up the location of the weapon. Then a crew can be sent to disable it and we'll be through."

Cabrillo didn't know it yet, but Al-Khalifa was on the bottom of the ocean.

Right next to a series of geothermal vents.

19

THOMAS DWYER WAS a name that sounded serious and staid. Even Dwyer's title, scientist of theoretical physics, made one imagine a pipe-smoking academic. An egghead, or a man who lived a carefully controlled existence. Nothing could have been further from the truth.

Dwyer was the captain of his darts team at the neighborhood pub, raced rally cars on the weekends, and chased single women with a purpose his forty years of age had not diminished. Dwyer bore a passing resemblance to the actor Jeff Goldblum, dressed more like a movie producer than a scientist, and read nearly twenty newspapers and magazines a day. He was smart, imaginative and bold, and was as up-to-date on current events and trends as a fashion maven.

His job title, however, could bring back the notion of a more serious side. His business cards read Central Intelligence Agency, Thomas W. Dwyer (TD)—Senior Scientist Theoretical Applications. Dwyer was a spook-scientist.

At the moment, Dwyer was hanging upside down in a pair of gravity inversion boots that were attached to a bar that was secured to the doorjamb leading into his inner office. He was stretching his back and thinking.

"Mr. Dwyer," a junior scientist said meekly.

Dwyer glanced toward the voice. He could see a pair of scuffed brown leather shoes over white athletic socks leading to a pair of pants with the hem a touch too high. Arching his back, Dwyer raised his head enough to see who was speaking.

"Yes, Tim?"

"I was assigned something I think is above my level," the scientist said quietly.

Dwyer reached up with his arms and grabbed the bar across the door. Then he twisted himself around like a gymnast, removed the ankle boots from the bar and dropped to the floor in one smooth motion.

"Saw that move in the last Olympics," Dwyer said, smiling. "What do you think?"

"Great, sir," the younger man said softly.

Walking into his office, Dwyer sat down behind his desk then bent over and started removing the boots from his ankles. The younger scientist followed meekly, holding in his hands a file stamped with the words "Echelon A-1." Dwyer finished removing the boots, tossed them in a corner of his office and reached out so Tim could hand him the file. He removed a sticker from the front, initialed it quickly and handed it back to the junior scientist.

"It's my problem now," he said, smiling. "I'll analyze it and write the report."

"Thanks, Mr. Dwyer," Tim said.

"Call me TD," Dwyer said, "everyone else does."

THOMAS "TD" DWYER was sitting in his office with his feet up on the desk.

In his hand was a thesis on the natural formation of Buckminsterfullerenes, more commonly called buckyballs, on meteorites. The spherical orbs—named for famed American architect R. Buckminster Fuller, who was most noted for designing the geodesic dome—are the roundest and most symmetrical large molecules known to man. Discovered in 1985 during a space experiment with carbon molecules, buckyballs have continued to astound scientists.

When the hollow area inside the sphere is filled with cesium, it produces the finest organic semiconductor that has ever been tested. Experiments with pure carbon buckyballs have created a lubricant with almost no drag. Possible applications included the development of nonpolluting engines, the timed introduction of medicines, and more advanced nanotechnology devices. The field of development was wide open and growing.

Though the future uses were interesting, Dwyer was not concerned with that. He was more concerned with the present. Naturally occurring buckyballs had been found in the location of meteorite craters. When these samples had been examined, both argon and helium gases had been found in the hollow area of the spheres.

Dwyer pondered this for a moment.

First he imagined two geodesic domes placed together to form an orb the size of a kick ball, or about the same size as the meteorite in the photograph. Then he imagined the void inside filled with gases. Next he imagined piercing the orb with a skewer or lopping off the top with a sword. Whatever gas inside would leak out. Then what? Helium and argon were harmless and existed in abundance in nature. But what if these gases contained something else? Something not of this world?

Opening the telephone directory inside his computer, he located a number and entered the command for the computer to dial. Once the computer signaled the line was ringing, Dwyer reached over and picked up his phone.

Across the country, three time zones distant, a man walked toward his ringing phone.

"Nasuki," a voice answered.

"Mike, you old hack, this is TD."

"TD, you Mensa reject you, how's the spy game?" Nasuki asked.

"I'd tell you, but it's so secret I'd have to kill myself."

"That's secret," Nasuki agreed.

"I have a favor to ask," Dwyer said.

Miko "Mike" Nasuki was an astronomer with the National Oceanographic and Atmospheric Administration. NOAA is a division of the Commerce Department. The agency had a broad base to conduct scientific research, though they usually worked with hydrography.

"Is this a *no one should know we had this conversation* favor?"

"That's right," Dwyer said, "all hypothetical and off the record."

"All right," Nasuki said, "let me have it."

"I'm looking into meteorites and particularly the formation of buckyballs."

"That's right up my alley," Nasuki said, "cutting-edge stuff."

"Have you ever heard any theories about the makeup of the gases inside the spheres themselves?" Dwyer said carefully. "Perhaps why helium and argon are prevalent?"

"Mainly, those are the most common gases that would occur on another planet."

"So," Dwyer noted, "the potential is there for the inside of the balls to be filled with other substances. Things not normally found on earth."

Nasuki thought for a moment. "Sure, TD. I attended a symposium a few months ago where someone presented a paper that made the argument that the dinosaurs had been wiped out from a virus from space."

"Brought in by a meteorite?" Dwyer asked.

"Exactly," Nasuki said. "There is one problem, however."

"What's that?"

"A meteorite sixty-five million years old has yet to be discovered."

"Do you remember any details about the theory?"

Nasuki searched his memory. "The gist was that extra-terrestrial microbes inside the helium were released on impact, and those that didn't burn up poisoned the life that existed at that time. There were two major points," Nasuki continued. "The first was that the microbes were a fast-spreading virus like a super-flu, SARS, or AIDS that attacked the dinosaurs physically."

"What was the second?" Dwyer asked.

"That whatever was trapped inside the helium actually changed the atmosphere itself," Nasuki said, "perhaps altered the molecular structure of the air itself."

"Like what?" Dwyer asked.

"Depleted all the oxygen, that sort of thing."

"So the dinosaurs actually choked to death?" Dwyer asked incredulously.

Nasuki gave a low chuckle. "TD," he said, "it's just a theory."

"What if a meteorite formed primarily of iridium existed in a complete form," Dwyer asked, "not shattered by impact?"

"Iridium, as you know, is both extremely hard and relatively radioactive," Nasuki said. "It would make an almost perfect delivery system for a gas-borne pathogen. The radiation might even mutate the virus and change it. Make it stronger, different, whatever."

"So," Dwyer said, "it's possible a mutant virus from millions of years and a billion miles away could be contained inside the molecules?"

"Abso-freaking-lutely," Nasuki said.

"I've got to go," Dwyer said quickly.

"Somehow," Nasuki said, "I knew you were going to say that."

20

AT ABOUT THE time Cabrillo had touched down in Greenland, two men met in an abandoned waterfront building in Odesa, Ukraine, half a world away. Unlike the Hollywood staged switches, where teams of armed men converge on an area to switch cash for munitions, this gathering was decidedly less exciting. Just a pair of men, one large wooden crate, and one large black nylon bag containing the payoff.

"Payment is mixed like you requested," one of the men said in English, "greenbacks, British pounds, Swiss Francs and Euros."

"Thanks," the second man said in Russian-accented English.

"And you had the records changed to show that this weapon was secretly sold to Iran in 1980?"

"Yes," the second man answered. "From the old communist government to the radical Khomeini forces that overthrew the shah, with the money from the sale being used to fund the Russian occupation of Afghanistan."

"The trigger?"

"We included a new one in the box."

"Mighty white of you," the first man said, smiling. He reached over and shook the second man's hand. "You have that number to call if there is any trouble."

"I will," the second man said.

"You're leaving the Ukraine, right?" the first man asked as he slid the crate along a roller ramp into the rear of a one-ton truck.

"Tonight."

"I'd get far away," the first man said as he pulled down the truck door and secured the latch.

"Australia far enough?"

"Australia would be just fine," the first man said.

Then he walked to the front of the truck, climbed into the seat, shut the door and started the engine. Less than an hour later at a different dock the crate was loaded aboard an old cargo ship for the transit of the Black Sea—the first leg of a much longer journey.

AFTER LEAVING ODESA, the Greek cargo ship *Larissa* bobbed on the swells as she steamed east through the Mediterranean. To the starboard, the rocky cliffs of Gibraltar rose into the sky.

"Dirty fuel," the grubby mechanic said. "I cleaned the filter and it should be okay now. As for the clunking, I think that's just piston slap. The diesels need rebuilding, badly."

The captain nodded and puffed on an unfiltered cigarette, then he scratched his arm. A rash had started forming off Sardinia that now extended from wrist to elbow. There was little the captain could do—the *Larissa* was still fourteen hundred miles and four days from her destination. He stared up as a large oil tanker passed alongside, then reached over and opened a jar of petroleum jelly and slathered some on the raw skin.

His deadline for delivering his mysterious cargo was New Year's Eve.

Now that the fuel problem was solved, he was starting to feel he'd make the London deadline. Once there, his plan was to make the delivery, drink in the New Year at a waterfront bar, then locate a doctor the following day to look at the rash.

The man had no way of knowing the next doctor he'd see would be a coroner.

21

THE VIEW FROM the front window of the helicopter was a field of lights. On Hanley's orders the crew of the *Oregon* had lit all the available lights and the ship looked like a Christmas tree against the dark sky. Flying with only instruments was nerve-racking, and Adams was glad they could soon touch down. Lining up behind the stern, he descended and hovered at the rear of the ship then gradually eased forward until the Robinson was over the landing pad.

Then Adams lightly touched down and began the shutdown procedure.

"Hard flight," Cabrillo said as he waited for the rotor blade to stop spinning.

"It was white knuckle most of the way," Adams admitted.

"Hell of a job, George," Cabrillo said.

Before Adams could answer, the *Oregon*'s medical officer, Julia Huxley, raced over and opened the door just as the rotor stopped and Adams engaged the brake. Right behind her was Franklin Lincoln.

"He's in back," Cabrillo said.

Huxley nodded and opened the rear door and quickly checked Ackerman's vital signs. Then she stood back and

Lincoln reached in and lifted the archaeologist, sleeping bag and all, into his arms. Carrying Ackerman in front at waist level, he raced for the sick bay with Huxley following closely. Hanley walked over as Cabrillo was climbing from the helicopter. He didn't waste time with pleasantries.

"Murph called from the *Akbar*."

"He's compromised?" Cabrillo asked expectantly.

"Nope," Hanley said as he steered Cabrillo toward the door leading into the interior of the *Oregon*, "he heard some noises and freed himself. After waiting a safe amount of time, he ventured from the cabin where he was being held and started searching around. The ship was empty and there was no sign where Al-Khalifa and his crew had gone, so he risked a call."

The men had exited the rear deck and were heading down the passageway to the control room.

"Did he recover the meteorite?" Cabrillo asked.

"It was gone," Hanley said as he opened the door to the control room. "We're receiving tracking signals from the bugs you left, but they're intermittent."

The men walked into the control room.

"Where are the signals originating from?" Cabrillo asked.

Hanley pointed to a monitor. "There," he said, "the track was heading north but now it's heading east in the sea above Iceland."

"He switched boats," Cabrillo said, "but why?"

"That's the question," Hanley said.

"How far are we from the *Akbar*?"

Without replying, Stone entered commands into the computer and an image came onto a monitor on the wall. A video camera that was lit by spotlights on the *Oregon*'s bow was filming.

The *Akbar* was dead ahead.

THE *FREE ENTERPRISE* was steaming at full speed through the tossing seas.

"Stop at the Faeroe Islands," a man said over a secure link. "I'll have someone at the local airport to pick up the package."

"Where do you want us after that?" the captain asked.

"Calais," the man stated, "the rest of the team is there."

"Very good, sir," the captain said.

The man added, "One more thing."

"Yes, sir."

"Explain to the team they each have a fifty-thousand-dollar bonus coming," he said, "and be sure they know that Hughes's family will be well compensated for their loss."

"I'll do that, sir," the captain said.

The man disconnected then reached for a folder on his desk. He removed the sale document for the British textile firm as well as the authorization for payment. He signed both, then fed them into a fax machine and awaited receipt.

Once he received the confirmation, he stood back for a moment.

The first part of his plan was now in place. Soon it would be time for the payback.

AT THE SAME time the fax was traveling to England over the telephone line, the cargo ship *Larissa* was rounding Cabo de Finisterre. The captain set a course for Brest, which was located on the point of France that led into the English Channel. The night air was cool and the skies overhead were clear with a blanket of billions of stars.

He watched as a comet streaked across the sky.

Nodding in approval, he lit a cigarette, sipped from a silver flask containing ouzo, and then scratched the itch on his arm. A thin trickle of blood oozed to the surface and he dabbed at it with a rag.

In two more days they'd reach London and then he'd have the rash examined.

USING THE COMPUTER-CONTROLLED thrusters, Hanley placed the *Oregon* directly alongside the *Akbar*. Cabrillo was the first across, followed by Seng, Jones, Meadows and Linda Ross. Murphy was waiting on the deck. Pieces of his vinyl mask were still visible near his hairline. As soon as Cabrillo was on deck, Murphy motioned to the open door.

"Tell me what you heard and what happened afterward," Cabrillo said as he followed Murphy into the main salon.

Murphy explained the light popping sounds and the masked man entering his cabin.

"It was all over in five minutes," he said as the rest of the team finished filing into the salon. "I waited another ten minutes before venturing out."

"Search every compartment," Cabrillo ordered. "I want some answers."

The team split up and fanned out through the vessel. Rifles and handguns were strewn about the staterooms, as well as clothing, personal items and suitcases. The beds were rumpled and some had the covers pulled back. Copies of the Koran were in every cabin and shoes were still sitting by the beds on the floor.

It was as if a UFO had come down and snatched the men into the heavens.

ON BOARD THE *Oregon,* Hanley made sure the thrusters were adjusted properly then turned to Stone. "Take the helm," he said, "I'm going across."

Stone slid into Hanley's seat and began to adjust the cameras on deck so he could watch what was happening.

Hanley stepped across to the *Akbar* and made his way into the main salon. Meadows was waving a Geiger counter around the long dining table.

"It was here," he said as Hanley passed through the room.

Just up the passageway Ross was holding a spray bottle containing blue liquid. She sprayed the walls then slipped on a pair of goggles as Hanley passed behind her. Hanley continued down to a stairway.

"If they transferred to another ship," Cabrillo was saying to Murphy just as Hanley opened the door to the cabin, "why didn't they take their personal belongings?"

"Maybe they didn't want anything with them that might be traced back to here," Hanley said.

"Doesn't make any sense," Cabrillo noted. "They go through the trouble to kidnap who they think is the emir of Qatar, then they leave him, as well as a multimillion-dollar yacht, unattended?"

"They must be planning on returning," Murphy offered.

Right then Seng popped his head inside the cabin. "Mr. Chairman, Ross has something she wants to show you," he said.

The four men filed down the passageway to where Ross was standing. On the wall were areas outlined with barriers of sprayed foam. The walls inside the barriers were tinted blue. Ross slid off the goggles and handed them to Cabrillo silently.

Cabrillo slid the goggles over his head and stared at the areas. The fluorescent glow of blood splatters looked like a Jackson Pollock painting. He slid off the goggles and handed them to Hanley.

"They tried to clean it off," Ross said, "but it was a fast and dirty job."

Just at that instant Stone's voice came out of a radio clipped to Cabrillo's belt.

"Mr. Cabrillo, Mr. Hanley," he said, "there's something you need to see."

The two men walked down the hallway out through the main salon, then onto the rear deck and across to the *Oregon*. They quickly walked down the hall to the control room.

Cabrillo opened the door. Stone pointed to a monitor on the wall.

"I thought it was a dead baby whale," he said, "until it flipped over and I saw a face."

Just then another body surfaced.

"Have Reyes and Kasim fish them out," Cabrillo said to Hanley, "I'm going back across."

Cabrillo left the control room and stepped across to the *Akbar*. Seng was in the main salon when Cabrillo entered. "Meadows thinks that the object was only in here," Seng said. "He's looking through the rest of the ship, but so far it's clean of radiation."

Cabrillo nodded.

"Ross has found blood in the pilothouse and staterooms as well as in and around the main salon and passageways. The captain was on duty, the posted guards and the rest were sleeping. That would be my guess."

Cabrillo nodded again.

"Whoever hit them, boss," Seng said, "came in hard and fast."

"I'm going to the pilothouse," Cabrillo said, walking away.

Once there he examined the ship's log. The last entry was only two hours old and it stated nothing out of the ordinary. Whoever the visitors were, they'd come unannounced.

After leaving the pilothouse, Cabrillo was walking down the hall when his radio was called.

"Mr. Cabrillo," Huxley's voice said, "come to the sick bay at once."

Cabrillo made his way through the *Akbar* and back across to the *Oregon* once again.

Reyes and Kasim were out on the deck with boat hooks in their hands. They were pushing a body toward a lowered net hung from a cable attached to a derrick. Cabrillo made his way inside and headed down the passageway to the sick bay and opened the door.

Ackerman was lying on an exam table covered by electric warming blankets.

"He's been trying to talk," Huxley said. "I wrote it all down, but it was mostly gibberish until a few minutes ago."

"What then?" Cabrillo asked, staring down at Ackerman, whose eyes had started to flutter. One eye cracked open just a touch.

"He started talking about the ghost," she said, "not *a* ghost, *the* Ghost, as if it were a nickname."

Just then Ackerman spoke again. "I should have never trusted the Ghost," he said in a voice growing weaker by the word. "He bought and paid for the un . . . ivers . . . ity."

Ackerman started convulsing. His body began to shake like a dog exiting the water.

"Mom," he said weakly.

And then he died.

No matter how much Huxley shocked him, his heart would not start again. It was just after midnight when she pronounced him dead. Cabrillo carefully reached up and closed Ackerman's eyes, then covered him with a blanket.

"You did the best you could," he said to Huxley.

Then he left the sick bay and walked down the *Oregon*'s passageway.

Ackerman's words were still ringing in his head.

Walking onto the stern of the ship, he found Hanley staring over a trio of bodies. Hanley was holding an eight-and-a-half-by-eleven-inch computer picture in his hand.

"I enhanced the photograph with a computer to distort the face in order to account for the swelling," he said as soon as Cabrillo walked closer.

Cabrillo took the photograph from Hanley, bent down next to the body, and held it to the face. He stared at the face of the corpse and then the photograph.

"Al-Khalifa," he said slowly.

"He must have been weighed down and tossed overboard," Hanley noted. "The only thing was that the killers didn't know that the bottom of the ocean around here is littered with geothermal vents. The hot water caused the bodies to quickly bloat and overcome the weight. If it weren't for that, we'd have never found them."

"Have you ID'd the others?" Cabrillo asked.

"I haven't found any records yet," Hanley said, "plus there are more surfacing as we speak. Probably just Al-Khalifa's minions."

"Not minions," Cabrillo said, "madmen."

"Now the question is . . ." Hanley said.

"Who is crazy enough," Cabrillo said, "to steal from other crazies."

22

LANGSTON OVERHOLT IV was sitting in his office, bouncing a red rubber ball off a wooden paddle. The telephone receiver was cradled to his ear. The time was barely 8 A.M. but he'd already been at work for more than two hours.

"I left a pair of my engineers on board," Cabrillo said to Overholt. "We're claiming salvage rights."

"Nice prize," Overholt said.

"I'm sure we can use it somehow," Cabrillo agreed.

"What's your current location?" Overholt asked.

"We are north of Iceland heading east. We're trying to track the bugs on the meteorite. Whoever killed Al-Khalifa and stole the meteorite must be aboard another ship."

"You're sure the body you recovered is Al-Khalifa?" Overholt asked.

"We're faxing you fingerprints and digital photographs of the corpse," Cabrillo said, "so your people can make a positive identification. But I'm ninety-nine percent sure."

"After you woke me up this morning, I ordered some of my men to try to check out the ID on the passenger aboard the Eurocopter. We got nothing. I'm sending a team to Greenland to recover the bodies, then hopefully we'll know more."

"Sorry about the midnight call, but I thought you should receive the news as soon as possible."

"No problem, I probably got more sleep than you."

"I managed to grab a few hours once we left the *Akbar*," Cabrillo admitted.

"What's your gut feeling, old friend?" Overholt asked. "If Al-Khalifa is dead, then the threat of the dirty bomb seems diminished. The meteorite is radioactive, but without a catalyst the danger is a lot less."

"True," Cabrillo said slowly, "but the missing Ukrainian nuclear bomb is still out there somewhere, and we don't know that several of Al-Khalifa's own people didn't kill him and will now try to mount the mission themselves."

"That would explain a lot," Overholt said, "like how the killers accessed the *Akbar* so easily."

"If it wasn't some of Al-Khalifa's own people, then we have another group to contend with. If that's the case, we should be wary. Whoever made the assault on the *Akbar* were highly trained and as deadly as vipers."

"Another terrorist group?"

"I doubt it," Cabrillo said. "The operation had none of the earmarks of religious fanatics. It was more like a military operation. No emotion or fuss—just a surgical and flawless elimination of the opposition."

"I'll dig around," Overholt said, "and see what I can find out."

"I'd appreciate that."

"Good thing you managed to bug the meteorite," Overholt added.

"The only card up our sleeve," Cabrillo agreed.

"Anything else?"

"Just before he died, the archaeologist started talking about the Ghost," Cabrillo said, "as if he were a man and not a disembodied apparition."

"I'm on it," Overholt said.

"This is turning into an episode of *Scooby-Doo*,"

Cabrillo said. "Find out who the Ghost is and we solve the caper."

"I don't seem to remember a *Scooby-Doo* episode dealing with nuclear weapons," Overholt said.

"Update it for the twenty-first century," Cabrillo said before disconnecting, "it's a much more dangerous world now."

THE *FREE ENTERPRISE* was steaming through the frigid ocean water on a course toward the Faeroe Islands. The team was starting to relax—after they delivered the meteorite they'd have a break for a while. Once they repositioned the ship to Calais, they would simply wait for a call if needed. The mood aboard the ship was light.

They had no idea a greyhound of the sea disguised as an old cargo ship was following.

Nor did they know that both the Corporation and the might of the U.S. government would soon be aligned against them. They were in ignorant bliss.

"IT'S IMPORTANT," TD Dwyer explained to the receptionist.

"How important?" the receptionist asked. "He's preparing for a White House meeting."

"Very important," Dwyer said.

The receptionist nodded and buzzed Overholt. "There's a Thomas Dwyer here from Theoretical Applications. He claims that he needs to see you immediately."

"Send him in," Overholt said.

The receptionist rose and walked over to Overholt's door and opened it. Overholt was sitting behind his desk. Closing a file, he swiveled around and slid the file into a slot in a safe behind his desk.

"Okay," he said, "come in now."

Dwyer slid past the receptionist and she closed the door behind him.

"I'm TD Dwyer," he said. "I'm the scientist tasked with the analysis of the meteorite."

Overholt walked from behind his desk and shook Dwyer's hand, then motioned him over to a pair of chairs around a seating pit. Once they were both seated, he spoke.

"What have you got?"

Dwyer was less than five minutes into his dissertation when Overholt stopped him.

He walked over to his desk and spoke into the intercom. "Julie, we need to schedule Mr. Dwyer to accompany me to the meeting at the White House."

"Could you ask him his clearance, sir?" Julie asked.

"One-A critical," Dwyer answered.

"Then we can go in the front," Overholt said to Julie, "as planned."

"I'll call over, sir."

Overholt walked back to the chair and sat down. "When it's our turn I want you to deliver your findings without hyperbole. Just lay out the facts as best you know. If you are asked for an opinion—and you probably will be—give it, but qualify it as such."

"Yes, sir," Dwyer said.

"Good," Overholt said. "Now, just between us, lay out the rest of it, harebrained theories and all."

"The gist of the theory is this: There is a possibility that if the molecular structure of the meteorite is pierced, a virus could be released that might have dire consequences."

"Worst case?"

"The end of all organic life on earth."

"Well," Overholt said, "I can safely state you've ruined my morning."

IN THE *OREGON*'S control room, Eric Stone was carefully watching a monitor. He would pin down the location of the meteorite, then it would seem to move. Using all the various locations, Stone was trying to vector in on the object. Then he punched in more commands on the computer keyboard and glanced at a different screen. Stone was using space the Corporation rented on a commercial satellite.

The image filled the monitor but the sea was hidden by a heavy cloud cover.

"Boss," he said to Cabrillo, "we need a KH-30 shot. The clouds are too thick."

The KH-30 was the Defense Department's latest supersecret satellite. It could peer through clouds, even into the water itself. Stone had been unable to hack into the system despite repeated efforts.

"I'll ask Overholt the next time we talk," Cabrillo said. "Maybe he can railroad the National Reconnaissance Office into giving him time. Good try, Stone."

Hanley was staring at the track map on another monitor. The *Oregon* was flying through the water but the other vessel had a good head start. "We can overtake them before Scotland anyway, if they stay at the current speed."

Cabrillo glanced at the monitor. "It looks to me like they're on a course for the Faeroes."

"If that's the case," Hanley said, "they'll reach port before we can overtake them."

Cabrillo nodded and considered this. "What's the location of our jets?"

Hanley pulled a world map up on the screen. "Dulles, Dubai, Cape Town and Paris."

"Which aircraft is in Paris?"

"Challenger 604," Hanley answered.

"Direct it to Aberdeen, Scotland," Cabrillo said. "The runway at the airport in the Faeroe Islands is not long enough to handle it, and Aberdeen is the next closest city. Have it fueled and ready if we need to use her."

Hanley nodded and walked over to a computer to enter the instructions. The door to the control room opened and Michael Halpert entered. He was holding a manila folder in his hands. He walked to the coffee machine, poured a cup and then approached Cabrillo.

"Mr. Chairman," he said wearily, "I've exhausted the database. There are no terrorists or other criminal elements that go by the nickname the Ghost."

"Did you find anything?"

"One Hollywood actor who fashions himself a proponent of the dark side, an author who does vampire books, an industrialist, and 4,382 various e-mail identities."

"The actor and the author are definitely out," Cabrillo

said. "All the ones I've met are too stupid to plan lunch, much less an assault on a terrorist ship. Who is the industrialist?"

"One Halifax Hickman," Halpert said, reading from the file, "an ultrarich Howard Hughes type with a vast variety of business interests."

"Find out everything you can about him," Cabrillo ordered. "I want to know everything from the color of his underwear on through."

"Will do," Halpert said as he walked out of the control room again.

It would be twelve hours before Halpert exited his office.

And when he did, the Corporation would know a lot more than it did right now.

IF TD DWYER claimed he was not nervous he'd be lying.

The group that was assembled around the conference table were the blue-ribbon winners in the nation's power struggle. More than a few of them appeared nightly on the news programs, and most were recognizable to anyone not living in a cave.

The people assembled were cabinet officials, the secretary of state, the president and his advisors, and a scattering of four-star generals and intelligence leaders. When it was Overholt's turn to address the group, he gave a quick overview of the situation and then introduced Dwyer for questions.

The first question came from the heaviest of hitters.

"Has this possibility ever been verified in a laboratory?" the president asked.

"It is believed isotopes of helium were detected in buckyballs that were inside fragments recovered at the meteor crater in northern Arizona as well as at an underwater site near Cancun, Mexico. However, the studies were conducted by university laboratories and the results were not completely conclusive."

"So this is all a theory," the secretary of state said, "not hard science."

"Mr. Secretary," Dwyer said, "the entire field is a new one. It has only been around since 1996, when the Nobel

Prize in chemistry was awarded to three men credited with discovering buckyballs. Since then, with funding cutbacks and such, the field has been mainly explored by corporations with an eye toward commercial applications."

"Is there a way to test this theory?" the secretary of state followed up.

"We could recover some debris and puncture the atoms in a controlled setting," Dwyer said, "but there is no guarantee that we would recover a sample with the virus intact. Some parts might contain it, some might not."

The president spoke. "Mr. Overholt, why did you dispatch contractors to Greenland and not some of our own agents?"

"Firstly," Overholt said, "at that time I believed we were dealing with a relatively harmless object and I had no way of knowing Echelon had been compromised. The information of the increased threat only came to me from Mr. Dwyer today. Secondly, we planned to confiscate the object, and I wanted to shield your administration from any negative blowback."

"I understand," the president said. "Who did we hire for the job?"

"The Corporation," Overholt said.

"They were in charge of the Dalai Lama's return to Tibet, were they not?"

"Yes, sir."

"I figured they'd all be retired by now," the president said. "They hit a financial home run with that operation. Anyway, I have no doubt as to their skill—if I had been you, I'd have done the same thing."

"Thank you, sir," Overholt said.

The air force chief of staff spoke next. "So the situation is that we have an iridium orb loose at the same time that there is a Ukrainian nuclear weapon missing. If one meets the other, we'll have a hell of a problem."

The president nodded. That was the situation in a nutshell. He paused.

"Here's what I want done," he said finally. "Mr. Dwyer should recover some of these extraterrestrial buckyballs and start experimenting. If there's a chance that an extraterrestrial virus can be unleashed, we need to know about it. Secondly, I want the military and intelligence unified in an effort to locate this meteorite. Thirdly, I want Mr. Overholt to continue to work with the Corporation—they've been on this since the onset, so I don't want them pulled. I'll budget whatever funds we need for their fees. Fourthly, I want this kept quiet—if I read about this tomorrow in the *New York Times,* whoever leaked it will be fired. Last is the most obvious: We need both the Ukrainian nuke and the meteorite recovered as quickly as possible so we don't start the New Year with a crisis." He paused and looked around the table. "Okay, everyone, you know what you're supposed to do. Just get the job done and let's wrap this up."

The room started to empty but the president motioned for Overholt and Dwyer to remain. Once the marine guard had everyone herded out, he shut the door behind him and stood guard outside.

"TD, isn't it?"

"Yes, sir," Dwyer said.

"Give me the sour milk."

Dwyer glanced at Overholt, who nodded.

"If there *is* a virus in the molecules that comprise the meteorite," Dwyer said slowly, "a nuclear detonation might be the least of our problems."

"Get me Cabrillo on the telephone," the president said to Overholt.

23

ON BOARD THE *Oregon* the conference room was full.

"At three hundred fifty miles out we can launch the Robinson," Cabrillo said. "If we fly at a hundred miles an hour against the headwind, we should be able to arrive in the Faeroe Islands around the same time as our mystery ship."

"The problem is," Hanley said, "with only you and Adams on site, there's no way you can storm the vessel. It would be suicide."

"These guys," Seng added, "are badasses."

Just then the door to the conference room opened and Gunther Reinholt, the *Oregon*'s aging propulsion engineer, poked his head inside.

"Mr. Chairman," he said, "there's a call you need to take."

Cabrillo nodded and rose from the head of the table, then followed Reinholt into the hall. "Who's calling?" he asked.

"The president, sir," Reinholt said, leading Cabrillo toward the control room.

Cabrillo said nothing—there was really nothing to say. Reaching the control room, he opened the door, made his way over to the secure telephone and lifted the receiver.

"This is Juan Cabrillo."

"Please hold for the President of the United States," the operator said.

A second or two later a voice with a twang came on the line. "Mr. Cabrillo," he said, "good afternoon."

"Good afternoon to you, sir," Cabrillo answered.

"I have Mr. Overholt here with me—he's already briefed me. Could you explain the current situation?"

Cabrillo gave the president a quick recap.

"I could scramble some planes out of England and take out the ship with a Harpoon missile," the president said when Cabrillo had finished, "but then the nuke is still out there, isn't it?"

"Yes, sir," Cabrillo agreed.

"We can't land troop transports at the Faeroe airport," the president continued. "I checked and the airport is too small. That means our only shot is to helicopter in a team, and my estimates are that to prepare and deploy a force up there would take six hours."

"We estimate we have three and a half to four hours tops, sir," Cabrillo said.

"I checked with the navy," the president said. "They have nothing in the area."

"Mr. President," Cabrillo said, "we have a locator placed on the meteorite. Until it is combined with the nuclear device, it is of limited threat. If you give us permission, we believe we can follow the meteorite to the location where it is to be mated with the nuke and recover both at the same time."

"That's a risky strategy," the president said.

The president turned to Overholt.

"Juan," Overholt said, "what are the chances your team can pull this off?"

"Good," Cabrillo said quickly, "but there is a wild card."

"What's the wild card?" the president asked.

"We don't know for sure who we're up against. If the

people that have the meteorite are a faction of the Hammadi Group, I think we can take them."

The president paused before speaking. "Okay," he said at last, "I say we go ahead as planned."

"Very good, sir," Cabrillo said.

"Now," the president said, "we have uncovered an entirely separate problem pertaining to the meteorite. I have a scientist here who will explain."

For the next few minutes, Dwyer explained his theory.

Cabrillo felt a cold chill rising on his back. Armageddon was close at hand.

"That raises the stakes, Mr. President," Cabrillo offered, "but the other side must be unaware of the possibility of a released virus. We just learned it was possible ourselves. The fact is that they would be ensuring their own destruction. The only scenario that makes sense is using the meteorite to construct a dirty bomb."

"That's all true," the president agreed, "and we've been hard-pressed to come up with a scenario where the molecules would be penetrated. They need to break the meteorite down somehow for that to happen. Still, the threat exists— and the consequences could be dire and permanent."

"If the Corporation had been hired to launch this operation," Overholt asked, "how would you go about it?"

"You mean if an evil twin to the Corporation existed and we wanted to kill as many people as possible?" Cabrillo asked. "We would want to introduce the radioactivity in the iridium to the largest possible population."

"So you'd need a delivery system of some sort?" the president asked.

"Correct, Mr. President," Cabrillo said.

"Then if we have the British seal off their airspace, the threat of aerial dispersal is eliminated," the president noted. "Then we just have the bomb to deal with."

"We will need increased security at the underground stations and public areas as well," Cabrillo added, "in case their plan is to dust public areas with radioactive dust. Maybe they have somehow dismantled the nuke and ground up the core, and their plan is to combine it with the iridium in a powdered form to poison the populace."

"Then the British will need to watch their mail and package delivery apparatus as well," the president added. "What else?"

The four men were silent as they thought.

"Let's pray you can recover the meteorite and the bomb together," the president said, "and protect England from ruin. Any other outcome is too horrible to consider."

The call ended, and Cabrillo started walking back to the conference room.

What he had no way of knowing was that while Great Britain was a target for one operation, the other target was three time zones away to the east.

Cabrillo opened the door and entered the conference room.

"I just got off the telephone with the president," Cabrillo said as he made his way to the head of the table. "We have the resources of the United States government behind us."

The group waited for Cabrillo to continue.

"There's one other thing," he continued. "A CIA scientist has advanced a theory that there might be traces of gases from deep space inside the molecules of the meteorite. These gases may have suspended in them a virus or pathogen that could prove deadly. No matter what, once we recover the meteorite it's not to be disturbed."

Julia Huxley spoke. As medical officer, she was tasked with the crew's safety. "What about exposure to the exterior of the meteorite?" she asked. "You were right next to the orb."

"The scientist said that if a virus was on the exterior it would have burned up upon entering the atmosphere. The problem could arise if the meteorite was drilled, for example. If the molecules have arranged themselves in a certain manner, they may have produced pockets larger than molecule size that contain the gases."

"How large might these pockets be?" Huxley asked.

"It's only a theory," Cabrillo said, "but the meteorite could be a hollow sphere much like a chocolate Easter egg. Or, there might be clusters of gas like naturally occurring geodes have, where there are pockets of crystal in various sizes. No one knows until it is recovered and studied."

"Any idea as to the type of virus?" Huxley asked. "Maybe I can prepare a serum."

"None," Cabrillo said carefully, "but if it's from space and it's released on Earth, it couldn't be good."

The room was so quiet you could hear a buzzing fly.

Cabrillo stared at Hanley.

"Adams is almost ready to leave," Hanley said, "and our Challenger 604 will be arriving in Aberdeen shortly."

"Where's Truitt?"

Richard "Dick" Truitt was the Corporation's vice president of operations.

"He was aboard the emir's plane," Hanley said. "He returned the emir safely to Qatar. I ordered our Gulfstream in Dubai to fly to Qatar and pick him up. They should have already left and are probably somewhere over Africa."

"Send him to London," Cabrillo ordered. "Keep him and the Gulfstream on standby."

Hanley nodded.

"I want all of you to continue planning the assault of our mystery ship," Cabrillo said. "If all goes according to plan, we can wrap this up in the next twelve hours. As usual, Hanley is in charge while I'm gone."

The crew nodded and returned to planning as Cabrillo left the room and headed down the passageway to Halpert's office and knocked.

"Come in," Halpert said.

Cabrillo opened the door and entered. "What have you found out?"

"I'm still doing research," Halpert said. "I'm running the various corporations he controls right now."

"Make sure you cover his personal life and make up a psych profile."

"I'll do it, sir," Halpert said, "but as of now, this guy seems to be a true-blue American. He has a DOD clearance, he's friends with a couple of senators and he was even invited to the president's ranch once."

"So was the North Korean president," Cabrillo noted.

"You have a point," Halpert said, "but be assured that if this guy has one bad wrinkle, I'll find it."

"I'm leaving the ship. Report your findings to Hanley."

"Yes, sir."

CABRILLO WALKED DOWN the passageway and up the stairs toward the flight deck.

George Adams was sitting in the pilot's seat of the Robinson and dressed in a clean khaki-colored flight suit. He had yet to start the engine, and the cockpit was cold. He rubbed his flight gloves together and finished writing in the log attached to a clipboard.

Flicking on the main battery power switch to check status, he looked up as Cabrillo approached and opened the passenger door. Cabrillo took a bag containing weapons, extra clothing, and electronics and another with food and drinks and placed them in the rear. Once these were safely stowed he looked over at Adams.

"You need me to do anything, George?" he asked.

"No, Chief," Adams said, "everything's already taken care of. I have a weather report, a flight plan, and the way-points are logged into the GPS. If you want to climb in and strap on a seat belt, I'll get this show on the road."

Over the years that Adams had worked for the Corporation, Cabrillo had never ceased to be amazed by the helicopter pilot's efficiency. Adams never complained and never got excited. Cabrillo had flown through some rough conditions with the man, but other than some glib casual comments, Adams seemed unflustered and without fear.

"Sometimes I wish I could clone you, George," Cabrillo said as he climbed in and fastened the seat belt.

"Why, boss," Adams said, glancing up from the instruments, "then I'd only have half as much fun."

Reaching down, Adams twisted the key and the piston engine turned over and settled into an idle. Adams watched the gauges until the engine reached operating temperatures, then radioed the pilothouse.

"Are we into the wind?"

"Affirmative," the reply came.

Then with a smooth motion he raised the collective and the helicopter lifted from the deck. The *Oregon* continued steaming until the helicopter was clear. Then Adams accelerated and passed alongside the ship. A couple of minutes later the *Oregon* was fading behind them in the distance. Now only clouds and the black sea filled the windshield.

"THAT'S WHAT WE have so far, Mr. Prime Minister," the president said.

"I'll raise the alert status," the prime minister replied, "and release a cover story to the press that the reason is that we believe a shipment of Ricin poison is loose. That way the terrorists continue with their plans."

"Hopefully we can wrap this up soon," the president said.

"I'll alert MI5 and MI6 to coordinate efforts with your people. However, once the meteorite reaches British soil, we're going to need to take over."

"I understand," the president said.

"Then good luck," the prime minister said.

"Good luck to you."

TRUITT STARED AT the side window of the Gulfstream as it streaked across the sky at over five hundred miles an hour. Far below, the coast of Spain sat glowing in the sunlight. Rising from his seat, he walked forward and knocked on the cockpit door.

"Come on in," Chuck "Tiny" Gunderson said.

Truitt opened the door. Gunderson was piloting and Tracy Pilston was in the copilot's seat. "How's it going up here?" he asked.

"Here's the score," Pilston said. "Tiny has eaten a turkey on rye, an entire bag of M&M's and half a can of smoked almonds. I'd keep my hands away from his mouth if I were you."

"There are two things that make me hungry," Gunderson offered. "Flying is one of them, and you know the other one."

"Salmon fishing?" Truitt offered.

"That too," Gunderson agreed.

"Dirt biking?" Pilston said.

"That too," Gunderson agreed.

"It's probably easier to find out what doesn't make you hungry," Truitt said.

"Sleeping," Gunderson said, slumping over and faking a nap.

"What did you need, Mr. Truitt?" Pilston asked as Gunderson continued to pretend he was asleep. The Gulfstream flew along untended.

"I was just curious if we were landing at Gatwick or Heathrow."

"Our last orders were Heathrow," Pilston said.

"Thanks," Truitt said as he turned to leave.

"Can you do me a favor?" Pilston asked.

"Sure," Truitt said, turning around.

"Order Tiny to let me fly, he always hogs the controls."

Gunderson's mouth barely opened as he spoke. "It's on autopilot."

"Play nice, kids," Truitt said, walking away.

"I'll give you a Snickers if you let me fly," Pilston offered.

"Shoot, woman," Gunderson said, "why didn't you say so?"

24

A WIND INFUSED with a fine powdery dust blew from east to west, coating all in its path with grit. Dust in Saudi Arabia was as constant as the tides in the ocean. Cool temperatures like today, however, were as infrequent as steaks at a Hindu wedding.

Saud Al-Sheik stared at the empty expanse of the giant stadium in Mecca.

Saudi Arabia was blessed with huge reserves of oil, fine hospitals and schools, and Islam's holiest site, Mecca. It is recommended that devout Muslims make the pilgrimage to Mecca, or hajj, at least once in their life as a statement of faith. Each year, thousands of the faithful converge, usually in early January, with most also taking a trip to nearby Medina, where the prophet Muhammad is buried.

The influx of so many pilgrims in so short a span of time is a logistical nightmare. Housing, feeding, caring for the sick and injured, and providing security for the masses is both mind-boggling and expensive.

Saudi Arabia bears the costs of the pilgrims visiting as well as the public scrutiny if something goes wrong.

With U.S. and British forces occupying both Iraq and

Afghanistan, the simmering hatred for the West that per-
meated the region was a powder keg ready to explode. Security this year at Mecca would be tight and unyielding.
Fundamentalist Muslims wanted the West crushed and
wiped from the planet like a plague.

The hatred was mirrored by the Western world, which
after 9/11 and numerous terrorist scares and attacks had
lost all patience with the fundamentalist message. If one
more attack was to occur with Saudi nationals involved,
most citizens in the United States would advocate an occupation of the oil-rich country. The lines in the Western
world had become more defined as of late. There were two
kinds of people in the world—friend or foe. Friendship
was rewarded—enemies should be eradicated.

Amid all this tension, hatred, violence, and anger,
everything needed to be in place for a safe and successful
hajj, which was due to start on January 10.

There was less than two weeks to accomplish all the
necessary preparations.

SAUD AL-SHEIK STUDIED a stack of documents on his
clipboard. There were still a thousand and one details, and
the time of pilgrimage was quickly drawing near. His latest
problem had just cropped up—the new prayer rugs he had
ordered from England. They were not finished yet and the
mill had just changed hands.

That, combined with the fact that England was not exactly held in esteem by his people because of the UK's
support of the United States in the occupation of Iraq, was
creating a hassle. Al-Sheik wondered if a bribe to the mill
was in order. He'd pay them extra to complete the order
and then run them through a broker in Paris to disguise
their country of origin.

That would take care of both problems at once.

Pleased with his idea, he took a sip of tea and reached
for his cell phone to place the call.

*   *   *

AT THAT MOMENT, the Greek cargo ship *Larissa* limped into the English Channel. The captain stared at his charts. He had been ordered to dock at the Isle of Sheppey, and he had never made port there before. His usual ports were Dover, Portsmouth and Felixstowe. What the captain had no way of knowing was that the British authorities had recently installed radiation detectors in his usual ports. By contrast, the Isle of Sheppey was as wide open as the Grand Canyon. And the people that had hired him knew this.

The captain studied his chart, then made his course correction. Then he scratched the scab on his arm. The *Larissa* plowed along, with smoke from the aging diesel engine venting out the single stack. She was a dying ship carrying a deadly cargo.

25

DWYER GLANCED DOWN at the dry desert ground as the Sikorsky S-76 helicopter flew above northern Arizona. Miles away to his left, he could see a snowcapped range of peaks. The view of the snow-covered mountains surprised him. Like most people who had never visited the state, Dwyer had been under the impression that the land would be an endless stretch of sand and cacti. Arizona, it now appeared, had a little of everything.

"How often does it snow here?" he asked the pilot through the headset.

"Those peaks are over near Flagstaff," the pilot said. "They receive enough to support a ski area. The tallest peak is Humphries—it's over twelve thousand feet."

"This was not what I expected," Dwyer admitted.

"Most people," the pilot said, "say the same thing."

The pilot had been a little reticent since first meeting Dwyer two hours ago in Phoenix. Dwyer couldn't blame him—he was certain that the higher-ups in charge of Arizona's homeland security had told the pilot nothing about Dwyer's position or the purpose of the trip. Most people preferred to have at least a vague idea of their mission.

"We're flying to the crater so I can remove some rock samples," Dwyer said, "to take to a lab for testing."

"That's all?" the pilot said, visibly relaxing.

"Yep," Dwyer answered.

"Sweet," the pilot said, "because you can't believe some of the assignments I've had lately. I almost hate to come to work some days."

"I'll bet."

"I've ended my shift in a chemical detox shower more than once," the pilot said, "not my idea of a good day at the office."

"This should be a piece of cake," Dwyer assured him.

The revelation loosened the pilot's jaw and he gave Dwyer a nonstop travelogue of the sights they were passing for the remainder of the flight. Twenty minutes later he pointed forward through the windshield. "There she is."

The meteor crater was a massive pockmark on the dusty terrain. Upon seeing the sight from the air, it was not difficult to imagine the force that would have been required to make such a deep penetration of the earth's crust. It was like a giant had taken a huge ball-peen hammer and whacked the earth. The dust clouds after the impact must have been visible for months afterward. The edge of the crater, a pie-crust-like circle, loomed ahead.

"Which side, sir?" the pilot asked.

Dwyer scanned the ground. "There," he said, "near that white pickup."

The pilot slowed the Sikorsky, then hovered and sat her down smoothly.

"I was ordered to remain aboard," the pilot said, "and monitor the radio traffic."

After the pilot had gone through his shutdown procedure and the rotor blade had stopped, Dwyer climbed out and walked over to a man in a cowboy hat and boots standing off to the side. The man extended his hand, and Dwyer shook it firmly.

"Thanks for agreeing to help," Dwyer said.

"Shoot," the man said, "you don't turn down a request from the President of the United States. I'm glad to be able to help."

The man walked back to his pickup, reached into the bed and removed a few hand tools and a bucket, then handed Dwyer a shovel. Then he pointed over to the rim.

"I think what you're looking for is right over there."

Climbing over the ridge of spoil that rimmed the crater, the two men headed down the side twenty yards. The temperature grew hotter as they descended.

The man in the cowboy hat stopped. "This is the far edge of the crater," he noted, wiping his brow with a bandana. "It's always yielded the biggest chunks for me."

Dwyer glanced around, located a likely spot, and began digging with the shovel.

AT THE SAME time that Dwyer started digging in Arizona, on the *Oregon,* in the sea off of Iceland, it was decidedly colder. Belowdecks in his office, Michael Halpert was staring at a printout from his computer. Halpert had been hard at work for hours, and his eyes were burning from staring at the computer screen. Punching commands into the keyboard, Halpert brought up the mission file and stared at Cabrillo's notes again.

Glancing at the printout again, he gathered his notes and walked to the control room.

"Richard," Hanley was saying as Halpert walked into the room, "have the Gulfstream fueled and ready. I'll call you as soon as we need you."

Hanging up the phone, Hanley turned to Halpert. "I take it you found something?"

Halpert handed Hanley the document and he read it quickly. "It might be significant," Hanley said slowly, "and it might not. That is a large sum that Hickman donated to the university, but he might have a habit of bequests like that."

"I checked," Halpert said, "he does. And they are all archaeologically based."

"Interesting," Hanley said.

"Plus what the archaeologist said when he was dying," Halpert added, *"he bought and paid for the university."*

"I see what you're getting at," Hanley said, "plus, I

thought it odd that Ackerman e-mailed Hickman first. He never even bothered to contact his department head with news of the find."

"Maybe Hickman and Ackerman put that together," Halpert said, "so Ackerman could be sure he grabbed the glory if anything was found—not his boss at the university."

"That doesn't explain how Hickman could be sure Ackerman would even find something," Hanley said, "or the chance that it would turn out to be a meteorite that was composed of iridium."

"Maybe Hickman's involvement was altruistic at the beginning," Halpert said slowly. "Ackerman makes his pitch and Hickman has an interest in Eric the Red so he decides to fund the expedition. Then, when the meteorite is discovered, he sees some opportunity."

"We don't even know Hickman is involved," Hanley said, "but if he is, what opportunity could make a rich man kill and risk all he has?"

"It's always one of two things," Halpert said, "love or money."

THE OUTLINE OF the Faeroe Islands was just coming into view through the haze when Hanley reached Cabrillo in the helicopter and explained what Halpert had discovered.

"Damn," said Cabrillo, "that's a twist out of left field. What are your thoughts?"

"I say we go with it," Hanley told him.

The islands started growing in size in the windshield.

"Has Dick arrived in London?" Cabrillo asked.

"I just spoke to him a few minutes ago," Hanley said. "The jet was being refueled, then he was going to a hotel in London to wait for our call."

"And the Challenger is standing by in Aberdeen?"

"On the ground," Hanley said, "fueled and waiting."

"Then call Truitt and his crew and tell them we need to have them fly to Las Vegas to see what they can find out about Hickman."

"Great minds think alike," Hanley said.

Through the windshield of the helicopter, the port was becoming defined as Cabrillo disconnected and turned to Adams. "Let's get on the ground, old buddy."

Adams nodded and started his descent.

THE *FREE ENTERPRISE* was just outside the breakwater as she slowed and stopped. A small open-deck fishing boat powered by a pair of 250-horsepower outboard motors pulled alongside. Pulling up next to the stairs that led to water level, the captain of the fishing boat slowed to a crawl, and one of his crew snagged the box from one of the *Free Enterprise*'s deckhands. The crewman slid the box into a fish hold as the captain steered away from the larger vessel and hit the gas.

Bouncing over the rough seas, the captain of the fishing boat steered his way into a small cove. The crewman climbed off the fishing boat and walked over to a road where a red van from a local package delivery service was waiting. Ten minutes later, the van had delivered the box to the airport.

There it sat awaiting transfer to a plane that was, at that instant, only a few miles away.

ADAMS TOPPED OFF both tanks and ran through his checklist. When that was finished he made notes in the log book. The helicopter had run fine on the trip in from the *Oregon,* so there was little to write—just flight times, weather conditions and a note of a tiny vibration. Adams was finishing just as Cabrillo drove up next to the helicopter in a tiny rental car. He pulled up next to Adams and rolled down the window.

"Hey, boss," Adams said, "did you get half off on the rental car?"

"It's called a Smart Car," Cabrillo said, brushing off the joke. "This was all they had—it was either this or walk. Now bring the binoculars and locator and climb inside."

From under the helicopter's seat Adams retrieved a pair of binoculars and the metal box that read the signals from the bugs sprinkled on the meteorite. Then he stepped over to the Smart Car and climbed into the passenger seat. The binoculars went on the floor. The metal box he kept on his lap. As Cabrillo pulled away, Adams began to tune in the signal from the bugs.

"The box says that the object is very close," Adams said.

Cabrillo crested a hill near the airport—the port was directly below.

In the other lane a red van approached, and the driver was flashing his headlights. Cabrillo realized he'd been driving on the right side of the road American-style, and he swerved over to the proper lane.

"Boss," Adams said, "we're right on it."

Cabrillo glanced over as the van passed—the driver gave a friendly wag of his finger at him for his poor driving, then continued on in the direction of the airport. Cabrillo glanced down the hill at a large ship just about to dock.

"There," he said, pointing. "That must be the vessel."

The vessel had the lines of a private yacht, but it was as black as a stealth bomber. Cabrillo could easily see the deckhands standing by with lines as the captain moved the ship over to the pier with the thrusters.

"The signal is fading," Adams said.

Cabrillo pulled over to the side of the road and watched the yacht through the binoculars as it was secured in its slip. The side nearest him had a stairway leading from the rear deck to almost the waterline. Then a revelation struck him.

He reached for his portable telephone and speed dialed the *Oregon*.

He put his hand over the mouthpiece while Hanley answered, and spoke to Adams.

"They made a switch at sea," he said quickly. "I'm going to drop you back at the helicopter and then follow the signal."

"Call Washington and ask them to have the Danish authorities impound the vessel that just docked."

After Hanley got his orders, Cabrillo switched the telephone off, then turned the steering wheel to the locks and hit the gas. The Smart Car roared around in a U-turn and Cabrillo headed back up the road. Entering the airport grounds again, he pulled alongside the Robinson. Adams quickly climbed out, leaving the locator on the passenger seat.

"Get her airborne, George," Cabrillo shouted. "I'll call you."

Then he hit the gas again and began following the signal.

JAMES BENNETT HAD learned to fly in the U.S. Army but he had never flown a helicopter. His rating was pilot fixed-wing. Because the U.S. Air Force guarded their domain carefully, he was one of the few pilots in the army with the rating. What few fixed-wing planes the army did have were used for observation, forward spotting, and a dozen or so corporate-type planes that were used to ferry generals around.

Bennett had flown Cessna observation planes while still on active duty, so the Cessna 206 model he was flying now was old hat. Bennett had been cruising the tired old prop plane at a hundred miles an hour on the flight north. Now he slowed to enter the pattern and glanced out the side window at the runway. The runway was short and ended at a rocky cliff, but that was okay. Bennett had landed on strips hacked out of jungles, tiny strips on the sides of mountains in Southeast Asia, and once in a farmer's field back home in Arkansas when he'd lost his engine.

Compared to those, the airport at Faeroe Islands was a piece of cake.

Bennett completed his circuit and lined up for landing. Drifting down in a light wind, he ruddered the Cessna straight at the last second. The Cessna touched down with only a light chirp from the tires. Bennett slowed the plane into a fast taxi as he stared at the directions that were written on a sheet of paper on his clipboard.

Then he slowed some more and turned down a side road toward a cargo terminal.

* * *

IN THE SMART Car, Cabrillo had his foot to the floor. Driving the tiny vehicle was like piloting a go-cart after a pot of coffee and half a pack of No-Doz. The Smart Car bounced over the pavement and lurched from side to side. Cabrillo raced alongside the row of hangars and carefully watched the locator. A Cessna had just exited the runway and was taxiing along. Cabrillo stared at the plane's tail, then stopped and pulled over to check the locator.

ADAMS HAD THE Robinson airborne three minutes after he was dropped off. They hadn't even been on the ground long enough for the engine to cool off. Flying along the side of the airport, he notified the tower that he was doing an equipment test and then he started to make low lazy circles in the sky.

The only plane visible was a Cessna that had just landed. He watched it slow to a stop in front of a hangar. Then he watched as Cabrillo in the Smart Car edged closer.

A UNIFORMED ATTENDANT walked out to the Cessna and shouted over the noise of the running engine, "Are you here for the oil-field parts?"

Bennett yelled back, "Yes."

The attendant nodded and raced back through the open hangar door. A moment later he returned with the box. Walking close to the hangar, he placed the box on the ground then shouted in the pilot's window.

"Front or back?"

"In the front on the passenger seat," Bennett shouted.

The attendant picked up the box and walked around the rear of the Cessna.

CABRILLO GLANCED AT the gauge again. The needle was maxed out, laying against the line marked ten. He glanced up from the gauge and through the windshield just as the attendant began walking around the rear of the plane

with the box. It was the same box Cabrillo had seen for a
split second in Greenland.

He hit the gas just as the attendant placed the box in the
plane and closed the door.

The Cessna started to taxi away. The plane had a head
start and was about to turn onto the runway when Cabrillo
reached full speed. Cabrillo steered the Smart Car with his
knees while he reached into a holster that hung down under
his arm. With his right hand he removed a Smith & Wesson
.50-caliber handgun. With his left he rolled down the driver's window.

Turning on the side road, Bennett turned to line up on
the runway. Glancing to the rear, he noticed the Smart Car
racing after him. For a second he thought it might be the attendant chasing after him to flag him down for some reason. Then Bennett noticed a hand come out of the window
with a nickel-plated revolver.

Bennett advanced the throttle and pulled onto the runway. Already cleared for takeoff, he took the Cessna up to
safe rotation speed. It would be a close race.

Cabrillo followed the Cessna onto the runway and gave
chase. The plane was accelerating hard, and it was obvious
the pilot was not considering stopping. As soon as Cabrillo
had the Smart Car cruising at fifty miles an hour, he set the
cruise control and slid himself through the window until he
was sitting on the windowsill.

Lining up his shots carefully, he began firing at the
plane.

BENNETT HEARD AND felt a bullet impact on his left
wing strut. That was followed by the report from more bullets being fired. Reaching proper takeoff speed, he rotated
by pulling back on the yoke. Lifting into the air, Bennett
waited until he was at three hundred feet of elevation before glancing back.

The Smart Car had stopped at the end of the runway.

And the man that had been driving the car was racing
toward a helicopter that had just touched down. Bennett ad-

vanced the throttle to the stops as Cabrillo climbed into the passenger seat in the Robinson.

"Think you can catch him?" he shouted to Adams as he lifted off.

"It'll be close," Adams said.

26

JUST TO THE south of the Faeroe Islands a layer of clouds lay almost to the sea. The leading edge of a storm heading from south to north, the clouds had pelted the British Isles with rain and snow for the last two days. As soon as the Robinson R-44 entered the maelstrom, it was as if Adams and Cabrillo had stepped inside a maze.

One minute they would have a stretch of clear skies, the next they would enter another cloud bank and lose all sight of the Cessna and the water beneath them. Winds buffeted the helicopter, changing directions and velocity like a puck on an air hockey table. The coastline of Scotland was just over two hundred and eighty miles to the south. Inverness, the first city where they might refuel, another seventy.

With both of the fuel tanks filled, Adams and Cabrillo could make land—but only if the headwinds cooperated. The Robinson had a range without reserves of four hundred miles, tops. The Cessna 206 could do just over eight hundred miles. Bennett had not refueled the 206 in the Faeroe Islands—as soon as he saw that Cabrillo was pursuing him, he had taken off as quickly as possible—so here both aircraft were evenly matched.

As for cruising speed, the ratings were equal at 130 miles per hour.

"There," Cabrillo said, pointing through an opening in the cloud bank, "he's a couple miles ahead."

Adams nodded; he'd been watching the Cessna appear and disappear for the last ten minutes. "I doubt he sees us," Adams said. "We're below him, and far enough back that we're out of his rear field of view."

"He can still pick us up on his avoidance radar," Cabrillo noted.

"I don't think he has one," Adams said. "That's an old-model Cessna."

"Can you speed up?"

"We're running dead out, boss," Adams said, pointing to the air speed indicator, "and so is he, I'd judge. I can't climb to dive down and gain speed that way. I'd lose too much forward air speed in the climb—he'd pull ahead out of sight."

Cabrillo considered this for a moment. "Then all we can do is follow along," he said, "and call for help."

"That's it," Adams said.

JAMES BENNETT FLEW along thinking he was alone in the sky. He was not familiar with the Robinson R-44's cruising speed but he knew most of the smaller helicopters topped out at around a hundred miles an hour. By his estimates, by the time he reached Scotland, the helicopter—if it was still following—would be at least a half hour behind him. Bennett reached for his satellite telephone and placed a call.

"I picked up the package," he said, "but I think I have a tail."

"Are you sure?" the voice asked.

"Not positive," Bennett answered, "but if I do, I think I can outrun him. The problem is, once I land, I'll only have a half hour or so to make the transfer. Is that a problem?"

The man on the other end of the line thought for a moment before answering. "I'll work something out," he said, "and call you back."

"I'll be here," Bennett said, disconnecting.

Adjusting the trim to keep the Cessna flying straight, Bennett scanned the instruments, paying particular attention to the fuel gauge. It was going to be close. Holding the yoke as the Cessna was lifted up by a thermal current, he waited until the plane settled back down to his cruising altitude. Then he reached over and poured himself a cup of coffee from a battered Stanley thermos he'd owned for close to twenty years.

"I'LL CALL OVERHOLT," Hanley said, "and have him get the British to scramble some fighter jets and force the plane down. That should wrap this up."

"Just make sure he has the British wait until the Cessna is over land," Cabrillo said. "I don't want to lose the meteorite now."

"I'll make sure he understands that," Hanley said.

"How far are you from port in the Faeroes?"

"About twenty minutes."

"Did the Danes impound the yacht yet?" Cabrillo asked.

"According to the last message from Washington, they don't have the manpower," Hanley said. "But they have a policeman on the hill near the airport watching the ship—that's the best they can do for right now."

Cabrillo thought for a second. "Has anyone recovered the nuclear bomb?"

"Not according to my last intelligence."

"It might be on the yacht," Cabrillo noted.

"The source Overholt had claims it was loaded on an old cargo ship."

"Whoever these guys are," Cabrillo said, "they seem to like to switch at sea. There's a good chance that they met up with the cargo ship somewhere and then took the weapon on board."

"What do you think we should do?"

"Let's recommend to Overholt that the yacht be allowed to leave port," Cabrillo said. "Keep the *Oregon* away from it—let's let the British or American navy deal with the problem. They can board the yacht at sea—there's a lot less risk that way."

"I'll call Overholt now," Hanley said, "and report our recommendations."

The telephone went dead, and Cabrillo sat back in his seat. He had no way of knowing that the meteorite and the nuclear bomb were possessed by two separate factions.

One group was planning a strike for Islam.

The second was planning a strike against Islam.

Hatred fueled them both.

27

AS SOON AS the Gulfstream landed in Las Vegas, Truitt left Gunderson and Pilston with the plane and hailed a cab. The weather was clear and sunny with a light breeze blowing down from the mountains outside Las Vegas. The dry air seemed to magnify the surroundings, and the mountains, though miles distant, seemed close enough to touch.

Tossing his bag on the rear seat, Truitt climbed in the front with the driver.

"Where to?" the driver asked in a voice that sounded like Sean Connery with a smoker's hack.

"Dreamworld," Truitt answered.

The driver put the cab in gear and sped off away from the airport.

"Have you stayed at Dreamworld before?" the cabbie asked as they were nearing the famed Strip.

"Nope," Truitt said.

"It's a high-tech paradise," the driver said, "a man-created environment."

The driver slowed and entered the rear of a line of cabs and personal automobiles waiting to pull into the entrance. "Be sure to catch the lightning storm out on the rear grounds this evening," he said, turning sideways to look at Truitt. "The display is every hour on the hour."

The line moved forward and the driver steered the cab onto a driveway leading toward the hotel. A few feet off the street, he drove through a portal with plastic strips hanging to the ground that reminded Truitt of the entrances to food cold-storage warehouses.

Now they were inside a tropical forest. A jungle canopy stretched overhead and the inside of the cab's windows began to fog from the humidity. The driver pulled in front of the main entrance and stopped.

"When you get out," he said, "watch for the birds. I had a customer last week who claimed he was dive-bombed and pecked."

Truitt nodded and paid the driver. Then he climbed out, opened the rear door and retrieved his bag, then closed the door again and motioned for the cabbie to pull away. Turning, he watched as a bellman shooed away a thick black snake from the main doors with a broom. Then he glanced up at the canopy overhead. There was no sunlight visible, and the sound of birds chirping filled the space.

Lifting his bag, Truitt walked over to the bellman's stand.

"Welcome to Dreamworld," the bellman said. "Are you checking in?"

"Yes," Truitt said, handing the bellman a fake driver's license from Delaware and a credit card that was tied to the false identity.

The bellman swiped both through a machine and then took an adhesive coded strip that printed out and slapped it on Truitt's bag. "We will send your bag to your room on our conveyor system," he said efficiently. "The room will be ready and the bag will be in the room"—he paused to stare at the computer screen—"in ten minutes. There is a front desk inside if you wish to arrange casino credit or for anything else you might need. Have a great stay here at Dreamworld."

Truitt handed the bellman a ten, took the card key for the door and walked toward the entrance. The twin glass doors opened automatically, and what Truitt saw inside as-

tounded him. It was as if the natural world had been
brought indoors.

Just inside the door was a man-made lazy river with
guests riding on small boats. In the distance to the left, Truitt could just make out the figures of people scaling an artificial alpine peak. He watched as snow cascaded down,
only to be swallowed up by an opening at the base. Truitt
shook his head in amazement.

Truitt continued on until he came to an information
desk.

"Which way to the nearest bar?" he asked the clerk.

The clerk pointed in the distance. "Just past Stonehenge
on the right, sir."

Truitt walked into a domed area and past an exact-sized
replica of Stonehenge. An artificial sun was mimicking the
summer solstice and the shadows formed an arm that
pointed to the center. Finding the door to the bar—a thick-
planked affair peering out from under a thatched roof—
Truitt opened it and entered the dimly lit room.

The bar was a replica of an old English roadhouse.
Walking over to a stool constructed from wood, leather,
and boar's horns, Truitt sat down and stared at the bar itself. It was a massive slab of wood that must have weighed
as much as a dump truck.

The bar was empty save Truitt, and the bartender approached from the side.

"Grog or mead, my lord," she asked.

Truitt considered this for a moment. "Mead, I guess," he
said finally.

"Good choice," the bartender said, "it's a little early for
grog."

"My thoughts exactly," Truitt said as the bartender
reached for a glass and began to fill it from a wooden cask
behind the bar.

The bartender was dressed in the costume of a serving
wench. Her bosom spilled out of the top of the uniform.
Setting the glass in front of Truitt, she made a half bow
then backed away down the bar. Truitt sipped the drink and
sat in the dark room thinking about the man who had created this man-made wonderland.

And how he would break into the man's office to search.

"How much do I owe you?" Truitt asked the bartender.

"I can put it on your room card," the bartender offered.

"I'll just pay cash."

"Morning special," the bartender said, "one dollar."

Truitt sat a few ones on the bar then walked through the dim room and out the door.

TURNING LEFT PAST Stonehenge, he entered a massive atrium. In the distance a chairlift led toward the top of a ski mountain with the crest covered in clouds. Walking past the base of the mountain, where people on skis were waiting to take the chairlift up, he watched a few skiers coming down the hill as the fake snow flew through the air like real powder. Continuing past, he came upon an information booth.

"Do you have maps of the hotel?" Truitt asked the clerk.

The man smiled and withdrew a map from below the counter and marked their location with a felt-tip pen. Truitt handed the clerk his door card.

"How do I find my room?" he asked.

The clerk ran the card through the scanner and stared at the details on the screen. Taking the pen again, he made notes on the margin of the map. "Take the River of Dreams to Owl Canyon and exit the boat at mine shaft seventeen. Then board elevator forty-one for the ride up to your floor."

"Sounds easy enough," Truitt said as he gathered up the map and slid his room card back in his pocket.

"That way, sir," the clerk said, motioning.

Thirty yards past the information kiosk, Truitt came to a railing along the river that led to a boarding station. There, a line of canoes were awaiting passengers. Attached to a cable like an amusement ride, the canoes circled the hotel on a river with no beginning or end. Truitt climbed into the first one in the line and stared at the control pad. Entering mine shaft seventeen on the keypad, he sat back and waited a moment as the canoe lurched from the stop. It headed down through a false canyon with rocky walls.

Once the canoe automatically stopped at his destination,

Truitt climbed out and walked toward a bank of elevators. Finding forty-one, he rode it up to his floor, then exited and walked down a long hallway to his room. Using the card key, he unlocked the door.

The room was decorated in a mining-town motif. The walls were paneled with weathered wood planks and accented with pressed tin. A sagging bookshelf with old books and novels was propped against the wall. On another side was an old gun rack with fake Winchester rifles bolted down. The bed was wrought iron, piled with what looked like antique quilts. It was as if Truitt had been transported back in time.

Truitt walked over to the window, parted the drapes and stared down at Las Vegas as if to ensure himself that the world outside was still the same. Then he closed the drapes again and walked into the bathroom. Although it was decorated to appear old, it featured a steam shower and tanning lamps. Splashing some water on his face, he dried himself off then walked back into the room to telephone Hanley.

"HICKMAN CAN PLAN a major operation," Truitt said when Hanley answered, "that's for sure. You would not believe this place—it's like a theme park with slots."

"Halpert is still researching him," Hanley said, "but he's secretive. Have you devised a plan to search his office yet?"

"Not yet, but I'm working on it."

"Be careful," Hanley told him. "Hickman is very powerful, and we don't want any backlash if it turns out he's not involved."

"I'll get in and out as quietly as possible," Truitt said.

"Good luck, Mr. Phelps," Hanley said.

Truitt started humming the theme to *Mission: Impossible* as he disconnected.

SITTING DOWN AT the rolltop desk in the room, Truitt studied the hotel map and the building plans that Hanley had faxed to the Gulfstream before they had landed. Then he took a shower, changed clothes and left the room. He took the elevator down, boarded a canoe and rode it to the main entrance. Then he walked outside and hailed a cab.

After explaining his destination to the driver, he sat back and waited.

A few minutes later, the driver pulled up in front of the tallest hotel in Las Vegas. Truitt paid the fare and climbed out. Then he walked into the lobby, purchased a ticket and rode a high-speed elevator to the hotel's observation deck. The entire city of Las Vegas was stretched out beneath him.

Truitt stared at the view for a few minutes, then walked over to one of the viewers and inserted a few coins. While most of the other tourists scanned the high-powered binoculars from side to side, Truitt kept his trained on just one spot.

ONCE THE RECONNAISSANCE was completed, Truitt rode the elevator down, hailed another cab, and returned to Dreamworld. It was still a little early, so he went to his room and took a nap. It was just after midnight when he awoke. Brewing a pot of coffee using the pot in the bathroom, he sipped the cup to help himself wake up. Then he shaved, showered again, and walked back into the room.

Digging into his bag, he removed a black T-shirt and black jeans and dressed. He removed a pair of rubber-soled black shoes from the bag and slid them on his feet. Then he repacked his bag and called the bellman to have it delivered to the front door. Gunderson had been told to pick it up in ten minutes. Before leaving the room, he removed a strangely padded jacket from his bag and slid it over his shoulders. After taking the boat to the lobby, he entered the casino.

Groups of vacationers, eyes red from lack of sleep, filled most of the seats at the tables and in front of the slot machines. Even this late at night the casino was a money-maker. Continuing on through the casino, he entered the mall inside the hotel.

The mall was a cornucopia of excessive consumption. Nearly seventy-five brand-name stores and boutiques were

located along a cobblestone walkway. Along with the
twenty or so designer clothing stores were shoe shops, a
luggage store, jewelry shops, restaurants and a bookstore.
Truitt still needed to kill some time, so he entered the
bookstore and flipped through the newest Stephen Goodwin novel. Goodwin, a young author from Arizona, had
spent the last few months at the top of the charts. Truitt
could not carry a book right now, but he made a mental
note to pick up the novel before he left Las Vegas. Leaving
the bookstore, Truitt entered a barbeque restaurant and ordered a plate of ribs and an iced tea. Once he finished
those, he decided it was time.

HICKMAN'S PENTHOUSE HIGH atop Dreamworld
featured decks on all four sides. Glass walls that slid back
allowed entrance to the decks, which had a forest of carefully trimmed trees in pots. The pinnacle of the penthouse
was pyramid shaped, with a copper roof still new and
gleaming. Tiny pinlights lit the trees and pinnacle.
    Riding the elevator up to the next-to-highest floor, Truitt
recalled the building plans. Exiting the elevator, he peered
down the hallway and found it empty. Then he walked to
the far end of the hall and found a white metal ladder
bolted to the wall. Truitt climbed the ladder until it ended
at a door locked with a padlock on a clasp. Taking a plastic
sleeve from a pouch in his pocket, Truitt slid the thin shaft
into the lock and twisted a small knob on the top.
    The knob released a catalyst that made the plastic sleeve
harden inside the lock. A few seconds later, Truitt twisted
the shaft and the lock sprung open. He removed the lock
from the clasp, opened the door upward into the crawl
space and climbed inside.
    The plans had called this area a service access walkway.
Cables for power, plumbing and communications filled the
space. Truitt closed the door again and turned on his flashlight. Slowly he crawled down the walkway toward where
the plans showed another door that led up to the deck.
    When observing the deck from the other hotel, Truitt
had noticed a sliding door cracked open. The open door

was his best chance to enter the penthouse undetected. Reaching the door beneath the deck, Truitt used another of the plastic sleeves to open the lock, then carefully swung it up and peered out.

There was no alarm, no indication he had been detected.

Keeping low to avoid being seen, Truitt climbed out onto the deck, closed the door, and crept toward the still-open door. Prying it slowly back, he peered inside. No one was visible—and he carefully entered.

Truitt was in the huge open living room of the penthouse. A half-round sunken conversation pit with padded benches encircled a rock fireplace. Off to one side, lit only by a light above the stove, was a commercial-style kitchen. To the other side was a massive wet bar with beer taps mounted into the wall. The room was lit by unseen lights into a sort of twilight. Bluegrass music played through invisible speakers.

Truitt crept down the hall toward where the plans showed Hickman's office.

28

THE *LARISSA* LIMPED into the Isle of Sheppey and tied up to the dock. The captain took his forged documents and walked up the hill toward the customs shack. A man stood at the door locking up for the night.

"I just need to note arrival," the captain said, showing him a paper.

The man unlocked the door again and entered the tiny shack. Without bothering to turn on the lights, he walked over to a chest-high table and removed a stamp from a rotisserie on the top. Opening an ink pad, he wet the stamp and motioned for the sheet in the captain's hand. Once he had it, he placed it on the top of the table and stamped it.

"Welcome to England," the customs official said, motioning for the captain to walk back outside.

As the official started to lock the door again, the captain spoke. "Do you know where there is a doctor nearby?" he asked.

"Two blocks up the hill," the customs official said, "and one block west. But he's closed now. You can visit him tomorrow—after you've come back here and made full declarations."

The customs official walked off. The captain returned to the *Larissa* to wait.

TO THE REGULARS at the waterfront bar on the Isle of Sheppey, Nebile Lababiti must have seemed like a gay man looking for a lover. And they didn't like the implications. Lababiti was dressed in an Italian sport coat, shiny woven silk pants and a silk shirt unbuttoned to show a neck encircled with gold chains. He smelled of hair pomade, cigarettes and too much cologne.

"I'd like a pint," he told the barkeep, a short, muscled and tattooed man with a shaved head who wore a grimy T-shirt.

"Sure you don't want a fruity drink, mate?" the barkeep asked quietly. "There's a place up the road that makes a mean banana daiquiri."

Lababiti reached into his sport coat, removed a pack of cigarettes and lit one, then blew smoke in the barkeep's face. The man looked like an ex–carnival worker who had been fired for scaring the customers.

"No," Lababiti said, "a Guinness would be fine."

The barkeep considered this but made no move to fill a glass.

Lababiti removed a fifty-pound note and slid it across the bar. "And buy the rest of these fine men a drink as well," he said, sweeping his hand along the bar toward the ten other customers. "They look like they've earned it."

The barkeep looked down to the end of the bar, where the owner, a retired fisherman who was missing two fingers on his right hand, was clutching a pint of ale. The owner nodded his okay and the barkeep reached for a glass.

Even if the Middle Eastern man was a swish on the prowl, this was a joint that couldn't afford to turn down cash-paying customers. Once the stout was placed on the bar in front of him, Lababiti picked it up and took a swallow. Then he wiped his upper lip with the back of his hand and stared around. The bar was a sty. Mismatched chairs sat in front of battered and scarred wooden tables. A coal fire was burning in a smoke-stained fireplace down at the end of the room. The bar itself, where Lababiti was standing, had been etched and scratched by numerous knives over the years.

The air smelled like sweat, fish guts, diesel fuel, urine and axle grease.

Lababiti took another sip and glanced at his gold Piaget wristwatch.

NOT FAR FROM the bar, on a rise overlooking the docks, a pair of Lababiti's men stood watching the *Larissa* through night-vision binoculars. Most of the crew had already left the ship for a night in town; only one light was still visible in the stern stateroom.

On the dock itself, another pair of Arabs were pushing a cart that appeared to be filled with trash along the pier. As they passed the *Larissa,* they slowed and swept a Geiger counter near the hull. The sound was turned off, but the gauge told them what they needed to know. They continued on toward the end of the dock slowly.

BELOWDECKS, MILOS COUSTAS, captain of the *Larissa,* finished combing his hair. Then he rubbed some salve on his arm. He wasn't sure why he was doing this— since he'd bought the salve, it had seemed to have little effect. He only hoped that the doctor he'd see tomorrow would come up with something more powerful.

Finished with his grooming, Coustas walked out of his stateroom then up to the deck.

He was due to meet his client at the bar just up the hill.

LABABITI WAS JUST starting his second pint of Guinness when Coustas walked into the bar. Lababiti turned to see who had entered and instantly knew it was his man. Had Coustas worn a T-shirt imprinted with "Greek ship captain" he could not have been more visible. He was wearing a pair of baggy peasant pants, a loose white gauze shirt with ropes through the hood and the sloped cap it seemed all Greeks who lived near the water favored.

Lababiti ordered Coustas ouzo from the barkeep then motioned him over.

THEY WERE TERRORISTS, but they were not incompetents. As soon as the men with the night-vision binoculars confirmed Coustas had entered the bar, the pair of men pushing the cart headed back down the pier and stopped alongside the *Larissa*. Quickly they climbed aboard and began searching. Within minutes they had located the crate containing the nuclear bomb and they radioed the lookout team, who were sitting behind the wheel of a rental van. The van rolled down to the end of the pier at the same time the two terrorists aboard the *Larissa* were sliding the crate over the side. Lifting up a plastic cover with trash glued on top, they slid the heavy crate into the reinforced cart.

With one pulling and one pushing, they headed down the pier.

LABABITI AND COUSTAS had moved to a table near the back of the bar. The smell from the nearby lavatory wafted across them. Coustas was now on his second drink and he was becoming more animated.

"Just what is this special cargo that you have paid so dearly to have delivered?" he asked Lababiti, smiling. "Since you are an Arab and the box is so heavy, I suspect you are smuggling gold."

Lababiti nodded, neither confirming nor denying the accusation.

"If that is the case," Coustas said, "I would think a bonus might be in order."

AS SOON AS the crate with the bomb was loaded in the rear of the van, the two lookouts sped away. The other pair of men wheeled the cart down to the water and pushed it in. Then they ran to a motorcycle nearby and both climbed aboard. Clicking it into gear, they started up the hill leading to the bar.

* * *

LABABITI DIDN'T HATE the Greeks as much as Westerners, but he didn't like them much.

He found them loud, brash and lacking in manners for
the most part. Coustas had already had two drinks but he'd
yet to offer to buy Lababiti one. Motioning to the barkeep
for another round, Lababiti rose from his chair.

"We'll talk about bonuses when I return," he said.
"Right now I need to visit the facilities. The barkeep is
making another round—why don't you make yourself useful and pick it up from the bar?"

"I still have some in my glass," Coustas said, grinning.

"You can finish it when you return," Lababiti said,
walking off.

Stepping into the lavatory was like hiding out below an
outhouse. It didn't smell good and the light was bad. Luckily, Lababiti knew exactly where he had placed the tablet
and he removed the foil-wrapped packet from his pocket
and unwrapped it in the dim light.

Then, clutching the tablet in his hand, he quickly
walked back to the table.

Coustas was still at the bar badgering the barkeep to
pour a little more ouzo into his glass. He watched as the
barkeep bent over and lifted the bottle to top off the drink
while, at the same time, a thin, dark-skinned man poked
his head into the bar, sneezed and left again. Lababiti was
just about to sit down again when he witnessed the signal
that the heist had gone smoothly.

He crushed the tablet and sprinkled the contents into the
last third of Coustas's glass.

Then he sat down as the Greek walked over carrying the
drinks. The sound of a motorcycle outside racing away filtered through the walls. "The bartender wants more
money," Coustas said, sliding into his seat, "said he's gone
through what you left."

Lababiti nodded. "I need to go out to my car and get
some more pounds. Just finish your drink and I'll be right
back."

"Then we can discuss bonuses?" Coustas asked, raising the partially filled glass to his lips and taking a sip.

"Bonuses as well as the transfer of cargo," Lababiti said, rising. "I assume you'll take payment in gold?"

Coustas nodded as Lababiti walked toward the door. He was high on ouzo and newfound wealth. Everything seemed perfect in his world—until he felt the pain in his chest.

LABABITI MOTIONED TO the barkeep that he was walking outside for a second, using a single raised finger, then he exited the bar and walked up the street to his Jaguar sedan. The street was empty, littered with trash, and barely illuminated by the few operational streetlights.

It was an avenue of broken dreams and misplaced hope.

Lababiti never hesitated or faltered. He unlocked the door of the Jaguar with his key fob and then climbed inside and started the engine. Adjusting the volume on the CD player, he slid the sedan into gear and pulled smartly away.

When the owner of the bar raced out onto the street to report to the smartly dressed foreigner that his friend had taken ill, all he caught was the sight of taillights as the Jaguar crested the hill and disappeared.

BRITISH POLICE INSPECTORS usually don't show up when people die in bars. It happens frequently and the causes are usually obvious. For Inspector Charles Harrelson to be summoned from bed required a call from the office of the coroner. And at first he was none too happy. After packing tobacco into his pipe, he lit the bowl and stared down at the body. Then he shook his head.

"Macky," he said to the coroner, "you woke me up for this?"

The coroner, David Mackelson, had worked with Harrelson for nearly two decades. He knew the inspector was always a little testy when he was awakened from a deep sleep.

"You want a cuppa, Charles?" Macky said quietly. "I can probably get the owner to make us one."

"Not if I'm going back to sleep," Harrelson said, "which I think I will be, judging by the looks of this unfortunate soul."

"Oh," Macky said, "I think you might need one."

Pulling back the sheet over Coustas's body, Macky pointed to the red marks on his arms.

"Know what that is?" he asked Harrelson.

"No idea," Harrelson said.

"Those are radiation burns," Macky said, removing a tin of snuff and snorting some into his nose. "Now, Charles, are you glad I woke you?"

29

ADAMS CAUGHT A glimpse of the Cessna, motioned to Cabrillo, and pointed at the moving map on the navigation system.

"He'll be crossing over land in the next few minutes," Adams said through the headset.

"Hopefully," Cabrillo said, "the RAF will be there to greet him. Then we can wind this up and be done with it. How's our fuel?"

Adams pointed to the gauge. The headwinds had taken their toll, and the needle was just above empty. "We are pretty far into the reserve, boss, but we have enough to reach land. After that there's no telling, however."

"We'll touch down and refuel," Cabrillo said confidently, "as soon as Hanley informs us that the jets have made the intercept."

But at that moment Hanley was fighting through layers of red tape on two continents.

"WHAT THE HELL do you mean there's no planes?" he said to Overholt.

"The quickest the British can scramble a jet is ten minutes from now," Overholt said, "from Mindenhall, which is
down south. They have nothing currently based in Scotland. To make matters worse, their assets in the south are
stretched like we are—most of their fighter wings are de-
ployed to help us in Iraq and Africa."

"Does the U.S. have a carrier in the area?" Hanley
asked.

"Nope," Overholt said, "the only vessel we have in the
sea close by is a guided-missile frigate that has been ordered
to intercept the yacht steaming from the Faeroe Islands."

"Mr. Overholt," Hanley said, "we have a problem. Your
friend Juan is probably on fumes by now—if we don't get
him some help soon we're going to lose the meteorite once
again. We're doing our job here, but we need some
backup."

"I understand," Overholt said, "let me see what I can do
and I'll call you back."

The telephone went dead and Hanley stared at the map
on the monitor in the control room. The blip from the radar
image of the Cessna was just crossing over the shoreline.
He began to dial.

"YES, SIR," THE pilot of the Challenger 604 sitting in
Aberdeen said. "We have been running the turbines every
half hour to keep them warm. We can be off the ground as
soon as we receive clearance."

"The target has just reached land at Cape Wrath," Hanley said, "so fly east first, then turn north. It appears his
present course is toward Glasgow."

"What do we do when we reach him?"

"Just follow him," Hanley said, "until the British jets
arrive."

While Hanley and the pilot had been talking, the copilot had received clearance for takeoff. He motioned to the
pilot.

"We just got clearance," the pilot told Hanley, "is there
anything else?"

"Keep an eye out for our chairman. He's aboard the Robinson helicopter and he's low on fuel."

"We'll do it, sir," the pilot said as he advanced the throttles and began to taxi toward the runway.

A light mist wet the windshield of the Challenger as the pilot steered down the access road toward the main runway. From the looks of the clouds to the north, it was only going to get worse. Lining up on the runway, the pilot ran through his checks.

Then he advanced the throttles to the stops and raced down the runway.

JAMES BENNETT STARED at his fuel gauge with concern. He wouldn't make Glasgow with the fuel onboard, so he adjusted his course slightly to port. Bennett's plan was to stay over land in case he had to make an emergency landing, so he decided his new course would be south to Inverness then almost due east to Aberdeen. He'd be lucky if he reached the Scottish port. But Bennett was not a lucky man.

Just then his telephone rang.

"We have a problem," the voice said. "We just intercepted a British communication stating they are scrambling a pair of fighter jets to intercept you. We have perhaps fifteen minutes until they reach you."

Bennett glanced at his watch. "That is a problem," he said quickly. "I've had to change course because of fuel. I can no longer make Glasgow like we'd planned. The best I can do is maybe Aberdeen—and I can't reach there before the jets arrive."

"Even if you had the chance to refuel in the Faeroes," the voice said, "it now turns out that Glasgow would have been out because of the British fighters heading your way. What about the helicopter? Do you think he's still following?"

"I haven't seen him since I left," Bennett said. "My guess is they turned back."

"Good," the voice said, "then my plan should work. Get out your chart."

Bennett opened the chart showing Scotland. "Got it," he said.

"Do you see Inverness?"

Bennett glanced at the chart. "Yep."

"Right south of there, do you see the large lake?"

"You're kidding," Bennett said.

"Nope," the voice said, "Loch Ness. Fly along the east side—we have a team on the ground in a truck. They are going to pop smoke so you can see them."

Popping smoke was a military term for igniting smoke grenades to mark a position.

"Then what?" Bennett asked.

"Come in low and drop the cargo out the door," the voice said. "They will retrieve it and bring it the rest of the way."

"What about me?" Bennett asked.

"You let the fighter jets force you down at an airport," the voice said. "Then once the Cessna is searched and found to be empty, they will think this was all just a mistake."

"Brilliant," Bennett said.

"That's what I thought too," the voice said before disconnecting.

THE ROBINSON HELICOPTER carrying Cabrillo and Adams passed over the rocky shoreline. Adams made a thumbs-up sign to Cabrillo, then turned on the microphone.

"Looks like we'll live," Adams said. "If we run out of fuel now, I can do an autorotation to the ground."

"I hope that if it comes to that, you've been practicing."

"I do a few every week," Adams said, "just in case."

The cloud cover was thickening the farther inland they flew. Every now and then the men could catch a glimpse of the snow-covered hills of Scotland below. Thirty seconds earlier, Cabrillo had caught a quick glimpse of the flashing taillight of the Cessna above.

"The jets should be out there now," Cabrillo said as he reached for the satellite telephone and called Hanley.

* * *

THE *OREGON* WAS steaming south from the Faeroe Islands at full speed. Soon a decision would have to be made about whether to steam west along Scotland and Ireland or east between the Shetland Islands and the Orkneys into the North Sea. Hanley was watching the projections flash across the monitors when his telephone rang.

"What's the status?" Cabrillo asked without preamble.

"Overholt had trouble getting the British jets scrambled," Hanley said. "Last word was they just left Mindenhall. If they travel at Mach one-plus, they should reach you in a half hour, give or take."

"We don't have a half hour of fuel left," Cabrillo said.

"I'm sorry, Juan," Hanley said. "I dispatched the Challenger from Aberdeen to take up the pursuit until the fighters arrive. They can track the Cessna and call me with the information. We're going to get this guy—don't worry about that."

"What about the yacht?"

"It steamed from the port in the Faeroe Islands ten minutes ago," Hanley reported. "A U.S. guided-missile frigate is on a course to intercept her out in the Atlantic."

"Finally," Cabrillo said, "some good news."

Hanley was staring at the monitor that showed the position of the Cessna and the Robinson. At the same time, he was listening to the copilot of the Challenger giving an update over the radio speaker in the control room. The Challenger was picking up the two aircraft on their radar scope and closing quickly.

"The Cessna is just now flying over Inverness," Hanley said. "The Challenger has him on their scope. How much fuel do you have left?"

Cabrillo spoke over the headset to Adams. "Can we make Inverness before we run out of fuel?"

"I think so," Adams said, "we picked up a tailwind once we crossed onto land."

"Enough to make Inverness," Cabrillo said to Hanley.

Hanley was going to recommend that Cabrillo and Adams stop and refuel but he never had the chance. Right at that instant the copilot of the Challenger called in to report again. All of a sudden the Cessna was descending.

"Juan," Hanley said quickly, "the Challenger just reported the Cessna is starting a descent."

On the moving map aboard the Robinson, Inverness was only a few miles ahead.

"Where is he trying to land?" Cabrillo asked.

"It looks like Loch Ness, along the eastern side."

"I'll call you back," Cabrillo said to Hanley before disconnecting.

The weather was turning worse and rain began running along the windshield of the Robinson in tiny streams. Adams turned up the fan on the defroster and stared at the fuel gauge apprehensively.

"Do you believe in monsters?" Cabrillo asked Adams.

"I believe in monster trucks," Adams answered, "why do you ask?"

Cabrillo pointed to the moving map. The cigar-shaped mark of Loch Ness was just coming into view. "According to Hanley, the Cessna is on a descent for a landing along the east side of Loch Ness."

In the last few minutes, Adams had been able to catch a few glimpses of the ground before the clouds closed in. "I don't think so," he said.

"Why not?" Cabrillo asked.

"Too hilly," Adams noted, "there's no place for a runway."

"Then that must mean—" Cabrillo started to say.

"He's making a drop," Adams said, finishing the sentence.

AS SOON AS he received Bennett's call that the Cessna had left the Faeroe Islands and was being followed, the leader of the operation ordered two of the four men waiting at Glasgow to drive north at breakneck speed. The two men had made the hundred-plus-mile trip to Loch Ness in less than two hours, and they awaited further instructions. Ten minutes ago the men had received word to head to the east side of the loch, find a desolate area, and then wait until they were notified. Two minutes ago, a call came in ordering them to light their smoke grenades and wait for a package to be dropped.

The men were sitting in the back of the van with the

doors open, watching the smoke being blown about by the rain. The plane was due to arrive any minute.

"Did you hear that?" one of the men asked, hearing the sound of a plane.

"It's growing louder," the second man said.

"I thought our guy was in a . . ."

Bennett fought the controls as the jet wash from the Challenger buffeted the air around the Cessna. Whoever was flying the corporate jet was a madman or an incompetent, he thought. Surely his tiny plane must have been on their radar scope.

"Two hundred feet," the copilot of the Challenger said. "We lose an engine now and we're toast."

"Watch out the window," the pilot ordered. "I'll make one pass and then pull up."

The Challenger streaked above the ground, barely clearing the hilltops. In the jet's wake, snow was blowing in vortices from the rear. A taller hill dominated the view out the windshield and the pilot pulled up on the yoke then dropped the altitude again when they'd crossed over. They were flying over the loch now.

"There," the copilot said, pointing to a van on the eastern shore nearest Inverness, "I see smoke."

The pilot glanced over, then pulled back on the yoke and began climbing into the sky again. *"Oregon,"* he said once they had reached a safe cruising speed again, "we have a van on the eastern shore with smoke markers ignited. How long until the fighters are due to arrive?"

"Challenger," Hanley said, "the fighters are still fifteen minutes distant."

"They're going to try a drop," the pilot of the Challenger said.

"Thanks for the report," Hanley said.

"THEY ARE GOING to try a drop," Cabrillo said as soon as Hanley answered.

"We know," he said, "I was just getting ready to call you. The Challenger just made a low-level pass and witnessed a van with smoke markers active along the eastern shore."

"We just caught a glimpse of the Cessna," Cabrillo said, "he's just in front of us. Both of us will be over the loch within minutes."

"How's the fuel situation?"

"Fuel?" Cabrillo asked Adams.

"I've never seen the gauge this low," Adams said.

Cabrillo repeated what Adams had said.

"Break it off," Hanley said quickly, "and land while you still can."

The Robinson flew through a patch of clearer air and Cabrillo stared down. The wind-whipped water of the loch was visible. "Too late for that, Max," Cabrillo said, "we just started over the loch."

THE TWO MEN waiting by the loch had been ordered to maintain radio silence until they recovered the meteorite and were a safe distance away from the drop zone. Because of this they did not report the low-flying jet. There was a good chance the business jet was just an oil company plane having problems—if not, there was little they could do about it anyway. They continued to listen and scan the skies for signs of the Cessna.

THE TORNADO ADV fighter passed over Perth, Scotland, and the British flight officer reported his position. They were less than six minutes from Loch Ness and closing fast.

"Watch for a Challenger corporate jet and a rotary helicopter in the area," the flight officer radioed his wingman. "They are friendlies."

"Acknowledged," the wingman said, "target is a Cessna 206 prop plane."

"Five minutes, out," the flight officer radioed to his base.

BENNETT STRAINED TO see the smoke marker he had been told to watch for once he caught sight of the northeast end of the loch. It was hazy and the fog over the water mixed with the smoke. He lowered the flaps and slowed the Cessna to a crawl, then looked again. Flashing lights appeared from across the loch, and he turned to fly closer.

"THERE'S THE LOCH," Cabrillo said.

The Robinson was closing fast on the Cessna and Adams slowed down. "He's slowing," he said through the headset to Cabrillo.

Cabrillo stared at the moving map on the dash. "There's no field showing, so he must be trying a drop, just like we thought."

The helicopter was halfway across the water, tracking the Cessna, which was turning to fly along the eastern shore. Adams had just moved the cyclic to head toward land when the engine started to sputter.

ON BOARD THE Cessna 206, Bennett looked ahead. He could now see the smoke, the flashing strobe lights, and the van. Flying lower to the ground, he reached over and unlocked the passenger door and slid the box containing the meteorite to the edge of the seat nearest the door. A minute or so longer and he could open the door, tilt the plane over on her side and then push the box out.

BILLY JOE SHEA drove along the eastern edge of Loch Ness in a black 1947 MG TC. Shea was an oil-field drilling-mud salesman from Midland, Texas, who had purchased the classic car only a few days before from a garage in Leeds. His father had owned a similar vehicle, bought in England when he was stationed there in the air force, and Billy Joe had learned to drive in it. It had been nearly three decades since Shea's father had sold the car, and Shea had always had a secret desire to buy one himself.

A search on the Internet, a second mortgage on his home, and the three weeks' vacation he had accumulated finally made the dream a reality. Shea had decided to tour Scotland and England for a couple of weeks, until he would need to drop the car off at the port in Liverpool to be shipped home. Even with the top up the rain was seeping in through the open side doors. Shea picked up his cowboy hat off the passenger side of the bench seat and flicked the rain off. Then he stared at the engine gauges and motored on. He passed a van by the side of the road and then the road was clear again.

It was quiet and peaceful, and the air smelled of wet peat and rain-slick roads.

"I HAVE THE fighters on radar," the pilot of the Challenger said to Hanley over the satellite telephone.

"How far away are you from the Cessna?" Hanley asked.

"Not far," the pilot said. "We're lining up to make a pass over the eastern shore from south to north right now. We're going to buzz him as close as we can."

BENNETT WAS CLOSE to the drop point. He reached over, unlatched the door, and started to tilt the Cessna on her axis. Out of the corner of his eye Bennett caught sight of an old car driving along the road. Then he concentrated on making the drop as close to the van as possible.

Just then the corporate jet appeared in his windshield.

"THERE'S A VAN down on the road on the eastern shore," the pilot of the Challenger said to Hanley as he screamed past Bennett at a low altitude.

"What does—" Hanley started to say before being cut off.

"There's the Robinson," the pilot shouted.

"Can he see the van?" Hanley asked.

"Probably," the pilot said, pulling out of the pass and climbing, "but he's still a distance away."

"Get out of there," Hanley ordered. "We just received word from the British authorities that their fighters are only a few minutes away. They can handle things now."

"Acknowledged," the pilot of the Challenger said.

* * *

ON THE GROUND near the van, the two men watched as the Cessna came closer.

"I think I see a helicopter farther back," one of the men said.

The other man stared into the mist. "I doubt it," he said. "If it was that close, we could hear the engine and the rotor slap."

They could see the door of the Cessna open.

THE TWO MEN could have heard the engine of the helicopter—if the engine had been running. Instead, the cockpit of the Robinson had grown eerily quiet, with only the sound of the air slipping past the fuselage as Adams initiated an autorotation. He angled toward land and prayed they would not fall short.

Cabrillo just caught a glimpse of the van and the flashing strobes as they dropped.

He didn't bother to tell Adams over the headset—he had his hands full right now.

BENNETT PUSHED ON the box and it flipped out of the open door. Then he righted the Cessna and turned to head for the airport in Inverness. He was climbing into the air to clear the hills at the far end of the lake when he caught a quick glimpse of the helicopter only five hundred feet off the ground.

As soon as he could get the Cessna stabilized and on course he'd call and report.

A ROCK IN a box falls straight to earth. The meteorite plummeted down and slammed into a spot of soggy peat without breaking. The two men raced over and were just starting to pull the box from the mud when the high-pitched whine from the engines of a pair of fighter jets grew louder. Raising their heads, they stared up as the jets streaked past.

"Let's get the hell out of here," the first man said as soon as he yanked the box from the peaty soil.

The second man raced ahead to start the van while the first followed with the box.

"I THINK I can make the road," Adams shouted over the headset.

The Robinson was in a depleting arc powered only by the air flowing up through the rotor blades and causing them to spin. Adams was controlling the helicopter to the ground—but he was losing air speed fast.

The edge of the loch and the road were fast approaching, and he started his flare.

THE FIGHTERS CAME up behind Bennett and the Cessna so fast it was as if they had appeared out of thin air. They crossed within feet to either side, then blew past him and initiated high-speed turns. Just then his radio squawked.

"This is the Royal Air Force," a voice said, "you are to make your way to the nearest airfield and land immediately. If you refuse to comply or take evasive action, you will be downed. Acknowledge receipt of this message."

The two jets had completed their turns and were approaching Bennett head-on.

He waved his wings in reply—then he reached for the satellite telephone.

SO CLOSE AND yet so far.

Cabrillo glanced out the side window before the helicopter dropped behind a hill. The van and the drop zone were less than a mile away. Even if Adams could get them to the ground alive, by the time they climbed from the Robinson and jogged to the site, the van—and the meteorite—would be gone.

He clutched his satellite telephone to his chest and braced to hit the ground.

* * *

THE DRIVER OF the van slammed it into gear and stepped on the gas. The rear tires pawed at the muddy soil and spit peat into the air. Fishtailing, he reached the pavement and started down the road to the south.

He glanced quickly in his rearview mirror and found the road empty.

ADAMS PLAYED THE Robinson with all the finesse of a concert violinist. Gauging his flare with precision, he pulled up on the cyclic at the last possible second when the helicopter was in an arc only a few feet off the ground. The change in pitch on the rotor blades bled off the last of the stored air speed and the Robinson stopped in the air and dropped the last few feet to the road on her skids. The airframe took a thump, but not a hard one. Looking over at Cabrillo, Adams exhaled in a loud burst.

"Damn, you're good," Cabrillo said.

"That was a rough one," Adams said, removing his headset and opening the door.

The helicopter was blocking the road almost completely.

"If we had a mile more fuel," Cabrillo said, opening the door and stepping out, "we'd've had them."

The men rose to their full height on the road and stretched.

"You'd better call Mr. Hanley and report that we've lost them," Adams said as Shea and the MG appeared over the hill and slowed because the road was blocked.

"In a minute," Cabrillo said, glancing at the MG as it pulled to a stop.

Shea poked his head out the side window. "You men need some help?" he asked in a Texas twang.

Cabrillo trotted over to the MG. "You an American?"

"Born and raised," Shea said proudly.

"We are working directly for the president on a matter of national security," Cabrillo said quickly. "I'm going to need your car."

"Man," Shea said, "I just bought it like three days ago."

Cabrillo reached in and opened the door. "I'm sorry, it's a life-or-death matter."

Shea pulled on the emergency brake and climbed out.

Cabrillo motioned to Adams with his satellite telephone as he started to climb into the MG. "I'll call the *Oregon*," he said, "and have them get ahold of somebody and have fuel delivered."

"Yes, sir," Adams said.

Cabrillo pushed the starter button and pushed in the clutch and popped the old MG into gear. Then he turned the wheel and started a U-turn.

"Hey," Shea said, "what am I supposed to do?"

"Stay with the helicopter," Cabrillo shouted out the side window. "We'll take care of everything later."

With the MG now straight, he punched the throttle and sped away. In a few seconds he was over the hill and out of sight. Shea walked over to Adams, who was checking the helicopter's skids.

"I'm Billy Joe Shea," he said, extending his hand. "You mind telling me who that was that took my car?"

"That man?" Adams asked. "I've never seen him before in my life."

30

RICHARD "DICK" TRUITT scrolled through Hickman's computer files. There was so much information that the going was slow. Finally he decided to just link onto the *Oregon*'s computer and send the entire contents of Hickman's machine. Establishing a link, he began to transmit the data to a satellite that relayed the data stream down to the ship.

Then he rose from the desk chair and began to search the office.

Truitt removed several sheets of paper and a few photographs from a desk drawer, folded them and placed them in his jacket. He was scanning the bookshelf along the wall when he heard the front door open and the sound of a voice fill the hall.

"Just now?" the voice said.

There was no answer—the man was speaking into a portable telephone.

"Five minutes ago?" the voice said, now growing louder. "Why the hell didn't you send up security immediately?"

The sound of footsteps in the hallway grew louder. Truitt slipped into the bathroom attached to the office and then ran through to a spare bedroom on the other side. Another hallway led through to the living room. He crept along slowly.

"We know you're in here," the voice said. "My security people are on their way up here now. They have the elevator blocked, so you might as well just surrender."

THE KEY TO a good plan is imagining the contingencies. The key to a great plan is imagining them all. The data from Hickman's computer was flying through the air and down to the *Oregon*. Three-quarters of the information had transferred when Hickman walked into the room. Truitt had missed one small point—he'd forgotten to turn off the screen. As soon as Hickman entered, he realized that the screensaver was not on and someone had been accessing the computer.

Racing to the machine, he turned it off. Then he checked and found the vial from Vanderwald undisturbed in his desk drawer.

TRUITT SLIPPED DOWN the hall and into the living room. The sliding glass door was still cracked open. He quickly made his way through the living room. He was almost at the door when he bumped a sculpture and it fell and cracked.

Hickman heard the noise and raced down the hall.

Truitt was through the sliding glass door and on the rear patio when Hickman entered the living room and saw him outside. The intruder was dressed in black and moved with a certain purpose. Still, he was trapped on the patio and the guards were on their way up the elevator.

Hickman slowed to relish the moment.

"Just stop where you are," he said, peering out of the glass door. "There's no escape now."

The man turned and looked directly at Hickman. Then he smiled, climbed on the chest-high wall surrounding the patio, nodded, then waved. Turning around, he leapt off the wall and into the darkness. Hickman was still standing there in shock when the security guards burst into the room.

BLIND FAITH IS a powerful emotion.

And that was all Truitt had at the instant he pulled the cord attached to the front of his jacket. Blind faith in the *Oregon*'s Magic Shop. Blind faith that Kevin Nixon's invention would work. A split second after pulling the cord, a small drag chute popped from the rear of the jacket and ripped the Velcro holding the back of the jacket together. An instant later, a pair of wings like those on a Chinese fighting kite unfolded and locked into place. Four-foot-by-four-foot flaps attached by shock cords dropped below the wings like air brakes on a plane.

Truitt slowed and began to gain control.

"GET READY," GUNDERSON said, "he's coming down fast."

Pilston stared up and caught sight of Truitt for just a second as he passed through a spotlight sweeping the sky near the volcano. Truitt made a 360-degree turn in the air then straightened out. He was ten feet above the sidewalk, twenty yards in front of the Jeep, racing away from them. Luckily the sidewalk was almost empty. This late at night most of the tourists were already in bed or bound tight to the gambling tables. Truitt continued in a straight line.

Gunderson twisted the key on the Jeep and the engine roared to life. He slammed it into gear and raced forward after Truitt. Nine feet, eight feet, but Truitt was having trouble bringing it down to earth. He raced along, his feet still hanging free in the air.

A pair of call girls stood ahead on the corner waiting for the light to change. They were dressed in latex dresses, perched on platform shoes, and their hairstyles were teased and high. One was smoking, one was receiving her next assignment over her cell phone. Truitt reached up and pulled the cords that allowed the air brake to remain inflated. With the air brakes disabled, he dropped to the ground like a rock. He just managed to windmill his feet before touching the sidewalk, and he ran along until he could regain balance and slow his forward movement. He was only five feet from the two ladies when he managed to slow to a walk.

"Evening, ladies," Truitt said, "nice night for a stroll."

Farther to his rear, a red SUV with the Dreamworld logo was pulling out of the driveway of the hotel. The security guard driving stomped on the gas and the tires chirped on the pavement.

At just that moment, Gunderson and Pilston pulled alongside in the Jeep.

"Get in," Gunderson shouted.

Truitt climbed onto the running board then up into the rear of the Jeep. As soon as Truitt was in back. Gunderson hit the gas and raced up the Strip. Truitt's bag was sitting on the seat next to him. He unzipped it and reached inside, pulling out a metal box.

"We're being followed," Gunderson shouted to the rear of the Jeep.

"I noticed that," Truitt said. "When I tell you to, place the Jeep in neutral and shut off the engine."

"Got it," Gunderson said.

They were racing along at ninety miles an hour but the red SUV was gaining. Truitt swiveled around on the rear bench seat and pointed the box at the SUV's grille.

"Now," he yelled.

Gunderson placed the Jeep in neutral and twisted the key off. The lights went dark, and the power steering ceased to operate, making the Jeep hard to steer. Gunderson was wrestling to keep it on the road. Truitt flipped a toggle switch on the box. A signal was sent out into the ether that fried the electrical control box on any vehicles that were operating nearby. The lights on the red SUV went dark and it started slowing. A few cabs that were on the road nearby also ground to a stop.

"Okay," Truitt yelled, "you can start her up again."

Gunderson twisted the key and the Jeep roared to life. He slid it into gear again and regained control. "Where to?" he shouted to Truitt.

"Do you two have your bags?"

"We just showered at the hotel," Pilston said. "We left our bags on the plane."

"To the airport then," Truitt said. "We'd better get out of Vegas."

MAX HANLEY STOOD alongside the computer in Michael Halpert's office on board the Oregon. The two men were staring at the screen intently.

"Then it cut off," Halpert said.

"How much data did we retrieve?" Hanley asked.

"I'll have to go through it all," Halpert said, "but it looks like a lot."

"Start analyzing it," Hanley said quickly, "and report back to me as soon as you find anything of value."

Just then Hanley's communicator beeped and Stone's voice came over the speaker.

"Sir," Stone said, "I just received word from the Gulfstream that they are departing Las Vegas."

"I'll be right there," Hanley said into the microphone.

Hanley made his way quickly along the passageway then opened the door to the control room. Stone was sitting in front of the monitors; he turned as Hanley entered, then pointed at the screen. A map of the western United States was displayed with a flashing red light marking the position of the Gulfstream. The jet was just about to cross over Lake Mead heading east. Right then Hanley's telephone rang, and he walked over to his console and answered it.

"Hanley."

"Did you receive the computer files?" Truitt asked.

"We got some," Hanley said. "Halpert's analyzing them now. It looked like the transmission was stopped midstream—did you run into problems?"

"The target returned when I was doing the download," Truitt said over the noise from the Gulfstream's jet engines. "He probably broke the connection."

"That also means that he knows someone might be on to him."

"Exactly," Truitt said.

"What else have you got?"

Truitt reached into his jacket on the seat across the aisle and removed the photographs he had stolen from Hickman's office. He turned on the fax machine that was attached to the air phone and started to scan them into memory.

"I'm sending you some photographs," Truitt said.

"Who are they?" Hanley asked.

"That's what I want you to find out."

31

"DAMN RIGHT IT'S a problem," the president said to Langston Overholt.

An hour earlier the British prime minister had informed the president that they had discovered a Greek ship captain with radiation burns at a location less than fifty miles from downtown London. As the president and Overholt spoke, the secure lines between the two countries were still burning with a flurry of transmissions.

"We've been working with the Russians as well as the Corporation to recover the weapon," Overholt said, "but it got into England anyway."

"Is that what you'd like me to tell our closest ally?" the president asked. "That we tried, but no cigar?"

"No, sir," Overholt said.

"Well, if whoever is behind this mates the nuke with the meteorite, London and the surrounding area is going to be turned into a wasteland. And whatever you think you might be able to argue about the nuke, the meteorite is *our* screwup."

"I understand, sir," Overholt said.

The president rose from his chair in the Oval Office.

"Listen to me carefully," he said in a voice tinged with anger, "I want results, and I want them now."

Overholt stood. "Yes, sir," he said.

Then he made his way to the door.

"CABRILLO'S STILL TRACKING the meteorite," Hanley told Overholt over the secure line, "at least according to our helicopter pilot who phoned in a few minutes ago."

"The president is up in arms," Overholt said.

"Hey," Hanley said, "don't blame us—the British jets were late to the party. If they'd arrived on time, the meteorite would be secure right now."

"The last communication the British sent mentioned that they had forced the Cessna down at Inverness and were preparing to search the plane."

"They won't find anything," Hanley said. "Our pilot said he and Cabrillo saw the pilot of the Cessna drop the package out the side."

"Why hasn't Cabrillo telephoned in," Overholt said, "so we can coordinate help?"

"That, Mr. Overholt, is a question I cannot answer."

"You'll let me know as soon as you speak to him?"

"Yes, sir," Hanley said as the telephone went dead.

THE MG TC rode like a buckboard wagon filled with grain. The thin tires, lever-action shocks and ancient suspension were no match for a modern sports car. Cabrillo was in fourth gear with the engine wound to her highest RPM and the old car was only doing a little over seventy miles an hour. Holding the wood-rimmed wheel with one hand, he slapped the side of his satellite telephone again.

Nothing. It might have been the landing—despite his best efforts to protect the device, it had hit the dashboard when they finally touched down. It might be the power supply—satellite telephones burned through power like a fat man's air-conditioning during a Phoenix summer. Whatever the case, Cabrillo could not get the green light to come on.

Just then he caught sight of the van a few miles ahead as it crested a hill.

EDDIE SENG GLANCED over at Bob Meadows as the car Meadows was driving neared the Isle of Sheppey. Plucked from the *Oregon* by the Corporation's amphibious plane, the two men had been flown to an airport on the outskirts of London, where the armored Range Rover had been left by the British intelligence agency MI5.

"It looks like we received the weapons we asked for," Seng said as he picked through the nylon bag that had been left on the rear seat.

"Now if we can just find where the Hammadi cell is hiding in London," Meadows said confidently, "and locate the bomb and disable it while our chairman secures the meteorite, we can call it a day."

"Sounds reasonably difficult."

"I give it a seven on the ten scale," Meadows said as he slowed to turn into the port.

SENG STEPPED FROM the passenger seat as Meadows was still shutting off the engine. He walked over to a lanky man with strawberry-blond hair and extended his hand.

"Eddie Seng," he said.

"Malcolm Rodgers, MI5," the man said.

Meadows was out of the Range Rover and approaching.

"This is my partner, Bob Meadows. Bob, this is Malcolm Rodgers from MI5."

"Pleasure," Meadows said, shaking his hand.

Rodgers began to walk toward the pier. "The captain was found at a local pub just up the hill. According to the customs slip, he had docked that evening."

"Did the radiation kill him?" Meadows asked.

"No," Rodgers said, "the preliminary autopsy showed traces of a poison."

"What kind?" Seng asked.

"Nothing we've been able to verify yet," Rodgers said, "some paralytic agent."

"Do you have a phone?" Meadows asked.

Rodgers slowed and removed a cell phone from his pocket then looked at Meadows.

"Call your coroner and have him get in touch with the Centers for Disease Control in Atlanta. Ask them to send the toxicology profiles for Arabian Peninsula scorpion and snake venoms and see if they get a match."

Rodgers nodded then made the call. While he was on the telephone, Seng studied the port area below. There were several old cargo ships, three or four pleasure crafts, and a single catamaran whose upper decks bristled with antennae and two davits. The rear deck of the catamaran was crowded with crates and electronic gear. A man was hunched over a table on the rear deck with his arms inside a torpedo-shaped device.

"Okay," Rodgers said, "they'll check."

The men continued walking down the hill and reached the dock. They walked out on the planks then turned and headed down another dock that abutted the first at a right angle. Three men were visible on the *Larissa*'s deck. You could be sure more were below.

"We've searched every inch," Rodgers said. "Nothing. The logs are falsified, but by interviewing the crew we learned that the cargo was picked up near Odesa in the Ukraine, and they steamed here without stopping."

"Was the crew aware of what they were transporting?" Seng asked.

"No," Rodgers said. "The rumor was that it was stolen artwork."

"They were just the delivery men," Seng said.

Meadows was staring back down the dock at the catamaran.

"Do you men want to go aboard?" Rodgers asked.

"Did anyone see the man leave the pub after he met with the captain?" Meadows asked.

"No," Rodgers answered, "and that's the problem. We don't know who he was or where he went."

"But the captain didn't take the bomb with him to the pub," Meadows wondered aloud, "so either someone on the crew made the switch, or it was stolen off this ship."

"No one saw the bomb at the pub," Rodgers said, "and the captain died there."

"And you've grilled his crew?" Seng said.

"What I'm about to tell you is classified," Rodgers said. Seng and Meadows nodded.

"What we did to the crew is illegal by world convention—they told us everything they know," Rodgers said quietly.

The British were not playing around—the Greeks had been tortured or doped or both.

"And no one in the crew made the switch?" Meadows said.

"No," Rodgers said. "Whoever that man was at the pub, he had accomplices."

"Eddie," Meadows said, "why don't you board the *Larissa* and check it out? I'm going to wander over there and talk to the guy on the catamaran."

"We've already questioned him," Rodgers said. "He's a little odd, but harmless."

"I'll be right back," Meadows said, walking down the dock.

Seng motioned to Rodgers and followed him on board the *Larissa*.

"SIR, WE NEED to call it," Stone said, "Atlantic or North Sea?"

Hanley stared at the moving map on the monitor. He had no idea which way Cabrillo was headed, but the time to decide was upon them.

"Where's the amphibious plane?"

"There," Stone said, pointing to a blip on the map that showed the plane over Manchester and flying north.

"North Sea, then," Hanley ordered. "London is the target. Order the amphibious plane to Glasgow to support Cabrillo."

"Got it," Stone said, reaching for the microphone.

"Hali," Hanley said over his shoulder to Kasim, who was sitting at a table behind the control chair, "what's the situation on the fuel for Adams?"

"I couldn't get the airport in Inverness to make a delivery," Kasim said, "so I contacted a gas station in Loch Ness to bring fuel out to the site in five-gallon cans. He should be arriving there shortly. As soon as he does, I'm sure Adams will report."

"Damn," Hanley said, "we need George up there to support our chairman."

Linda Ross, the *Oregon's* security and surveillance expert, was sitting at the table with Kasim. "I linked up with the British authorities and told them what we know—that we have a white van heading south on the road from Loch Ness that we think is carrying the meteorite, and that Mr. Cabrillo is chasing in an old black MG. They're sending helicopters, but it will be an hour or so until they reach the area."

"Can the Challenger fly high cover and report?" Hanley asked the room.

For a second no one spoke. Stone punched commands into his keyboard then pointed at the monitor. "That's real time from the area," he said.

The blanket of fog looked like a gray wool sheet. On the ground in northern Scotland, visibility was being measured in feet, not yards. Help from the air would not be coming anytime soon.

HALIFAX HICKMAN WAS fuming. After berating his security team, he turned to the head of the detail. "You're fired," he said loudly.

The man walked to the door and exited the penthouse.

"You," he said to the fired man's second in command, "where's the thief that broke in here?"

"Our men saw him land on the ground up the street from Dreamworld," the man said. "He was picked up by two people in an open-topped Jeep. Two of my men were giving chase when their vehicle suffered a massive electrical failure. They lost them at that point."

"I want every person we have scouring this city to find that Jeep," Hickman said. "I want to know who has the balls to break into my apartment on top of my hotel."

"We'll get on it right away, sir," the newly appointed head of security said quickly.

"You damn well better," Hickman said, as he walked up the hallway to his office.

The security men filed out of the penthouse. And this time they remembered to lock the door. Hickman dialed a number on the phone and spoke.

IN HIS OFFICE on board the *Oregon,* Michael Halpert was cataloging the contents from Truitt's transmission. The files were a jumbled mess of corporate documents, bank and brokerage records, and property holdings. Either there were no personal files or they had not been transmitted before the link was disabled.

Halpert set the computer to search for keywords then stared at the photographs Truitt had faxed from the Gulfstream. Rolling his chair over to another computer, he fed the pictures into a scanner, then linked onto the U.S. State Department computer and began searching passport photos. The database was huge and the search might take days. Leaving the computers to work, he left the office and walked up the hall to the dining room. Today's special was beef Stroganoff—Halpert's favorite.

"SIR," THE VOICE said loudly over the phone, "we are being hailed by a United States Navy guided-missile destroyer."

"What do you mean?" Hickman said.

"We've been ordered to heave to or be sunk," the captain of the *Free Enterprise* said.

Hickman's plan was unraveling faster and faster.

"Can't you outrun them?" he asked.

"No way."

"Then engage them," Hickman ordered.

"Sir," the captain said loudly, "that would be suicide."

Hickman thought for a second before answering.

"Then delay the surrender for as long as possible," he said at last.

"Yes, sir," the captain said.

Hickman disconnected and sat back. The team on the *Free Enterprise* had been given a false story from the start. To get the team to cooperate, he'd told them that his plan was to use the meteorite, combined with a nuclear device, for an attack on Syria. Then he told them he was going to blame the attack on Israel and create a full-scale war in the Middle East. By the time it was all over, he'd said, the United States would control the region and terrorism would be snuffed out.

His true plan was much more personal. He was going to avenge the death of the only person he had ever really loved. And God help those that stood in his way.

Reaching for the phone again, he dialed his hangar.

"Get my plane ready for a trip to London."

"AHOY," MEADOWS SAID to the man on the deck of the catamaran.

"Ahoy," the man answered.

The man was tall, a shade over six foot four inches in height, and slim. His face was framed by a trimmed goatee and a tangled mess of graying eyebrows, and his eyes were clear and twinkled as if possessing a secret no one else knew. The man, who appeared the wrong side of sixty years of age, still had his hands inside the torpedo-shaped object.

"Permission to come aboard?"

"Are you the sonar guy?" the man said, grinning.

"No," Meadows said.

"Come on aboard anyway," the man said with a trace of disappointment.

Meadows climbed onto the deck and approached the man. He looked vaguely familiar. Then Meadows placed the face. "Hey," Meadows said, "you're that author, that—"

"Retired author," the man said, smiling, "and yes, I'm him. Forget about that for a moment—how are you with electronics?"

"My oven is still on daylight savings time," Meadows admitted.

"Damn," the author said, "I blew the motherboard in this sonar and I need to get it fixed before the weather clears and we can go out again. The repairman was supposed to be here an hour ago. He must be lost or something."

"How long have you guys been docked here?" Meadows asked.

"Four days now," the author said. "Another couple more and I'll need to spring for new livers for my team—they've been sampling the local flavor. That is, except for one guy—he swore it off years ago and now he's hooked on coffee and pastries. The question is, where do I find these guys? These expeditions are like a floating insane asylum."

"Oh, yeah," Meadows said, "you like to do underwater archaeology."

"Don't say 'archaeology' on this vessel," the author joked. "Archaeologists are on the same plane as necrophilia on this boat. We're adventurers."

"Sorry," Meadows said, smiling. "Hey, we're looking into a theft on these docks a couple of nights ago. Did you guys lose anything?"

"You're an American," the author said. "Why would you be investigating a robbery in England?"

"Would you believe national security?"

"Oh, sure," the author said. "Where were you when I was still writing? I had to make everything up."

"Seriously," Meadows said.

The author considered this for a moment. Finally he answered. "No, we didn't lose anything. This boat has more cameras on it than a Cindy Crawford swimsuit shoot. Underwater, above water, down in the cabins on the instruments, hell, probably in the head for all I know. I rented it from a film crew."

Meadows looked astonished. "Did you tell the Brits that?"

"They didn't ask," the author said. "They seemed a lot more interested in explaining to me that I hadn't seen anything—which I hadn't."

"So you didn't see anything?"

"Not if it was late at night," the author said. "I'm over

seventy years old—if it's past ten at night, there had better be a fire or a naked girl if you want to wake me."

"But the cameras?" Meadows asked.

"They run all the time," the author said. "We're making a television show about the search—tapes are cheap, good footage is precious."

"Would you mind showing them to me?" Meadows asked.

"Only," the author said, walking toward the door leading into the cabin, "if you say 'pretty please.' "

Twenty minutes later, Meadows had what he had come for.

32

NEBILE LABABITI GLANCED at the nuclear bomb sitting on the wood floor of the apartment just off the Strand with excitement tempered by apprehension. It was an inert object—mainly machined metal and a few copper wires—but it emitted a feeling of awe and danger. The bomb was more than just an object—it had a life. Like a painting or sculpture infused with the life force of its creator, the bomb was not simply a hunk of metal. It was the answer to his people's prayers.

They would strike directly at the heart of the British.

The hated British that had stolen artifacts from the pyramids, oppressed the citizens of the Middle East, and fought alongside the Americans in battles they had no place mounting. Lababiti was smack-dab in the center of the lion's den. Downtown London was all around him. The City, where the bankers that funded the oppression resided; the art galleries, museums, and theatre districts of downtown were nearby. Number 10 Downing Street, the Houses of Parliament, Buckingham Palace.

The palace. Home to the queen, the ancient symbol of all he despised. The pomp and circumstance, the righ-

teousness and ceremony. Soon it would all burn with the
fires from the sword of Islam—and when it was over, the
world would never be the same. The heart would be cut
from the beast. The hallowed ground seeping with history
would become a barren wasteland where the human soul
would find no purchase.

Lababiti lit a cigarette.

It wouldn't be long now. Sometime today the young
Yemeni warrior who had agreed to deliver the payload to
the target would arrive in the city. Lababiti would wine and
dine the boy. Supply whores and hashish and tasty treats.
He could do no less for a man willing to commit to the
cause with his life.

Once the boy was acclimated and knew the route,
Lababiti would make a hasty retreat.

The key to leadership, he thought, was not to die for
your country—it was to make the other man die for his.
And Nebile Lababiti had no designs on becoming a martyr
himself. By the time the bomb exploded, he'd be safely
across the English Channel in Paris.

He only wondered why he had not heard from Al-Khalifa.

"I DON'T KNOW how we missed it," Rodgers said.

"No matter," Meadows said, "now you have a plate
number on the truck. Track it down and the bomb will be
close."

"Can I have the tape?" Rodgers asked.

Meadows didn't disclose that he'd had the author make
two copies and that one of them was safely inside the borrowed Range Rover. "Sure," he said.

"I think we can take it from here," Rodgers said, re-
asserting his authority. "I'll make sure and have my boss
notify the head of American intelligence to praise you for
your contribution."

The constant struggle between people and agencies was
exerting itself. Rodgers must have been briefed by his su-
periors that whatever might happen, MI5 needed to receive
credit for recovering the bomb. Now that he had what he

believed would allow them to recover the bomb, he was trying to push the Corporation into the background.

"I understand," Seng said. "Do you mind if we keep the Rover for a few more days?"

"No, please, help yourself," Rodgers said.

"And would it be all right if we questioned the owner of the pub?" Meadows asked, "just so we can complete our file and all?"

"We've already extensively grilled the man," Rodgers said, considering the request for a long moment, "so I can't see how it can hurt."

Rodgers reached for his cell phone to call in the van's plate number, then stared at the two Americans with expectation.

"Thank you," Seng said, motioning to Meadows to walk toward the Range Rover, leaving Rodgers alone.

Rodgers gave a semi-salute and dialed the phone.

Meadows opened the door and climbed behind the wheel as Seng slid into the passenger seat.

"Why'd you give him the tape?" Seng said when the doors were closed.

Meadows pointed to the copy on the floor then started the Range Rover and spun it around in a U-turn.

"Let's go visit the pub owner," he said, "and see what else we can find out."

"Are you thinking what I'm thinking?" Seng asked a few minutes later as Meadows stopped in front of the bar.

"I don't know," Meadows said. "Does it have to do with the motorcycle that was also on the tape?"

"Why don't I call it in," Seng said, "while you go inside?"

Meadows climbed out of the Range Rover. "You've got a damn good memory," he said.

Seng held up his palm, where the number was scrawled in ink.

Meadows closed the door and walked to the pub entrance.

THE TREES IN St. James's and Green Parks near Buckingham Palace were devoid of leaves, and the dormant grass was dusted with a thick frost. Tourists watched the changing of the guards with puffs of steam coming from their mouths. A man on a scooter came down Piccadilly then turned on Grosvenor Place and drove slowly past the lake inside Buckingham Palace Gardens. Continuing on, he rounded the corner onto Buckingham Palace Road to where it met the Birdcage Walk. Pulling to the side of the road alongside the lake inside St. James's Park, he recorded his travel times and the traffic conditions.

Then he slid the small notebook back into his jacket pocket and puttered away.

CABRILLO POKED HIS head out the side window of the MG. An hour ago, when he had driven past Ben Nevis, the tallest mountain in Scotland, he had been gaining on the van. Now as the MG labored up the Grampian Mountains the van was pulling ahead once again. Something needed to happen soon. Cabrillo expected to see Adams in the Robinson, the British army or air force, or even a police car any minute. He was sure the *Oregon* was sending help—he was unarmed in an underpowered chase car.

Surely someone had figured out where he was by now.

ON BOARD THE *Oregon,* they were working on the problem with limited success.

The ship was still a hundred miles from Kinnaird Head, steaming south at full speed. In a few more hours she'd be off Aberdeen, a few more and she'd cross a point offshore Edinburgh.

"Okay," Kasim shouted across the control room to Hanley, "Adams reports he has enough fuel loaded on board to make it to the airport in Inverness. Once there, he'll top off the tanks and head south along the road."

"How much range will he have then?" Hanley asked.

"Hold on," Kasim said, repeating the question to Adams.

"Most of England," Kasim said, "but he won't be able to make London without refueling."

"We should have this wrapped up before then," Hanley said.

"Okay," Kasim shouted, "Adams said he has the engine going."

"Tell him to follow the road until he finds Cabrillo."

Kasim repeated the orders.

"He said the fog is as thick as a winter coat," Kasim said, "but he'll fly right above the road."

"Good," Hanley said.

Linda Ross walked over to Hanley's chair. "Boss," she said, "Stone and I reworked the tracking frequencies on the bugs on the meteorite. We're getting a more complete signal now."

"Which monitor?"

Ross pointed to one on the far wall.

The meteorite was almost to Stirling. Soon the driver of the van would need to signal his intentions with a turn. East toward Glasgow, or west toward Edinburgh.

"Get me Overholt," he said to Stone.

A few seconds later Overholt came on the line.

"I'LL HAVE THE British seal off the roads just outside Glasgow and Edinburgh," Overholt said, "and search every truck."

"We're blessed there's not that many roads they can pick from," Hanley said. "They should be able to snag the truck."

"Let's hope," Overholt said. "Now on another note, I got a call from the head of MI5 thanking Meadows and Seng for the work they are doing on the nuclear bomb problem. Apparently Meadows located a videotape that gave them a license-plate number they think will lead them to the bomb."

"I'm glad," Hanley said.

Overholt paused before speaking again. "Officially they also asked if your people could back off now—they want to handle it from here."

"I'll let Meadows and Seng know when they phone in," Hanley told him.

"Well, Max," Overholt said, "if I were you, I wouldn't be in a rush to take their call."

"I get your drift, Mr. Overholt," Hanley said as he hung up.

"Overholt says the British want Meadows and Seng to back off and let them handle the stray nuke," Hanley said to Stone.

"You should have told me," Stone said. "They just telephoned in to have me run a British motorcycle plate."

"Did you locate the owner?"

"Name and address," Stone said.

"What else did they need?"

"I faxed several dossiers to Meadows's laptop. The land line he used was a number listed in the directory as Pub 'n Grub on the Isle of Sheppey."

MEADOWS HAD LEARNED long ago that threats only worked when someone had something to lose. The agents from MI5 and the local police had made it clear to the owner of the pub what might happen if he did not cooperate. They forgot to mention what might happen if he did. It's easy to gather bees with honey. For information, money works better.

"Gold watch, huh," Meadows was saying as Seng walked inside and nodded.

"Piaget custom," the owner said.

Meadows slid five hundred-dollar bills across the bar as Seng walked over and sat down at the bar. "What do you want to drink?" Meadows asked Seng.

"Black and tan," Seng said without hesitation.

The owner went off to draw the drink. Meadows bent down and whispered to Seng, "How much cash do you have?"

"Ten," Seng said, meaning thousand.

Meadows nodded and slid the laptop around so both he and the owner could see the screen. "Now for five thousand American and our heartfelt thanks, I'm going to scroll through some pictures. If you recognize the man that was with the ship captain, you tell me and I'll stop."

The owner nodded and Meadows began going through the photographs of Al-Khalifa's known accomplices. They had scrolled through over a dozen before the owner shouted to stop. The pub owner stared at the digital photograph intently.

"I think that's him," he said at last.

Meadows turned the laptop back around so the owner couldn't see. Then he unlocked the file showing the pictured man's personal habits.

"Did he smoke?" Meadows asked.

The owner thought back for a second. "Yes, he did."

"Remember the brand?" Meadows asked, showing Seng the information, as if they were engaged in a board game and not a life-and-death situation.

"Oh, hell," the owner said, thinking back.

Meadows pointed to the line that mentioned Lababiti had a gold Piaget watch.

"I got it," the owner shouted. "Morelands, and he had a fancy silver lighter."

Meadows folded the laptop closed and stood up.

"Pay the man," he said to Seng.

Seng reached into his jacket pocket and removed a wad of bills, then broke the paper seal. Counting out fifty, he handed them to the owner. "Bob," Seng shouted to Meadows, who was almost at the door, "verify for me."

"You gave him five," Meadows said, "duly noted."

33

THE *OREGON* WAS racing through the North Sea like a whale on speed. In the control room, Hanley, Stone, and Ross were staring intently at a monitor that showed the location of the meteorite. The signals had calmed down since the frequency adjustment. Other than the occasional distortions that occurred when the bugs passed near high-powered electrical lines, they were finally receiving a clear image.

"The amphibious plane just landed in the Firth of Forth," Stone noted, glancing at another screen. "It's too foggy for him to locate Mr. Cabrillo."

"Have him stand by," Hanley said.

Stone relayed the message over the radio.

Reaching for the secure telephone, Hanley called Overholt.

"The truck turned toward Edinburgh," Hanley said.

"The British have cordoned off the inner city as well as the highways leading south," Overholt told him. "If they start toward London, we'll have them."

"It's about time," Hanley said.

* * *

THE DRIVER OF the van disconnected and turned to his partner. "There's been a change in plans," he said easily.

"Flexibility is the key to both sex and stealth," the passenger said. "Where are we headed?"

The driver told him.

"Then you'd better take a left up here," the passenger said, staring at the road map.

CABRILLO DROVE ALONG, tracking the truck with his remote detector. It had been nearly twenty minutes since he'd seen the truck, but once they reached the series of villages around Edinburgh he'd sped up and was closing the gap.

Taking his eyes off the metal box, he stared at the countryside.

The fog was thick as he drove along the road, which was lined with fences built from rocks and stones. The trees were barren of leaves and appeared as stark skeletons against a gray backdrop. A minute or so before, Cabrillo had caught a glimpse of the Firth of Forth, the inlet that cut into Scotland from the North Sea. The water was black and tossing; the span of the suspension bridge near the edge of the water was barely visible.

Pressing down on the gas pedal, he stared at the box again. The signal was growing closer by the second.

"I WAS ORDERED to drop you in front and take off," the driver said. "Someone will meet you farther down the line."

The driver slowed in front of the Inverkeithing Railroad Station, then came to a stop near a porter with a baggage cart.

"Anything else?" the passenger asked as he reached to open the door.

"Good luck," the driver said.

Stepping onto the sidewalk, the passenger waved his hand at the porter. "Come here," he said, "I have something to load aboard."

The porter wheeled the cart over. "Do you have your ticket already?"

"No," the passenger said.

"Where's the baggage?" the porter asked.

The passenger opened the rear of the van and pointed at the box.

The porter reached down and hoisted the box. "This is heavy," he said. "What's inside?"

"Specialized oil-field testing equipment," the passenger said, "so be careful."

The porter placed the box on the cart and stood up.

"You'd better head inside and purchase your ticket," the porter said. "The train leaves in less than five minutes. Where are you headed?"

"London," the passenger said, walking to the door.

"I'll meet you at the train," the porter said.

AS THE METEORITE was being pushed through the station on the cart, the driver of the van was turning left out of Inverkeithing Station. He had traveled only a few miles in the direction of Edinburgh when the traffic began to slow. There was a tie-up ahead. Looking down the road, he tried to see the problem. It looked like a checkpoint.

He idled forward.

"GO NOW," HANLEY said over the radio to the pilot of the amphibious plane.

The pilot finished duct-taping a note to his heavy coffee thermos, then advanced the throttles. The plane started bumping and jolting as it taxied across the choppy water.

With a lurch the plane lifted off.

The pilot flew as low as he dared. He stared at the ground for some sign of the strange-looking car Hanley had described. He was only feet above the power lines when he found the road he was looking for.

* * *

THE SIGNAL HAD stopped. The problem was that Cabrillo had no map of the area, so his only hope was driving in circles looking for the strongest reading.

"LAST CALL FOR the number twenty-seven train to London," the loudspeaker blared, "all passengers should board now."

"All I have is American money," the passenger said. "Is twenty enough?"

"That's fine, sir," the porter said. "Let me place the package in your cabin."

Walking onto the train, the porter located the cabin and opened the door. Then he set the box containing the meteorite on the floor. Once he had backed out, the passenger, still clutching his ticket, entered.

"WHAT'S THE SCHEDULE?" Hanley shouted to Stone.

"There's a train leaving for London right about now," Stone said, staring at his computer.

"Pull up the route," Hanley ordered.

"I'm nearing Edinburgh," Adams radioed in. "No sign of Mr. Cabrillo yet."

"Watch for the seaplane," Hanley radioed back.

"Roger," Adams answered.

SHEA SPOKE OVER the headset to Adams. "My car better not be damaged."

"Don't worry," Adams said, "if anything has happened, my people will make it right."

"You'd better," Shea said.

"Just keep an eye out for it on the ground."

ON BOARD THE *Oregon,* Hanley reached for the radio and called the amphibian.

"I think I see him," the pilot said.

"Add *train to London* on the note," Hanley said, "and *Adams is closing in,* then buzz him so he can see you and make the drop."

"Got it, boss," the pilot said.

Scribbling the extra line on the note with a felt-tip pen, he angled down between the power lines and passed directly over Cabrillo in the MG at a height of ten feet.

"WHAT THE . . ." CABRILLO said as the rear of the amphibious plane appeared in his windshield.

The pilot wagged the wings then accelerated ahead and made a sweeping turn to make another pass. As soon as Cabrillo saw the side of the plane in the turn he recognized it as the Corporation's and pulled to the side of the road.

Lowering the convertible top, Cabrillo craned his neck around and stared up at the sky. The amphibian was back down the road and coming in low and slow. Once it had almost reached him, Cabrillo saw a tube fly out of the window and bounce on the pavement.

The thermos cartwheeled along until it came to a stop ten feet in front of the MG.

Cabrillo jumped out and raced forward.

"SEAPLANE 8746," EDINBURGH air control reported, "be alert for a helicopter in your immediate area."

The pilot of the Corporation's amphibian was pulling out of his steep climbing turn and took a second to answer.

"Tower, seaplane 8746, helicopter in area," the pilot said, "please report make."

"Seaplane 8746, make is a Robinson R-44."

"Seaplane 8746, I have a visual."

"THE BRITS HAVE the van surrounded," Overholt said to Hanley.

"I think they switched the meteorite onto the train to London," Hanley reported.

"You've got to be kidding," Overholt said in exasper-ation. "I'll need to call the head of MI5 and report. What train?"

"We're not positive yet, but the next train leaving is for London," Hanley said.

"I'll call you back," Overholt said, slamming down the phone.

But a few seconds later another call reached Overholt—and this one was from the president.

THE PILOT OF the amphibian raised Adams on the radio. "Follow me and I'll lead you right to him."

"Fly on," Adams said.

Angling around in a turn, the amphibian lined up over the road and started another pass. The Robinson came in on his tail.

"There," Shea shouted as his MG came into view.

Adams glanced down. Cabrillo was in front of the old car, walking back.

Adams set the Robinson down in a field across the street, leaving the engine idling. Cabrillo raced over with a thermos and his satellite telephone tucked under his arms. Opening the passenger door, he placed the two items in the back. Shea was fumbling with the seat belt. Cabrillo unfas-tened it and helped him out.

"The keys are in your car," he shouted over the noise from the engine and rotor blade, "we'll be in contact soon to pay you for the rental."

Then he slid into the passenger seat of the Robinson and closed the door. Shea ducked down and walked out from under the helicopter blade. Once he was clear he crossed the road and approached his treasured MG. He started in-specting the vehicle as Adams lifted off. Other than a nearly empty tank the car appeared fine.

Adams was 150 feet in the air before Cabrillo spoke.

"My phone is dead," he said over the headset.

"So we gathered," Adams said. "We think they moved the meteorite onto the train."

"So this message is unnecessary," Cabrillo said, ripping off the paper taped to the thermos.

"Is there any coffee in there?" Adams asked. "I could use a cup."

"Me too," Cabrillo said as he cracked the top and steam came out.

34

"I UNDERSTAND, MR. Prime Minister," the president said. "I'll have them notified immediately."

He hung up the phone and buzzed his secretary. "Get me Langston Overholt over at the CIA."

Then he sat back in his chair and waited for the call to be connected.

"Yes, Mr. President," Overholt said when he came on the line.

"I just spoke to the prime minister," the president said. "They were none too happy. It seems you and the Corporation have had them running all over their little isle on what the prime minister described as 'goose chasing and near misses.' The prime minister ordered the roads leading into two cities in Scotland closed, and now they've entered the van you told them contained the meteorite and found it empty. They want the Corporation to back off and let them handle the situation."

"Sir," Overholt said, "I believe that would be a grave mistake at this point. Cabrillo and his men have faced a tough situation. In the first place, they've stuck to the stolen meteorite like paste on paper. They have not recovered it yet, but they haven't lost it either. In the second place, they have traced the movement to a London-bound train—Cabrillo is back in the air and preparing to intercept."

"Turn your information over to MI5," the president ordered, "and let them handle it."

Overholt paused for a minute before speaking. "We still have the Ukrainian bomb loose. The Corporation has a team near London searching for it now—can they proceed with that?"

"The Ukrainians hired the Corporation for that job," the president said, "not agencies of the United States government. I don't see how it is within our power to order them off."

"I asked MI5 to cooperate with them," Overholt said. "In some ways, that gives the Corporation sanction."

The president thought before answering. "The prime minister didn't mention the stray nuke specifically," he said slowly. "He was more concerned about the events in Scotland."

"Yes, sir," Overholt said.

"So tell them to continue the search," the president said finally. "If they *can* recover the bomb, the threat of a dirty bomb using the meteorite is nullified."

"I think I understand what you're saying, Mr. President."

"Tread lightly," the president said, "and have them move quietly."

"You have my word, Mr. President," Overholt said as the phone went dead.

ADAMS FLEW ABOVE and to the rear of the number twenty-seven train. He was edging forward to drop Cabrillo on the roof when Hanley reached the men on the radio.

"We've been ordered off," Hanley said. "The British are planning to intercept the train in a remote area along the coast near Middlesbrough."

"We're right there, Max," Cabrillo argued, "another five minutes or so and I'll be inside the train and searching for the meteorite."

"It came directly from the president, Juan," Hanley said. "We defy a presidential order and I have a feeling there won't be any more work coming our way from the Oval Office. I'm sorry, but from a company standpoint it's just not worth it right now."

Adams heard the conversation and started slowing the Robinson. He stayed close to the tracks in case Cabrillo wanted to go ahead. Looking over at Cabrillo, he shrugged his shoulders.

"Back away, George," Cabrillo said over the headset.

Adams moved the cyclic to the right and the helicopter moved away from the railroad tracks and over some farmland. Pulling back, Adams started climbing to reach a safe altitude.

"All right," Cabrillo said wearily, "you're right. I guess we should get your location so Adams can fly us back to the ship."

"We're passing offshore of Edinburgh and traveling south at full speed," Hanley said, "but if I were you, I'd have Adams drop you in London. I have Meadows and Seng on their way there and they've turned up some interesting leads pertaining to the missing nuclear bomb."

"We're still a go on that?" Cabrillo asked.

"Until we're told otherwise," Hanley said.

"So the Corporation recovers the bomb," Cabrillo said slowly, "and we let the Brits handle our meteorite. Seems backward."

"Backward is all we have right now," Hanley said.

ON THE RAIN-SOAKED deck of the ferry boat sailing from Goteborg, Sweden, to Newcastle upon Tyne, Roger Lassiter was speaking into a satellite telephone. Lassiter had worked for the CIA before being terminated a number of years before, after it had been discovered that vast amounts of funds had gone missing from accounts in the Philippines. The money was intended to be used for payoffs to the locals for information on Muslim terrorist groups operating in the southern provinces. Lassiter had lost the money gambling in a Hong Kong casino.

Once he had been fired, the CIA uncovered a few more facts. Lassiter was not above using unauthorized torture, misappropriating U.S. resources for his profit, or outright deceit and deception. Lassiter had operated in areas with little Langley control—and he had abused his privileges to the limits and beyond. There was also talk of him being a double agent for China, but once he had been fired, nothing was done.

Lassiter now resided in Switzerland, but he hired out to the highest bidder.

In Sweden, he'd stolen blueprints from a marine manufacturer who'd designed a revolutionary drive system. The party that had hired him for the theft was Malaysian. The drop was to take place in London.

"Yes," Lassiter said, "I remember talking to you. You weren't sure you'd need my services."

The Hawker 800XP was just reaching New Jersey, where it would be refueled for the trip across the Atlantic Ocean. Hickman was making plans as he went.

"Turns out I do," Hickman said.

"What's the job?" Lassiter said as he glared at a tourist who walked past on the deck. The man headed back inside.

"Pick up a package and take it to London for me."

"That's a long ways out of my way," Lassiter lied.

"Not according to the man I had following you in Sweden," Hickman said. "He mentioned you got on board the ferry bound for the east coast of Britain quite a few hours ago. Was that someone else?"

Lassiter didn't bother to answer. When two liars are speaking, brevity is critical.

"Where's the package?" he asked.

"You'll need to pick it up at the train station," Hickman said. "It'll be in a locker."

"You want me to fly it down," Lassiter asked, "or drive?"

"Drive," Hickman said.

"Then it's something that won't stand up under an X-ray," Lassiter said. "That raises the risk."

"Fifty thousand," Hickman said, "on delivery."

"Half now," Lassiter said, "and half upon completion."

"One third, two thirds," Hickman said. "I want to be sure you deliver on time."

Lassiter considered this for a moment. "When do I get my first third?"

"I can wire it right now," Hickman said. "What account?"

Lassiter rattled off an account in the Channel Islands. "I can't verify the funds are there until morning. Can I trust you?"

"By the time you're near London tomorrow morning," Hickman said, "you can call your bank. You'll know you've been paid before the delivery."

"And how will I receive the last two thirds?"

"I'll hand it to you," Hickman said, "in person."

"Leaving the sun and sand for the foggy British Isles," Lassiter said. "It must be big."

"You worry about your end," Hickman said. "I'll worry about mine."

"WE INTERCEPTED A British communication," Hickman told the man on the train. "They are stopping the train at Middlesbrough."

"So they are onto the switch?" the man asked.

"They caught your partner entering Edinburgh," Hickman said. "He must have given you up."

The man considered this for a moment. "I doubt that," he said, "at least not this soon. Someone else must be following us."

Hickman didn't tell the man about the break-in at his office. The less the man knew the better. So far he had lost his team on the *Free Enterprise* as well as one of his men inside Great Britain. Hickman was running out of assets he could use. And he'd need the man in Maidenhead.

"Whatever the case," Hickman said, "I've taken care of the problem. You exit the train in Newcastle upon Tyne and place the package in a locker. Then proceed to the nearest restroom and place the locker key in the farthest toilet tank from the door. I have arranged for someone to pick up the package and take it the rest of the way."

"What should I do then?" the man asked as he stared out

the train window. The sign said Bedlington. He was thirty miles from his new stop.

"Make your way to this location in Maidenhead by rental car," Hickman said, reading off an address, "and meet up with the rest of the team coming in from Calais."

"Sounds great," the man said.

"It will be," Hickman agreed.

AT THE SAME time that Adams and Cabrillo were flying toward London, the *Oregon* was passing through the fifty-five-degree latitude, offshore of Newcastle upon Tyne. In his office, Michael Halpert was staring at a stack of documents he'd printed from the files Truitt had sent. Halpert was underlining sentences with a yellow highlighter when one of the computers in his office beeped and the printer started.

Halpert waited until the document was finished, then removed it and read.

The pictures Truitt had stolen had been matched on a U.S. military database. The face belonged to one Christopher Hunt of Beverly Hills, California. Hunt had been a captain in the U.S. Army until he had been killed in Afghanistan. Why did Halifax Hickman have a photograph of a dead soldier in his office? What possible tie could it have to the theft of the meteorite?

Halpert decided to dig deeper before contacting Hanley.

NEBILE LABABITI STARED at the bomb, bathed in the light from a flashlight, with glee. It was sitting on the floor in a ground-floor office/showroom on the Strand that was located below Lababiti's apartment. The office had been vacant for the last few months, and Lababiti had jimmied the lock last week then changed it so he had the only key. As long as no one wanted to show the office in the next few days, he was home free.

The showroom had an overhead garage door for deliveries. The space was perfect for loading the bomb into a vehicle for the run down to the park. Out of sight, but with a fast exit. It was all coming together, he thought.

Turning off the flashlight, he slipped out the door and walked across the street to a pub near the Savoy Hotel. Then he ordered a pint and dreamed of death and destruction.

35

THE DATE WAS December 30, 2005. Bob Meadows and Eddie Seng were on the road to London. The traffic was thick and the roads were slick with rain. Seng adjusted the radio to receive a weather report, then listened as the announcer gave a detailed outlook. The dashboard of the Range Rover glowed in the dim light and the heater was blowing.

Seng clicked the radio off.

"Rain turning to sleet in the next hour," he said. "How do people live here?"

"It's dismal, that's for sure," Meadows said, staring out at the growing darkness, "but the people are surprisingly upbeat."

Seng ignored the comment. "Friday-night traffic," he said, "people must be going into London for the shows or something."

"I'm surprised Mr. Hanley has not called back yet," Meadows said.

After leaving the pub, Meadows had called in to report their findings.

"The *Oregon*'s probably in some rough seas right about

now," Seng said as he slid to a slow crawl behind a line of traffic that stretched for miles ahead.

IT WAS COLD on the North Sea, but not as rough as it could have been. The storm that was advancing from the north was laying down the seas and, other than a ten-degree decrease in temperature in the last hour, those on board the *Oregon* had noticed little change.

Belowdecks in the Magic Shop, Kevin Nixon was actually warm. The last few days he had been working on Al-Khalifa's recovered satellite phone. The unit had been immersed in seawater when his body had been thrown overboard. Since the thermal vents had bloated the body quickly and it had floated to the surface with the phone still in the pocket, the insides had not had a chance to corrode much.

Nixon had taken the unit apart and cleaned it thoroughly. But when he reassembled the phone it still did not work. He'd decided to bake the chip boards in a small toaster oven to make sure that all trace of moisture was gone. Removing the parts from the oven carefully with medical forceps, he reassembled the unit then added the freshly charged battery.

The unit lit up and the message icon flashed.

Nixon smiled and reached for the intercom.

HANLEY AND STONE had been working on Seng and Meadows's information. They had managed to hack into the British Motor Vehicles Registry and match a name and address with the motorcycle license plate. Then they ran the information on Nebile Lababiti through a different database and located bank information and his visitor visa information. Stone was cross-checking everything now.

"His rent checks don't match the address he gave passport control," Stone noted. "I ran the name of the building his rent checks are made out to through a mapping program and found the location. He told passport control he lives in the Belgravia section of London. The building he pays rent to is a few miles away, near the Strand."

"I know the Strand," Hanley said. "Last time I was in London I ate at a restaurant on the Strand named Simpson's."

"Any good?" Stone asked.

"It's been in business since 1828," Hanley said. "You don't stay around that long if the food is bad. Roast beef, mutton, good desserts."

"What's the street like," Stone asked, "the Strand itself?"

"Busy," Hanley said, "hotels, restaurants, theaters. Not the perfect place for a covert operation."

"Sounds like an excellent place for a terrorist to strike."

Hanley nodded. "Find me the closest heliport."

"I'm on it," Stone said.

Then the intercom buzzed and Nixon asked Hanley to come down to the Magic Shop.

LABABITI HAD FINISHED two pints of ale and a double shot of peppermint schnapps. He stared at his gold wristwatch then smoked a cigarette. When that was finished he snubbed it out in the ashtray, tossed some pound notes on the bar and walked outside.

The Yemeni who would drive the bomb to the location was due to arrive on the bus from the airport in the next few minutes. Lababiti found the bus stop just up the street, then leaned against the building and smoked another cigarette while he waited.

London was alive with holiday cheer. The shop windows were decorated for the season and people crowded the streets. Most of the hotels were booked solid as people arrived in London for the New Year's Eve celebration. There was an Elton John concert planned for Hyde Park. And at both Green and St. James's Parks near Buckingham Palace, the trees had been adorned with thousands of colored lights. The streets near Hyde Park would be closed, and food courts, temporary pubs and outdoor restrooms would be placed on the streets for the massive party. Fireworks would be launched from barges anchored in the River Thames. And the sky would burn with celebration.

Lababiti smiled with a secret only he knew. He would be supplying the most powerful fireworks, and when it was done the party, and all who attended, would cease to exist. The bus pulled up and Lababiti waited as it unloaded.

The Yemeni was nothing more than a child, and he appeared scared and confused by the unusual surroundings. Stepping timidly off the bus after most of the others at the stop had disembarked, he clutched a cheap suitcase in his hands. He was dressed in a tattered black wool overcoat that must have been bought used. The thin outline of a mustache that would never have time to fill in adorned his upper lip like the mark left from a glass of chocolate milk.

Lababiti stepped forward. "I'm Nebile."

"Amad," the boy said quietly.

Lababiti steered him down the street toward the apartment.

They had sent a child to do a man's job. But Lababiti didn't care—there was no way he would do it himself.

"Have you eaten?" Lababiti asked when they were away from the crowd.

"I had some figs," Amad said.

"Let's get your bags in my apartment and I'll show you around."

Amad simply nodded. He was visibly trembling, and speech would not come.

HANLEY LISTENED TO Al-Khalifa's messages, then saved them.

"His voice prompt is short," Hanley noted.

"It may be enough," Nixon said.

"Get on it then," Hanley said.

"You got it, boss."

Leaving the Magic Shop, Hanley walked back to the elevator and took it up. He walked along the passageway and entered the control room. Stone pointed to a screen with a map of downtown London being displayed.

"We can put them right there," he said, "Battersea Park."

"How far is it from Belgravia and the Strand?" Hanley asked.

"The heliport is built on pilings on the Thames," Stone

said, "between the Chelsea Bridge to the east and the Albert Bridge to the west. If they cross over the Albert Bridge on the Queenstown Road, they're in Belgravia. From there it's only a short drive to the Strand."

"Beautiful," Hanley said.

MEADOWS REACHED FOR the telephone on the first ring.

"Go to Battersea Park," Hanley said without preamble, "there's a heliport there out in the Thames. Cabrillo will be arriving shortly in the Robinson."

"Have you made arrangements for a hotel?"

"Not yet," Hanley said, "but I'll book several rooms at the Savoy."

"So you located our man?" Meadows asked.

"We think so," Hanley said. "He should be right across the street."

"Perfect," Meadows said, disconnecting.

NEXT HANLEY CALLED Cabrillo to report. After giving him the locator numbers for the heliport, he explained that Meadows and Seng would meet him there.

"George will need to hangar the helicopter at Heathrow," Cabrillo said. "I'm sure they won't let us leave it on the helipad."

"I'll make the arrangements," Hanley said.

"Be sure to book him a hotel as well," Cabrillo said, "he's exhausted."

"I'll put him up right near Heathrow, close to the Robinson."

"What else?" Cabrillo asked.

"Nixon got Al-Khalifa's satellite telephone working."

"Can he match the voice so we can call his contacts?" Cabrillo asked excitedly.

"We'll know soon."

36

ROGER LASSITER SAT on a bench outside the restroom in the train station at Newcastle upon Tyne. He had been watching the door and the areas nearby for the last twenty minutes. Nothing seemed amiss. He waited until the man who had just entered had finished and left. Now the facility should be empty. Glancing around one last time, he stood up and walked inside.

Then he made his way down to the far stall and took the lid off the tank.

The locker key was inside, and he quickly removed it and slid it in his pocket. Then he walked from the facility and located the locker. After watching the area for another half hour and finding nothing out of place, he waited until a luggage porter walked past and hailed him.

"I have a rental car in the parking structure," Lassiter said, smiling, with a twenty-pound note in his hand. "If I pull it up to the doors, will you bring out a package I have?"

"Where is it, sir?" the porter asked.

Lassiter handed him the key. "Over there," he said, "in a luggage locker."

The porter took the key. "What kind of rental car should I look for?"

"It's a black Daimler sedan," Lassiter said.

"Very good, sir," the porter said, wheeling his cart toward the locker.

Lassiter walked out of the lobby and crossed the road to the parking structure. If he got in the car, started it, and was allowed to exit the garage, he was home free. If anyone was on to him, they'd make their move by then.

No one came. No one stopped him. No one knew.

After paying the parking fee, Lassiter drove around the loop to the front of the train station. The porter was waiting alongside the curb with the box on his cart. Lassiter pulled alongside, then popped the trunk release inside the glove box.

"Put it in the boot," he said, as he rolled down the passenger window.

The porter lifted the box into the rear of the Daimler and closed the lid. Lassiter placed the sedan into gear and pulled away.

THE CIA'S LIAISON to MI5 sat inside an office at MI5's headquarters in London.

"Your contractors gave us a tape that shows a license number for the van that we believe left with the nuclear device," he said. "We have a team descending on the rental agency as we speak. As soon as we retrieve the information about the renter, we should be able to recover the bomb."

"Excellent," the CIA agent said evenly. "Now, what is the status of our missing meteorite?"

"That should be resolved shortly," the MI5 agent said.

"Do you need our help?" the CIA agent asked.

"I think not," the MI5 agent said. "We have the Royal Army and Marines on the job."

The CIA agent rose from his chair. "Then I'll just wait for you to contact me," he said, "after you've made the recovery."

"Once we have it, I'll contact you immediately."

As soon as the CIA man left his office, the MI5 agent reached for the telephone.

"How long until we intercept?" he asked.

"The train is five minutes away," a voice said.

IN A WOODED area one mile north of the village of Stockton, the nearest train station to Middlesbrough, it looked as if a war was commencing. A pair of British army Challenger tanks sat on each side of the railroad tracks. Farther up the tracks to the north, approximately where the end of the train would be after it was stopped, two platoons of Royal Marines in camouflage hid in the woods, waiting to enter the train from the rear door. Farther to the left and right of the tracks, in cleared fields hidden behind the rows of trees that lined the tracks, were a single Harrier jet and an Agustawestland A-129 Mongoose helicopter with a weapons pod attached.

From the distance to the north the sound of the number twenty-seven train grew louder.

The British army colonel in charge of the operation waited until he could see the nose of the locomotive. Then he called the engineer over a radio and ordered him to stop. As soon as the engineer caught sight of the Challengers he slammed on the brakes and the train started sliding to a stop, with sparks flying from the wheels. The Harrier and Agustawestland, which had both been hovering, popped up over the trees and assumed a fire support role at the same time that the Royal Marines slid from the woods and boarded at all the doors.

A methodical search would be made, but they would find nothing.

AT THE SAME time, Roger Lassiter was driving south on the highway leading to London. Passing Stockton, he noticed the commotion in the distance and took the exit to the right toward Windermere. Once he reached the main north-south highway that passed through Lancaster, he would continue on through Birmingham and access southern England. Lassiter lit a cigar and stared out at the rain.

APPROACHING THE THAMES from the air, Adams studied the GPS for his exact location. Cabrillo was glancing out at a park across the river. A huge tent, lit by spotlights, was swarming with workers completing the installation.

"To your left, sir," Adams said over the headset.

The square outline of the heliport pad was lit with flashing lights. Then a car nearby flashed its headlights. Adams lowered the collective and started down.

"Seng and Meadows are here," Cabrillo said. "I'm going to have them take me to the hotel so we can regroup. Hanley is having someone meet you at the executive air terminal at Heathrow with your hotel key. What else will you need, George?"

"Nothing, sir," Adams said. "I'll refuel and head to the hotel. When you need me, just call."

"Get some sleep," Cabrillo ordered, "you've earned it."

Adams was on his final approach and didn't bother to answer. Dropping down over Battersea Park, he edged forward to the pad and then lightly touched down. Cabrillo opened the door and grabbed his telephone. Ducking down, he crab-walked away from the Robinson. Once he was clear he stood upright. He was nearing the Range Rover when Adams lifted off and flew across the Thames.

Meadows climbed from the passenger seat and opened the rear door for Cabrillo.

"Where are we at?" Cabrillo said as he slid into the rear and closed the door.

"We forwarded what we have to Mr. Hanley," Seng said. "He said you'd fill us in."

Seng steered away from the heliport and out of the park. He stopped at the light and waited to turn onto Queenstown Road to cross the Chelsea Bridge.

Cabrillo began to explain as Seng drove them toward the Savoy.

*   *   *

THE *OREGON* WAS racing south. It was almost midnight on December 30 and the ship was scheduled to reach the docks near London at around 9 A.M. local time. The conference room was crowded. Hanley was writing notes on a dry-erase bulletin board. The board was becoming crowded.

"Here's what we know," he said. "We now believe that the theft of the meteorite and the missing Ukrainian nuclear bomb are not related. We believe that Al-Khalifa and his group got wind of the meteorite through an officer that was bribed at the Echelon listening post and then decided to combine it with their existing plan, which we believe is a terrorist strike in the heart of London."

"Who was originally after the meteorite?" Murphy asked.

"The latest information, which was recovered by Mr. Truitt in Las Vegas, seems to point to Halifax Hickman."

"The billionaire?" Ross asked.

"Correct," Hanley said, "we just don't know why yet. Hickman has interests in hotels, resorts, casinos, arms manufacturers, household products. Along with that he has a string of funeral homes, a hardware manufacturer that makes tools—nails and fasteners. He also has railroad and oil interests, and a satellite television operation."

"An old-fashioned tycoon," Pete Jones said. "Not like today, when the truly rich make their money from one source, like software or pizza chains."

"Isn't he a recluse?" Julia Huxley asked.

"Sort of like Howard Hughes," Hanley answered.

"I'll run a psych profile," Huxley offered, "so we know what we might be dealing with."

"Halpert's digging through the computer files as we speak to see if we can determine motive."

"What's the status of the meteorite now?" Franklin Lincoln asked.

"As you all know, Juan and Adams witnessed it leaving the Faeroe Islands aboard a Cessna that they followed. Once the helicopter ran out of fuel, Juan chased the Cessna by car to a railroad station near Edinburgh. He was ready to intercept when the president, through Overholt, ordered him off to let the British authorities handle the problem.

They were planning to stop the train an hour or so ago, but we've yet to hear the outcome."

"So if they have recovered it," Hali Kasim said, "our only involvement would be to return it to the United States."

"Correct," Hanley said, "and that's why I want to concentrate on the nuclear device. We believe that it was shipped through the Black Sea to a port named the Isle of Sheppey on a Greek cargo ship. There, we believe operatives of Al-Khalifa's terrorist organization grabbed the weapon without paying and drove away. Seng and Meadows were on the ground there and found a videotape that gave us leads to the possible current location."

"It seems odd," Jones said, "that after Al-Khalifa's death, the others didn't scrub the mission. Their leader is killed and they're still planning to go ahead?"

"That's the beauty of it," Hanley said. "We don't think they know that Al-Khalifa is dead yet."

"He obviously has not been in contact with them," Ross noted.

"True," Hanley said, "but apparently he's done that before—at least according to the reports we've amassed over the years."

"So one of us is going to become Al-Khalifa?" Meadows said.

Hanley motioned to Nixon, who nodded and reached for a tape recorder. "We recovered Al-Khalifa's satellite telephone from his pocket. There was a short message on his voice mail. I matched that with an existing surveillance tape we had and printed his voice on the computer."

Nixon turned the tape player on and Al-Khalifa's voice floated into the air.

"We think we can call his contact with his telephone and arrange a meeting," Hanley said, "then recover the bomb."

"How much time do we have?" Kasim asked.

"We think they will strike tomorrow at the stroke of midnight," Hanley said.

"New Year's Eve," Murphy said, "those grandstanding bastards. Any idea where?"

"There's a celebration and concert in a park right near Buckingham Palace," Hanley said. "Elton John will be performing."

"Now I'm really pissed," Murphy said. "I love that guy's music."

"All right, everyone," Hanley said, "I want you to all make your way to your cabins and get some sleep. Most of you are going into London tomorrow to work the operation. We're going to meet here in the conference room at seven a.m. for assignments, and as soon as we near London, you'll be off-loaded and sent into the city. Are there any more questions?"

"Just one," Huxley said. "Does anyone know how to defuse a nuclear bomb?"

37

"LEAVE IT IN front," Seng ordered as they pulled in front of the Savoy and climbed out. Peeling off a hundred-dollar bill, he handed it to the valet. "And do not block it in."

Cabrillo walked inside and headed to the check-in desk.

"May I help you?" the clerk asked.

"My name's Cabrillo," he said, "my company made a reservation."

The clerk entered the name, then stared at the note the general manager had written. The note was succinct: *Extremely valued repeat customer—unlimited credit verified—Bank of Vanuatu—four river-view suites tonight—additional rooms as needed.*

The clerk reached for the keys, then snapped his finger and a porter trotted over. At the same time Meadows and Seng entered the lobby.

"I see you have no luggage, Mr. Cabrillo," the clerk noted. "Will you need us to arrange shopping?"

"Yes," Cabrillo said, reaching for a slip of paper and a pen. He began jotting down notes. "Call Harrods tomorrow morning. There is a Mr. Mark Andersen in men's clothing—ask him to deliver these items. He already has my sizes."

Meadows and Seng walked over to the desk carrying a pair of bags each. Cabrillo handed each of the men a key. "Do you need anything from Harrods?" he asked.

"No," both men replied.

The porter reached for Seng's and Meadows's bags but Seng raised his hand and stopped him. "You'd better let us take care of those," he said, slipping the man a twenty-pound note. "Just follow us up and take the cart back."

The bags were loaded with weapons, communication devices and enough C-6 to level the hotel to rubble. The unknowing porter nodded, pushed the cart closer and waited to follow the men up to the suite.

"What are you men hungry for?" Cabrillo asked as Seng and Meadows placed the bags on the cart.

"I could do breakfast," Meadows said.

"Send three full English breakfasts to my suite," Cabrillo said, holding up his key to the clerk, "in forty-five minutes."

"Let's shower and clean up," Cabrillo said to his men, "and meet in my suite at one-thirty."

Then, followed by the porter, they pushed the baggage cart toward the elevator and rode up to their rooms. At the door to Cabrillo's suite, he unlocked the door and stopped.

"Wait here, please," he said. "I want these clothes taken down to the laundry and cleaned and pressed."

He walked inside, undressed, slid into one of the robes in the closet and returned to the door with a pile of the clothing he had been wearing. Handing them to the porter in a plastic laundry bag along with a hundred-dollar bill, he smiled. "Get these back to me as soon as possible."

"Will you need your shoes shined?" the porter inquired.

"No, thank you," Cabrillo said, "they will be fine."

As soon as the porter left, Cabrillo climbed into the shower and scrubbed himself clean. When finished, he dressed again in the robe and walked back to the front door and opened it. A basket of toiletries had been left, and he took this inside the bathroom and shaved, splashed his cheeks with expensive aftershave then brushed his teeth and combed his hair. Then he walked back into the suite and dialed the control room on the *Oregon*.

AT THE SAME time Cabrillo was finishing his grooming, it was just past 8 P.M. Washington time. Thomas "TD" Dwyer had spent the last few days working double shifts inside the infectious agents laboratory at Fort Detrick, Maryland, which was located in the mountains north of Washington, D.C., near Frederick. Dwyer was exhausted and almost ready to call it quits for the night. So far he had subjected the samples from Arizona to ultraviolet light, acids, combinations of gases, and radiation.

And nothing had happened.

"Ready to wrap it up for the night?" the army technician asked.

"Let me just cut off a sample for tomorrow," Dwyer said, "then we can start again at eight a.m."

"Do you want me to warm up the laser?" the technician asked.

Dwyer stared through the thick glass viewing window at the sample, which was clamped in a vise on a workbench inside the tightly sealed room. Dwyer had placed a diamond-tipped portable air-powered saw into the entry port earlier, then moved it over to the bench by reaching through the wall with his arms inside the thick Kevlar gloves. The saw was now sitting in the pincer arms of a robotic device that Dwyer could control with a joystick.

"I'm going to use the saw," Dwyer said, "stand by."

The technician slid into a chair behind a large control panel. The wall in front of him, including the area around the small windows that looked into the sealed area, was covered with gauges and dials.

"We're negative," the technician noted.

Dwyer carefully moved the joystick and started the saw spinning. Then he slowly lowered it down to the sample. The saw started smoking, then ground to a halt.

It would not be until noon tomorrow that it could be repaired.

* * *

TINY GUNDERSON THROTTLED the Gulfstream down and entered the pattern at Heathrow. He and Pilston had taken turns sleeping on the flight from Las Vegas. Truitt had napped in the rear and was now awake and drinking his second pot of coffee.

"Fill up?" he asked through the door of the cockpit.

"I'm okay," Gunderson said. "How about you, Tracy?"

Pilston was talking to the tower on the radio but she motioned no with her hand.

"Hanley arranged a hotel near the airport for you two," Truitt said. "I'm taking a cab into the city."

Gunderson made his turn to final approach. "We'll fuel up, then stand by at the hotel," he said.

"Sounds like a plan," Truitt said.

Something had been bothering Truitt for the entire flight and he couldn't put his finger on what it was. He had been trying to remember the interior of Hickman's office for hours but, try as he might, the picture was not clear. Sitting back in his seat, he buckled the seat belt and waited for the Gulfstream to set down.

Ten minutes later he was inside a cab heading through the deserted streets for the Savoy. The cab was driving past Paddington Station when it hit him.

OVERHOLT WAS PLANNING to sleep in his office on the couch. Win, place or show, something would be happening in the next forty-eight hours. It was almost ten at night when the president called again.

"Your boys screwed up," the president said. "There was nothing on the train."

"Impossible," Overholt said. "I've worked with the Corporation for years—they don't make mistakes. The meteorite was on the train—it must have been moved again."

"Well," the president said, "now it's loose somewhere in England."

"Cabrillo is in London right now," Overholt said, "working on the missing nuke."

"Langston," the president said, "you'd better get control of this situation, and soon, or you'd better start figuring if you can make it on your retirement pay."

"Yes, sir," Overholt said as the phone went dead.

"WE HAVE THE meteorite headed south on the road just south of Birmingham," a weary Hanley said to Overholt's question. "We'll be off shore of London tomorrow morning and then we can off-load our operatives and track it down."

"We'd better," Overholt replied. "My ass is in the wind here. What's the status on the bomb recovery?"

"Cabrillo and his team plan to pinpoint the location tomorrow and then call MI5," Hanley said.

"I'm sleeping here in my office tonight," Overholt said. "Call me if anything changes."

"You have my word," Hanley said.

DICK TRUITT GOT his key from the desk, then tipped the doorman to place his bag in his room. He walked down the hall to Cabrillo's suite and knocked on the door softly. Meadows answered.

"Easy money," Meadows said when he saw who it was. He stood aside to allow Truitt to enter. Truitt walked into the suite. Half-eaten plates of food sat around a table along with open files and notes.

"Morning, boss," he said to Cabrillo.

Then he walked over to the telephone and called room service for a club sandwich and a Coca-Cola. Returning to the table, he slid into a chair.

"Halpert learned the identity of the soldier in the photographs you swiped," Cabrillo said, "but how he's tied to Hickman we've yet to determine."

"He's his son," Truitt said simply.

"Well, hell," Seng blurted, "that explains a lot."

38

"HE HAS TO be," Truitt said. "When I was in Hickman's office I saw something that registered in my mind as odd but I didn't have time to investigate it before he returned to the penthouse. On a shelf near his desk there was a set of bronze baby shoes."

"That's odd," Cabrillo said. "Hickman has no known offspring."

"Yes," Truitt said, "but wrapped around them was a set of dog tags."

"Did you have a chance to read the tags?" Seng, a former marine, asked.

"Nope, but I bet someone from the Las Vegas police could. The thing is, why would he have another man's dog tags?"

"Unless they were from someone close," Meadows said, "and that person was dead."

"I'll call Overholt and ask him to have the Las Vegas police check," Cabrillo said. "You men get some rest. I have a feeling tomorrow will be a long day."

Meadows and Seng filed out but Truitt remained. "I slept on the Gulfstream, boss," he said. "Why don't you give me the addresses you have and I'll do a little late-night recon."

Cabrillo nodded and handed Truitt the information. "Meet back here at eight a.m., Dick," he said. "The rest of our people will be arriving then."

Truitt nodded, then walked down the hall to change clothes. In five minutes he was riding down the elevator.

HALPERT WAS PULLING an all-nighter. The *Oregon* surged toward London with only a minimum crew handling navigation. The operatives were asleep in their cabins and the ship was quiet. Halpert liked the solitude. Setting the computer to search the Department of Defense records, he walked down the hall to the galley and toasted a bagel while he brewed a fresh pot of coffee. Smearing the bagel with cream cheese, he wrapped it up and slid it under his arm, then took the pot back with him to his office.

A single sheet of paper was sitting in his printer tray, and he picked it up and read it slowly. Christopher Hunt's next of kin was his mother, Michelle Hunt, who was a resident of Beverly Hills, California.

Halpert entered her into the computer to see what he could find.

IT WAS FOUR A.M. London time when the Hawker 800XP carrying Hickman touched down at Heathrow. He was immediately met on the runway by a black Rolls-Royce limousine. The limousine set off through the deserted streets toward Maidenhead.

Hickman wanted to be at Maidenhead Mills when it opened. The rest of his team was due in from Calais soon and he had much to accomplish. He stared at the vial of plague he had bought from Vanderwald. A little of this and a little meteorite dust and voila.

THE INTERIOR OF the house was plush considering its location in London's East End. Long the grittiest section of

London proper, in the last few years the East End had become more upscale as high prices in Central London had forced the citizens farther away from the city center.

The three-story house on Kingsland Road, not far from the Geffrye Museum, had survived the bombings of World War II nearly unscathed. After years of life as a rooming house for the immigrants who had settled in the area in the late twentieth century, it had, for the last few years, been resurrected as a high-class whorehouse run by an old-line East End crime family named for its leader, Derek Goodlin.

The lower floor was a salon area with sitting rooms and a pub. The second floor was comprised of a casino with another bar along the wall, and the top floor contained the bedrooms, which were outfitted for a variety of tastes and fetishes.

As soon as Lababiti had pulled the Jaguar in front and climbed out with Amad, Derek Goodlin, who was operating the house this evening, had been alerted to his arrival. Goodlin, who was called "Bugs" behind his back because of his beady eyes and pockmarked skin, smiled, raced to the door and in his mind started counting his money.

Goodlin had dealt with the Arab before and he knew the house would make thousands before Lababiti called it a night.

"Chivas and Coke," Goodlin ordered the bartender as he raced to greet his guest.

Swinging the door open, he smiled, showing thin, pointed teeth. "Mr. Lababiti," he said with all the warmth of a snake encased in ice, "how good of you to join us this evening."

Lababiti detested Goodlin. He was all that was wrong with the West. Goodlin sold sin and depravity—the fact that Lababiti was a frequent buyer made little difference.

"Evening, Derek," Lababiti said quietly, taking the drink from the waiter who had raced over. "Still running your crooked game, I see."

Goodlin smiled his evil smile. "I just supply what people want," he said.

Lababiti nodded and motioned for Amad to follow him

inside. Walking over to the ornate carved mahogany bar in the pub room, he slid into a chair alongside a round table with a lit candle on top. Goodlin followed behind like a lapdog.

"Will you be gaming this evening?" Goodlin asked once the pair was seated.

"Maybe later," Lababiti said, "but for now, bring my friend here an Araq and then have Sally brought down."

Goodlin signaled the waiter to find the bottle of the strong licorice-flavored Middle Eastern alcoholic drink, then looked down at Lababiti. "Sally Forth, or Sally Spanks?"

"Forth for him," Lababiti said, pointing, "and Spanks for me."

Goodlin raced off to alert the women. A few seconds later the waiter slid the bottle of Araq and a glass onto the table. Amad, who was due to die in a day, looked scared.

DEREK GOODLIN CLOSED the door behind Lababiti and his friend, then walked back to his office. He sat down and began counting a pile of bills while he sipped from a snifter of brandy. It had been a good night. The Arab and his silent friend had added five thousand pounds to the nightly take. That, along with a Japanese regular who had lost heavily at the roulette wheel, gave him a 30 percent increase over last night's business.

He was wrapping a pile of pound notes with a rubber band to hide in the safe when there was a knock on his door. "Hold on," he said as he placed the cash in the safe and then closed it and spun the dial.

"Okay," he said once the safe was closed, "come in."

"I'm here for my pay," Sally Forth said, "my final pay."

The socket around her left eye was purple and swollen.

"Lababiti?" Goodlin asked. "I thought you were supposed to be with the kid."

"I was," Sally said. "He got a little mean after . . ."

"After what?" Goodlin asked.

"After he couldn't get it up," Sally Forth answered.

Goodlin reached into his desk drawer for one of the envelopes he had prepared for the girls who had worked that night and handed it over. "Take a few days off," he said, "and be back at work Wednesday."

Nodding a weary nod, she left the office and walked down the hallway.

LABABITI WAS DRIVING the Jaguar west on Leadenhall Street. Amad was sitting in the passenger seat quietly.

"Did you have a good time?" Lababiti asked.

Amad grunted.

"Are you going to be ready tomorrow?"

"Allah is great," Amad said quietly.

Lababiti turned and glanced over at the Yemeni, who was staring out the side window at the buildings they passed. He was beginning to have his doubts about Amad, but he kept them to himself. Tomorrow morning he'd give the Yemeni his last instructions.

Then he'd drive to the Chunnel and escape to France.

TRUITT WALKED DOWN the Strand to the side street where the records showed Lababiti rented an apartment. On the lower floor, a vacant shop abutted the lobby. The three floors above, where the apartments were located, were dark, the residents sleeping. Truitt jimmied the lock on the door to the lobby then walked over to examine the row of mailboxes. He was staring at the names when a Jaguar sedan pulled up in front of the building and two men climbed out. Truitt slid past the elevator to where a stairway led to the upper floors, then listened as the men entered the lobby and walked over to the elevator.

He waited while the elevator descended, opened and closed, and began to rise again, then walked out and stared up at the number on the panel above the doors. The elevator stopped on the third floor. Truitt returned to the stairs and climbed the three flights. Then, removing a small microphone from his pocket, he slid the earpiece into his ear and slowly walked down the hallway outside the apart-

ments. At one apartment he heard the sound of a man snor-
ing, at another a cat's quiet meow. He was halfway down
the hall before he heard voices.

"That folds out into a bed," the voice said.

Truitt could not make out the reply. Noting the number,
he visualized where the windows of the apartment would
be from the street. Then he swept across the closed door
with a small Geiger counter he had brought with him.

There was no sign of radiation.

He climbed quietly down the stairs, exited the lobby,
then stared up at the window of Lababiti's apartment. The
shades were drawn. Truitt slipped under the rear of the
Jaguar and attached a small magnetic disc to the fuel tank.
Then he scanned the car with the Geiger counter and found
it clean.

Noting the arrangements of the other buildings nearby,
he walked back to the Strand.

The street was nearly deserted; only a few cabs passed
and there was a single truck making a delivery to a Mc-
Donald's restaurant that was open twenty-four hours. Truitt
walked along the north side of the Strand, reading the play-
bills outside the theaters. He walked almost to Leicester
Square before he turned around and crossed over to the
south side.

There he passed a shop with classic British motorcycles
for sale. He stopped and stared in the window at the bikes,
lit by spotlights, on display. Ariels, BSAs, Triumphs, even
a legendary Vincent. A candy store for the motorhead.

He walked back to the McDonald's and ordered a Danish and coffee.

AT 5:30 A.M. LONDON time—9:30 in the evening in Las
Vegas—Captain Jeff Porte of the Las Vegas Police Department was having a tough time convincing the head of security for Dreamworld to allow him to enter the penthouse.

"You'll need a warrant," the head of security said,
"that's the only way I can let you inside."

Porte considered this. "We understand you've had a

break-in," he said, "so we're investigating an active crime."

"I still can't let you in, Jeff," the security chief said.

"Then I'm going to wake a judge and get a warrant," Porte said, "and when I do, I'll be back with television cameras. That should help your casino take—police and reporters throughout the lobby and common areas."

The head of security considered this for a moment. "Let me make a phone call," he said at last.

HICKMAN HAD ALMOST reached Maidenhead when his satellite telephone rang. After the head of security explained what was happening, Hickman spoke.

"Tell them they need a warrant," he said, "and order our counsel to start working on quashing it now. Whatever you do, delay them going inside as long as possible."

"Is there a problem, sir?" the security man asked.

"Nothing I can't handle," Hickman said, disconnecting.

The net was closing around him and he could feel the strings drawing tight.

MICHAEL HALPERT WAS widening the search. Logging on to the FAA computer, he pulled up the flight records for Hickman's jet. As soon as he saw the records, he knew he had their man. One of Hickman's jets, a Hawker 800XP, had recently filed a flight plan for Greenland. The latest plan filed was for a Las Vegas–London jaunt that placed Hickman's plane in London right now.

Printing them, Halpert began to search the British property records.

Nothing came up under Hickman's name so he began to search using the long list of Hickman's companies. Hours would pass before the search would bear fruit. While the computer was searching, Halpert tried to imagine why one of the richest men in the world would want to conspire with Arab terrorists to explode a nuclear bomb in London.

It was always love or money, Halpert thought.

There was no way Halpert could envision that Hickman

could make money off a disaster like an atomic bomb
blast. Halpert tried for an hour to find some financial motive but came up short.

It had to be love then, he thought.

And who does one love enough to kill for but family?

39

THE *OREGON* DOCKED at Southend-on-Sea at the mouth of the Thames just past 6 A.M.

The operatives were all awake and showered. One by one they filed into the dining room for breakfast. They were due to meet in the conference room at seven. Hanley had grabbed a few hours' rest and then had been back at work by 5 A.M., planning the logistics for the coming operation.

Just after 6:00 he telephoned Overholt and woke him.

"Our team is going into London soon," he said. "We think we have the principals located, but so far we have yet to detect traces of radiation."

"Are you coordinating with MI5?" Overholt asked.

"Mr. Cabrillo will contact them soon and turn over command of the operation. He just wants to make sure our team is in place as a backup."

"Sounds reasonable," Overholt said wearily. "What's the status on the meteorite?"

"We're doing things one at a time," Hanley said. "As soon as the threat of the bomb is gone, we'll switch our team over to that problem."

"What's the current location?"

"Just south of Oxford," Hanley said, "headed south. If it comes within the outskirts of London, we'll move on it. If not, we'll deal with it when the bomb is recovered."

"The Las Vegas police have been stymied," Overholt said, "so I issued a national security directive that gives them authority to do whatever we need. They should be entering the penthouse soon. You know that if you're wrong, and Hickman is not behind this, by the time the fallout settles I'll be out of a job."

"Not to worry, Mr. Overholt," Hanley said, "we are always looking for qualified applicants to join our team."

"You're a regular barrel of laughs, Mr. Hanley," Overholt said as he disconnected.

Hanley replaced the telephone in the cradle on his command chair and turned to Stone.

"How are the arrangements coming?"

"As usual, Mr. Truitt has been Johnny-on-the-spot," Stone said. "He's been working since early this morning. He's purchased sets of British clothing and overcoats for the people we're sending to London. He's also arranged for a tour bus to pick them up here. Last I spoke with him, he was on the bus on his way here."

"Good man," Hanley said. "What about Nixon?"

"Nixon has the equipment ready and is completing the final checks as we speak."

"Halpert?" Hanley asked.

"Still hard at work, last I checked. He claims he's pursuing a different angle and should have the details in another few hours."

"Go over the roster," Hanley said.

"We have four in London already," Stone said, reading from a printed sheet. "Cabrillo, Seng, Meadows and Truitt. The six to be transported are Huxley, Jones, Lincoln, Kasim, Murphy and Ross."

"That gives us a force of ten inside London," Hanley noted.

"Correct," Stone said. "Air support at Heathrow is Adams in the Robinson and Gunderson and Pilston in the Gulfstream. Judy Michaels just flew in from her leave and is taking over the amphibian piloting."

"Operations on the *Oregon*?" Hanley asked.

"The vessel will be crewed by Gannon, Barrett, Hornsby, Reinholt and Reyes."

"Who does that leave?"

"You, me, Nixon in the Magic Shop, Crabtree here on logistics, and King," Stone finished.

"I forgot about King," Hanley said. "We need him in there as support."

"Do you want me to include him in Truitt's group?"

Hanley thought for a moment. "No," he said finally. "Have Adams pick him up and put them both on standby. I want them close to the scene and ready to take to the air at a moment's notice. Adams and King can provide air cover."

"I'll make the arrangements," Stone said.

"Excellent."

"TRUITT CASED THE principal's apartment building early this morning," Cabrillo said.

Cabrillo, Seng and Meadows were eating breakfast in the chairman's suite.

"Where is he now?" Meadows asked.

"He's on his way to the port where the *Oregon* is docked to pick up the rest of the team."

"Then I guess he didn't detect traces of the bomb," Seng said, "or we'd have already moved by now."

"Correct," Cabrillo said.

"So we have to wait until they move?" Meadows asked.

"If the bomb is in London," Cabrillo said, "and the principals realize someone is on to them, they could blow it at any time. They might not be at their primary target yet, but with a nuclear warhead—even a small one like this—the destruction would be horrific."

"So we try to flush them out," Seng asked, "then make the grab and defuse the weapon?"

"I'm sure that's not what MI5 wants," Cabrillo said, "but that's what I will recommend."

"When do you meet with them?" Meadows asked.

Cabrillo wiped his mouth with the linen napkin and

stared at his wristwatch. "In five minutes," he said, "in the lobby."

"What would you like us to do?" Seng asked.

"Walk the area near the apartment and get the lay of the land."

EDWARD GIBB WAS not happy. Being awakened on New Year's Eve and ordered into work was not his idea of a pleasant holiday. An attorney had telephoned this morning and asked if he could meet the new owner of the mill and unlock the doors. Gibb had almost refused—he'd decided on retirement and was planning to tell the Human Resources Department as soon as they all returned to work—but the idea of meeting the mysterious buyer of Maidenhead Mills intrigued him.

After showering, dressing and eating a quick breakfast of tea and toast, he drove over to the mill. A limousine was idling near the front doors, the exhaust creating puffs of smoke in the chill air. Gibb approached and knocked on the rear window. The window slid down and a man smiled.

"Mr. Gibb?" he asked.

Gibb nodded.

"Halifax Hickman," the man said, climbing out of the rear and standing on the asphalt near the doors. "Allow me to apologize for taking you away from your family on a holiday."

The men shook hands.

"No problem, sir," Gibb said, walking toward the door. "I can understand you might want to see what you spent your money on as soon as possible."

"I was on my way to Europe," Hickman lied, "and am limited in time."

"I understand, sir," Gibb said as he reached into his pocket and removed a set of keys and unlocked the door.

"Thank you," Hickman said as Gibb opened the door and stood aside.

"Keep these," Gibb said, handing Hickman the keys. "I have another set."

Hickman slid them into his pocket. Gibb walked past

the reception area and through the doors into the massive shop floor where the mills and fabric were stored. Reaching over to a breaker switch on the wall, he flipped it on. The interior of the massive room lit up. Gibb looked over at Hickman. The man was scanning the various machines.

"This is the final stage shaver and vacuum unit," he said, pointing to a machine that looked like a large version of the broiler unit used at Burger King. "The material is fed in on the belt, it's treated, and then it comes out here on these series of rollers."

The metal frame that contained the rollers was waist high and went to an area for packing, then it stretched in a half circle to end near the loading dock. Bolts of cloths could be pushed along until they were boxed or wrapped, and then taken along to the trucks for shipment.

Hickman's eyes were scanning the area nearby. "Are those the prayer rugs for Saudi Arabia?" he asked, staring at three large metal shipping containers near the milling machine and next to the door to the docks. "Can I see them?"

"Yes, sir," Gibb said, unlocking each of the containers and swinging the doors open, "and they are overdue to be delivered."

Hickman peeked inside. Each of the metal containers was as large as a semitrailer. They were designed to be loaded aboard a 747 cargo plane. The rugs were hanging from vises on the ceiling of the containers and stretched forward as far as the eye could see. Each container held thousands.

"Why aren't they stacked?" Hickman asked.

"We have to spray them with insecticide and disinfectant before they are allowed into Saudi Arabia. They don't want Mad Cow disease or some other airborne pathogen brought in—every country makes that mandatory now," Gibb said.

"Leave them open," Hickman said, "and give me the keys to the containers."

Gibb nodded and handed Hickman the keys.

"When are the workers due back from holiday?" Hickman asked.

"Monday, January second," Gibbs said, following Hickman, who was walking back through the machines toward the lobby area again.

"I've got some guys from the U.S. coming in to help. We'll make those a top priority," Hickman said as they neared the lobby and front offices. "Now, can you show me to an office where I might use a telephone?"

Gibb pointed to stairs that led to a glass-enclosed office overlooking the shop floor. "You're welcome to use mine, sir. It's unlocked."

Hickman smiled and reached out for Gibb's hand. "Mr. Gibb," he said easily, "why don't you get back to your family. I'll see you on Monday."

Gibb nodded and started for the door, then stopped. "Mr. Hickman," he said slowly, "would you like to come over this evening and celebrate the New Year with us?"

Hickman was halfway to the stairs and turned back to look at Gibb. "That's a kind offer," he said, "but for me New Year is always a time for quiet reflection."

"No family, sir?" Gibb asked.

"I had a son," Hickman said quietly, "but he was murdered."

With that, he turned and walked toward the stair.

Gibb turned and walked through the door. Hickman was nothing like the newspapers said. He was just a lonely old man, as ordinary as white rice. Gibb might reconsider his plans to retire—with Hickman as owner, big things might be afoot.

Hickman entered the office and reached for the telephone.

CABRILLO ENTERED THE lobby with Meadows and Seng in tow. A blond man dressed in a black suit and polished shoes approached immediately.

"Mr. Fleming has cordoned off a quiet area of the dining room so you can meet in private," the man said, referring to the head of MI5. "It's right this way."

Seng and Meadows headed for the front door. Like magic, several men in the lobby reading newspapers rose and followed. They would not be alone for their reconnaissance.

Cabrillo followed the blond man into the dining room.

Taking a hallway to the left, they entered a private room where a man was seated at a table with a pot of tea and a silver platter of pastries.

"Juan," the man said, rising.

"John," Cabrillo said, reaching out to shake hands.

"That will be all," Fleming said to the blond-haired man, who walked back through the door and closed it behind him.

Fleming motioned to a chair and Cabrillo sat down. Fleming poured Cabrillo a cup of tea and waved his hands over the platter of pastries.

"I've eaten," Cabrillo said, taking the cup of tea.

Fleming looked over into Cabrillo's eyes and held them for a minute. "Well, Juan," he said, "what the hell is going on?"

IN THE CONFERENCE room on the *Oregon* all the seats were filled. Hanley entered last and walked over to a podium and set a file on top.

"Here's the situation right now," Hanley began. "We believe we have the location of the bomb pinned down to the general area of the West End of London. Mr. Truitt has checked out the apartment building that the principal, Nebile Lababiti, has secretly rented, and he managed to observe Lababiti and another man coming home late last night. After they entered the apartment, Mr. Truitt swept the area outside the door with a Geiger counter but found no traces of radiation. You six will be going in as support for Mr. Cabrillo, who is already present along with Mr. Meadows and Mr. Seng. Mr. Truitt also placed a locator on Lababiti's Jaguar, and as of right now, there has been no movement."

"What do we think the timetable is?" Ross asked.

"We still think the plans call for a midnight New Year's Eve attack," Hanley said, "as a symbolic gesture."

"Will we receive our actual assignments once we're in London?" Murphy asked.

"Correct," Hanley said. "Mr. Cabrillo will be coordinating with MI5. They and Mr. Cabrillo will assign your actual duties as they unfold."

Hanley's beeper vibrated, and he removed it from his belt and stared at the readout.

"Okay, people," he said, "Mr. Truitt has arrived to take you into London. He's in front right now. Be sure and take the crates of supplies that Nixon has prepared along with you, they are stacked alongside the gangplank. Any other questions?"

No one spoke.

"Good luck, then," Hanley said.

The six filed out and down the hallway.

CABRILLO FINISHED BRIEFING Fleming then took a sip of tea.

"The prime minister will have a problem keeping the public in the dark about this," Fleming admitted.

"You know that if the Hammadi Group realizes that their cover is blown, they could detonate at any time," Cabrillo told him. "Our best chance is to try to make contact using our voice tape of Al-Khalifa, or simply to wait for them to move and follow them to the bomb, then defuse it."

"We should cancel the concert," Fleming said. "That reduces the number of people in the area at least."

"I think that will clue in the Hammadi Group," Cabrillo said.

"We need to at least remove the royal family and the prime minister to safe locations," Fleming said.

"If you can do it undetected," Cabrillo said, "by all means do."

"Prince Charles is scheduled to announce Elton John before his performance, but he could plead sickness," Fleming said.

"Use a decoy," Cabrillo offered.

"If the plan is to hit the concert," Fleming said, "and the weapon is not already in place, then they have to deliver it to the site."

"If you have teams covertly check all the areas near the concert with Geiger counters and no radiation is found, hen we have to assume they are planning to deliver the warhead to the site by vehicle."

"So we eliminate the areas near the concert, and if we find nothing," Fleming said slowly, "we just need to control the roads leading into the Mayfair and St. James areas."

"Exactly," Cabrillo said. "The traffic is already horrible in the area. You just station trucks on the side streets that can be moved into place to seal off the roads. I don't think it will come to that. If we're correct and Lababiti *is* in control of the bomb, we know it is not in his Jaguar but it must be close. I think our only hope is to keep surveillance on him as thick as flies on a carcass. Then grab him when the time is right."

"If we're wrong and he doesn't lead us to the bomb," Fleming said, "then our only hope to stop it is the ring around Mayfair and St. James."

"If you place your trucks correctly, there isn't a car in the world that can make it through those streets."

"But then will we have time to defuse the bomb?" Fleming asked.

"The farther away from the concert we locate it, the more time we'll have. Make sure all your men have diagrams so they know what wires to cut in order to stop the timer from running through its cycle."

"Lord," Fleming said, "if only we knew exactly where the bomb was."

"If we did," Cabrillo said, "this would be a hell of a lot easier."

40

OVERHOLT WAS BRIEFING his commander in chief.

"So that's where we are, Mr. President," Overholt said early on New Year's Eve morning.

"And you offered the British any help we might have?" the president asked.

"Absolutely," Overholt said. "Fleming, who heads MI5, said there's nothing we can do at this point other than have a couple of our nuclear experts from Mindenhall Air Base on standby."

"And you did that, of course," the president said.

"The U.S. Air Force helicoptered them down an hour ago," Overholt said. "They are in London now and should be linking up with the Corporation and MI5."

"What else can we do?"

"I have contacted the Pentagon," Overholt said. "They are preparing relief and medical supplies if it goes badly."

"I've ordered all nonessential personnel evacuated from the embassy in London," the president said. "There were only a few because of the holiday."

"I don't know what else we can do," Overholt said, "but pray for a positive outcome."

* * *

ACROSS THE POND, Fleming was briefing the prime minister.

"That's the latest," he finished. "We need to evacuate you and your family as soon as possible."

"I'm not one to run from a fight," the prime minister said. "Evacuate my family, but I'm staying. If it goes bad, I can't let my countrymen die when I knew of the threat."

The debate raged for the next few minutes as Fleming pleaded for the prime minister to allow himself to be taken to safety. The prime minister held firm to his decision.

"Sir," Fleming finished, "you becoming a martyr cannot help in any way."

"True," the prime minister said slowly, "but stay I will."

"At least allow us to take you to the bunkers under the Ministry of Defence," Fleming pleaded. "They are case-hardened and have fresh air generators."

The prime minister rose. The meeting had ended.

"I'll be at the concert," the prime minister said. "Arrange the security."

"Yes, sir," Fleming said, rising and heading for the door.

OUTSIDE THE APARTMENT on the side street bordering the Strand, four parabolic microphones were hidden on nearby buildings and directed at the windows of Lababiti's residence. The dishes picked up vibrations on the glass of the windows and magnified the sounds until everything inside the apartment could be heard as clearly as a high-definition recording.

A dozen MI5 agents were posing as London cab drivers and patrolled the streets nearby, while others walked the street staring into shop windows and eating in restaurants. At the hotel directly across the street from the apartment, agents sat in the lobby reading newspapers, waiting for something to happen.

* * *

TRUITT STOOD UP from his seat near the driver as the bus came to a stop in front of the Savoy. He had called Cabrillo from his cell phone, and Meadows and Seng were waiting in front of the lobby doors. Truitt filed off the bus, followed by the rest of the team, and walked toward the lobby doors.

"We're supposed to meet in Cabrillo's suite," Meadows said, opening the door.

As the team filed past, Seng handed each a room key. A few minutes later they were all crowded into Cabrillo's suite. Once they all found seats, he spoke.

"MI5 has decided that there will be no attempt to intercept the device until there is movement," he said. "We will be working a support role in the off chance the weapon somehow makes it close to the area of the concert."

"What's the status of the principal right now?" Murphy asked.

"We have listening devices trained on the apartment," Cabrillo answered, "and right now they are sleeping."

"What exactly will we be doing?" Linda Ross asked.

"Each of you is trained in disabling the device, so you will be placed along the possible routes into the area of the concert. We will wait there in case we're called upon."

Cabrillo walked over to a cork bulletin board on an easel. A large map of London was tacked on the board and a series of lines had been highlighted with a yellow marker.

"Based on where the apartment is located, these are the highest probability routes," Cabrillo said. "We believe that, wherever the bomb is now, whoever has it will stop by and pick up Lababiti and the other man so they can place the nuke at the concert together."

"You believe that they're going to hide the device, then set the timer and escape?" Kasim asked.

"That's what we're hoping," Cabrillo admitted. "This type of device has a fail-safe switch that requires ten minutes from arming to detonation to avoid unwanted explosions."

"So you can't just flip the switch and start the fission process?" Julia Huxley asked.

"No," Cabrillo said, "the Russian devices are similar to ours in that respect—they require a series of steps before the device is operational. The one we believe they purchased is a 'baby bomb' designed for targeted destruction. The entire device could fit in a crate five feet long by three feet wide by three feet deep."

"What's the weight?" Franklin Lincoln asked.

"Under four hundred pounds."

"So we know they can't carry it or transport it by something like a bicycle," Pete Jones said.

"They'll need some type of vehicle," Cabrillo said, "so that means they'll need to travel over the roads."

Cabrillo pointed to the apartment on the map.

"From the apartment," he said, "there are a couple of routes they might take. The first is right behind us. Turn off the strand down Savoy Street toward the Thames and turn on Victoria Embankment heading south. Once on Victoria Embankment, they have several choices. Turn at Northumberland Avenue then head down the Mall, or they could continue on to Bridge Street and Great George Street, then drive down Birdcage Walk. The second possibility is for the driver to head straight down the Strand to the Mall, but that takes him through the Charing Cross section as well as Trafalgar Square, where the traffic is usually very heavy. Thirdly, they have a variety of side streets they could cut across and piece together a route that, while not as direct, would be harder to follow. At this point we're really just guessing."

"What's your gut feeling, boss?" Truitt asked.

"I don't think they are trucking the bomb in from some other part of London," Cabrillo said quietly. "I think it's close to Lababiti right now. The starting point has to be the apartment, or somewhere very near, and if I was the driver I'd want to get it over as quickly as possible and try to escape the primary blast zone. I'd drive down Victoria Embankment, make my way to the park where the concert is being held, then initiate the firing sequence and make my escape while watching the time. At nine minutes I'd be looking for a sturdy building to hide inside."

"How far does the primary blast zone extend?" Truitt asked.

Cabrillo took the highlighter and made a circle. At the

north end was the A40 and Paddington, at the south end was Chelsea almost to the Thames. The eastern border was Piccadilly Circus, the west was the far edges of Kensington and Notting Hill.

"Everything inside this circle will cease to exist completely. One mile diameter outside the circle, including most of the British government offices, will be heavily damaged, and in a circle five miles from the center of the blast, buildings will be damaged and the radiation fallout heavy."

Everyone stared at the map.

"That's almost all of London," Murphy said finally.

Cabrillo simply nodded.

"And we'll all be toast as well," Huxley, the medical officer, noted.

"Is that a medical term," Jones said, "toast?"

LARRY KING WALKED out to where Adams had set down in a field near the *Oregon*. Ducking under the spinning rotor blade, he opened the rear door of the Robinson R-44, slid his cased rifle in the rear and several boxes in back, then closed the door, opened the front, and climbed into the passenger seat. Slipping on a headset, he closed the door and locked it before speaking.

"Morning, George," he said laconically.

"Larry," Adams said, pulling up on the collective and lifting the Robinson from the ground, "how's it going?"

Adams pushed the cyclic forward and initiated forward flight.

"Good day for hunting," King said as he stared out the side window at the scenery.

Hanley had arranged for them to station the helicopter on top of a bank that was closed for the holidays. The helipad on the top was used by courier helicopters that made nighttime pickups and deliveries during the week.

But first they had a delivery to make to Battersea Park.

MEADOWS, SENG AND Truitt sat in the borrowed Range Rover and scanned the sky. As soon as the Robinson appeared, Meadows turned in his seat and spoke to Truitt.

"Your Majesty," he said, "your face has arrived."

Substituting Truitt for Prince Charles had been Cabrillo's idea, and Fleming had gone along. In the first place, the Magic Shop on the *Oregon* had the capability to produce a latex mask that exactly matched Prince Charles's features, and could make it fit any member of the Corporation team using the computer scans of their faces that Nixon already had stored. In the second, Cabrillo wanted a steady hand in the role and he knew that Truitt was as unflappable as they came. In the third, of all the men in the Corporation, Truitt most closely matched the heir to the throne in physical size and stature.

"Well then," Truitt said, "why don't one of you commoners retrieve it—it's damp and cold out there and I'm quite warm inside here."

Meadows laughed and opened the door. He ran over to the helicopter as it set down and took the box containing the mask from King. He walked back to the Range Rover and turned and watched as Adams lifted off again.

ADAMS CROSSED THE Thames again then flew north a little into Westminster. There, just off Palace Street, he found the bank and set down on the roof. Once the rotor blade had stopped spinning, King climbed out and walked over to the edge and peered over the waist-high wall surrounding the roof. Just in the distance to the northwest he could see Buckingham Palace Garden and Hyde Park to the north.

Vendors were already setting up for the evening concert.

The large truck from Ben & Jerry's ice cream did not hold much appeal, but the Starbucks display did. King walked back to the Robinson and smiled at Adams.

"There's food, bottles of water, soda, and thermoses of coffee prepared by the dining room in one of those packages," he said, motioning to the rear seat, "and I bought a pile of books and current magazines and put them in the other."

"How long you figure we'll wait?" Adams asked.

King stared at his watch. It was 10 A.M. "The most it will be is fourteen hours," he said, "let's hope they find it sooner."

BACK AT THE Savoy, the team was dressing in the clothes Truitt had purchased. One by one they filed back into Cabrillo's suite for their assignments. Each of them had high-powered microradios with earpieces to communicate. The send units were strapped across their necks near their voice boxes. To talk they simply touched their finger to their throat and spoke. Each person could then hear what they said.

The three two-person teams would form a half circle around Green Park with the closed part nearest the strand and the open part facing Green and St. James's Parks.

Farthest to the northwest, Kasim and Ross would take up station on Piccadilly between Dover and Berkley Streets. They left the Savoy and were taken to the area by a driver from MI5. Next, in the center of the semicircle, were Jones and Huxley. They were assigned a position directly across the street from Trafalgar Square, near the Charing Cross subway station. If the bomb traveled straight down the Strand, it would pass right by them. The last team, Murphy and Lincoln, were assigned to the area in front of the War Cabinet Room on Great George Street and Horse Guards Road. If the bomb came along the Victoria Embankment, they would intercept. Depending on where they would stand, they could have a clear shot across St. James's Park.

Since they had the only clear shot, Murphy had a bag full of small handheld missiles, rifles and smoke grenades. The other teams were armed with handguns, knives and sharp spikes to toss on the road and flatten any vehicle's tires.

Cabrillo would stay close to the apartment. Along with him, the street was swarming with agents from MI5. Morning became afternoon and still no movement.

41

LABABITI WAS A rake and a cad but he was also a highly trained terrorist. Today was the most critical day, and he was leaving nothing to chance. Waking Amad in early afternoon, he slipped his hand across the Yemeni's mouth and then held up a slip of paper. It read *No speaking from here on, communicate in writing only,* in Arabic. Amad nodded and sat up in bed.

Taking a pad of paper and a pen from Lababiti, he scratched out a message.

Are the infidels listening?

We never know, Lababiti wrote.

For the next few hours the two men communicated by notes. Lababiti laid out the plan. Amad made sure he understood the mission. Darkness had fallen over London before they were finished. Lababiti's last note was succinct.

I have to leave soon—you know where the sword of Allah is located and what to do with it—best wishes on your journey.

Amad swallowed and nodded. His hands were shaking when Lababiti handed him a glass of Araq to calm his nerves. It was only a few minutes later when Cabrillo decided to finally use Al-Khalifa's telephone to call the apartment. But by then the two had taken the vow of silence. The telephone rang four times until it was picked up by the answering machine. Cabrillo chose to leave no message.

The Corporation's much-vaunted ace-in-the-hole turned out to be of zero value.

"THERE'S MOVEMENT," ONE of the MI5 men assigned to monitor the parabolic microphones said over the radio.

The time was just before 9 P.M., and a light snow had started falling in London. The temperature was just at the freezing point, and the snow was not sticking to the roads, merely wetting them. If the temperature dropped any more, they would become an icy mess. The buildings were becoming lightly shrouded and puffs of steam escaped from the numerous roof vents. The remaining Christmas decorations in the windows added a festive nature to the scene, and the streets were crowded with holiday partiers.

Except for the fact that a nuclear weapon was nearby, it was tranquil.

LABABITI RODE DOWN the elevator. He had explained to Amad the way into the shop; the vehicle that would transport the bomb had been gassed and checked a week before. The Yemeni knew how to activate the timer. There was nothing else to do.

Nothing else but to escape.

Lababiti's plan was simple. He'd drive the Jaguar through the city to the M20. That would take him forty-five minutes or so. Once on the M20 he would drive south to the train terminal at Folkestone, a distance of sixty miles, give or take. Once there, arriving a half hour early, as was required, he would drive the Jaguar onto the train scheduled to leave at 11:30 P.M.

The train would just be exiting the underwater tunnel at midnight for its arrival at Coquelles, near Calais, at five past the hour. Lababiti would be out of danger from tunnel collapse just as the bomb ignited—but he would still be able to witness the fireball from the window of the train.

It was a well-planned and well-timed escape.

Lababiti had no way of knowing that several dozen MI5 agents, as well as the Corporation, were watching his every move. He was a hare and the hounds were drawing near.

Lababiti exited the elevator and walked through the lobby and onto the side street. He glanced around but noticed nothing amiss. Other than a nagging sense that unseen eyes were watching, he felt confident and at ease. The feeling was just paranoia, he thought, the burden from the knowledge of the upcoming destruction. Lababiti shrugged off the thoughts, opened the door to the Jaguar and climbed inside.

Starting the car and allowing it to warm up for a minute, he placed it in gear and drove down the few feet to the Strand and turned right.

"I've got tracking," one of the MI5 men said through the radio.

THE BOX TRUITT had attached to the gas tank was operating perfectly.

Near the entrance to the Savoy, Fleming and Cabrillo stood on the sidewalk and glanced at the Jaguar waiting to turn the corner. Fleming turned his back to the car and spoke into the microphone attached to his throat.

"Teams four and five follow at a distance."

The Jaguar turned and a cab pulled from the side of the street and trailed at a safe distance. The Jaguar passed a small panel van marked with the logo of an overnight freight company a block down—the van pulled into the traffic and took up station a discrete distance behind.

"The Jaguar was clean, the bomb was not in it," Fleming said to Cabrillo, "so just where do you think Lababiti is going?"

"He's running," Cabrillo said, "leaving the kid to do the man's job."

"When should we move to intercept?" Fleming asked.

"Let him get to his destination," Cabrillo said. "The air-

port, the train terminal—wherever. Then tell your men to
grab him. Just make sure he has no chance to make a call
before they take him into custody."

"What then?" Fleming asked.

"Have him brought back here," Cabrillo said in a voice
that chilled the already cold air. "We wouldn't want him to
miss the party."

"Brilliant," Fleming said.

"Let's see how bad he's ready to die for Allah," Cabrillo
said.

THE CLOSER IT came to midnight the more the tension
increased.

The microphones at Lababiti's apartment were picking
up the sound of Amad praying aloud. Fleming was stationed in the hotel across the street with a dozen men from
MI5. The three Corporation teams had been at their stations for just over thirteen hours. They were growing tired
of the wait. Cabrillo was walking back and forth near Bed-
ford Street; he'd passed the classic motorcycle dealership,
a take-out curry restaurant and a small market hundreds of
times as he paced back and forth.

"We have to go in there," one of the MI5 agents said to
Fleming.

"What if the bomb is a few blocks away," Fleming said,
"and someone else has started a delayed timer? Then we've
missed it—and London burns. We wait—there is nothing
else we can do."

Another MI5 agent walked into the lobby. "Sir," he said
to Fleming, "we now have twenty vehicles prowling the
roads nearby. As soon as the principal climbs into whatever
car he's going to use, we can stop traffic in an instant."

"And the bomb experts are nearby, ready to move?"

"Four British experts"—the man nodded—"a couple
from the United States Air Force."

At that instant Amad's praying stopped and the sound of
him walking across the floor of the apartment came over
the microphone.

"We have movement," Fleming said into the radio to the

dozens of men in wait. "*Do not* move on him until he is at his final destination."

Fleming prayed it would soon be over. The time was 11:49 P.M.

THERE WERE MI5 agents at the front, rear and all sides of the apartment building. Every car on the street had been tagged with a locator; each had an electronic disabling device attached. Each had been scanned with a Geiger counter and found to be clean.

Everyone believed Amad would be driving to another location to retrieve the bomb.

But the bomb was downstairs right now. It was resting in the sidecar attached to a Russian-made Ural motorcycle— just like the one Amad had trained on in Yemen.

AS SOON AS the door to the apartment opened and Amad exited, an MI5 agent passed through the lobby and stared at the elevator button. It showed the elevator going to Lababiti's floor, and then it started down. The elevator stopped on the second floor.

The MI5 agent whispered the information over the radio, then quickly walked from the lobby. Everyone who was listening tensed up—the time was now and this was the place.

THE FOOD AND beer and fun had not been diminished by the cold and scattered snow. The areas around Hyde and Green Parks were crowded with tens of thousands of holiday partygoers. Backstage, a liaison from MI5 was explaining to a rock star the cold reality.

"You should have warned us," his agent said loudly, "so we could have canceled."

"He explained that," Elton John said. "That would have alerted the terrorists."

Dressed in a yellow sequined jumpsuit, jeweled sunglasses and black platform boots with lights in the soles, it would be easy to dismiss John as just another spoiled and overindulged musician used to a life of pampered elegance. The truth was far from that. Reginald Dwight had clawed his way up from a hardscrabble existence with strength, perseverance and decades of hard work. No one can dominate the pop charts for decade after decade if they're not both tough and realistic. Elton John was a survivor.

"The royal family has been evacuated, right?" he asked.

"Come in here, Mr. Truitt," the MI5 agent shouted outside the trailer.

Truitt opened the door and stepped inside.

"This is the stand-in for Prince Charles," the agent said.

John glanced at Truitt and grinned. "Looks just like him," he said.

"Sir," Truitt said, "I want you to know we're going to recover the bomb and disable it before anything happens. We appreciate you going along with this."

"I have faith in MI5," John said.

"He's with MI5," Truitt said. "I'm with a group named the Corporation."

"The Corporation?" John said. "What's that?"

"We're private spies," Truitt said.

"Private spies," John said, shaking his head, "imagine that. You guys any good?"

"We have a one hundred percent success record."

John rose from his chair—it was time to go backstage. "Do me a favor," he said, "give this one a hundred and ten percent."

Truitt nodded.

John was at the door but he stopped. "Tell the cameraman not to do close-ups on Prince Charles—the bad guys might be watching."

"You're going out there?" the agent asked incredulously.

"Damn straight," John said, "that's a crowd of my countrymen and they came to see a show. Either these men"—he swept his hand at Truitt and the MI5 agent—"handle this problem, or I'm going out singing."

Truitt smiled and followed John out the door.

* * *

THERE ARE SIX ways to enter a room. Four walls, the floor, or through the ceiling. Amad was using the latter. At the end of the second floor of Lababiti's apartment building there was a utility closet. Two months prior, Lababiti had carefully sawed the four corners of the wood-planked floor and removed it, revealing the subfloor. Then, using a two-foot-diameter round hole saw, he'd bored a hole into the lower shop. Between the subfloor and the wood hatch above he'd hidden a rope ladder. After cleaning up the dust below, he retrieved the round section of floor and reattached it above with twin plates. Next he filled the edges around the wall in the closet with wood putty so it could not be detected. The hatch had been left alone until now.

Amad opened the utility closet using a key Lababiti had copied.

With the door open and the hallway empty, he pried off the hatch with a screwdriver. Setting the wood-planked section against the wall, Amad entered the closet and shut the door behind him. He took a pair of hooks from his pocket and screwed them into a wall, then attached the rope ladder. After removing the plates holding the round section of floor in place, Amad pulled it up into the closet and tossed it to the side.

He dropped the ladder into the hole and climbed down.

EVERY MI5 AGENT on the rooftops nearby had their scopes trained on the second floor.

"Nothing," they called in one by one.

The MI5 agent who had walked through the lobby then out again reentered the building. Walking over to the elevator, he saw the indicator light still on number two.

"Still on two," he radioed to Fleming.

In the hotel across the street, Fleming was staring at his watch. Four minutes had passed since the principal had stopped the elevator on the second floor. "Go up the stairs," he ordered the agent.

* * *

AMAD STARED AT his instructions written in Arabic, then flipped back the hinged panel over the arming mechanism. The symbols were Cyrillic but his diagram was easy to follow. Amad turned a toggle switch up and an LED light began to flash. Turning a knob, he adjusted the time to five.

Then he climbed on the Ural and kicked the engine to life. Once it started, he reached for a garage door opener duct-taped to the handlebars, and pushed the button. He shifted into first and was doing nearly ten miles an hour as the door rose six feet in the air and continued up.

Everything began to happen at once.

THE AGENT REACHED the second floor and reported it empty at the same instant the garage door began to open. "We have a door opening," Fleming said into the radio as he raced through the lobby for the door.

He was just at the inner glass doors when the motorcycle appeared and drove onto the street. Amad was at the corner crossing onto the Strand in a second.

"The principal is on a motorcycle," he shouted into the radio.

The sharpshooters followed Amad, but he turned before the order to fire came.

On the Strand, three taxis driven by MI5 agents heard the radio call. They pulled from the side of the street and tried to block the Ural. Amad swerved and took to the sidewalk to pass them, then angled back onto the road and twisted the throttle to the stops. Gaining speed, he swerved in and out of traffic like a madman.

Ahead, a truck driven by an MI5 agent tried to block the road, but Amad squeezed past.

They're on to me, he thought. Now he just had to deliver the bomb to the chosen area or die trying. Either way, he'd be a martyr. Either way, London would burn.

CABRILLO STARED DOWN the street and saw the vehicles from MI5 were being outfoxed. They had not planned on the principal using a motorcycle, and it threw a screw into the operation. There was only one thing to do—and Cabrillo did not hesitate.

Yanking a newspaper rack off the sidewalk, he threw it through the window of the classic motorcycle dealership's front window. The burglar alarm started blaring. Cabrillo climbed through the broken glass. The 1952 Vincent Black Shadow on display had the key in the ignition. Using his boot to clear the edges of glass from the frame, Cabrillo stomped on the kick start and the engine roared to life. He lifted the front end of the Vincent over the windowsill, clicked it into gear, and rode over the windowsill and down to the sidewalk.

The Ural pulled abreast of the dealership then headed down the Strand.

Cabrillo twisted the throttle and leapt in behind. The Ural was fast, but there is no motorcycle like a Black Shadow. If the Ural had not had a block head start, the Shadow would have caught him within seconds.

"THE PRINCIPAL IS on a dark green motorcycle with a sidecar, he's heading down the Strand," Fleming shouted over the radio, "he has the bomb aboard. Repeat, the bomb is in the sidecar."

The Robinson with Adams and King took to the air. Near Trafalgar Station, Jones and Huxley drew their weapons and aimed down the road. Hundreds of people were milling about and they angled for a clear shot but could find none. In front of the War Cabinet Room, Murphy and Lincoln turned away from the Victoria Embankment and started sighting down on Hyde and Green Parks. On Piccadilly Street, Kasim and Ross separated and began covering both ends of the street.

TRUITT WAS KEPT away from the others backstage until it was time to walk in front of the microphone. Stepping from foot to foot he waited.

"It's time," John's agent said.

Truitt glanced over at the MI5 agent, but he was talking

on the radio, so Truitt walked onto the stage and approached the microphone.

"Ladies and gentlemen," he said, "could you please join me in welcoming in the New Year with England's favorite musician, Sir Elton John."

The stage was dark except for Truitt. Then a spotlight appeared on Elton John sitting at an elevated piano. Still dressed in the yellow jumpsuit, his head was covered with a British army Kevlar field helmet.

The introduction music for the song "Saturday Night's Alright for Fighting" started to play. A second later, John began to sing.

Truitt walked off-stage and approached the MI5 agent.

"He's headed this way on a motorcycle," the agent said.

"I'm going into the crowd," Truitt said.

THE URAL RACED past Nelson's Column with Cabrillo and the Vincent Black Shadow hot on its heels. Cabrillo wanted to open his coat so he could get to his shoulder holster, but he couldn't take his hands off the handlebars to get at the weapon. Twisting the throttle, the Vincent shot ahead and came abreast of the Ural just as they passed Charing Cross. Huxley and Jones ran into the street and tried to line up shots as the two motorcycles passed, but Cabrillo was too close and the crowds too great.

At the intersection of the Strand and Cockspur Street, Cabrillo pulled up next to the Ural and kicked at Amad with his boot. The Yemeni swerved but retained control.

"They're going straight down the Mall," Jones shouted over the radio.

Kasim and Ross started running down Queen's Walk toward the concert.

Murphy could become excitable, but with a sniper rifle in his hands he was always quite calm. Lincoln was spotting for him and scanned the parks in front. "The only clear shot through the trees is when they almost reach the Queen Victoria Memorial," Lincoln said.

"The street around the memorial runs clockwise, right?" Murphy said.

"Correct," Lincoln said.

"I'll plink the bastard as he slows for the turn—JFK style," Murphy said.

"I've got them," Lincoln said, just catching the front end of the motorcycles.

ADAMS MADE A left turn above the Old Admiralty Buildings and started down the Mall to the rear of the racing motorcycles.

"Head and shoulders," King said through the headset.

"Shampoo?" Adams said.

"No," King said, "where I'm going to shoot this little shit."

He sighted in his scope and regulated his breathing. The cold wind through the open door of the helicopter was making his eyes tear, but King hardly noticed it at all.

CABRILLO GLANCED AHEAD. There was a line of food vendors and booths ahead lining the circular drive where the Queen Victoria Memorial sat. They were nearing the edge of the concert grounds. He pulled alongside in preparation to leap over to the Ural.

"FOUR, THREE, TWO, one," Lincoln said.

Murphy squeezed off a round at the same time King let loose a quick volley from the helicopter. Amad was almost to the circle when blood burst from his head, chest and shoulders. He was dead a second later, almost exactly the same time Cabrillo jumped from the Vincent across to the Ural. His hands grabbed a lifeless corpse.

The Vincent hit the pavement in a shower of sparks and rolled end over end before stopping. Cabrillo tossed Amad to the ground; he bounced across the pavement like a crash dummy dropped off a table. Reaching for the clutch, he took the Ural out of gear and applied the brakes. The motorcycle rolled to a stop near the line of vendors.

Cabrillo looked over at the timer. The countdown has just passed two minutes. He only hoped it was regular time and not metric time.

Truitt had made all of twenty yards into the crowd when he realized the mask had to go. As Prince Charles, everyone wanted to touch him—once he'd peeled the mask off, people backed away.

"Mr. Cabrillo has control of the bomb at the Queen Victoria Memorial," Lincoln reported over the radio.

Whooping sounds filled the air as the MI5 teams in the decoy cars attached their portable lights and sirens and raced toward the memorial. Blockers moved into place to stop traffic and an air-raid siren started to blare. Truitt ran across the road to Cabrillo just as he was snipping the wire.

"She's still active," Cabrillo shouted as soon as he saw Truitt.

Truitt glanced up quickly. There was a Ben & Jerry's ice cream truck alongside the road. He ran over and opened the rear door. The attendant started to say something but in a second Truitt was in the rear. Grabbing a block of dry ice in his gloved hands, he ran back across the street to where Cabrillo was rapidly taking apart the nose cone with a pair of Leatherman pliers.

Cabrillo had just pulled back the panel when Truitt arrived.

"Let's try freezing the firing mechanism," Truitt said.

The timer was at one minute twelve.

"Go," Cabrillo yelled.

Truitt's gloves were frozen to the block of dry ice and he could not feel his hands. He tossed the block, gloves and all, onto the nose cone and then slid his gray hands under his armpits. The timer clicked a few more times then stopped cold.

Cabrillo looked over at Truitt and smiled. "I'm surprised that worked," he said.

"Necessity," Truitt said through gritted teeth, "is the mother of invention."

Cabrillo nodded and reached for the voice microphone at his throat. "I need the bomb guys at the Queen Victoria Memorial ASAP."

Fireworks erupted over the park and throughout London as the New Year came.

Two minutes later a car pulled up and a British officer climbed out. Soon another car arrived containing an expert from the U.S. Air Force. Five minutes later the two men had the firing mechanism removed and stowed. Now the bomb was just a housing for an orb of enriched uranium.

Its heart was ripped from its body, and with it went the life force that could bring death.

WHILE THE BOMB experts were rendering the device inert, Cabrillo and Truitt walked over to Amad's body, which was lying in a pool of blood on the pavement. The radio had reported that Lababiti had been detained and was now being brought back to London by helicopter. Elton John was still singing and the sound filled the air. The scene around the motorcycle was being cordoned off by British military and intelligence officials, and most at the concert were unaware of what had happened.

"Nothing but a kid," Cabrillo said, looking down.

Truitt nodded.

"Let's get you to the medic to look at your hands."

Kasim and Ross, who had arrived a few minutes after the timer was stopped, were wheeling the smashed Black Shadow over toward Cabrillo. The classic motorcycle was a mess. The tanks and side panels were scratched, the handlebars bent and one tire was flat. A perfect specimen of motorcycle history had been destroyed. Cabrillo looked at the motorcycle and shook his head.

"I want you two to go back to the dealership," he said to Ross and Kasim, "and pay the man whatever his asking price was. Then I want you to ask him where to send it to be restored again."

"You're keeping it, boss?" Ross asked.

"Damn straight," Cabrillo said.

Right then Fleming appeared and Cabrillo walked over to brief him. Lababiti was being brought back to downtown London, but it would be weeks before he filled in the pieces.

PART TWO

42

ON BOARD THE U.S. Navy guided-missile frigate, Scott Thompson and his team from the *Free Enterprise* had yet to crack. Although they had been grilled by the navy commander of the ship since the time of their surrender, they had yet to disclose a thing.

In the pilothouse, Commander Timothy Gant was awaiting the arrival of a helicopter from shore. The sky was black and the wind was whipping the seas into a white froth. On the radar scope a blip indicating the incoming helicopter moved nearer.

"She's on final, sir," the helmsman said, "winds twenty to thirty from the north and northwest."

Gant reached for his radio. "Get her secured to the deck the minute she touches down," he said to the head of his deck operations.

"Roger that, sir," the man answered.

The helicopter appeared out of the haze with her landing light illuminated. She came straight for the ship and barely slowed as she neared. "I'm coming in hot," the pilot said over the radio. One hundred yards, eighty, sixty, forty, twenty before the pilot slowed. Once he was just above the deck one-third of the way down the ship he saw the men with flashlights. Then he saw the open spot on the deck and dropped the helicopter down. As soon as the skids touched, a quartet of deckhands bent over at the waist ran out and secured the skids with chains. The rotor blade had not yet stopped when a single man carrying a valise climbed out and was led over to the door inside. Gant had come down to meet him and opened the door.

"Come on inside out of the weather," Gant said as the man entered the ship. "I'm Commander Timothy Gant."

The man was tall and lanky with a slightly pockmarked face and a hook nose. "Dr. Jack Berg," the man said, "Central Intelligence Agency."

"The prisoners have yet to disclose anything," Gant said, leading the doctor down the passageway toward the brig.

"Don't worry," Berg said quietly, "that's what I'm here for."

FINDING A TECHNICIAN to fix the saw during the holiday had not been an easy task. Finally, Dwyer had just gone into the isolation room wearing a contamination suit and done it himself. Luckily, the problem had turned out to be simple—a belt that drove the saw blade had slipped and Dwyer had merely needed to tighten the pulley with a wrench. After testing his repairs inside the room and finding that the saw worked fine, Dwyer exited through the isolation lock, washed his contamination suit under the chemical bath, then removed the suit, hung it on a hook, and exited back into the control area.

The technician who was monitoring the gauges looked up as he entered.

"No leaks," he said, "and it looks like you got the saw fixed."

Dwyer nodded, then pushed the button to start the saw again. As soon as the blade was spinning, he walked over to the joystick control and lowered it down to the sample taken from the Arizona crater. The blade bit into the lemon-sized metal chunk and sparks began to fly in the air like the flickering tendrils from a Fourth of July sparkler.

Dwyer was halfway through the chunk when the alarm sounded.

"Negative pressure," the technician shouted.

"Add air," Dwyer shouted.

The technician turned a dial and stared at the gauges on the wall. "We're still sinking," he yelled.

Inside the isolation room, vortices like that from a small tornado began forming. Several of the samples began to lift in the air and swirl about as if weightless, while the wrench Dwyer had left inside was sucked off the bench and danced in the air near the saw. It was like a giant drain had been opened and the air in the room was being sucked into nothingness.

"Full air," Dwyer shouted.

The technician spun the air control valve to full on. Still the negative pressure grew.

The inner layer of thick glass windows began to spider web. If they went, there was only one more layer of glass between Dwyer and the technician and certain death. The Kevlar gloves that poked through the wall were completely sucked in on themselves. Dwyer quickly slammed round metal plates over the arm openings then flipped down the hatches that held them in place. The workbench in the room was bolted to the floor with one-inch-diameter bolts. One of them sprung loose and shot toward the center of the bench. The workbench started to rock as the other bolts began to work loose.

"Sir," the technician shouted, "we're going to lose it. I'm at full positive pressure and the vacuum is growing."

Dwyer stared into the room. He was seconds away from a maelstrom. Then it hit him like a fist. Taking a step over to the board, he flipped on the laser. The laser lit up and the firing end began to wildly spin. Smoke filled the room as it gyrated around then touched down on the sample. Wherever the laser touched, it burned.

"The pressure is dropping," the technician yelled a second later.

"Back off the incoming air," Dwyer ordered.

The objects in the room began to settle as the pressure was restored. A few minutes later, things were back to normal. Dwyer shut down the laser and stared into the room.

"Sir," the technician said a moment later, "would you mind telling me what just happened?"

"I think," Dwyer said, "there is something in those samples that likes the taste of our atmosphere."

"Good God," the technician said quietly.

"Luckily for us," Dwyer said, "we just found both the disease and the cure."

"There is more of that out there?" the technician said warily.

"A hundred pounds."

SOON THE PILGRIMS would begin pouring into Saudi Arabia on chartered planes, buses from Jordan and ships crossing the Red Sea from Africa. Saud Al-Sheik still had a thousand details to attend to, foremost of which was arranging delivery of the prayer rugs. He had been promised that the new owner of the mill would call him tomorrow. So he called the Saudi National Airline and arranged for transportation space on a 747 cargo plane in two days' time.

If the prayer rugs did not get here on time, not even his family connections could spare him from the wrath he would face. He stared around the warehouse in Mecca. Pallets of food and bottled water stretched to the ceiling. A forklift truck drove in and lifted the first container of tents from the floor to load into the truck for delivery to the stadium.

Tomorrow the first of the tents would be erected.

From then on, things would move very fast.

Making a note to make sure the poles, stakes and guidelines were taken, Al-Sheik walked toward the door to make sure the driver loaded the truck properly.

JEFF PORTE GATHERED up the items he was taking from Hickman's office and stared at the head of security.

"Our warrant gives us the right to any and all items we determine might be of value."

The large manila folder in Porte's hand contained documents, the dog tags and a few stray hairs he'd found on the desk.

"I understand, Jeff," the head of security said.

"Two of my men will remain here," Porte said, "in case we need anything else."

The security chief nodded.

Porte headed for the door and walked down the hall toward the living room, where his two detectives were waiting.

"No one in or out," Porte said, "unless I okay it."

Walking from the penthouse, Porte rode down in the elevator, exited the lobby and climbed into his car. As soon as he returned to the Las Vegas Police Department he copied the dog tags and the other documents, then faxed them to the CIA.

As soon as Overholt received them he forwarded them on to the *Oregon*.

HANLEY WAS READING the stack of papers when Halpert entered the control room.

"Mr. Hanley," he said, "I have my report."

Hanley nodded and handed him the papers Overholt had sent. Halpert read them, then handed them back.

"This confirms my findings," Halpert said. "I found Hunt's birth certificate. His mother, Michelle, did not list the father but I managed to access the old hospital records and learned that the bill had been paid by one of Hickman's companies. There's no doubt now that Hunt was Hickman's son."

"So what does that have to do with the meteorite?" Hanley asked.

"Look at this," Halpert said, handing Hanley a file.

"Hunt was killed by the Taliban in Afghanistan," Hanley said after he had finished reading.

"Right after that, Hickman started exhibiting strange behavior," Halpert said, reading from his notes.

"So he blames the Arab world for the death of his only son," Hanley said.

"So how did he come to fund the expedition to Greenland?" Stone asked.

"Apparently, since the death of his son, Hickman has funded numerous archaeological departments across the country. Ackerman's expedition for UNLV was one of several slated for the year. The primary one was an expedition to Saudi Arabia by a scholar who is trying to discredit the legend of Muhammad as a myth. Ackerman's was outside that realm but he received funds anyway. I think that the recovery of the meteorite was just a stroke of luck."

"So Hickman decided at first to use history to attack the Arab world," Hanley said slowly, "then, as if from the gods themselves, the meteorite drops in his lap."

"But that has nothing to do with Islam or Muhammad," Stone noted.

Halpert nodded. "At that point I think Hickman decided more direct retribution was needed. I found records he pulled up on his computer dated right after Ackerman's finding. They explain the radioactive nature of iridium and the dangers it poses."

"So he decides to grab the meteorite and then what," Hanley said slowly, "combine it with an existing warhead and bomb some Arab country?"

"That's what has taken me so long," Halpert admitted. "At first I was following that same train of thought—that the meteorite was to be used somehow in a nuclear fashion. That was a dead end—there is simply nothing to tie him to the Ukrainian nuclear device or any other—so I started to branch out in my thinking."

"Radioactive dust?" Hanley asked.

"That's the only other logical use," Halpert said.

"What else have you found?"

"I found records that Hickman just purchased a textile mill in England, near the town of Maidenhead."

"That's right about the current location of the meteorite according to the tracking data," Stone said.

"He's planning to sprinkle it onto clothes and send them to the Middle East?" Hanley asked.

"I don't think so, sir," Halpert said slowly. "The mill has

a large order from Saudi Arabia for a shipment of woven prayer mats that has yet to be delivered."

"So he's planning to sprinkle the dust on the prayer rugs and infect the Muslims while they pray," Hanley said. "Diabolically evil."

"He arrived in London on his jet early this morning," Halpert said. "I think—"

Right then Hanley's telephone rang and he motioned to Halpert to wait while he answered. It was Overholt and he got right to the point.

"We have a problem," Overholt began.

"NO," THE HEAD of security for Dreamworld said, "I'm calling from my home phone. I don't think it's tapped."

Continuing, he explained about the warrant and the items the detectives had removed.

Hickman listened.

"Where are you now, sir?" the head of security asked. "They would really like to speak to you."

"It's better that you don't know," Hickman said.

"Is there anything you want us to do?"

"Right now," Hickman said, "there's nothing anyone can do but me."

Disconnecting, Hickman sat back in the chair in the office at Maidenhead Mills.

Someone in the government was hard on his trail. It would not be long until they traced him to his current location. Reaching for the telephone, he dialed.

THE CREWMEN FROM the *Free Enterprise* that had remained in Calais when the vessel sailed north had arrived in London this morning. There were four men, a skeleton crew really, but they were all Hickman had left. He telephoned them with their orders.

"You will need to steal a trio of trucks," Hickman said. "Nothing will be available to rent because of the holiday."

"What type?" their leader asked.

"The cargo are standard forty-foot shipping containers that slide aboard flatbed trailers," Hickman said. "I called my man at Global Air Cargo and he recommended a few different types of trucks."

Hickman read off the list to the man.

"Once we have them, where do we go?"

"Look at your map," Hickman ordered. "There is a town named Maidenhead just north of Windsor."

"I see it," the man said.

"Once you're in Maidenhead, drive to this address," Hickman said, reading off the mill's address and general directions.

"How soon do you need us?" the man asked.

"ASAP," Hickman said. "I have a Global Air Cargo 747 jet waiting at Heathrow for the cargo."

"How'd you arrange that on New Year's Eve?" the man blurted.

"I own the company."

"Give us at least an hour," the man said.

"The faster the better."

The noose was closing, but Hickman had yet to feel it tightening around his neck.

JUDY MICHAELS TAXIED the amphibian alongside the *Oregon*, then turned off the engine and walked back to the cargo door. Waiting for the plane to float forward on the tide, she waited until she saw someone on the deck then tossed up a rope. The deckhand secured the plane to the side and Cliff Hornsby climbed down the ladder.

"Evening, Judy," he said as he began to take supplies that were being passed down to him, "how's the weather up high?"

"Snow and sleet," Michaels said as she too grabbed several of the bags and crates.

Rick Barrett climbed over the side clutching a bag. Once on the deck he turned to Michaels. "There's some dinner and coffee in there," he said, "I made it myself."

"Thanks," Michaels said, taking the last package.

Halpert and Reyes crossed over.

"Any of you men have any piloting experience?" Michaels asked before going forward to the cockpit.

"I'm taking classes," Barrett said.

"Chef and a pilot," Michaels said, "hell of a combination. Come forward then—you can help with radios and navigation."

"What do you need us to do?" Halpert asked.

"Once the deckhand throws off the rope, use that boat hook to push us away. Then close and latch the door and take seats. I'll fire her up when you tell me we're clear."

Sliding into the pilot's seat, she waited until Barrett was seated next to her, then turned back to the cargo area. "Ready when you are," she said.

Hornsby grabbed the rope that was tossed, Halpert pushed them away, and Reyes fastened the door closed. "Fire her up," Halpert said a moment later.

Michaels turned the key and the engines roared to life. Idling away from the *Oregon,* she waited until they were fifty yards away and advanced the throttles. The seaplane raced along the water then lifted into the air.

Michaels gained altitude, then made a sweeping left-hand turn.

She was still climbing when they reached the outskirts of London.

HANLEY WATCHED THE amphibian taxi away on the remote cameras, then turned to Stone.

"How are you coming?" he asked.

Halpert had left his notes in the control room. Stone was following up on leads.

"I'm running through Hickman's companies now," Stone said.

"I'll check to see if Hickman's pilot has filed any other flight plans," Hanley said.

AT THE HEATHROW Airport air cargo annex, a pair of pilots were sipping tea and watching the television in the lounge at the spacious Global Air Cargo hangar.

"Have you pulled the latest weather?" the pilot asked the copilot.

"Fifteen minutes ago," the copilot replied. "The storm breaks up over France. The Mediterranean is clear, and it stays that way into Riyadh."

"Clearances and papers in order?" the pilot asked.

"We're good to go," the copilot said.

"I have the distance at thirty-one hundred miles," the pilot said.

"Just over five and a half hours flight time," the copilot offered.

"Now, if we just had our cargo."

"If the owner tells you to wait," the copilot said, "you wait."

The pilot nodded. "What's on the telly tonight?"

"The replay of the Hyde Park Concert with Elton John," the copilot said. "The opening acts are starting soon."

The pilot rose and walked over to the kitchen area. "I'll microwave us some popcorn."

"Extra butter on mine," the copilot said.

MICHAELS LINED UP over the river and landed. After steering over to the shore, the men secured the plane with ropes to some nearby trees, then off-loaded the cargo and stood on the shore.

MI5 had all their assets tied up in London, so there was no one to meet them.

"Anyone know how to hot-wire a car?" Halpert asked.

"I do," Reyes said.

"Cliff," Halpert said, "go with Tom and find something big enough to transport us and the gear."

"Will do," Hornsby said, climbing the bank with Reyes and walking toward town.

Halpert studied the map as he waited. He'd had Michaels fly over Maidenhead Mills on the way here— now all he had to do was find the route on the map. Once he had that done, he turned to Michaels, who was still on the plane.

"Can you spare a cup of that coffee?" he asked.

Michaels slipped inside the cockpit and poured a cup, then handed it to Halpert on shore. "What's the plan?" she asked.

"First we watch," Halpert said, "then we pounce."

At that moment, Reyes pulled alongside the bank in an old British Ford flatbed truck. Several chicken coops were on the bed near the cab, along with some rusty tools and a length of chain.

"Sorry about the ride," Reyes said, climbing out, "but beggars can't be choosers."

"Let's load it up," Halpert said, handing Reyes the marked map.

"I'll be monitoring the radio," Michaels said as the men transported the cargo to the flatbed. "Good luck."

Halpert smiled but didn't say a word. Once everyone was aboard, he pounded on the bed. "Let's roll."

With a swirl of snow the truck lurched away from the bank in the direction of the mill.

43

IT WAS PAST 1 A.M. on January 1, 2006, when Cabrillo finally called the *Oregon* to report.

"We recovered the weapon," Cabrillo said.

"How's MI5?" Hanley asked.

"Ecstatic," Cabrillo answered, "there's talk of making me a Knight of the British Empire."

"You made the final grab?" Hanley asked incredulously.

"I'll fill you in when we return to the ship. What else is happening?"

"While your team was working the bomb, Halpert dug up more information tying the meteorite to Halifax Hickman. We now believe that because his son was killed by the Taliban in Afghanistan, he's planning to strike at the entire Islamic religion. He recently purchased a mill to the west of London that is filling an order for prayer rugs to be used during the hajj," Hanley said.

"Refresh my memory," Cabrillo asked, "the hajj is the pilgrimage to Mecca, right?"

"That's correct," Hanley said, "this year it falls on the tenth."

"So we have plenty of time to shut down his operation."

"That might have been the case," Hanley said, "but a lot happened today while you were tied up in London."

Hanley recounted what Overholt had explained about the tests on the meteorite fragments. Then he recapped all Halpert had discovered.

"Where are we at right now?" Cabrillo asked.

"I've dispatched Halpert and three others to the mill," Hanley explained. "It's in the town of Maidenhead."

"And the bugs on the meteorite?" Cabrillo asked.

"They show that it is still in the general area at the moment."

"So if Hickman does something to disturb the integrity of the orb, we could have a worse situation than from the nuke," Cabrillo said.

"Stone checked with some sources and discovered there's no machine in a standard textile mill that's strong enough to crush or grind iridium," Hanley said. "If that *is* Hickman's plan, he must have some way to achieve that goal at, or nearby, the mill."

Cabrillo was silent for a second.

"Halpert is going to need some help," Cabrillo said. "I'm leaving Seng and Meadows here—they've been coordinating with MI5 on the operation and they can handle the mop-up and cover-up of our involvement."

Hanley was writing notes on a pad. "Got it," he said. "What about the rest of you?"

"Call Adams and have the Robinson at the heliport across the river in half an hour," Cabrillo ordered, "and tell Halpert we're coming."

"Consider it done," Hanley said as the telephone went dead.

"THE CORPORATION STOPPED the bomb, Mr. President," Overholt reported. "It's in the hands of British intelligence."

"Good job," the president said heartily, "offer them my heartfelt congratulations."

"I'll do that, sir," Overholt said, "but there is another problem you need to be aware of."

"What's that?" the president asked.

Overholt explained about the tests done with the meteorite samples.

"That's not good," the president said. "It could be easily argued the meteorite got in the wrong hands as a result of a CIA screwup."

"I need you to do me a favor then," Overholt said. "We need to take the mother of Hickman's son secretly into custody—no warrants, no lawyers."

"Suspend her rights under the Patriot Act?" the president asked.

"That's it, sir," Overholt said.

The president thought for a moment. As much as he wanted this over, snatching U.S. citizens from their homes or businesses without explanation always smacked of dictatorship to him. The president only used the power when the threat was great.

"Go ahead, then," he said at last, "but make the snatch smoothly."

"Trust me, sir," Overholt said, "no one will know she's gone."

SIX MEN FROM the CIA's Directorate of Operations surrounded Michelle Hunt's Beverly Hills home later that same afternoon. As soon as she returned from the gallery after work they grabbed her as she pulled into her garage. By 7 P.M. that same evening she had been taken to Santa Monica Airport and loaded on a government jet bound for London. The plane was just crossing the Colorado River above Arizona when one of the CIA men started to explain the situation. When he finished she spoke.

"So what—I'm bait?" she asked sweetly.

"We're not sure yet," the CIA man admitted.

Michelle Hunt nodded her head and smiled. "You don't know my son's father," she said. "To him, people are like properties to be used and disposed of as need be—threatening me will do you no good."

"Do you have a better idea?" the CIA man asked.

Michelle Hunt thought about the question.

* * *

STEALING THREE TRUCKS on New Year's Eve had been an easy operation. The trucking district outside London had been nearly deserted. A single freight yard that serviced the cargo carriers had been open, and it was manned by a crew of one. The remaining team from the *Free Enterprise* had merely waltzed in, tied up the attendant and taken the keys they needed. No one would check on the man until morning.

By then the cargo would be moved and the trucks discarded.

SCOTT THOMPSON, THE leader of the *Free Enterprise* crew, had showed a steely resolve up to now. He remained defiant until the orderly on the guided-missile frigate strapped him to a table and made sure his arms were secure.

"I demand to know what's happening," Thompson said as dots of sweat began breaking out on his forehead.

The orderly simply smiled. Then the door opened and Dr. Berg walked into the sick bay. He was clutching a valise. He walked over to the sink and began to wash his hands. Thompson strained to see the man but he was tightly bound and could barely move his neck. The sound of the running water was like a knife to Thompson's heart.

THE THREE TRUCKS pulled into the parking lot of Maidenhead Mills and then drove around to the rear of the buildings, where the loading docks were located. Backing up to the bay doors, the men shut off the engines and climbed out.

Halpert and Hornsby were assigned to the rear of the building, with Barrett and Reyes watching the front. Other than a Rolls-Royce and a Daimler sedan in the parking lot near the front door, the mill appeared deserted. Halpert waited until the men went inside the mill and then whispered into his radio.

"We're moving closer," he said, "to see what we can see."

"We'll move on the front," Reyes replied.

INSIDE THE MILL, Roger Lassiter was sitting in the front office, staring at Hickman. "Of course, because of the holiday I couldn't verify the funds being transferred."

"You knew that when you took the job," Hickman said. "You'll just have to trust me."

The box containing the meteorite was sitting on the desk between the two men.

"I'm not much for trust," Lassiter said, "but you must be."

"I can assure you," Hickman said, "you'll be paid."

"Where's the meteorite headed?" Lassiter asked.

Hickman wondered if he should answer. "The Kaaba," he said quickly.

"You're rotten to the core," Lassiter said, rising, "but then again, so am I."

Lassiter walked from the office and out the front door. And as Lassiter climbed into the Daimler, Reyes secretly took photographs.

WALKING ONTO THE mill floor carrying the meteorite, Hickman saw two of the men from the trucks approaching from the back of the building. They met halfway across the expanse.

"Did you see the shipping containers?" Hickman asked.

"The three by the door?" one of the men asked.

"Yes," Hickman said, walking closer to the docks with the men now following. "After I prep them, I want you to load them on the trucks and take them to Heathrow."

Hickman was almost at the rear door now.

"Here's the coating you ordered," one of the men said, holding it aloft.

"Perfect," Hickman said, reaching the milling machine. "Hand it to me."

One of the men lifted a sack off the floor, started shaking it, and handed it over.

44

CABRILLO AND HIS team were waiting in the borrowed Range Rover at the Battersea heliport when Fleming reached him by cellular telephone. Adams was just descending over the Thames and making his turn to land.

"Juan," Fleming said, "we just learned something you're going to find interesting—it pertains to your meteorite. Call it repayment for helping us with the bomb."

The sound of the approaching helicopter grew louder. "What is it, sir?" Cabrillo shouted.

"This comes from our lead agent in Saudi Arabia," Fleming said. "The actual spot that Muslims pray to five times a day in Mecca is named the Kaaba. It's a special temple that houses an interesting artifact."

"What's the artifact?" Cabrillo asked.

"A black meteorite supposedly recovered by Abraham. The site is the very heart of the Islamic faith."

Cabrillo sat in stunned silence.

"Thanks for alerting me," Cabrillo said. "I'll be in touch soon."

"I thought you should know," Fleming said. "Be sure to call MI5 if we can help. We owe you one."

* * *

HALPERT REACHED INTO a backpack he'd brought
from the *Oregon* and attached locators to all three trucks.
Then he attached a microphone to the bottom of the wall
near the overhead door. Motioning to Hornsby, the two
men retreated back to the tree line.

Once he was again safely hidden, he whispered into the
radio.

"Tom," he said, "what's your status?"

Reyes and Barrett had attached a similar microphone
near the front glass doors. They had just returned to safety
behind a wall around the edge of the parking lot.

"We're wired," he whispered back.

"Now we just wait and listen," Halpert said.

HICKMAN'S TEAM WAS working in silence. After using
the portable paint sprayer to make an airtight seal over the
containers with a liquid plastic, one of the men drilled a
pair of small holes directly through the metal sides of the
containers. One hole was near the top, about chest high, the
other farther down at about ankle height.

Next, the holes were threaded and small pipes installed.

Once that was done, Hickman spoke. "Masks," was all
he said.

Reaching into bags they'd brought along, the five men
placed gas masks over their mouths and noses. Then one
of the men attached an air pump to the pipe on the bottom of the container and started it up. Air started to be
sucked from the interior of the container. Making two
marks on the vial of poison to divide it into thirds, Hickman poured the liquid into a small stainless steel holding
tank that screwed into the upper fitting. Carefully watching his wristwatch, he timed the introduction of the virus
into the container, then removed the holding tank and
screwed an airtight cap on the end.

Leaving the air pump running for another thirty seconds
to create a slight vacuum, he removed the pump and
capped the end off. While he moved down to the next con-

tainer, one of the men sprayed the pair of end caps with the liquid plastic to make sure they were airtight. At the same time Hickman was spraying the poison into the containers, another member of the team sprayed the meteorite with a second layer of specialized coating on the floor of the mill. He rotated the orb to reach all the sides, and when he finished he lifted it and placed it in the box.

Hickman was just finishing with the containers. Taking the empty vial away from the area they were in, he found an empty spot on the floor. Sprinkling the vial with gasoline, he lit a match and tossed it on the floor. Flames burst out.

Back at the containers, the remaining four men removed small butane torches like those used by plumbers to sweat pipes together. They lit them, turned the flames on high and waved them through the air for a full five minutes.

"Okay," Hickman said, "open the doors but keep the masks on."

One of the men walked over to the overhead doors and pushed the electric lifts on all three bays. Then the drivers walked out, pulled the winch cables from the rear of the cabs of the trucks and started to winch the containers into place. Once they were secured, Hickman climbed into the passenger side of the lead truck and motioned for the driver to pull out.

HALPERT AND HORNSBY watched the exodus from their hiding spot. They snapped as many photographs as they could with their infrared cameras, but there was little else they could do. They watched as the trucks pulled from the docks one by one with the doors open to the weather.

The snow had turned to rain and the tires of the trucks splashed through the parking lot as they drove from the rear to the front of the building, then headed up the road leading away from the mill.

"Tom," Halpert said quickly, "do not try to enter the building; the men that just left were wearing gas masks."

"I understand," Reyes said.

"I'm going to call the *Oregon*," Halpert said, "and ask what to do."

* * *

AS SOON AS he hung up after talking with Fleming, Cabrillo phoned Hanley to report what he had learned.

"I'll have Stone start looking into it immediately," Hanley said.

"Maybe Hickman is not planning to destroy the meteorite at all," Cabrillo said, "but do something else entirely."

Just at that instant Halpert radioed. "Hold on," Hanley said to Halpert, "I'll put you on a three-way with Mr. Cabrillo."

Once they could all hear one another, Halpert explained what had happened.

"ARE YOU READING the locator signals from the trucks?" Cabrillo asked Hanley.

Hanley glanced over at the screen Stone was pointing at. Three moving dots were illuminated. "We have them," he said, "but there's another problem."

"What's that?" Cabrillo asked quickly.

"We lost the signal from the meteorite a few minutes ago."

"Damn," Cabrillo said loudly.

The line was silent for a moment as Cabrillo thought. "Here's what we are going to do," he said after the pause. "I'm sending Adams and Truitt back to the ship in the Robinson for chemical exposure suits—Michael, you and the others wait until they arrive."

"Okay, boss," Halpert said.

"Jonesy and I will stay here in the Range Rover," Cabrillo continued. "As soon as the trucks have a definite direction selected, we'll try to intercept them. Has the other team reached Heathrow yet?"

"They just met up with Gunderson and Pilston at the Gulfstream in the last five minutes," Hanley said.

"Good," Cabrillo said. "Make sure Tiny keeps the plane warm—they may need to move at any second."

"I understand," Hanley said.

"Have Nixon prepare the suits," Cabrillo said. "The helicopter will be there in ten minutes."

"We'll do it."

"Now just keep this line open and keep telling me the direction of the trucks," Cabrillo said.

"Okay," Hanley said.

Sitting in the Range Rover, Cabrillo put his hand over the telephone. "Dick," he said, "I need you to fly with Adams to the *Oregon* and pick up a crate of chemical exposure suits. We think Hickman has introduced some sort of chemical agent into the mill. After you pick up the suits, go directly to Maidenhead—Halpert and three others are waiting there."

Truitt didn't ask any questions; he simply opened the door of the Range Rover and raced through the darkness to where Adams had the Robinson idling on the heliport and climbed inside. After he explained the plan to Adams, the helicopter lifted off and started flying toward the *Oregon*.

"THEY HAVE TURNED onto the main motorway, the M4, that leads into London," Hanley reported to Cabrillo.

"Mr. Jones," Cabrillo said, "can you find us the quickest route to the M4?"

"With everyone in central London for the New Year celebrations," Jones said, "I'd say quick might be a stretch."

Sliding the Range Rover into gear, he backed up and then headed down the road leading out of Battersea Park. His plan was to cross the Battersea Bridge and take Old Brompton Road over to West Cromwell to the A4, which led to the M4. Even at this late hour the going would be slow.

HICKMAN AND THE trio of trucks had it easier. They drove through Maidenhead on the Castle Hill Road, which was also the A4, then turned onto A308, which led directly to the M4. Fourteen minutes after leaving Maidenhead Mill they were approaching exit number 4 to Heathrow Airport.

* * *

AT THE SAME instant the trucks were slowing to exit the M4, Truitt and Adams touched down on the rear deck of the *Oregon*. Nixon was waiting with a wooden crate containing the chemical suits and he raced out, opened the rear door, and stowed them across the rear seats while Adams kept the rotor turning. After closing the rear door, Nixon opened the front door and handed Truitt a printed sheet with directions to make sure the suits were airtight, then secured the front door and backed away.

Once clear, he gave Adams a thumbs-up sign and the Robinson lifted from the pad.

Within minutes the helicopter was back over London racing in the direction of Maidenhead. The distance was twenty-six miles and their arrival time was twelve minutes away.

THE PAIR OF pilots were still in the lounge at Global Air Cargo when the trucks pulled in front of the facility and slid to a stop. The 747 was sitting out front with the nose cone lifted in the air, awaiting loading. The rear ramp was also down to allow easy access. Hickman walked in a side door and found the pilots still watching the television.

"I'm Hal Hickman," he said, "we brought the priority cargo."

The head pilot rose and walked toward Hickman. "I'm honored to meet you, sir," he said, extending his hand. "I've worked for you for years—it's great to finally meet you."

"The pleasure is all mine," Hickman said, smiling. "Now, like I said over the phone, I have a priority cargo that needs to be on its way immediately. Are you ready?"

"We don't have any loaders," he said. "They won't arrive for another hour—holidays and all have thrown a wrench in the works."

"No problem," Hickman said. "My men and I will drive the containers on board and secure them into place. Have you received clearances yet?"

"I can call and have them in a few minutes," the pilot said.

"Do that," Hickman said. "We'll get the cargo aboard."

Hickman walked back through the door and the pilot turned to the copilot. "Call for weather and plot the course. I think London over France across the Mediterranean and into Riyadh. That's if the weather cooperates—if not, divert us as necessary."

ONCE OUT OF the hangar again, Hickman picked up the gas mask he had left on the ground and placed it over his mouth and nose. The drivers had been briefed on the loading procedures, and as soon as Hickman motioned to them to start, the first drove his truck carrying the container from the front to the back of the 747. Stopping with his truck going down the rear ramp, the man unhooked the cable holding the container to the flatbed then slightly tilted the bed so the container rolled backward on the steel rollers built into the bed. He was pulling away from the rear of the 747 as the next driver backed under the nose cone and placed his container's end to the one already at the rear of the plane. Sliding the container off the truck, he pulled out again. Turning away from the third truck, which was backed up waiting to enter, he pulled ahead and stopped.

The third truck backed in and started to unload as Hickman entered the 747 with the first driver. As they had practiced, the two men began to secure the containers to the floor with long canvas straps. One would attach the strap and pulley into slots built into railings on the floor, then toss the strap over the container to the other man, who attached it to the railing in the floor then winched the strap tight. One by one they attached three straps to each container.

The last driver was unhooked and pulling out of the 747 as they reached the container.

One, two, three and they were done.

Hickman walked out of the 747, motioned for the trucks to line up a distance away from the plane, then walked back toward the hangar.

* * *

"HERE ARE THE documents," he said, handing a clipboard of declarations over to the pilot. "The containers are in and fastened down. We're taking off."

"How bad do you want to push this through, sir?" the copilot asked. "We have some weather over the Mediterranean that looks bad. It would be a lot safer if we could wait until morning to start out."

"I need it there yesterday," Hickman said.

"Okay," the copilot said, "it'll be a bumpy ride."

Hickman turned and walked away. The copilot watched him heading for the door. There was something odd about the man, but it was not a bizarre personal appearance, as some of the pulp magazines claimed the elusive billionaire fostered. In all respects Hickman appeared quite nomal— ordinary, in fact. It was that tonight Hickman had a slight red ring shaped like a triangle with rounded sides around the area of his mouth.

The copilot brushed it off; he had a lot to get done and a short time to do it.

"PULL UP A detailed map," Hanley ordered Stone.

The locators on the containers had stopped moving a few minutes ago. Hanley wanted to know where. Stone punched commands into the computer and waited as the screens loaded. Slowly homing in on the area that showed the beeping lights, he gradually reduced the maps down to smaller scale.

"Heathrow air cargo annex," Stone said.

Hanley reached for the file Halpert had left and flipped through the sheets of paper. He remembered Hickman had a freight company. There it was. Global Air Cargo. Finding the telephone number of the hangar at Heathrow, he handed it to Stone.

"Call and see what you can find out," he said quickly. "I'll call Cabrillo."

"THAT'S IT," THE pilot said, "we're cleared."

The copilot gathered up his weather reports and the log

book and started to follow the pilot to the door. They had opened the door and were headed out when the telephone started to ring.

"Leave it," the pilot said as the copilot started to turn back, "I've got a flat to pay for."

"WE'RE MOVING THAT way, but slowly," Cabrillo said.

"No answer," Stone shouted across the control room of the *Oregon.*

"We're trying to reach the hangar by telephone," Hanley told Cabrillo, "but no one is answering."

"Alert Gunderson in the Gulfstream to be ready to lift off," Cabrillo said. "I'll try to reach Fleming."

Cabrillo hit the speed dial on his telephone just as the pilot secured the nose cone of the 747 and started the engines. Fleming came on the line and Cabrillo explained.

"And you think the cargo may be radioactive?" Fleming said after Cabrillo explained.

"Somehow poisoned," Cabrillo said. "One of my teams witnessed the people in control wearing gas masks. We need you to shut down Heathrow."

Fleming was silent for a second. "I think it better they left England," he said.

ADAMS TOUCHED DOWN on the parking lot in front of Maidenhead Mills and shut the Robinson down. Once the rotor had stopped spinning and the rotor brake was locked, he climbed out, walked around to the other side and began to help Truitt unload the crate. Halpert and the others walked over. Prying the top off with a screwdriver from his tool pouch, Adams set it on the ground.

"Here's your space suits, boys," Adams said, smiling. "Looks like Kevin packed four."

"We'll dress," Truitt said. "You tape our wrists and ankles."

Adams nodded.

"Barrett," Truitt said, "you sit this one out. The rest of you suit up."

Eight minutes later, Truitt, Halpert, Hornsby and Reyes
were ready. Walking around to the back of the building, they
entered from the rear door. Truitt held a chemical detection
device in his gloved hand. Almost immediately he got a positive reading.

"Spread out," Truitt said, "and search everything."

Hornsby raced for the front door, unlocked the dead-
bolts and walked out.

THE TRAFFIC HAD loosened as Cabrillo and Jones got
farther from central London, and once they reached the
M4, Jones accelerated to just over ninety miles an hour.
Cabrillo hung up after talking to Fleming and dialed the
Oregon again.

"Fleming won't shut down Heathrow," Cabrillo said
over the speaker phone as soon as Hanley answered.
"What's the closest exit to Global Air Cargo?"

Stone read off the exit number and Cabrillo repeated it
to Jones.

"We're right there, boss," Jones said as he started to
slow and pull off the M4.

"Follow the signs to Global Air Cargo," Cabrillo said to
Jones.

Jones stepped on the gas and raced down the side
streets. In a few seconds he could see a large hangar with
the name painted on the side in ten-foot-tall letters. A 747
was taxiing away from the building.

"Can you take us any closer?" Cabrillo asked.

Jones looked around but a chain-link fence secured the
entire area. "No way, boss," he said. "They have it secured."

The 747 was turning to enter the taxiway.

"Drive up there to that spot between the buildings,"
Cabrillo said.

Jones accelerated and then pulled to a stop. Cabrillo
reached for a pair of binoculars in the side pouch and
stared at the cargo plane. Then he read the tail numbers off
to Hanley, who quickly wrote them down.

"Have Gunderson follow them in the Gulfstream,"
Cabrillo said dejectedly. "That's all we can do right now."

"I'll do it," Hanley said.

Just then Hornsby radioed in and Stone took the call. After he explained what they had found, Stone wrote it down and handed it to Hanley, who read the notes.

"Mr. Chairman," Hanley said, "I'm calling up the Challenger 604. I think you're going to want to travel to Saudi Arabia at once."

45

AT ROUGHLY THE same time the Global Air Cargo 747 was lifting off the runway at Heathrow, the truck carrying Hickman was stopping at another section of the airport.

"Meet up with the others, ditch the trucks, and disappear," Hickman said to the driver who was dropping him in front of the private jet terminal. "I'll reach you if I need you."

"Good luck, sir," the driver said as Hickman climbed out.

Hickman waved at the driver, then walked through the front door.

The driver steered the truck out of the parking lot, then reached for his radio. "The big man is clear," he said. "I'll meet you at the rendezvous."

Twelve minutes later, the three trucks met up at an abandoned factory on the west side of London where they had stashed their getaway car. Climbing from the trucks, they quickly wiped down any surfaces they had touched with ungloved fingers then climbed into a nondescript British sedan.

Their plan was to drive through the city toward the English Channel, leave the rental car in a lot and board the ferry for Belgium. The plan would go off without a hitch.

* * *

"PREPARE THE *OREGON* to sail," Cabrillo ordered Hanley as Jones steered into the executive air terminal at Heathrow. "Set a course for the Mediterranean and then through the Suez Canal into the Red Sea. I want the ship as close to Saudi Arabia as possible."

Hanley sounded an alarm throughout the ship. Cabrillo could hear the whooping sound over the telephone link. "Gunderson and the others are in the air," he said. "The cargo plane is headed toward Paris."

"Jones and I are going to board the Challenger 604 in a few minutes," Cabrillo said quickly. "Have the team at Maidenhead withdraw and board the amphibian. Then have Michaels fly out and meet the *Oregon* in the English Channel."

"What about the mill?" Hanley asked.

"Tell Fleming what we found," Cabrillo said, "and turn it over to him."

"Sounds like we're swapping playing fields," Hanley noted.

"The action," Cabrillo said, "has switched to Saudi Arabia."

THE COPILOT OF Hickman's Hawker 800XP was waiting in the terminal.

"The pilot has fueled, finished the preflight and received the necessary clearances," the copilot said as he steered Hickman through the terminal and toward the runway. "We can leave now."

The two men walked out to the Hawker and boarded. Three minutes later they were taxiing toward the north-south runway. Three more minutes and they were airborne. Once they were over the English Channel, the pilot opened the cabin door.

"Sir," he said, "at the speed you want to fly, we're going to burn up a ton of fuel."

Hickman smiled. "Don't spare the engines," he said, "time is critical."

"As you wish, sir," the pilot said as he closed the door again.

Hickman felt the engines throttle up and the plane gain speed. The flight plan called for the Hawker to travel across France along the border with Belgium, then over Switzerland above Zurich. Continuing on across the Alps, they would race down the eastern coast of Italy, then Greece, Crete, and over Egypt. Crossing the Red Sea, they would be in Riyadh, Saudi Arabia, by early morning.

AS SOON AS Hanley called, Truitt and the others started preparing to leave. After making sure they had carefully photographed everything, they strung tape across the doors and windows of the mill and left handwritten signs warning people not to enter.

Once that was done, they climbed back in the beaten-down truck and headed back to the river and the amphibious plane.

FROM THE EDGE of the trees a young red fox made tentative steps from his cover in the brush. Sniffing at the air, he started across the cargo loading area at the rear of the mill. Warm air was blowing out of the mill through the open cargo doors and he raised his snout and felt the heat. Carefully moving forward, he stopped near the open middle door.

Then, feeling no threat, the fox wandered inside.

Raised near people, he knew that their presence equaled food.

Smelling human scents, he started to forage for scraps of food. He stepped in a strange black substance on the floor that coated his paws. Then he continued on across the floor, the sticky black coating picking up traces of the virus.

Just then the overhead heaters clicked on and the noise scared him. He raced back to the cargo door. When nothing happened, he decided to lie on the floor and wait. Lifting his paw up to his mouth to clean it, he began to lick the blackness away.

Within minutes his body began to convulse. His eyes grew bloodshot and liquid ran from his snout. Twitching as if he were being electrocuted, he tried to rise on his legs and run away.

But his legs would not work, and white foam was running from his mouth.

The fox lay down to die.

THE SOUND OF the whooping horn was filtering throughout the *Oregon*.

The team members raced to their stations and the ship was a blur of activity. "Lines are away, Mr. Hanley," Stone said.

"Take her away from the dock," Hanley said over the intercom to the wheelhouse.

The *Oregon* started to move away from the dock and gradually gained speed.

"Have you plotted the course?" Hanley asked Stone.

"Just finishing it, sir," Stone said, pointing to the large monitor on the wall.

A large map of Europe and Africa was displayed with a thick red line showing the route. Time intervals were displayed alongside the line.

"What's the quickest we can reach the Red Sea?" Hanley asked.

"January fourth, at eleven a.m.," Stone said.

"Coordinate the pickup with Michaels on the amphibian and get Adams back on board," Hanley said, "then arrange the schedule of watches for the journey."

"Yes, sir," Stone said.

Then Hanley reached for the telephone.

THE INSISTENCE THAT the cargo of prayer rugs be documented as coming from France would help one side and hurt the other. The Global Air Cargo 747 was quickly cleared to land. After less than an hour on the ground, the cargo was retagged and the plane was off the ground again.

* * *

GUNDERSON AND THE team on the Gulfstream would
not be as lucky. They were boarded by French customs officials as soon as they landed. Hickman had retrieved a list
of all the private planes that had been at McCarran Airport
in Las Vegas at the time of the break-in of his penthouse.
From there it had been a simple matter of searching flight
plans to locate any that had traveled to England thereafter.

The Gulfstream had been the only one.

Hickman then made an anonymous call to Interpol
claiming that the plane was carrying drugs. It would take
two full days and multiple calls from Hanley and others
before his people were released. The French could be difficult to deal with.

CABRILLO WAS LUCKIER. The Challenger 604 with
him and Jones aboard left Heathrow within thirty minutes
of Hickman's departure. The pilot immediately set a
course for Riyadh, the capital city, at her maximum speed
of 548 miles per hour. They streaked through the sky at an
altitude of 37,000 feet.

A half hour ahead and now over France, Hickman's
Hawker 800XP was at her maximum speed of 514 miles
per hour. The Challenger carrying Cabrillo and Jones at a
faster speed should have arrived first, but that would not be
the case. Hickman had known his destination for some
time—Cabrillo had become aware of it only recently.

On a good day, getting a visa to visit Saudi Arabia is
difficult. The process is slow and arbitrary, and tourism is
not only discouraged but outlawed. Several of Hickman's
companies did business with the kingdom, and he was a
known entity. His application for visiting took mere hours
to approve.

Cabrillo would not be so lucky.

EARLY THE MORNING of January 1, Saud Al-Sheik was
awakened by the chirping of the computer in his home of-

fice, indicating an e-mail had arrived. The mill in England was reporting that the prayer rugs he had been waiting for had cleared customs and were documented in Paris. They were now en route to Riyadh via 747.

Once at the air cargo terminal in Riyadh, they needed to be trucked across Saudi Arabia to Mecca. There the containers would be opened, and the rugs would be sprayed with pesticide, then left to air out for a day or so before being placed in the stadium.

Al-Sheik stared at the clipboard on his desk. With the exact date the rugs would appear an unknown, he had scheduled all his trucks for other duties. The earliest he could truck the rugs was January 7. He'd arrange it so they were sprayed on the eighth, left to air out for a few hours, and then moved into place on the ninth.

That still gave him twenty-four hours before the official start of the hajj. Al-Sheik was cutting it close, but what choice did he have? He had a million details to cover and only so much time to do the impossible.

It would all come together, he thought as he rose to leave the office and climb back into bed—it always did somehow. *Inshallah*—God willing. Lying in bed, Al-Sheik's brain bubbled with a thousand details. Deciding further sleep would not be forthcoming, he rose and walked into the kitchen to make a pot of tea.

THE CHALLENGER 604 was over the Mediterranean when the pilot opened the cockpit door and shouted to the rear.

"Mr. Chairman," he said, "Saudi is refusing us entrance until we have the proper documents. We have to decide what to do now."

Cabrillo thought about it for a few moments. "Divert to Qatar," he said. "I'll call the emir's representative in a couple of minutes. Don't worry, he'll honor our request."

"Qatar it is," the pilot said, closing the door again.

* * *

IT WAS SUNRISE when Hickman's Hawker crossed over the Red Sea into Saudi Arabia and across the desert to Riyadh. Touching down smoothly, the pilot taxied over to the jet terminal and slowed.

"Keep her fueled and ready," Hickman said.

As soon as the door opened he walked out, down the steps and onto Saudi soil carrying the boxed meteorite.

"So this is the country I will ruin," he whispered as he looked around at the dry hills near the airport, "the heart of Islam."

Spitting on the ground, he smiled an evil smile.

Then he walked to where a limousine was waiting to take him to the hotel.

HICKMAN WAS ALREADY checked in and sleeping before the Challenger raced up the Indian Ocean, turned and crossed atop the Strait of Hormuz into the Persian Gulf en route to Qatar. The emir had come through with flying colors. His representative had smoothed out entry into the country and a suite of hotel rooms was awaiting Cabrillo and his team. It was arranged that Cabrillo would meet with the emir himself at noon today. First Cabrillo would grab a few hours' sleep. Then he'd explain the problem in person.

The pilot opened the door again and shouted back, "The tower has cleared us, sir."

Cabrillo stared out the window at the azure waters of the gulf. Dhows, the strangely shaped boats that carried fisherman and cargo across the water, bobbed peacefully. In the distance to the north, Cabrillo could make out the long expanse of an oil tanker heading south. The wake trail from the tanker's massive propellers trailed back for miles.

Cabrillo heard the engines on the Challenger start to slow.

Then they began to descend for landing.

46

TWELVE HINDUS WERE clustered into a cheap apartment in an aging building in downtown Riyadh. They had arrived in Saudi Arabia a week prior using work visas listing their occupations as laborers. Once through customs and immigration they had disappeared, never meeting with the employment agency that had arranged their entry.

One by one they had made their way to the apartment that Hickman had had stocked with food, water and supplies enough to last for several weeks. Never venturing out or communicating with anyone, they were to lie in wait until contacted.

The twelve men would be the only forces that Hickman would use in Saudi Arabia for the plan he was about to initiate. What Hickman had in mind was simple on the surface, considerably more complex in application. He and the twelve Hindus were first planning to make their way to Mecca. Once there, Hickman was planning to steal the most sacred artifact to Islam, the meteorite inside the Kaaba that had allegedly been discovered by Abraham, and switch it with the one from Greenland.

Then he would take Abraham's meteorite elsewhere to destroy.

Hickman was planning to stab Islam in her heart.

IN HIS HOTEL room in Riyadh, Hickman stared at his notes.

Mecca is the center of Islam. The city was the birthplace of Muhammad and the religion he founded. Located forty-five miles from the Red Sea on a dusty plain studded with hills and mountains, the city was once an oasis on a trade route that linked the countries along the Mediterranean with Arabia, Africa and Asia. There, according to legend, some two thousand years before the time of Jesus Christ, God ordered Abraham to build a shrine. Over the centuries the shrine was destroyed and rebuilt numerous times. In 630 the prophet Muhammad took control of Mecca and rid the structure of all false idols. All that Muhammad left was the Kaaba and the sacred stone housed inside. He made this the centerpiece of his new religion.

Over the centuries that followed, the area housing the stone was ringed by a series of walls and larger, increasingly more elaborate structures. The last major rebuilding, in the twentieth century, was funded by the Saudi royal family. This construction resulted in the surrounding mosque, al-Haram, the largest on Earth.

In the center of the mosque lies the Kaaba, a small structure draped in a black silk covering that is embroidered with passages from the Koran in gold thread. The silk covering is changed yearly, and once each year in a show of humility the floor around is swept by the king of Saudi Arabia.

Pilgrims come to kiss the sacred stone and drink from the spring of Zamzam nearby.

In less than a week, over a million people would pass alongside the Kaaba.

For now, however, it was closed in preparation.

Hickman turned on the computer in his hotel suite and logged on to a mainframe at one of his aerospace companies in Brazil. He had stored his most important files there.

Downloading the pictures and documents, he scanned through them.

He stared at an aerial photograph of the mosque at Mecca.

The al-Haram, also known as the Great Mosque, is a massive structure. Huge walls and arches made of stone ring the area and are tiered to additional levels with the same curved arches. The walls are ringed by seven minarets that soar into the air for hundreds of feet. A total of sixty-four gates allow the pilgrims entrance; the entire area has a floor space of nearly 200,000 square feet.

The mosque dwarfs the Kaaba, which is only some sixty feet by sixty feet in dimension.

All Hickman and his team had to do was get inside the curtain surrounding the Kaaba, remove the sacred stone, which was mounted in a silver frame in a wall in the southeast corner of the structure some four feet off the ground, and replace it with the one from Greenland. Then they had to try to make their escape.

All in all it seemed fairly impossible.

HIS ROOM PHONE rang. The front desk clerk was alerting him to an overnight package that was waiting for him at the front desk. Hickman asked that a bellman bring it up to him. A few minutes later, there was a knock at the door.

Hickman opened the door, slipped the bellman a tip and took the package.

THE *OREGON* SLOWED in the water off France.

"I've got her on radar," Stone said to Hanley.

Hanley nodded and watched the exterior cameras as the amphibious plane appeared out of the gloom. Slowing, the plane dropped down and landed in the water and taxied toward the ship. Hanley watched as the deckhands secured it to the side and the team aboard climbed off. Then he reached for the radio.

"Ms. Michaels," he called out to the pilot.

"Yes, sir."

"The ship is bound for the Red Sea. How much sleep have you had recently?"

"Not much," Michaels admitted.

"Make land at Spain and find a hotel room," Hanley said. "After you're fully rested, start making your way south. I'd take up refuge at an airport in southern Italy for now—you should be close enough there that we can call you if we need you."

The amphibian had proved a useful tool, but it was just too large to take aboard the ship.

"Very good, sir," Michaels said.

"One of the men is coming out to you with two stacks of hundred-dollar bills," Hanley said, "ten thousand dollars in total. Can you safely fly alone or do you want someone to go with you?"

"No, sir," Michaels said, "I'll be fine."

"If you need more funds, just call," Hanley said. "We can wire to you wherever you move. Now get some rest, but keep the plane fueled and ready to go at all times."

"Yes, sir."

"And Michaels," Hanley said, "you did a hell of a job. I know this was your first pilot-in-command mission and I want you to know the Corporation couldn't be happier."

"Sir," Stone said, "we have Adams inbound in the Robinson."

Michaels poked her head at the side door of the plane and glanced up at where she knew a remote camera was mounted. She gave Hanley a thumbs-up, then climbed back inside and secured the door. Walking back to the cockpit, she started the engines then keyed the microphone.

"I hear Adams on the radio," she said, "so I'll clear out now."

The lines were taken back aboard the *Oregon* and Michaels idled away from the ship. Once clear, she hit the gas, took the amphibian up to speed and lifted off. Making a slight arc to the left, she headed toward Spain.

"Let's get Adams safely aboard," Hanley said, "and get back up to speed."

Two minutes later the Robinson appeared over the fantail and dropped onto the pad.

As soon as the helicopter was secured to the deck, Hanley ordered full speed again.

CABRILLO SLEPT LIKE a rock until 11 A.M., when the hotel front desk telephoned to wake him. Cabrillo ordered breakfast, then telephoned Jones's room.

"I'm awake, sir," Jones said.

"Shower, change and meet me in my suite for breakfast," Cabrillo said.

"I'll be there in twenty minutes," Jones said.

Cabrillo had already showered, and he was shaving when the room service waiter knocked on the door. Dressed in his robe, he answered the door and motioned for where the waiter should place the cart. Walking over to his wallet on the dresser, he removed a bill and attempted to hand it to the man.

"Sorry, sir," the waiter said, "the emir has taken care of everything."

The waiter disappeared out the door before Cabrillo could argue. He finished shaving and dressed in clean clothes. He was adjusting the television to watch the news when Jones knocked on the door. Cabrillo let him in and the two men started on breakfast. Jones was halfway through his omelet before he spoke.

"I haven't met the emir, boss," he said. "What's he like?"

"The emir is in his mid-fifties and very progressive in his thinking," Cabrillo said. "He's allowed the United States military to maintain a base here for a few years. In fact, the entire Second Gulf War was based from the airfield here."

"How are his connections with Saudi Arabia?" Jones asked.

"Usually good," Cabrillo said, "but that can change day by day. The Saudis are always running a fine line between appearing pro-Western, which most of the Arab world thinks the emir is of late, and placating the large body of religious fundamentalists in their own population. The line has been stretched almost to the breaking point more than once."

Cabrillo was just finishing his last bite of potatoes when the room phone rang.

"The limo is downstairs," Cabrillo said after he hung up. "Let's go meet him and you can form your own opinion."

Rising from the table, Jones followed Cabrillo out the door.

IN LANGLEY, VIRGINIA, Langston Overholt was reading a report from MI5 about the nuclear warhead the Corporation had disabled. Britain was now secure, but the meteorite had still not been recovered. Michelle Hunt had been transported to England, but, as yet, Overholt was not sure how they would use her.

Hanley had reported in an hour ago and updated Overholt on the situation, but a recent flap with the U.S. government over support to Israel had made the Saudis increasingly difficult to deal with. Overholt had called his counterpart at the Saudi secret police to report the theory about the poisoned prayer rugs but had yet to receive a reply.

He was beginning to think he might need to call the president to intercede.

The thing that puzzled Overholt most of all was that when the Corporation had searched Maidenhead Mill they found no trace of the meteorite or any residue that it might have been processed like they originally theorized.

Just then the telephone rang.

"I have the satellite data you ordered, sir," an officer from the National Security Agency said. "I'll send it over now."

"Do that," Overholt said, "but tell me over the telephone where the Hawker went."

"Riyadh, Saudi Arabia, sir," the man said. "Arrived early this morning and remains there. We have a shot of the plane on the runway and the aerial tracks—that's what I'm sending."

"Thanks," Overholt said and hung up.

Sitting back in his chair, Overholt reached in his desk drawer and removed a tennis ball. He began to bounce it against the wall. After a few minutes he began to nod.

Then he reached over and dialed a number.

"Research," a voice answered.

"I need a quick overview on the Islamic faith and in particular sacred sites in Mecca." Overholt had remembered something about a meteorite and Islam from a history class taken years before.

"How detailed and how soon?" the voice asked.

"Brief and within the hour," Overholt said, "and find me an Islamic scholar inside the Agency and send him to my office."

"Yes, sir."

While Overholt was waiting, he bounced the ball against the wall over and over. He was trying to think like a parent with the ghost of a dead son clawing at his brain. How far would he go to revenge the death? How could he strike at the heart of the beast itself?

THE EMIR'S PALACE, sitting on a hill overlooking the Persian Gulf, was opulent. Surrounded by a high stone wall that housed a courtyard with garages, a large parklike grass area, and several pools, the palace grounds seemed surprisingly friendly—not like the drab and dreary edifices situated throughout much of Britain and Europe.

As the limousine pulled through the gate and headed around the circular drive toward the front doors, several peacocks and a pair of flamingos scattered. Off to one side, a mechanic dressed in a khaki jumpsuit was soaping off a Lamborghini off-road vehicle, while two gardeners were harvesting nuts from a pistachio tree nearby.

The limousine stopped in front of the door, and a man dressed in a Western businessman's suit walked out. "Mr. Cabrillo," he said, "I'm Akmad al-Thani, special assistant to the emir. We've talked before on the telephone."

"Mr. al-Thani," Cabrillo said, taking the man's extended hand and shaking it, "pleasure to finally meet you. This is my associate, Peter Jones."

Jones shook al-Thani's hand and smiled.

"If you men could come this way," al-Thani said, walking toward the door, "the emir is awaiting you in the drawing room."

Cabrillo followed al-Thani with Jones on their heels.

They entered a large foyer with marble floors and a pair of arching staircases on both sides leading to the upper floors. There were several marble statues tastefully arranged around a large polished mahogany table in the center, with a massive floral arrangement on the top. A pair of maids dressed in uniforms bustled about, and in one corner a butler in black coat and tails was motioning at a workman who was adjusting a spotlight that pointed to a painting that looked like a Renoir.

Al-Thani continued past the foyer through a hallway that led into a large room with an entire wall of glass looking out on the water. The room had to be over eight thousand square feet, with numerous seating areas clustered around tall potted plants. Several plasma televisions were placed around the room, and there was even a grand piano.

The emir was sitting at the piano, and he stopped playing when the men walked in.

"Thank you for coming," he said, rising.

Walking over to Cabrillo, he extended his hand. "Juan," he said, "always good to see you."

"Your Excellency," Cabrillo said, smiling and turning to Jones, "my associate, Peter Jones."

Jones took the emir's extended hand and shook it firmly.

"Pleasure," the emir said, motioning to nearby couches. "Let's sit over here."

The four men took their seats, and if by magic a waiter appeared.

"Tea and cakes," the emir said.

The waiter disappeared as quickly as he had arrived.

"So what was the end result in Iceland?" the emir asked.

Cabrillo filled him in on the details. The emir nodded.

"If you men hadn't been there and made the switch," the emir said, "who knows where I'd be right now."

"Al-Khalifa is dead now, Your Excellency," Cabrillo said, "so that is one less worry."

"Nonetheless," the emir said, "I want the Corporation to do a full-scale assessment of my security and the threats to my government as soon as possible."

"We would be happy to do that for you," Cabrillo said,

"but right now there is a more pressing matter we'd like to discuss."

The emir nodded. "Please, by all means."

Cabrillo started to explain.

47

THE THREE SHIPPING containers filled with poisoned prayer rugs sat off to the side of the cargo terminal at Riyadh Airport behind a chain-link fence that covered the space of several football fields. If the time had not been so close to the hajj, the rugs would have already been moved and unloaded. As it was, arriving late as they had, they had moved down the list in priority. As long as they were in place on the ground around the Kaaba the day before the start of the hajj, Al-Sheik would consider it a success.

Right now, the planner was concerned with more pressing matters.

Along with the prayer rugs, there were nearly one million plastic bottles of water that needed to be placed, ten thousand portable toilets to supplement those already at the site, six complete tented first-aid stations that would ring the perimeter, and ten thousand portable trash cans.

Boxes of printed flyers and memorabilia, complimentary Korans and postcards, and boxes containing tubes of sunscreen sat on pallets. Food for the pilgrims, six thousand brooms for the workers to use to sweep up the daily mess, portable umbrellas in case of rain. Twelve large crates of fans to be placed inside the massive structure around the Great Mosque for ventilation.

But Al-Sheik had nothing to do with the security arrangements.

That was handled by the Saudi Arabia secret police.

At a separate area of the air cargo terminal, trucks were already moving the security supplies to Mecca—a complete command-and-control facility with radios and live video capabilities; one hundred thousand rounds of ammunition and tear gas in case of disturbances; one thousand portable plastic handcuffs; forty trained dogs with pens, food, and extra leashes and collars; and a dozen armored personnel carriers, four tanks and thousands of troops.

The yearly hajj was a massive undertaking and the Saudi royal family footed the bill.

Al-Sheik stared at his clipboard then marked off a truck leaving the compound.

THE EMIR HAD been sipping his hot tea and listening to Cabrillo speak for nearly twenty minutes without interrupting. Finally there was silence.

"Will you allow me to indulge you with a short history of Islam?"

"By all means," Cabrillo said.

"There are three important sites to the Islamic religion, two in Saudi Arabia, the third in Israel. The first and most sacred is the mosque of al-Haram in Mecca, where the Kaaba is located; the second is Masjid al-Nabawi, the Prophet's Mosque in Medina, which has the tomb of Muhammad. The third is Masjid al-Aqsa, in Jerusalem, the Dome of the Rock, the site where Muhammad ascended on a horse to speak to Allah." The emir paused and sipped his tea, then continued.

"The Kaaba is of critical importance to Muslims; it is the spot they pray toward five times daily. It is the very beacon of our faith. Behind the sheets that hang down over the sacred site of the Kaaba, inside the building itself, is a black stone that Abraham recovered and placed there many centuries past."

Cabrillo and Jones nodded.

"As you mentioned, the stone is widely believed to be a meteorite sent from Allah to the faithful," the emir added.

"Could you describe the stone?" Jones asked.

The emir nodded. "I have touched it myself many times. The stone is round, approximately one foot in diameter, and black in color. If I was to guess the weight I would say about one hundred pounds, give or take."

"Those are the approximate dimensions of the meteorite recovered in Greenland," Cabrillo said.

The emir's face showed alarm.

"There's something I failed to mention, Your Excellency," Cabrillo said. "Our scientists have reason to believe that there might be a virus contained in the Greenland meteorite that could be released if the orb is split."

"What type of virus?" the emir asked.

"One that consumes oxygen at an alarming rate," Cabrillo said, "creating a vacuum that sucks everything nearby into the center."

"Armageddon," the emir said.

"I have to get into Saudi Arabia," Cabrillo said quickly, "to stop him."

"That, my friend, is harder than it appears," the emir said. "Since the Gulf War of 2003, King Abdullah and I have had a touchy relationship. My close and continued support of the United States, allowing troops and the large airfield here to be constructed, has placed a rift in our friendship—at least publicly. To appease the hard-liners in his country and to keep himself in power, he has found it necessary to publicly condemn my actions."

"Surely if you explain the threat he will come around," Jones said.

"I will try," the emir said, "but at this point we only speak through intermediaries. The process is slow and tedious."

"Will you try?" Cabrillo asked.

"Of course. But even if he did allow you to help," the emir said, "we have another problem. And this is quite serious."

"What is that?" Cabrillo asked.

"Only Muslims are allowed in the city of Mecca itself."

* * *

SCOTT THOMPSON WAS drenched in a cold sweat.

Dr. Berg had just strapped what looked like a video-
game headset over his eyes and adjusted the strap to fit
firmly. So far, Thompson had held firm. He'd been injected
with truth serum, which had not worked; grilled endlessly
over the past few days; and subjected to telephone calls
from family in the United States explaining what they'd
been told would happen to them if he did not cooperate.

Nothing had made him talk.

Thompson had been trained for such instances and a
doctrine had been drilled into his head.

He'd learned how to fight off the truth serum, been endlessly briefed on how to handle questioning, and internal-
ized the fact that, whatever he was told, the United States
would not harm innocent people to make him talk.

But no one had briefed him about this.

Thompson felt Berg's breath near his ear. "Scott," Berg
said, "you are going to see some colored lights in a minute
in front of your eyes. In time these will induce epileptic-
like seizures and a fierce burning that feels like nails are
being driven into your brain. If you need to vomit, and you
will, you probably won't be able to move your head, so try
and be careful not to inhale your own vomit. I have a
nurse standing by who will vacuum out any residue. Do
you understand?"

Thompson moved his head slightly.

"Now I want to give you one last chance to come clean
before this starts. I want you to know we rarely use this
technique because we've had a fair amount of patient failure with this therapy. By that I mean inducing vegetative or
catatonic states and even a percentage of outright expira-
tions. Do you understand what that means?"

Commander Gant was off to one side of the hospital
suite. He could not stand to watch what was happening and
motioned that he was going to leave. Berg waved as he
walked out. Then he walked over to a computer terminal
and entered the commands.

Thompson began to twitch and then arched his back up against the straps.

He began to flop around on the table like a fish out of water.

IT WAS 2 P.M. in Qatar, 9 A.M. in Washington, D.C., when Overholt answered his telephone. Cabrillo wasted no time.

"I'm in Qatar," he said. "We now think that Hickman might try to strike at one of the three most important sites to Islam."

"The Kaaba, Muhammad's Tomb, or the Dome of the Rock," Overholt said. "I've been studying."

Overholt had spent hours yesterday with the Agency's Islamic scholar and read pages of documents prepared by the research department.

"Well done," Cabrillo said.

"I've also had the National Security Agency tracing all communication to and from Hickman for the last few weeks and finally got the results," Overholt said. "He's been in communication with Pieter Vanderwald—in fact, an overnight package was just sent to Saudi Arabia from one of Vanderwald's front companies."

"Pieter the Poisoner?" Cabrillo said.

"The same," Overholt said.

"Somebody should take care of him," Cabrillo said.

"I issued a directive," Overholt replied. "A 'wet team' is seeking him now."

"Have you spoken to Hanley recently?" Cabrillo asked.

"Yes," Overholt said, "he explained what your men found at the mill in Maidenhead. We're sure it's some toxin Vanderwald supplied."

"And they sprayed it on the prayer rugs," Cabrillo said.

"I'm sure he sealed the containers, or the pilots would have been sickened on the flight from England and crashed the plane. Hickman's crazy, but he's not stupid. It's once the containers are opened that we have a problem."

"Which could be any hour now," Cabrillo said.

Just then the fax machine in Overholt's office started

printing. He wheeled his chair over to it, lifted off the papers, rolled back to his desk and scanned them.

"I'd say he'll strike at the Dome of the Rock and blame the Israelis for the entire affair," Overholt said.

"How'd you come up with that?" Cabrillo asked.

"Remember the yacht that transported the meteorite to the Faeroe Islands and was boarded by our navy guided-missile frigate?"

"Sure," Cabrillo said.

"I sent a specialist on board from the Agency," Overholt said. "He finally got their ringleader to talk."

"And?"

"A couple of weeks ago, Hickman sent a separate team to Israel to wire the Dome of the Rock with video cameras and explosives. If he is able to recover the stone of Abraham, it looks like he plans to take it to Jerusalem and destroy it in the explosion, then display the video worldwide."

"What about the operations in Saudi Arabia?" Cabrillo asked. "Did he disclose anything about that?"

"Apparently he knew nothing. Hickman must have compartmentalized that and used a different group."

"I need you to do me a favor," Cabrillo said.

"What is it?"

"Pull up the service records of all the United States military personnel in Qatar."

"What for?"

"I need every Muslim we have," Cabrillo said.

"Who will lead them in Mecca?"

"Don't worry," Cabrillo said, "I have just the man."

THE *OREGON* WAS just entering the Strait of Gibraltar when Hanley hung up the telephone after talking to Cabrillo. He reached for the intercom button and pressed it down.

"Kasim and Adams to the control room, immediately," he said. "Kasim and Adams to the control room, immediately."

As he waited for the men to arrive, he turned to Stone.

"Change the course to Israel, the nearest spot offshore of Jerusalem you can find."

Stone pulled a map up on the monitor. The port of Ashdod was nearest. He entered the commands and the ship control program reset itself. Just then Adams walked into the control room.

"Yes, sir," he said.

"I need you to prepare the helicopter to drop off Kasim in Tangier, Morocco."

"Then where do you want me to go?" Adams asked.

"Refuel and fly back out to the *Oregon*."

"I'll get on it right now," Adams said and walked out.

A few minutes later Kasim walked into the room.

"Are you up for leading an operation?" Hanley asked.

"Yes, sir," Kasim said, smiling.

"Only Cabrillo has access to the personnel files," Hanley said, "but he told me you're a Muslim. Is that correct?"

"Yes, sir."

"Good," Hanley said. "We have the Challenger on the way from Qatar to Morocco. We need you to lead a team into Mecca."

"What's the purpose, sir?" Kasim asked.

"You," Hanley said slowly, "are going to save Islam's holiest sites."

"It would be an honor, sir," Kasim said.

48

HICKMAN HAD NO trepidations about being a non-Muslim inside Mecca.

He hated the Islamic religion and all it stood for. After meeting with the dozen Indian nationals in the house in Riyadh at 4 P.M. and briefing them, they set out on the ten-hour drive to Mecca and the Kaaba in a stolen panel van marked with Islamic writing that read "Kingdom Cleaning" on the side. They were dressed in long white flowing garments and each had a broom, bucket, putty knife and brushes.

Hickman had paid a forger to write a letter in Arabic explaining that they were here to remove any chewing gum found on the grounds. Inside a bright yellow plastic janitor's cart, behind a white canvas curtain, Hickman had placed both the meteorite and some aerosol cans that Vanderwald had sent in his latest shipment. Each of the Hindus had a molded hunk of C-6 explosive with a tiny timer duct-taped to the small of his back. On each of their legs, hidden under the robes they wore, was a handgun just in case things went bad.

The van pulled up to a gate leading into the vast mosque.

Hickman and the others climbed out, pulled out the cart, buckets, and brooms and then walked toward the guard. Hickman had trained for this tirelessly, learning both Arabic and how to read body language. He handed over the sheet of paper and then spoke.

"In the name of merciful Allah, we come to clean the holy site," he said.

The time was late, the guard was tired, and the mosque was closed.

There was little reason for him to believe the men were anything other than what they said they were—he waved them through without comment. Wheeling the cart in front of him, Hickman pushed it under an arched passageway that led to the interior of the shrine.

Once inside the passageway, Hickman slipped a small mask and filter over his mouth and nose, then wrapped his headdress over that so only his eyes showed. Motioning to the Hindus to spread out and place the charges around the perimeter, he headed directly toward the Kaaba.

Four tall men in ceremonial uniforms were walking guard on each corner. Every five minutes they walked from the corner outside the black shroud with exaggerated steps that raised their feet in the air like Beefeaters at Buckingham Palace. Each guard moved from the corner where he was standing to the next in a clockwise direction, then stopped and waited. They were just finishing a repositioning when Hickman wheeled close with the cart.

Reaching into the cart, he popped one of the aerosol cans to open, then pushed it near the guard. The guard remained motionless for a second, then dropped to his knees, onto his chest, and finally facedown on the marble floor. Hickman quickly slipped under the curtain with the cart and pushed it inside.

Then he ran over to Abraham's Stone and pried it from the silver frame with a short iron rod he had hidden in the cart. Quickly switching it with the meteorite from Greenland, he placed Abraham's Stone under the white canvas curtain around the janitor's cart. He then hid explosive charges around the perimeter and slipped back under the shroud.

Vanderwald had explained that the knockout gas he had supplied only had effects for between three and four minutes. After that time anyone who had breathed the gas would start to come around. Hickman pushed the cart toward the arched passageway.

The Hindus worked quickly; the six assigned pillars closest to the passageway were already waiting in the tunnel. Two more arrived a few minutes later, then two more.

Hickman watched as the last pair hurried across the large expanse of marble.

Followed by the Hindus, Hickman pushed the cart past the guard at the entrance.

"What are you doing?" the guard asked.

"A thousand apologies," Hickman said in Arabic, still pushing the cart toward the van, "they told us inside we are supposed to clean tomorrow night."

HICKMAN AND THE others piled into the van and were just pulling away when the guard awoke. Shifting around until he was sitting on the marble, the guard glanced about to see if anyone had noticed. Apparently no one had. The guard on the other corner was facing away, as ceremony dictated. He rose to his feet and stared at his watch. One minute thirty seconds until the change. The guard decided to keep the fact he had passed out a secret. He knew if he told anyone they would replace him before the hajj.

The guard had dreamed his entire life of being a ceremonial guard. A slight case of heat stroke or food poisoning would not end his dream.

HICKMAN DIRECTED THE driver to the road that led to the town of Rabigh on the Red Sea.

Once there, the Hindus would hide out in a house he had rented. Tomorrow night they would drive to Medina. Hickman would not spend the night in Rabigh; a boat was waiting for him at the port. By first light he would be on board and steaming north.

OVERHOLT WAS SITTING in the Oval Office. He finished his briefing and sat back in his chair.

"This is one hell of a mess, Langston," the president said.

Overholt nodded slowly.

"Our relationship with Saudi Arabia is at an all-time low," the president continued. "Ever since Senator Grant passed the bill condemning the kingdom for being home to the September eleventh hijackers, and Congress passed the special tax on Saudi crude oil, our diplomats have hardly been able to even arrange meetings. The latest polls show a majority of the U.S. citizens think we should have attacked Saudi Arabia and not Iraq, and now you tell me that a crazy American billionaire is planning to strike at the country's holiest sites."

"I know it's a powder keg, Mr. President."

"Powder keg!" the president exploded. "It's much worse than that. If Hickman has poisoned prayer rugs and switched Abraham's Stone and something like you theorize happens to it, I see three major things that could happen. The first is a given—the Saudi's cut off oil shipments to the U.S. That will plunge us into another recession and we're barely out of the last one—that would be a shock that our economy just could not stand. Second, the fact that Hickman is an American will fan the flames with the terrorist elements. They will be swimming to the U.S. to wreak havoc. Let's face it, the U.S.-Canadian and U.S.-Mexican borders are sieves. Short of us erecting walls, there's not much we can do if someone is determined to enter our country. The third is possibly the worst. If the Greenland meteorite is shattered and releases a virus similar to the one that was in the Arizona sample, then the other two might be mute points. The oxygen could be sucked out of the atmosphere like water down a drain, then we'll all be breathing dust."

Overholt nodded slowly. "The first two are easily handled if what the CIA doctor learned from the captured combatant is true. That Hickman is planning to blame the entire affair on the Israelis."

"Unfortunately, as much as I've tried to wean the Israelis from American aid, I've been mostly unsuccessful. The Arab world believes the United States and Israel are closely tied—and we are. If the blame goes to Israel, it would be overrun with Arab troops from any nation that has troops. And we know what would happen then."

"The Israelis would go nuclear," Overholt said.

"So what are we left with?" the president asked. "Give me the out."

"The only way we can put this thing to bed is to eliminate the prayer rugs, capture Hickman and somehow replace the meteorites if he has already switched them, then search the holy sites for explosives."

"All without the Saudi Arabian government knowing what we're doing," the president said. "That's a tall order."

"Mr. President," Overholt said, "do you have a better idea?"

ON JANUARY 4, 2006, at 5 A.M. Qatar time, the telephone in Cabrillo's hotel room rang and woke him.

"It's me, Juan," Overholt said. "I've finished meeting with the president and have your orders."

Cabrillo sat up in bed. "What's the verdict?"

"He wants to do it all without Saudi cooperation," Overholt said. "I'm sorry but that's the only way we see this working."

Cabrillo exhaled and the sound carried over the telephone line. "We have six days until the hajj, when two million pilgrims will be all over Mecca and Medina, and you want me to send a team inside for what?"

"First, you find Hickman," Overholt said, "and determine the status of the meteorite—if he has switched it with Abraham's Stone, you switch it back. Then you search al-Haram and al-Nabawi mosques and make sure they are not wired to blow during the hajj. Then you and your team get out of Saudi Arabia before anyone knows you're there."

"I hate to talk business when you are talking fantasy," Cabrillo said, "but do you have any idea what this is going to cost the United States?"

"Eight figures?" Overholt guessed.

"Maybe nine," Cabrillo said.

"So you can do it?"

"Maybe, but I'll need all the resources of the Department of Defense and the entire intelligence community on our side."

"You call," Overholt said, "I'll make sure they jump."

Cabrillo hung up and dialed a number.

AN HOUR LATER, while Cabrillo was still back at the hotel showering, Hali Kasim walked out onto a runway in front of a hangar on the edge of the U.S. Air Force base in Qatar. Thirty-seven men were milling about—the entire number of Muslim U.S. military men from Diego Garcia in the Indian Ocean to the continent of Africa. All had been flown in yesterday from their various postings on military jets to Qatar.

Not one man had been told why they were sent for.

"Gentlemen," Kasim said, "form ranks."

The men lined up and waited at parade rest. Kasim studied a sheet of paper.

He looked up and addressed the men. "My name is Hali Kasim. I served seven years in the United States Navy as a warrant officer W-4 in underwater demolition before joining the private sector. I have been recalled to active duty by presidential decree and given a field rank of commander for the purposes of this operation. According to my docket, the next highest ranking man here is a United States Air Force captain named William Skutter. Would Captain Skutter please step forward."

A tall, thin black man dressed in a blue Air Force uniform took two steps forward.

"Captain Skutter," Kasim said, "is my second in command. Please come over here next to me and face the troops."

Skutter walked over and pivoted on his heel and stood alongside Kasim.

"Captain Skutter will be dividing you into teams according to your various service ranks in the next few hours," Kasim said. "Right now I want to explain why each of you was selected to appear here today. First and foremost, all of you are United States military personnel; secondary and very important to this mission, each of you listed Islam as your religion on your military records. Is there anyone here who is now *not* a Muslim? If there are, please step forward."

No one moved.

"Very good, gentlemen," Kasim said, "we have a special operation we need you for. If you could follow me into the hangar, we have assembled chairs and a briefing area. Once you are all seated I will begin to explain."

Kasim, followed by Skutter, walked toward the hangar.

The men filed behind. There was a series of blackboards surrounding a podium, several long folding tables with various weapons and devices displayed, a water cooler and several rows of black plastic folding chairs.

The men filed into their seats as Kasim and Skutter walked to the front.

49

EVEN IN A country as steeped in tradition as Saudi Arabia, the modern world has a way of intruding upon the past. The Prophet's Mosque in Medina was one such example. A massive construction project initiated in 1985 and completed in 1992 expanded and updated the facilities. The area was enlarged fifteenfold to cover an area of nearly 1.8 million square feet. The additional space allows almost three-quarters of a million visitors to be in the site at the same time. Three new buildings were added, along with a massive courtyard built from marble and inlaid with geometric designs. Twenty-seven additional courtyards topped with intricate retractable domes now graced the skyline, along with two more large areas that are topped with six large mechanical umbrellas that could be opened or closed depending on the weather.

Six minarets, soaring 360 feet in the air, were constructed around the perimeter—each topped with giant brass crescents weighing nearly five tons. Ornate tiled and gold gilding were added to various areas, and spotlights and beacons illuminated the various architectural details.

The physical plants were completely reworked. Escalators were installed to move the pilgrims to the upper levels, and a gigantic air-conditioning system was built. The cooling system, one of the largest ever constructed, pumps seventeen thousand gallons per minute of chilled water through pipes that were tunneled in under the lower level.

The entire system is managed from a control center a little over four miles from the mosque.

The rebuilding of the Prophet's Mosque and the additional construction around the Kaaba in Mecca were estimated to cost the Saudi Arabian government nearly $20 billion. The primary contractor for the massive construction project at the Prophet's Mosque was a company owned by the family of Osama bin Ladin.

THE LEADER OF the Indian mercenaries stared at the diagrams again. Before he boarded the ship in Rabigh, Hickman had made it clear he wanted the tomb of Muhammad at the Prophet's Mosque destroyed. The fact that bin Ladin had profited from the rebuilding galled him—Hickman wanted to erase the work from the planet.

A bonus of ten times their agreed-upon fee awaited the Hindus if they were successful.

They had been paid one million in gold so far—a king's ransom in their own country. Even split up among twelve men it was enough for each of them to live out the rest of their days in comfort. The additional ten million they had been promised would make them utterly rich.

All they needed to do was make it to Medina and sneak into the underground tunnels where the chilled water pipes ran under the mosque, lay the charges where the diagram directed them, and make their way back to Rabigh, where Hickman had another ship waiting to transport them across the Red Sea to Port Sudan, Egypt.

There a jet would be waiting with the gold and several guards. They would pass the next three days in Port Sudan. Once the Prophet's Mosque was destroyed on the morning of the tenth, the start of the hajj, the jet would fly them back to India with their gold. Performance before final payment was a lesson Hickman had learned decades before.

* * *

IF THERE IS one single key to a successful operation, that
key is to never rely on a single system. The Desert One affair during the Iranian hostage crisis in 1980 had proved
that doctrine. The president wanted to go in with the minimum number of helicopters, and once the first aircraft began to fail, the entire mission unraveled.

When faced with a question of having one weapon or
one thousand, you should always go for the largest possible
number. Systems fail, bombs can be duds, and weapons
jam.

Both Kasim and Skutter were aware of this fact.

"Sir, the primary threat right now is the shipping containers in Riyadh," Skutter said. "You have already verified
that they were delivered. And as soon as they are opened—
which has to be sometime before the start of the hajj,
which we believe everything else keys off—this entire operation could fall apart."

"The first case of viral poisoning and Saudi Arabia will
clamp down on everything," Kasim agreed.

The two men were standing in front of a map tacked to
a bulletin board in the hangar. On a table nearby were
stacks of Qatari passports and pilgrim documents for
Kasim and each of the thirty-seven team members. The
emir's government officials had been working on them all
night. Because they were real and not forgeries, they would
withstand any inspection by Saudi authorities. Since Saudi
visas were usually given to Qatari nationals without question, the men now had a way to gain access to the kingdom.

"Then we send in two teams of four men each," Kasim
continued. "That leaves us with thirty men to enter
Mecca."

Skutter pointed to an aerial map that the NSA had faxed
to Kasim in Qatar. The photograph showed the contain-
ment pen at the Riyadh Airport Cargo Facility. "Using the
tracking numbers your people recovered from the shipment in England, we can place the containers here."

Skutter circled the three containers with a highlighter.

"Damn good thing," Kasim said, "they paint stencil

identification numbers on the roofs of all the containers so the crane operators can see them. Otherwise we'd waste a lot of time searching through that mass of supplies."

"Once we have the two teams there," Skutter asked, "how do you want to handle it?"

"Secure and remove," Kasim said. "Once we establish that they are still sealed, we need to load them onto trucks and take them out into the desert until we determine what to do with them—either destroy them at that site or move them to a safe location."

"I read the personnel files," Skutter said. "We have a U.S. Army warrant officer whose name is Colgan. He's in Army Intelligence and has done some undercover work."

"Colgan?" Kasim said. "Sounds Irish."

"He converted to Islam in college," Skutter said. "His file shows an exemplary service record and notes that he is level-headed and methodical. I think he can handle this."

"Go ahead and brief him," Kasim said, "and handpick the rest of his team. Then get them on the next plane leaving Qatar for Riyadh. According to the emir's people, there is a shuttle flight that leaves here at six p.m."

"Very good, sir," Skutter said.

"That leaves us with the mosques in Mecca and Medina," Kasim said. "I'll lead the team into Mecca and you'll handle Medina. We'll each have fourteen men at our disposal, and our primary purpose will be to detect and disarm whatever type of destructive devices we believe Hickman has placed. We go in, search and remove, and get out again without being detected."

"What if Hickman has switched the meteorites?"

"The rest of my people are working on that as we speak," Kasim said.

THE INDIAN LEADER stared out the window of the house in Rabigh. The sun was set low in the sky and night would soon be upon them. It was about two hundred miles from Rabigh to Medina, or nearly four hours' drive time. Once there they'd need a few hours to check the lay of the land, find the access panel to the underground tunnel outside the mosque Hickman had marked on the diagram, and then enter.

It would take less than an hour to place the charges and exit the tunnel again.

Then there was the four-hour drive back to Rabigh. If the Hindus wanted to be on the boat to Egypt by sunrise tomorrow, January 6, as scheduled, they'd need to get moving.

After checking the crate of explosives again, the leader motioned for it to be carried outside to the truck. Eight minutes later they were driving down the road to Medina.

HANLEY WAS FINDING that Overholt's word was gold this time around. He was getting whatever he asked for. And he was getting it fast.

"We're ready to start beaming," Overholt said to Hanley over the phone. "Open up the link and check the picture quality."

Hanley motioned to Stone, who brought the images up on a monitor. Cameras at the entrance and exit to the Suez Canal were showing the passing ships as clear as if you were standing on the shore.

"Beautiful," Hanley said.

"What else do you need?" Overholt asked.

"Does the Agency have a Muslim agent in Saudi Arabia?"

"We have half a dozen," Overholt said.

"We need to know if the meteorite has been switched already," Hanley said.

"Even our people can't get inside the curtain," Overholt said. "There are four guards that walk the perimeter continuously."

"But they can get inside al-Haram mosque," Hanley said. "Have him come as close to the curtain as he can with a Geiger counter and then have him bow down and pray. If the Greenland meteorite is inside the curtain already, he should pick up radioactivity."

"Excellent," Overholt said. "We'll get on it right away and report back as soon as we know anything. What else?"

"We need overhead satellite shots of both mosques as

detailed as possible along with any engineering diagrams, floor plans, layouts or whatever else you can locate."

"I'll have a package assembled as soon as possible, and I'll have it sent by satellite transmission and followed up by a courier," Overholt said.

"Good," Hanley said. "The plan is for the Corporation to imagine we were Hickman and proceed as he would. Once we have the documents, we're going to assemble our team and plan how we would go about destroying the mosques if that was our mission."

"I'm staying in my office for the duration," Overholt said. "If you hear anything—or need anything—call at any hour."

"Thank you, sir," Hanley said. "We'll get this done for you."

UPON LANDING IN Tel Aviv, Cabrillo rented a car and drove as close as he could get to the Dome of the Rock. He entered through the gate near the al-Aqsa Mosque then crossed over into the courtyard where the Dome of the Rock was centered. The entire complex was some thirty-five acres in size, with garden and fountains and various shrines. The courtyard was crowded with tourists and scholars.

Cabrillo walked into the Dome building and stared at the spotlighted rock.

It was easy to see this was once the top of the hill—the rough outcropping jutted up, surrounded by a viewing area—but it was the history, not any particular physical attribute of the rock, that made it such a sacred site. For all intents and purposes, the rock looked like thousands of others nearby.

Cabrillo left the Dome building and headed underground to the Musalla Marwan.

The Musalla Marwan lies under the paved courtyard in the southeast corner of the complex. A vast underground area also known as Solomon's Stables, the subterranean space is domed and bisected by long walls with columns and arches. For the most part, the space is open floor and is now used as an overflow area for Friday prayers.

Here, in the cool underground, Cabrillo could feel the history seep into his bones.

Millions of souls had passed through here over the centuries, seeking a closer contact with their God. The area was quiet, with only the sound of water dripping from some faraway spring, and for a moment Cabrillo was hit with the gravity of Hickman's plans. Somewhere right now was a man so bound in hatred and infused with revenge for his dead son that he wanted to rid the world of three such places. Cabrillo felt a chill. Millions of men had fought and died nearby and their spirits felt close.

Cabrillo turned to leave.

Whatever nefarious plan Hickman had in store would start here—and it was up to Cabrillo and the Corporation to stop him in his tracks. He climbed up the stone steps and reentered the courtyard area. A dry wind brushed across him. He walked for the gate.

AT AN AIRFIELD near Port Said, Egypt, Pieter Vanderwald taxied to a stop in an ancient Douglas DC-3. The plane had served a long and useful life hauling cargo throughout the African continent. The twin-engine DC-3 is a legendary aircraft; thousands were built over the years, starting in 1935, and hundreds are still in service. The military version of the plane, the C-47, was used extensively in World War II, Korea, and even Vietnam, where they were outfitted as gunships. Also known as the Dakota, the Skytrain, Skytrooper, and Doug, it was most often referred to as Gooney Bird.

The Gooney Bird Vanderwald was piloting had one foot in the aviation graveyard.

Destined for the scrap yard in South Africa and lacking an air worthiness certificate, Vanderwald had purchased her for a song. Quite frankly, he was surprised she had made the trip north, but she had. Now, if the old plane had but one more flight in her bones, she could die a noble death.

The DC-3 is a tail dragger. The cockpit sits high to the front with the cargo compartment stretching back in an angle toward the runway. Her length is sixty-four and a half feet, her wingspan ninety-five.

Powered by a pair of 1,000-horsepower radial engines, she has a range of fifteen hundred miles and a cruising speed of between 155 and 190 miles per hour. With flaps extended, she can slow to almost a crawl before landing.

In an age when planes are as sleek and smooth as a knife, the DC-3 is an anvil. Solid, unyielding, and always ready, the plane asks little and goes about her job with little fanfare. She is a pickup truck in a parking lot full of Corvettes.

Vanderwald shut off the engines and slid back the cockpit window.

"Chock the wheels, fill her up," he shouted to the Egyptian attendant who had guided him to the spot on the runway. "And top off the oil. Someone will be here to pick her up soon for the next leg."

Then Vanderwald walked down the slanted cockpit area, unfolded the stair, and stepped onto the runway. Two hours later, he was in Cairo waiting for a flight back to Johannesburg. As soon as the funds were wired to his account, his part would be over.

CABRILLO ANSWERED HIS phone just as he was reaching the rental car.

"The Hawker just crossed over the edge of the Mediterranean," Hanley said. "It looks like she is bound for Rome."

"Call Overholt and have the plane impounded when it lands in Rome," Cabrillo ordered. "Maybe Hickman has decided to pull out."

"I doubt it," Hanley said.

"Me, too," Cabrillo said. "In fact, I'll bet that's not the case."

"Then how is he planning to make his escape?"

Cabrillo paused. "I don't think he is—I think he's planning a suicide mission."

The line was silent. "We'll factor that in," Hanley said at last.

"I have to go meet with the Mossad," Cabrillo said. "I'll call you after."

THE SUN WAS setting as the old pearling ship carrying Hickman entered the Khalij as-Suways at the northern end of the Red Sea. The five-hundred-mile trip from Rabigh had been slow but steady, and the ship would be entering the Suez Canal this evening as planned. The ship was cramped and Hickman had spent his time alternating between the small cockpit where the helmsman steered and the rear deck where the air was not polluted with the thin cigars the pilot chain-smoked.

Abraham's Stone was wrapped in a tarp on the deck next to Hickman's single bag, which contained a change of clothes, some basic toiletries, and a three-ring folder that he had been studying off and on the entire voyage.

"HERE'S WHAT I have," Huxley said as she walked into the control room. "I took the photographs Halpert and the others shot at Maidenhead, then erased the gas mask and used the biometric computer program to create a composite."

Hanley took the disc and walked over to Stone, who inserted it into the drive on the main computer. An image popped up on the monitor.

"Hell," Hanley said, "he doesn't look anything like the rumors."

"It's weird," Huxley agreed, "but it makes sense. If I was a recluse like Hickman, I would want to foster the most normal appearance I could have—that way I could blend in wherever I went."

"I guess the Howard Hughes rumors were just that," Stone said, "rumors."

"Click forward, Stoney," Huxley said.

Stone entered the commands. A 3-D image of the outline of a man appeared.

"This is a re-creation of his movements," Huxley said. "Each individual has unique mannerisms. Do you know what the security teams at casinos use to identify cheaters?"

"What?" Stone asked.

"Their walk," Huxley said. "A person can use disguises, alter his appearance, even some personal mannerisms—but no one ever thinks to change the way they walk or carry themselves."

Stone played with the computer and the image walked, turned and moved his arms.

"Let's make a copy and send it to Overholt," Hanley ordered. "He can distribute it to the Israeli officials."

"I can overlay this with the live cameras from the Suez," Stone offered.

"Do it," Hanley said.

AT THE SAME time Hanley was staring at the pictures of Hickman, eight men exited a commercial flight from Qatar to Riyadh and walked through customs without a hitch. Meeting outside the baggage claim area, they climbed into a white Chevrolet Suburban that the State Department had borrowed from an oil company official.

Then they made their way to a safe house to wait for nightfall.

"WE CAN DO what you need this evening," the head of Mossad, the Israeli intelligence agency, said, "but we can't use dogs—we'll have to do it with agents carrying chemical sniffers. Dogs in a mosque are a no-no."

"Will there be any problems?" Cabrillo asked.

"A few years ago when the Israeli prime minister went to the Dome of the Rock there was rioting for weeks afterward," he said. "We'll need to do it swiftly and quietly."

"Can your people completely cover the entire area?"

"Mr. Cabrillo," the man said, "Israel is faced with terrorist bombings on a weekly basis. If there are any explosives inside Haram al-Sharif, you'll know about it by sunrise tomorrow."

"And you will defuse anything you find?" Cabrillo asked.

"Defuse or remove," he said, "whatever is safer."

* * *

"MEN, PLEASE TAKE your seats," Kasim said.

The twenty-eight remaining men sat down. Skutter stood alongside Kasim at the blackboard. "Who here has never ridden a motorcycle?" Kasim asked.

Ten of the men raised their hands.

"This is going to be tough for you," Kasim said, "but we've assembled some instructors for a crash course. After we finish here, you ten will need to go outside and start practicing. In four hours' time you should all have a basic knowledge of the fundamentals."

The ten men nodded.

"Here's the situation," Kasim continued. "We cannot enter Saudi Arabia using a commercial flight. The risk of interception is simply too great. From here in Qatar to Mecca is over eight hundred miles, and that route is across bad desert with no fuel supplies, so what we came up with is this: the emir has arranged a cargo flight that will take us to Al-Hidayah in Yemen, and from there it is less than five hundred miles to Jeddah, Saudi Arabia, along a paved road that runs along the Red Sea. The emir paid off the Yemeni authorities and cleaned out a motorcycle distribution warehouse here in Qatar for our transportation. The motorcycles have a couple of advantages—the first is that we can cross the border above the checkpoint to avoid detection by driving across a stretch of desert then back to the road once we're inside Saudi Arabia. The second is the gas mileage—there are several cities along the road for fueling but they are far apart—the motorcycles can make it from city to city. The third is the most important. Each of us will be alone on our bikes—if the authorities stop one person, the entire mission is not compromised."

Kasim stared at the men.

"Does anyone have a problem with this?"

No one spoke.

"Good," Kasim said, "then if the men needing practice would follow Captain Skutter out onto the tarmac, we have cycles and instructors standing by for your training. The rest of you get some rest, we leave at ten tonight."

* * *

VANDERWALD DABBED SOME cologne under his nose. The first leg of his flight home was from Cairo to Nairobi, Kenya, and it was packed. The interior of the jet smelled like sweaty bodies and the lamb they had served for dinner.

AT THE SAME time Vanderwald was falling asleep, a pair of men approached his home in a Johannesburg suburb. Slipping around to the back, they slowly disabled the elaborate security system and unlocked the rear door and entered. Then they slowly and methodically began to search the inside.

Two hours later they were finished.

"Let me call and load his telephone onto the mainframe," one of the men said, "so they can scan for call records."

Dialing a number in Langley, Virginia, the man entered a code and waited for a beep. A CIA computer would take the number and search the South African telephone company's mainframe for a record of all calls out of and into the number for the last month. The results would be available in a few hours.

"What now?" the other men asked.

"We can take turns sleeping while we wait."

"How long are we going to be here?"

"Till he returns," the first man said, opening the refrigerator, "or someone else takes care of him first."

50

THE HINDU MERCENARIES arrived outside the hatch that led down to the water cooling pipes under the Prophet's Mosque in Medina. The hatch was located in an open space next to an apartment building on the far edge of a dirt lot used for overflow parking.

The lot was nearly empty, with only a dozen or so cars near the building itself.

The leader of the Hindus simply backed the truck up next to the hatch, cut the padlock with bolt cutters, and then led a team down the iron ladder into the tunnel. Once they were inside, the driver and another man who had stayed behind backed up on top of the hatch and waited.

The concrete tunnel was six feet in diameter with a series of pipes marked in Arabic that denoted their purpose. The pipes were propped up from the bottom of the tunnel on brackets, and there was a thin walkway along the side for inspections. The inside was dark and cool with the smell of wet concrete and mold. The leader turned on his flashlight and the other men followed suit.

Then they began walking single file toward the mosque. They had traveled nearly a mile underground before they came to the first fork. The leader stared at a handheld GPS. The signal was weak because of the concrete sheathing above his head, so he pulled out the tunnel diagram Hickman had provided and whispered to his men.

"You five go that way," he said, quietly pointing to the men. "The tunnel will arc around and eventually form a rectangle. Set charges as you go at the intervals we discussed, then meet up with us at the far side."

The one group set off along the tunnel to the right, the leader and his men to the left.

Forty-seven minutes later they all met up on the far side.

"Now we switch sides," the leader said. "You men go down our tunnel and check our charges as you go. We'll take yours and do the same."

The men set off in opposite directions, their flashlights waving through the tunnel.

At each of six spots along each passage, C-6 and sticks of dynamite were wrapped together in bundles almost a foot in diameter and attached to the pipes with duct tape. On each of the stations was a digital timer that was counting down the hours.

The first timer read 107 hr: 46 min. The charges were set to go off midday on the tenth, when the mosque would be crowded with nearly a million pilgrims. The amount of explosive force the Hindus had stowed would reduce the mosque to near rubble. The largest charge they placed, with double the C-6 and dynamite, was directly under the spot on the diagram showing Muhammad's tomb.

If the charges worked, in less than five days, centuries of history would be erased.

THEY MADE THEIR way back through the tunnel to the hatch that led up to the surface, and the leader climbed under the truck and slipped out the side. Stepping over to the driver's window, he tapped and the driver rolled it down.

"Pull forward," he said.

Once the men were back in the truck, the leader took out a padlock he had brought and relocked the hatch.

Four minutes later, under a thin sliver of moon, they set off back to Rabigh.

AT 6 A.M. THAT same morning, Hanley assembled the Corporation operatives in the conference room of the *Oregon*. The ship was offshore of Tel Aviv in the Mediterranean, making slow, lazy circles in the water. Hanley stared at a television screen showing the Robinson approaching from the bow.

"That's the chairman," he said, pointing. "He'll be leading the briefing. Until he makes it down here I want each of you to go over your notes. There's coffee and bagels on the side table. If you need something to eat, get it now. Once Mr. Cabrillo starts, I don't want any interruptions."

Hanley walked out to go to the control room for the latest updates. He picked them up from Stone and was just exiting the room again when Cabrillo and Adams walked past.

"Everyone's waiting for you in the conference room," he said, following the pair.

Reaching the conference room, Cabrillo opened the door and the three men walked inside. Adams, dressed in his flight suit, took a seat at the table. Hanley positioned himself next to Cabrillo, who walked behind the podium.

"Good to see you all again," Cabrillo began, "especially Gunderson and his team. It's nice to see they finally let you go," he said, smiling to Gunderson. "We'll need everyone for what is about to happen. I just returned from Tel Aviv and a meeting with the Mossad. They sent a large team into the mosque around the Dome of the Rock early this morning to search for explosives. Nothing of any type was located. Nothing conventional, nuclear or biological. They did locate a video camera that was not supposed to be there, however. It was hidden alongside a building inside a garden in a tree."

No one spoke.

"The camera was hooked to a wireless uplink that sent the images out to a processing unit outside the mosque, then on through a conventional cable to a nearby building.

The Mossad was making plans to enter the building when I left. They should have an update for me soon."

The group nodded.

"The interesting thing about the camera was that it was positioned to point up at the sky above the Dome of the Rock, just catching the top of the structure. This indicates to me that Hickman, if he has recovered Abraham's Stone, is planning some type of aerial assault that destroys the stone and damages the Dome of the Rock at the same time. His plan is to tape the destruction and somehow televise it to the world."

The team nodded.

"The situation with Mecca and Medina is this," Cabrillo continued. "Kasim and a United States Air Force officer will be leading a pair of teams, all comprised of U.S. military men who are Muslims, to check for bombs. I left Pete Jones in Qatar to coordinate things with the emir, who has offered to help us any way he can. I'll let Mr. Hanley explain those efforts."

Cabrillo stood away from the podium and Hanley took his place. Walking over to the coffeepot, Cabrillo poured two cups and took one over to Adams, who nodded his thanks.

"As you all know, Mecca and Medina are the two holiest sites to Islam. Because of that, they are off-limits to any non-Muslims. Kasim is the only member of our team who practices the Islamic faith, so he was selected to lead the teams. The emir arranged for a cargo plane and a fleet of multipurpose street and trail motorcycles to be shipped along with the members of Kasim's group to Yemen. They arrived early this morning and slipped across the border to Saudi Arabia by driving along a wadi, or dry streambed. The latest update shows them already past the Saudi town of Sabya and driving north. Then they will board public buses to take them to the two mosques. Once there, they will spread out and search for explosives."

"What about the shipping containers?" Halpert asked.

"As you all know," Hanley continued, "the team that was in Maidenhead discovered traces of a toxin that we believe was sprayed onto the prayer rugs inside the containers. Kasim dispatched eight men on a commercial flight to Riyadh and they have already taken up positions around the cargo area where the shipping containers are stored, awaiting delivery to Mecca. Quite simply, we caught a break there. If those containers had arrived on time, they probably would have been unloaded by now and the toxins would have been released into the air. As it was, Hickman was so late with the delivery that the trucks were rescheduled for other tasks. According to the schedule the NSA intercepted from the planner's PDA, he moved the delivery date to tomorrow, the seventh. The plan is to have the team at the cargo depot hook up the containers themselves and start down the road to Mecca. Somewhere between Riyadh and Mecca, we'll need to destroy them or move them out of the country."

Just then the telephone in the conference room buzzed, and Cabrillo walked over and answered. "Got it," he said, and hung the receiver back in the cradle. Hanley looked at him in expectation.

"That was Overholt," Cabrillo said. "His agent detected radiation near the curtain around the Kaaba. Hickman somehow managed to switch the meteorites."

IN LONDON, MICHELLE Hunt had spent the last few days cooped up in a hotel room being grilled by CIA agents. She was tired but still cooperating. Quite frankly, the CIA was beginning to realize there was little she could do to help their efforts. Right from the start they had dismissed the idea of her calling Hickman. Even if he was carrying a portable telephone, once he saw that she was not phoning from her usual number he'd know something was up.

A plane had been scheduled to fly her back to the United States, and it was scheduled to leave within the hour. For the most part, all Hunt had been able to do was shed some light on Hickman's life.

And that she had done in minute detail. They had asked her about everything, and she had complied. The agent in charge just needed to wrap up details on a few more points and he could submit his report.

"Now, back to the beginning," the agent said. "When you first met, you said he flew into Los Angeles to inspect an oil property he was thinking of purchasing."

"Yes," Michelle Hunt said, "we met that day at lunch at Casen's. I had a gift certificate from a girlfriend for a recent birthday. I was not in a position to afford expensive meals—even lunch—at that time."

"What happened next?"

"He came over to my table, introduced himself, and I asked him to join me," Hunt said. "We were there all afternoon. He must have known the owners because when the lunch crowd cleared out, they left us alone. They were setting the tables for dinner around us—but no one said anything."

"Did you eat dinner there that night?"

"No," Hunt said, "Hal arranged for us to fly over the oil field at sunset so he could check it out. I would guess he was trying to impress me."

"So you flew over the field and glanced at it from the window of the plane?"

"No windows," Hunt said. "It was a biplane. I sat in the seat behind."

"Hold on," the agent said, "it was a two-seater?"

"An old Stearman, if I remember correctly," Hunt said.

"Who was flying?" the agent asked.

"Well, Hal was," Hunt said, "who the hell else?"

"Mr. Hickman is a pilot?" the agent asked quickly.

"Well, he was back then," Hunt said. "If Howard Hughes did it, then Hal tried it too."

The agent raced for the telephone.

"THIS ADDS ANOTHER layer to the picture," Hanley said. "Now we not only need to recover Abraham's Stone from Hickman, we have to switch it back without being detected. The president has advised us that he wants to keep the Saudi government out of this operation if at all possible."

At that moment one of the hundred-inch monitors in the conference room lit up. The screen was split in half vertically, and Stone could be seen on the left side. "Sir, I'm sorry," he said, "I know you asked not to be interrupted, but this is important. Watch the other half of the screen."

An image filled the right half.

"This is from a pair of cameras the CIA stationed at the locks on the Suez Canal. The image was recorded within the last fifteen minutes."

The camera panned across an old work ship. A couple of crewmen were working the lines as the ship passed through the locks. A single man stood on the rear deck drinking coffee. The camera caught him looking up.

"I overlaid it with the program Ms. Huxley created," Stone said.

Everyone in the room watched as the 3-D image floated over the man. The edges of the lines matched up perfectly. When the man in the boat moved, the computer-generated re-creation tracked along.

"Sir," Stone said quickly, "that's Halifax Hickman."

"Where's the ship now, Stoney?" Cabrillo said.

The left side of the screen showed Stone in the control room glancing at another monitor. "She's out of the locks and slowing to come into Port Said, Egypt."

"George—" Cabrillo started to say.

"We should be fueled and ready by now," Adams said, rising from his seat.

Four minutes later the Robinson lifted from the deck. It was two hundred miles from the *Oregon*'s position to Port Said. But the Robinson would never reach Egypt.

51

VANDERWALD'S PLANE CAUGHT a tailwind and they arrived a half hour early.

Traffic was nonexistent; it would be another hour before commuters began to clog the roads heading to work, and he arrived in front of his house only fifteen minutes after stepping off the plane. He gathered a pile of mail from the mailbox on the street, slid it under his arm and carried his single bag to the front door.

Once he was inside the entryway, he set the bag on the floor and placed the mail on a desk.

He was just turning around to close the door when a man appeared from the side and the sound of footsteps came from the hall leading to the kitchen.

"Morning, shitbird," the first man said, pointing a gun with a silencer screwed to the barrel at Vanderwald's head.

The man said nothing else. He simply lowered the weapon and shot Vanderwald in both knees. Vanderwald dropped to the floor and began to scream in pain. The second man was in the entryway now, and he crouched by Vanderwald, who was rolling on the floor. "Do you want to explain this invoice we found on your computer for a DC-3?"

Two minutes and two well-placed shots later, the men had their answer.

A minute later the first man delivered the coup de grace.

The two men exited by the rear door and made their way through an alley off the rear of the house, then down a side street to where they had stashed their rental car. They slid into the seats, and the passenger peeled off his gloves and dialed his cell phone.

"The target just returned from delivering a DC-3 to Port Said, Egypt. He won't be a problem any longer."

"I understand," Overholt said. "You can come home now."

"I NEED A real-time shot of the airfield at Port Said, Egypt," Overholt said to the head of the National Security Agency. "We are looking for a DC-3 airplane."

The head of the NSA shouted instructions to his satellite technicians.

"We're redirecting," he said. "Hold on."

While he waited, Overholt reached in his desk drawer and removed his wooden paddle with the red rubber ball attached and began to furiously bang it back and forth. The wait, which took but a few minutes, seemed to stretch for hours. Finally the NSA head came back on the line.

"Stand by, we're directing the picture to you."

Overholt watched his monitor. An image of the airfield from high above filled the screen. Then it started to reduce itself until the DC-3 was visible. The image slowly reduced down and increased in detail. There was a man walking across the runway carrying what looked like a blanket close to his chest. He walked directly toward the DC-3 and, as Overholt watched, he began to open the side door.

"Keep on the DC-3," Overholt ordered. "If it lifts off, try to track it along."

"Will do," the NSA head said, disconnecting.

HANLEY WAS SITTING in the control room with Stone when the telephone rang.

"Here's where we're at," Overholt said quickly. "Ms. Hunt just disclosed to my agents that Hickman used to be a pilot. Two of my men met with the South African weapons broker a few minutes ago and he disclosed that he delivered a DC-3 for Hickman to Port Said yesterday. I have a satellite image up on the screen now that shows a man the approximate size of Hickman and matching the 3-D profile you sent, who is opening the door as we speak."

"That's it, then," Hanley interrupted. "He's going for the Dome of the Rock."

"We can't shoot him down or we lose Abraham's Stone," Overholt said. "We have to let him do the drop."

"Okay, sir," Hanley said, "let me warn Cabrillo."

HANLEY HUNG UP with Overholt and radioed out to the Robinson.

"Turn it around," Cabrillo said to Adams once Hanley explained.

Adams started a wide turn to the left.

"I want everyone but Murphy and Lincoln on the ground and at the Dome of the Rock ASAP," Cabrillo said. "Have those two start targeting the missile battery."

"It will be done right away," Hanley said.

"Call back Overholt and have him keep the Israelis at bay," Cabrillo said. "I want no planes in the air or any indication to Hickman that we are on to him."

"Roger."

"Then have Kevin Nixon call me back ASAP. I want to go over this thing of his one more time."

"WHERE TO, SIR?" Adams asked.

"Downtown Jerusalem," Cabrillo said, "the Dome of the Rock."

Adams punched commands into the GPS as the Robinson came over the coastline again.

* * *

THE OPERATIVES ON the *Oregon* were racing through the halls in preparation as Nixon made his way down the passageway to the control room. He opened the door and slipped inside.

Hanley hit the microphone button and Cabrillo instantly answered.

"I have Nixon here," Hanley said, handing him the microphone.

"Kevin?" Cabrillo said.

"Yes, sir."

"Are you sure what you have created will work? If you have doubts I need to know now."

"I calculated the weight and doubled the height estimate you gave me and it was still within limits," Nixon said. "As you know, nothing is perfect—but I'd have to say yes, it'll work."

"How long does it take for it to be load bearing?"

"Less than a minute," Nixon said.

"And you have enough of the material?"

"Yes, sir," Nixon said, "I produced more than we should need."

"Okay," Cabrillo said, "we're going with your idea. There is no backup plan, however, so this has to work."

"It will, sir," Nixon said, "but there is one problem."

"What?"

"We could lose the stone if it strikes the Dome."

Cabrillo was silent for a second. "I'll take care of that," he said.

HICKMAN HAD NOT flown a plane for more than two decades but it came back to him like it was yesterday. After he climbed into the pilot's seat, he went through the preflight and stoked up the engines. Puffs of smoke blew from the aging power plants as they were fired, but in a few minutes they settled down to a rickety fast idle.

Staring at the control panel, he located the various switches and made sure the crude autopilot was still hooked to the controls. Then, edging the old DC-3 forward, he called the control tower for clearance.

The airfield was quiet and he was given a runway immediately.

Easing the DC-3 forward, he tried the brakes. They were spongy but worked.

Hickman didn't mind the soft brakes—this would be the last time they would ever be used. The DC-3 was on her last journey. He rolled forward and did a slow turn onto the runway and lined up.

Checking the gauges one last time, Hickman rolled on the throttles, raced down the runway and rotated. The DC-3 lifted into the air and struggled to climb. Hickman had just over two hundred miles to travel.

At full speed, and with a slight tailwind, he'd be there in an hour.

"I HAVE THE shore boats in the water," Stone said, "and I've arranged an Israeli transport helicopter to ferry the team of ten from Tel Aviv to a location near the Dome of the Rock. The chopper is too large to use our pad. That's it there."

Stone pointed to a monitor that showed a camera image from the bow of the *Oregon*. The large double-rotor helicopter was just touching down on the sand in the distance.

"I'm going to the conference room," Hanley said.

He sprinted down the hall and opened the door of the conference room and burst inside. "Okay, people," he said, "the boats are ready and we have a chopper onshore to fly you the rest of the way. Is everyone up-to-date on what we're doing?"

The ten people all nodded.

"Mr. Seng is in charge," Hanley said. "Good luck."

The team began to filter out of the conference room, each holding a large cardboard box. Hanley stopped Nixon as he passed.

"Do you have the rope ladder?" he asked.

"It's here on this box on the top."

"Okay then," Hanley said, following him down the hall to the rear deck.

Hanley watched from the rear deck until the two boats were loaded and had set off the short distance toward shore.

Then he walked back inside to check on Murphy and Lincoln.

"WHERE AM I going to drop you off?" Adams asked.

"We're going right to the Dome of the Rock," Cabrillo said. "By then the team from the *Oregon* will have arrived."

"Then what?"

"Let me explain," Cabrillo said.

A couple of minutes later, when Cabrillo had finished, Adams whistled lightly. "With all the high-tech toys the Corporation has in its arsenal it's come down to this."

"It's like a high-wire act in the circus," Cabrillo agreed.

THE TEAM FROM the *Oregon* climbed off the helicopter on a closed street near the Dome of the Rock. Israeli tanks blocked all the side streets nearby and Israeli army platoons were sweeping the streets and the mosque of people. Crowds of Palestinians, not knowing their revered shrine was in jeopardy, began to protest and the Israelis had to keep them back with water cannons.

Seng led the team to the entrance to the mosque. "Spread out and take your positions," he told his team. "Kevin, make sure the rope is in place first."

"Yes, sir," Nixon said as the team trotted off into the mosque courtyard.

Seng turned to an Israeli army officer standing nearby.

"I need hoses attached to the fire hydrants on all sides and then run inside the mosque," Seng said. "Make sure we have enough hose to reach anywhere inside we want."

The officer began shouting orders.

HICKMAN FLEW ALONG over the Mediterranean. He was filled with a sense of a life at an end. And the life had been a failure. All his riches, the fame, and successes meant nothing in the end. The one thing he had wished to do right he had butchered. He had never been a good father to his son. Preoccupied with grandiosity and infused with a self-importance that allowed no other human being to come too close, he was never able to allow the love of a child for a parent to penetrate his shell.

Only Chris Hunt's death had caused it to open.

For Hickman the stages of grief had stopped at cold hatred. Anger toward a religion that fostered fanatics who killed without qualms, an anger toward the symbols they cherished.

Soon those symbols would be gone—and while Hickman would only see the first fruits of his labors, he knew he would die happy in the knowledge that the rest would soon crumble.

It would not be long now, he thought, as he glimpsed the first sight of the coastline.

Not long until Islam was ripped asunder.

NIXON AND GANNON unpacked a rope ladder from a cardboard box and quickly stretched it out on the courtyard alongside the Dome of the Rock. There was no way it would be long enough.

"I'll open the backup," Nixon said, cutting the tape on a second box with his knife and pulling out the second coiled ladder. "How are you with knots?"

"I own a sailboat," Gannon said, "so I guess I qualify."

Gannon began to splice the ends of the two ladders together. Around the Dome of the Rock, the other members of the team began to remove large plastic bags containing white powder from other cardboard boxes.

Near the entrance by the Silsila Minaret, Seng watched as the Israelis pulled hoses through the opening. "Leave them there," Seng ordered. "My people will take them the rest of the way inside."

Walking to all four sides of the massive mosque complex, Seng repeated the instructions. Soon, teams from the Corporation began pulling the hoses inside.

"Okay," Gannon said a few minutes later, "it's all together."

"Now we need to start at this side and carefully coil it up," Nixon said.

With Gannon pulling, Nixon formed the ladder into an orderly pile.

MURPHY STARED AT the trajectory lines on the computer screen, then turned and stared at Hanley. "Is there any budget on this little party?" he asked.

"None," Hanley said.

"Good," Murphy said, "because this little barrage is close to a million if you want guaranteed success."

"Go big or go home," Hanley said.

Lincoln was staring at a track line that showed the inbound DC-3. "Let's hope this course remains the same," Lincoln said, "and that what you hypothesize is true."

"From the angle of his camera," Hanley said, "it seems like he's going to come in low for the drop. That would make the destruction of Abraham's Stone more visible. If he dropped it from up high, he'd need to have the camera lens set on wide-angle and it wouldn't give the picture much detail when it shattered."

"I'm not worried about that," Lincoln said. "I'm worried about the second pass."

"To make sure the DC-3 destroys the Dome," Hanley said, "he has to know he'll need to climb up several thousand feet then dive down."

"We entered the climb rate of the DC-3 into the computer," Murphy said, "and set the parameters for two thousand feet extra elevation. That takes the flight out here."

Murphy pointed to the monitor.

"Perfect," Hanley said.

Murphy smiled. "Me and Lincoln think so too."

HICKMAN WAS STILL nine minutes away when Adams passed over the courtyard surrounding the Dome of the Rock and lowered the helicopter down to where Nixon was waving. Nixon raced under the spinning rotor blade and handed Cabrillo the end of the rope through the open door, then raced back away.

"Slow and steady," Cabrillo said through the headset.

"That's my middle name," Adams said confidently.

Carefully lifting off, Adams manipulated the controls with all the finesse of a surgeon. Bringing the Robinson up slowly, Adams crabbed sideways as Cabrillo played out the rope. A thin web began to form over the Dome. Reaching the far side, Adams hovered a few feet off the ground and Cabrillo dropped the end of the ladder. Meadows and Ross each took a side and pulled out the slack, then stood there holding the ladder taut. Nets hung down from the rope ladders.

"Now if you could drop me off on the top," Cabrillo said, smiling across the cockpit, "I'd appreciate it."

Adams lifted up slowly and carefully came close to the Dome. Cabrillo opened the door cautiously and stepped out onto the skid. Then with a little wave at Adams, he stepped across and grabbed the rope rung of the ladder.

Adams carefully backed away then landed on a street nearby.

Cabrillo was atop the Dome. He stared up at a large silver plane approaching in the distance. He pulled the nets as tight as he could.

"GO, GO, GO, go, go," Seng shouted to the seven members of the team.

They quickly began to spread the powder across the courtyard like farmers of old sowing seeds. Once they were finished, they ran to the fire hoses and waited for the orders to spray.

Nixon and Gannon were manning a hose. Nixon had the nozzle, Gannon was behind him holding the hose in place. "You're sure this will work, old buddy?" Gannon asked.

"It'll work," Nixon said. "It's the cleanup that will be a problem."

HICKMAN DIDN'T NOTICE that no Israeli jets had been scrambled to intercept him. He simply thought that his coming in low had brought the DC-3 under the radar.

Setting the autopilot, he walked back to the cargo bay and opened the door.

Abraham's Stone was still wrapped in the blanket. Hickman removed it and clutched it in his hands.

"Good riddance," he said quietly, "to you and all you stand for."

Through the side window he could see the mosque complex approaching. He had calculated that at the speed the DC-3 traveled, to hit the Dome itself he would need to toss out the meteorite just as the nose of the plane reached the edge of the first wall.

Hickman would never see the stone strike the Dome, but that's why he had cameras.

"NOW, NOW, NOW," Seng shouted as he heard the noise of the approaching DC-3.

The teams at the hoses opened the nozzles and sprayed the powder on the ground. The water was the catalyst. As soon as it hit the dust, the tiny grains of powder began to expand and interlock into a dense foam material. The dust grew to nearly two feet in height. Gannon felt himself rise in the air as the spray from the hose he was handling wet the dust beneath his feet. The weight of his body made an imprint of his feet in the foam.

HICKMAN STARED OUT the side window and timed the release. As soon as he saw the wall around the mosque he tossed out Abraham's Stone. Then he ran back toward the cockpit to start his climb for the suicide run while the heavy stone dropped through the air, end over end, toward the Dome.

IF THIS HAD been a movie, Cabrillo, clutching the ladder, would have batted the stone away from the Dome and saved the day. Or Abraham's Stone would have landed in the net and been saved. As it was, Cabrillo's presence atop his perch would prove unnecessary.

Hickman's toss fell short.

Had the foam not been applied to the courtyard, the stone would have shattered as it struck the marble flooring. Instead, it tumbled down and stuck in the foam a good ten feet from the edge of the Dome. Penetrating the surface of the foam almost a foot, it lay cradled and protected like a fine firearm in a custom-built case.

Seng raced over and stared down at the stone. "Nobody touches it," he shouted. "We have a Muslim CIA agent outside that will handle it."

SENG REACHED FOR his radio and called out to Hanley on the *Oregon*.

"I'll explain later, but the stone is secured," Seng said. "Could you radio Adams to pick the chairman back up?"

Hanley turned to Stone. "Make the call, please."

While Stone was on the radio, Hanley stood alongside Murphy and Lincoln at the firing station. One deck above off the rear of the *Oregon,* a computer-guided missile battery was slowly tracking the DC-3.

The DC-3 was traveling at three miles per minute. By the time Hickman had made his way back to the cockpit and gotten back into the pilot's seat to start the climb, he was ten miles past Jerusalem and about an equal distance from the Dead Sea.

Pulling back on the yoke, Hickman climbed higher.

"Thirty more seconds and any wreckage will be away from any Palestinian settlements," Lincoln said.

Hickman was far from an innocent; still, the Corporation were not murderers. If Hickman continued on toward Jordan, they'd try to catch him on the ground there. If he started a turn, they would have no choice. The only reason Hickman would turn back toward Jerusalem was to make a suicide run.

The DC-3 was seconds from crossing above the Dead Sea.

"Sir," Murphy said, "the computer detects the turn starting."

"You have sanction," Hanley said quietly.

"Time note," Lincoln said, reading off the date and time.

"Missiles away," Murphy said a split second later.

"Tracking," Lincoln said.

TWO MISSILES LEFT the firing platform, two packages of four from each side of a small glass dome that housed a radar tracking unit. The time interval between the two packages was but milliseconds, and they streaked from the ship across Israel and directly toward the DC-3. Like arrows shot from a warrior's bow they ran straight and true toward the target.

Adams was plucking Cabrillo off the Dome as the missiles streaked overhead. Quickly removing the rope and dropping it down to those on the ground, Adams pulled up on the collective and climbed above the mosque then edged the Robinson forward.

Hickman was almost sideways when for the briefest of seconds he saw two pinpoints of light coming from the distance. Before his mind could register what they were, they slammed into the fuselage of the DC-3.

Death came instantaneously as the shattered aircraft fell into the Dead Sea.

THE GLASS NOSE cone of the Robinson was facing the DC-3 far in the distance when the missiles found their mark.

"Secure the stone," Cabrillo radioed to Hanley on the *Oregon*. "I'm going out to the crash site."

52

"IT'S A MIXTURE of starches taken from rice powder along with the addition of a naturally occurring accelerant that makes it plump up," Nixon said.

Seng was staring at the courtyard surrounding the Dome of the Rock. A Muslim CIA agent who was assigned to Israel was carefully removing Abraham's Stone from the crust. The heavy object had penetrated the surface over a foot but was still cushioned by inches of the white blanket.

The CIA agent looked up at Seng and nodded that the stone was secure.

"How do we get this stuff off the courtyard?" Seng asked.

"I didn't have much time to test that," Nixon said, "but vinegar should do the trick."

Seng nodded, then reached onto his belt and removed a folding knife. He reached down and cut a square into the white blanket. Prying with the knife, he pulled up the chunk and held it in his hand.

"It's like a rice cake," he said, tossing the feather-light square in the air and catching it again.

"If we have someone cut it up with shovels," Nixon said, "then remove the biggest pieces, followed by wetting

the area with vinegar and brushing it with brooms, I think
all it will need then is a good hosing off."

THE SOUND OF the Robinson grew louder. The helicopter passed over the mosque then landed on a nearby street.
Seng was giving the Israelis instructions on the cleanup
when Cabrillo walked through the arched gate and into the
courtyard.

"The wreckage of the DC-3 landed in the Dead Sea,"
Cabrillo said to Seng. "The largest piece we could see on
the surface was about the size of a loaf of bread."

"And Mr. Hickman?" Seng asked.

"Whatever remains exist," Cabrillo said, "sleep with the
fishes."

Seng nodded and the men stood quietly for a moment.

"Sir," Seng said a moment later, "the stone is secured
and the cleanup of the mosque has been initiated. The
teams are ready for extraction."

Cabrillo nodded. "You're cleared for extraction," he
said, turning to the CIA agent. "Bring the stone and come
with me."

Placing the carefully wrapped stone into a wheelbarrow
used by the gardeners at the mosque, the CIA agent
grabbed the handles and followed Cabrillo toward the gate.

AT THE SAME time Cabrillo was walking toward the
Robinson, Hanley was conferring with Overholt over the
telephone.

"We've secured the stone and are withdrawing from Israel," Hanley said. "How are your contacts in Egypt?"

"Excellent," Overholt said.

"And the Sudan?"

"Our man there is top-notch."

"Here's what we need," Hanley said.

Overholt made notes as Hanley explained. "Okay," he
said when Hanley finished, "Al Ghardaqah, Aswan, and
Ras Abu Shagara, Sudan. I'll arrange the clearances and
have one-hundred-octane fuel at each stop."

* * *

HANLEY WAS JUST disconnecting as Halpert walked into the control room holding a file folder stuffed with papers. "I think I have Medina figured out," he said. "I lifted the blueprints from the contractor's computer base and studied them for the last hour."

"Blueprints?" Hanley asked. "It was built hundreds of years ago."

"But enlarged and modernized 1985 through 1992," Halpert said. "At that time they bored underground tunnels to run water lines for an air-conditioning system. You told me to think like Hickman—if I was him, that's where I'd place charges."

Hanley stared at the diagrams for a moment. "Michael," he said a second later, "I think you nailed it."

"Remember that," Halpert said, smiling, "at bonus time."

Halpert walked out of the control room and Hanley reached for a telephone. While the number was ringing, he turned to Stone. "Pull up a satellite shot of Medina for me."

Stone began to enter commands into the computer just as the phone was answered.

"YES, SIR," KASIM said.

"What's the progress?"

Kasim was standing just off to the side of a crowd of people at the Jeddah bus terminal.

"Both teams made it safely here," Kasim said. "We stashed the motorcycles in a dry wash outside of Jeddah and made our way into the city. Skutter, who's heading the Medina operation, and his team have already boarded a bus for the city. My team are I are waiting for ours now."

"And Skutter has a satellite phone with him?"

"Yes, sir."

"How long until his bus arrives?" Hanley asked.

"Four to five hours," Kasim said.

"I'll wait until he arrives to call him, but we think we know where the charges were placed at the Prophet's Mosque."

The bus was just pulling up.

"My bus is here," Kasim said. "What do you want us to do?"

"You'll be met by a CIA contact in Mecca and taken to a safe house," Hanley said. "I'll call you there."

"Got it."

PETE JONES LOOKED over to the emir of Qatar. "Your Excellency," he said, "how are your relations with the Bahrainis?"

"Great," the emir said, "they are dear friends."

"Can you have trucks waved through customs without any problems?"

"I'm sure I can."

"Do you have a cargo ship available that can pick them up at the port in Bahrain?"

The emir stared over at his aide, al-Thani.

"I'll arrange one here or in Bahrain immediately," al-Thani said.

"We have about six hours before everything needs to be in place," Jones said.

"It shall be done, Mr. Jones," the emir said. "It shall be done."

INSIDE THE FENCED cargo area alongside Riyadh Airport, U.S. Army Warrant Officer Patrick Colgan and his team were still awaiting instructions. They had spent three nights hiding under the containers, eating from their food supplies and drinking their bottled water. Now supplies were running low on both, and the containers around them that gave them cover were growing thinner and thinner.

Something needed to happen—and happen quickly.

JONES STUDIED THE file taken from Al-Sheik's PDA, then reached for the telephone.

"Sir," he said when the phone was answered, "have you

received any changes to the shipping time for the cargo containers?"

"No changes," Hanley said.

"Okay, then," Jones said, "I've got the out."

Hanley listened while Jones explained.

"I like it," Hanley said, "simple and sweet."

"I'm cleared?"

"Do it," Hanley said.

THE AREA AROUND the three shipping containers where the men were hiding was gradually being cleared. There was still a scattering of containers to the left, but to the right was only bare sand and gravel.

Colgan's telephone rang quietly, and he pushed the button to answer. "Colgan," he said.

"This is Jones in Qatar."

"What have you got for us, Mr. Jones? We are nearly out in the open here. We need to do something quick."

"In ten minutes three trucks are due to arrive to pick up the containers," Jones said. "The trucks all have GPS locators attached to the rear of the cabs. The locators are about the size of a pack of cigarettes and are secured by a magnet. Have three of your men act as lot workers helping the trucks hook up. Have the men remove the locators as the trucks back in, otherwise you'll be tracked."

"Okay," Colgan said.

"Tell the three men with the locators to attach them to an uncontaminated container, then have them jump into another truck and catch a ride to Mecca. The people tracking the shipment should just think that the trucks are following close behind each other."

"What should my men do when they reach Mecca?"

"Jump out of the trucks before they reach the unloading terminal and discard the locators in the first trash cans they see. Then they need to catch a bus down to Jeddah and make their way to the port area. Once there, they will find a shore launch marked *Akbar II*. Have them board the boat and they will be transported offshore."

"*Akbar II,*" Colgan repeated.

"Now the five of you that remain will have to overpower the drivers and take the trucks yourselves. Bind and gag the drivers and place them on the passenger side on the floor. Then simply drive through the gate, and when you reach the main road, go east instead of west. Your ultimate destination is Bahrain."

"Okay," Colgan said.

"Now," Jones said, "since after the three leave for Mecca you still have five men, you'll be crowded in two of the trucks—your driver and passenger, plus the bound-and-gagged one you've overpowered. Make sure your extra man ducks under the blanket when you pull from the gate so they don't notice."

"Won't they stop and check us?" Colgan asked.

"We've had someone watching the gate today," Jones said. "They check for the correct truck on the way in, then they just mark down the container number as it passes loaded through the gate."

"But what happens when the cargo is missing and they find the locators?" Colgan asked. "Won't they start looking for us then?"

"The trip from Riyadh to Mecca takes six hours," Jones said. "It's only four to Bahrain. Once they figure out the containers are missing, you'll be on a cargo ship bound for Qatar."

"And you're sure we can make it through the border checkpoint into Bahrain?"

"It's all been taken care of."

"Sweet plan," Colgan said.

"Good luck."

FIFTEEN MINUTES LATER, Colgan and the four other men bound for Bahrain made it safely out of the cargo terminal and started down the road. Seven minutes after that, a Coast Guard petty officer named Perkins, along with two others, attached the locators to three trucks in a six-truck convoy, then climbed inside the last truck.

The truck was filled with bottles of water, so at least

they would not be thirsty on the six-hour haul to Mecca. If only the truck had had a pallet of M&M's aboard, the ride would have been more enjoyable.

IT WAS ALMOST noon when Adams, Cabrillo and the CIA agent handling Abraham's Stone landed at the first fuel stop at Al Ghardaqah, Egypt, at the mouth of Khalij as-Suways on the entrance to the Red Sea.

Overholt not only had the promised fuel, but food, water, coffee and a U.S. Army helicopter mechanic to check the R-44. The mechanic added half a can of oil to the piston engine and did a quick check of the craft, then pronounced the Robinson fit as a fiddle. The three men made a quick bathroom stop then took off again.

The next leg of the flight, some two hundred miles to Aswan, was made in less than two hours at a speed of 125 miles per hour. The helicopter was fueled and checked again and the trio set off.

Aswan to Ras Abu Shagara, the dangling peninsula of land that jutted into the Red Sea across from Jeddah in Saudi Arabia, was the longest leg of the flight. Some 350 miles in length, the flight would take nearly three hours.

The Robinson was thirty minutes out of Aswan high above the desert when Adams spoke. "Sirs," he said, "it will be a couple of hours until the next stop. If you want to get some sleep it's okay by me."

The CIA agent in the rear seat nodded, crouched down and pulled his hat down over his eyes.

"You okay, George?" Cabrillo asked. "You've been flying a lot lately—how are you holding up?"

"I'm ten by ten, boss," Adams said, smiling. "I'll take us down to the Sudan, then across the Red Sea and drop you—once I'm back in Sudan I'll get some shut-eye."

Cabrillo nodded. Slowly, as the helicopter droned south, he fell into a sleep.

THE TIME WAS just after 4 P.M. when Hanley on the *Oregon* made the satellite call to Skutter. With no clear direction yet on how to proceed, Skutter and his team had been milling around the bus terminal waiting for a contact.

"My name is Max Hanley, I'm Mr. Kasim's superior."

"What do you want us to do?" Skutter asked quickly.

Several people had approached his team already and only one of the men with him could speak even a smattering of Arabic. If they stayed here any longer they might be detected.

"To your left," Hanley said, "is a beggar with an old tin plate who looks like he's sleeping. Do you see him?"

"Yes," Skutter said.

In between bouts of what looked like napping, the man had been staring at his team for the last twenty minutes.

"Go over to him and place a coin in his plate," Hanley said.

"We don't have any coins," Skutter whispered. "We were only issued bills."

"Then use the smallest bill you have," Hanley said. "He will hand you what looks like a religious pamphlet. Take the pamphlet, walk a safe distance away from the terminal to a side street, then find somewhere you can read it without being observed."

"Then what?"

"Your instructions are inside."

"Is that all?" Skutter asked.

"For now," Hanley said, "and good luck."

SKUTTER DISCONNECTED THEN whispered to one of his men. Then he walked over to the beggar, removed a bill from a stack in his pocket, bent over, and slipped it on the plate.

"Allah will reward you," the beggar said in Arabic, handing him the pamphlet.

Skutter was bending back to an upright position when the briefest of winks flickered across the beggar's left eye. Suddenly Skutter was feeling a renewed hope. Making his way away from the bus station followed by the other men, he found a deserted area and read the instructions. It was only a few blocks to his destination and he ate the entire pamphlet as he walked.

"DO NOT GO outside," the CIA contact said to Kasim and his team at the safe house in Mecca, "do not do anything to draw attention to yourself. There is food, water, and soft drinks in the kitchen."

"How do we reach you if we need to?" Kasim asked.

"You don't," the contact said. "You wait for your people to give you any further instructions. I was told to stock the house, meet you at the terminal and bring you here. That ends my involvement. I wish you luck and Godspeed."

The CIA man made his way to the door and exited.

"THAT SEEMS ODD," an army private in Kasim's team offered.

"Everything is compartmentalized," Kasim said. "Each piece of this operation will remain separate until it is time to bring it together. Now we all need to get some rest and take turns getting cleaned up. I want everyone to eat a good meal and try to relax. Soon we will be called, and when we are, it'll be go time."

The team nodded.

THE SUN WAS setting as Adams approached the *Akbar* from the Red Sea. Passing over the yacht once to alert the crew, he lined up over the stern and dropped slowly down. Al-Khalifa's Kawasaki helicopter was still on the heliport, so he hovered a few feet above the yacht, just above a clear spot on the stern. The CIA agent dropped Abraham's Stone safely packed in a box with padding to the deck, then leapt off.

"Overholt's men are waiting for you back at Ras Abu Shagara," Cabrillo said. "Will you be okay?"

"Yes, sir," Adams said.

The CIA agent was carrying the box toward the rear

door of the *Akbar*. Cabrillo stepped off and crab-walked
out from under the rotor blade. Adams lifted off again.

AT JUST THAT moment Cabrillo's phone rang.

"Threat one is eliminated," Hanley said. "The cargo
containers are on board a ship just now leaving Bahrain for
Qatar."

"No problems?"

"All went as planned," Hanley said. "Three men will meet
the *Akbar*'s shore boat in Jeddah. You'll need to have them
transported out to the yacht—their part in the operation is
finished."

Kent Joseph, part of a Florida team who had been contracted to handle the *Akbar* for the Corporation, poked his
head out of the door, and Cabrillo smiled and raised his finger for the captain to wait a minute.

"Skutter?"

"He has the diagrams and we're sending him and the
team in this evening," Hanley said. "If that's successful,
it'll be two down, one to go."

"How are you coming on that plan?" Cabrillo asked.

"I'll call you back soon."

The telephone went dead and Cabrillo placed it in his
pocket. Then he smiled and reached his hand out to Joseph.

"Juan Cabrillo," he said, shaking. "I'm with the Corporation."

"Is that like *the Agency*?" Joseph asked.

"Heck, no," Cabrillo said, smiling. "I'm not a spy."

Joseph nodded and motioned to the door.

"But he is," Cabrillo said, waving toward the CIA agent.

53

IT WAS DARK when Coast Guard Petty Officer Perkins and the other two men inside the last truck in the convoy felt their vehicle begin to slow. Perkins peered out the crack between the cargo doors. There were scattered buildings along the road and the lights of a car following. He waited almost five minutes before the car, finding a clear spot in the road to pass the trucks, accelerated and sped past.

"Okay, guys," Perkins said, "we need to jump out."

Upon climbing inside, Perkins had rigged the door to open again so exiting was not a problem. The problem was the speed of the truck—it was still moving at over thirty miles an hour. He watched the side of the road out the rear.

"Men," he said a minute later, "there is really no easy way to do this. Our best shot is to wait until we see sand along the left side of the truck, then you two grab the top of the door and I'll push it open. The swing should get you near the side of the road—just drop off as soon as possible."

"Won't the driver notice?" one of the men asked.

"Maybe if he's staring in the rearview mirror at that exact instant," Perkins admitted, "but the door should swing back afterward, and if he *doesn't* notice it immediately, he should be farther down the road before he catches on that the door is open."

"What about you?" the third man asked.

"All I can do," Perkins said, "is run and jump as far as I can."

The buildings were giving way to a less populated area just outside Mecca. Perkins stared through the gloom. "I don't know, guys," he said a second later. "I guess this is as good a spot as any."

Perkins boosted them up so they could grab the top of the door frame. Then a second later he pushed it out. The door swung outward, the two men dropped to the ground and rolled end over end in the sand. Perkins backed up as far as he could in the crowded shipping container and ran from the right side of the container toward the left then leapt into the air. Perkins's legs windmilled through the air as he flew.

The truck, door flapping, receded into the distance. They were alone, with only the lights of Mecca a few miles away lighting the desert sky.

Perkins tore some skin off his knee and realized that he had also wrenched it upon landing. He lay on the ground just off the road. The other two men, one bleeding from an elbow abrasion, the other with a red spot on his face where he had scraped it against the sand, helped Perkins to his feet.

Perkins's knee gave out and he crumbled to the ground.

"Take the phone I was given," he said, reaching into his pocket and handing it to one of the men, "and push number one. Explain what happened to whoever answers."

BACK ON THE *Oregon*, Hanley reached for the ringing telephone.

"Okay, hold on a second," he said after the man explained.

"Get me GPS on this signal," he shouted to Stone, who punched the commands into the computer.

"Got a lock," Stone said a minute or so later.

"Is there a spot off to the side of the road where you're not visible?" Hanley asked the man.

"We're right alongside a wash," the man said. "There's a dune above."

"Start climbing the dune and take cover," Hanley said. "Leave the line open—I'll get back to you in a second."

Reaching for another phone, Hanley dialed the number of the CIA station chief for Saudi Arabia on the number Overholt had given him. "This is the contractors," he said when the man answered. "Do you have any agents in Mecca right now?"

"Sure," the station chief answered. "We have a Saudi national on the pad."

"Does he have a car?"

"He drives a Pepsi delivery truck."

"We need him to drive to these GPS coordinates," Hanley said, "and pick up three men. Can you do that?"

"Hold on," the station chief said as he dialed the Pepsi driver's cell phone.

Hanley could hear him explaining in the background.

"He's leaving now," the station chief said, "he thinks it's about twenty minutes away."

"Tell him to honk when he reaches the area," Hanley said. "Our men will come out of hiding then."

"Where is he taking them?" the station chief asked.

"Jeddah."

"I'll call if there are any problems."

"No problems," Hanley said. "We don't like any problems."

Hanley hung up on the station chief, then grabbed the other phone and explained the plan.

HANLEY MAY NOT have liked problems but that was exactly what he was faced with.

The conference room was filled with Seng, Ross, Reyes, Lincoln, Meadows, Murphy, Crabtree, Gannon, Hornsby and Halpert. All ten of them seemed to be talking at once.

"We can't do anything from the air," Lincoln said, "they'll see that coming."

"No time to tunnel," Ross said.

"The key," Halpert said to Crabtree, "was how Hickman got it out in the first place."

"I can arrange a pyrotechnic display to divert them," Murphy said, smiling at Hornsby, "but we're here on the *Oregon,* in the Mediterranean, and they're there, in Saudi."

"Tear gas?" Reyes offered to the room.

"Cut the power?" Meadows mentioned.

Seng stood up. "Okay, people," he said, "let's get some order here."

As the highest-ranking man, he was in charge of the brainstorming session.

Seng walked over to the coffeepot to pour another cup. He was talking as he walked. "We have less than an hour to come up with a cohesive plan the team on the ground can execute if we want to do this thing tonight—and we do."

He finished pouring the coffee and walked back to the table. "Like Halpert said—how did Hickman get the meteorites switched in the first place?"

"He had to somehow disable the guards," Meadows said. "There is no other way he could have pulled if off."

"Then why wasn't the theft discovered soon after," Seng asked, "and reported?"

"He had an inside man," Murphy said, "that's the only way."

"We checked out the guards," Seng said. "If one of them was on to what was happening, he'd be out of Mecca by now. They're all still on the job."

The conference room was quiet for a moment as the team thought.

"You said you checked out the guards," Linda Ross said, "so you have the schedules and such?"

"Sure," Seng said.

"Then the only way I see this going down is to switch all four," Ross said.

"That's good," Halpert said, "hit them at shift change—replace the oncoming guards with our team."

"Then what?" Seng asked.

"Turn off the power to all of Mecca," Reyes said, "and have them make the switch."

"But then we have four guards that will be found at the next shift change," Seng said.

"Boss," Gannon said, "by then the teams from Qatar will be safely away and the Saudis can do what they will."

The room was quiet for a second as Seng thought.

"It's crude," he said at last, "but doable."

"Sometimes you need to split a coconut with a rock to get to the milk," Gannon said.

"I'll take it to Hanley," Seng said, rising.

WHILE THE PLANNING session on the *Oregon* was finishing, Skutter and his team found one of the hatches leading into the tunnel beneath the Prophet's Mosque and slipped inside. They were only five minutes underground when the first of the explosive packages was located.

"Spread out up the tunnel," Skutter said to the others, "and find out how many of these there are in here."

Then he turned to the only man on his team with any training in demolition. "What do you think?"

The man smiled, reached in his pocket for wire cutters and pulled them out. Reaching down, he pulled up a wire and snipped it in two. Finding a few others, he cut those as well, and then started unwrapping the duct tape from the pipe.

"Crude but damned powerful is how I'd describe these," the man said, laying the C-6 and the dynamite separately on the ground of the tunnel.

"That's it?" Skutter said in exasperation.

"That's it," the man said. "One thing, however."

"What's that?"

"Be careful and don't kick or drop the dynamite or anything," the man said. "Depending on its age, it could be unstable."

"Don't worry," Skutter said, "we're leaving it here."

Within two hours the charges would all be disabled and the tunnel would be checked then double-checked to make sure. Then Skutter could call and report.

* * *

WHILE THE DEMOLITION man was snipping the wires on the first explosive package, Hanley was phoning Cabrillo on the *Akbar*.

"That's what we've got, boss," he said after he finished filling Cabrillo in on the plan they had come up with. "It's crude, I'll admit."

"Have you spoken to Kasim yet?" Cabrillo asked.

"I wanted you to clear it first."

"I'm with it," Cabrillo said. "Why don't you fax me everything you have so I can brief the CIA man. Meanwhile, I'll call Kasim and report what we came up with."

"I'll send it now."

"YOU'LL NEED TO move fast," Cabrillo explained to Kasim. "Shift change is at two a.m."

"What about any explosives?" Kasim asked.

"The CIA man who's delivering Abraham's Stone will have a dozen chemical sniffers. Have the rest of the men in your team spread out and search while you do the switch."

"Okay," Kasim said.

"You have an hour and forty minutes for you and your team to make your way to the Great Mosque, observe the guards so you understand the procedures, then find the incoming guards, disable them and take their places. Can you do it?"

"It would seem we have no choice."

"This is all riding on you, Hali," Cabrillo said.

"I won't let you or my religion down," Kasim said.

"I'll finish briefing the CIA agent and send him on his way," Cabrillo said. "There's a car and driver waiting to take him to Mecca as we speak. He'll enter the Great Mosque at ten minutes after two if he doesn't hear gunfire."

"We'll be there," Kasim said.

The telephone went dead, and Kasim turned to his team. "Listen up," he said, "we have our orders."

CABRILLO TOOK THE sheets from the fax and quickly briefed the CIA agent. Once that was done, he boarded the shore boat with the agent for the ride across the water to the port of Jeddah. It was a pleasant night, seventy-five degrees with almost no breeze. The moon was waning and cast a pale glow on the water as the boat skimmed across the placid sea.

The lights of the *Akbar* faded and the ones of Jeddah loomed larger.

AS SOON AS the Pepsi truck pulled up by the dune and honked, Perkins and the other two men in hiding peered over the dune, waited until there was no traffic coming down the road, then made their way to the road. Perkins's knee was heavily swollen and one of the men supported him as the other approached the truck.

"You here for us?" the man asked the driver.

"Hurry up and get in," the driver said, reaching across the cab and opening the passenger door.

Once the three men were situated, the driver spun around in a U-turn, then headed toward the lights of Mecca. Skirting the main part of the city on an expressway, he was two miles down the road to Jeddah before he spoke.

"You guys like the Eagles?" he asked as he slid a CD into the player.

The first cut on *Hotel California* began to play as they drove through the night.

AS SOON AS the shore boat reached land, the CIA agent climbed off and raced to a waiting Chevrolet Suburban. A minute later the Suburban spun off, throwing gravel from the rear tires as he raced away.

"What now brown cow?" one of the Florida mechanics who was piloting the shore boat asked.

"Now we back off and wait for a Pepsi truck," Cabrillo said.

The mechanic put the drive in reverse and started backing away. "So you men are Pepsi smugglers?" he asked.

"Is there a radio aboard?" Cabrillo asked.

The mechanic turned a dial on the dash. "What's your poison?"

"Find the news," Cabrillo said.

Cabrillo and the mechanic sat in the moonlight, bobbing in the bay.

A CHEVROLET SUBURBAN blew past the Pepsi truck headed in the opposite direction just as the driver exited off the main road onto the one to Jeddah's port. The driver steered down the road he was instructed to take, then pulled to a stop with the nose of the truck facing the sea. He flashed the lights three times, then waited.

A SHORT DISTANCE out in the water, the tiny red lights from the bow of a boat answered.

"Okay, men," the driver said, "I'm done here. There's a boat coming in to get you."

The first man climbed out of the cab and helped Perkins to the ground. Once the two men had stepped away from the cab, the last man climbed down.

"Thanks for the ride," he said, closing the door.

"I'll send you the bill," the driver shouted through the open window as he started his engine and backed out.

The three men made their way out to the edge of the water just as the *Akbar*'s shore boat edged itself on land. Cabrillo slipped over the side and helped the three men aboard, then climbed back inside.

"Home, James," he said to the mechanic.

"How'd you know my name was James?" the mechanic asked, backing away from shore.

As soon as Perkins and his men were safely on board, Cabrillo ordered Joseph to begin steaming north up the coastline at high speed.

ON THE *OREGON*, Hanley was monitoring the various operations. It was just after 1 A.M. when the truck that had been dispatched to pick up Skutter and his men reported that they had left Medina and were racing toward Jeddah.

The distance was a little less than a hundred miles.

Barring any surprises, part two was almost completed.

Hanley reached for the phone and called Cabrillo.

"Jones met up with the group with the prayer rugs and all is well," he said. "They have been doused with antiviral agents, given clean clothes, and are now sleeping. Team two in Medina has completed their mission and is on their way toward you now. They should be arriving in a few hours."

"They found explosives?" Cabrillo asked.

"Apparently enough to level the Prophet's Mosque," Hanley said. "They disabled them and left them in the tunnel. The CIA or someone will eventually need to handle that."

"Then it's all up to Kasim," Cabrillo said.

"So it seems."

AT THAT EXACT instant, Kasim and his team were approaching the mosque containing the Kaaba. Even being U.S. citizens did not provide the team much comfort—they were deep inside a foreign country whose capital punishment was beheading. And they were entering the holiest of the country's sites for a mission that could be easily mistaken for a terrorist action. The fourteen servicemen and Kasim were very conscious of that fact.

One mistake, one misstep, and the entire operation would unravel.

AT THE SAME time Kasim was walking through one of the gates leading into the courtyard where the Kaaba was sheathed in cloth, a C-17A troop transport plane was lifting off the runway in Qatar. The Boeing-built jet, a replacement for the venerable Lockheed-Martin C-130 prop plane, could carry 102 troops or 169,000 pounds of cargo.

Designed to land on either short or rough dirt airfields, she was manned by a crew of three. The C-17A had a range of three thousand miles and tonight she would need that.

After leaving Qatar on the Persian Gulf, she was scheduled to fly out over the Gulf of Oman and into the Indian Ocean. There she would turn, fly over the Arabian Sea, into the Gulf of Adan, then through the gap between Yemen and Djibouti, Africa, and into the Red Sea. She would loiter there until called or released.

The C-17A was the ace everyone hoped they would not need to deal.

KASIM WALKED FARTHER inside the mosque, then he and four others hid off to the side and watched the guards walk through their routine from a distance. It seemed simple enough. Every five minutes the guards would walk from one corner to the next in a clockwise direction. The exaggerated steps they used looked simple enough to duplicate.

Kasim studied the plans he had, seeking out the small stone building inside the mosque that the guards used to change from their street clothes into their uniforms. Locating it on the hand-drawn diagram, he motioned for the men with him to stay in place, and then he walked back to where the rest of his group was hiding.

"You stand guard," he said to one of the men, "and whistle if you need to attract our attention."

"What am I looking for?" the man asked.

"Anything that doesn't look right."

The man nodded.

"I want the rest of you to follow me. We are going to sneak over to that structure," he said quietly, "and wait for the first incoming guard to arrive. I'll take him down as soon as he unlocks the door to the building."

The men nodded their assent.

Then they fanned out across the mosque, slowly sneaking toward the small stone building. A few minutes later they were all in place.

ABDUL RALMEIN WAS tired. His schedule as a guard rotated throughout each month. Sometimes his four-hour shift took place in the heat of day, sometimes at sunrise—

the time he liked best—and sometimes at 2 A.M., like tonight. It was the late-night shifts he had never learned to adjust to—his personal clock stayed the same, and when his time came to work through the night, it took everything he had to fight off sleep.

Finishing a steaming cup of coffee flavored with cardamom seed, he slid his bicycle into a rack on the street near the Great Mosque and locked it with a chain and padlock.

Then he walked toward the entrance and through the gate.

He was partway across the courtyard when the shrill whistle from a bird sounded.

Rubbing the sleep from his eyes, he slid the keys from his pocket as he neared the building. He grasped the padlock and slid the key in the slot. He was just twisting the lock open when he felt a hand across his mouth and a tiny prick on his arm.

Ralmein grew even more sleepy.

KASIM OPENED THE door to the room and dragged Ralmein inside. Flipping the light switch on the wall, a single bulb lit up and illuminated the crowded space. The inside of the building wasn't much—a rack against the wall holding uniforms in plastic sleeves to keep them clean, a large laundry-type sink, and a toilet behind a curtain.

On the wall, attached with tacks to a corkboard, was the schedule for the coming week. On the wall next to it was a framed photograph of King Abdullah and another of the Great Mosque during the hajj, taken from the air, showing crowds of people. The only other thing was a round black-edged clock. It read 1:51 A.M.

KASIM HEARD WHAT sounded like the hoot of an owl. He turned off the light and waited.

The second guard walked through the open door and reached for the light switch. He flicked in on, and for the briefest of seconds saw Kasim standing there. The image was so shocking to his mind that it didn't register for a second. By the time it did, Kasim had wrapped his arms around him and pricked him with the needle.

The guard was placed alongside Ralmein.

Right at that instant, Kasim heard the voices of two men approaching. He had no time to reach the light switch to turn it off, no time to hide. The two men walked through the open door and stared at him.

"What the—" one started to say just before two of Kasim's team hiding outside blocked the exit.

The fight was almost over before it began.

"You," Kasim said to one of the men, "go back to the gate and bring the others here."

The man raced off.

"You six fan out and start searching for bombs," Kasim said. "When the sniffers arrive, we'll send them over to you. For now, just look. If you find anything, leave it alone."

The six men crept away into the night.

"The rest of you stay here with me. After we dress the replacement guards and they take their stations, we'll need to deal with those going off shift."

Three minutes later the replacement guards were dressed.

"Now," Kasim said, "you watched what the others did, right?"

The men nodded vigorously.

"Just do the exact same thing."

"Do we all go out together?" one of the men asked.

"No," Kasim said, "the plan says the switch takes place one at a time. Starting at the northeast corner and moving counterclockwise."

The clock read 1:57.

"You're the first," Kasim said, motioning to one of the men. "We'll all follow and watch from a distance."

The first faux guard walked through the courtyard. Kasim and his men hid at the edge of the building closest to the Kaaba and watched. He approached the northeast corner.

* * *

SOMETIMES EVEN THE best-thought-out plans are just that—plans. This one, cobbled together in a rush and lacking the Corporation's usual finesse, was about to unravel like a cheap sweater. The guard Ralmein was due to relieve happened to also be his best friend. When someone else showed up instead, it raised more than concern. The real guard knew something was wrong.

"Who are you?" the guard said loudly in Arabic.

Kasim heard it and knew the problems were starting. The guard reached for a whistle on a chain around his neck. But before he could blow it the fake guard wrestled him to the ground.

"It's a free-for-all," Kasim yelled to his men. "Just don't let anyone escape."

KASIM, THE REMAINING three fake guards, and the four other men raced from their hiding spot and ran across to the Kaaba. They quickly subdued two more of the real guards but one managed to escape and ran toward the gate.

Kasim raced after him but the guard was fast. He had cleared the courtyard and was almost under the arch leading outside when one of the men looking for explosives stepped out of the shadows and clotheslined him with his arm.

The guard hit the stone flooring and was knocked out. A thin trickle of blood ran from the back of his head.

"Drag him over to the guard shack," Kasim said as he raced over, "and wrap his head."

The men grabbed the guard under his armpits and started dragging him away.

KASIM RACED BACK toward the Kaaba, made sure the fake guards were in place, then began to help remove the real ones to the guards' building. When that was finished he stared at his wristwatch. The time was 2:08 A.M. Kasim raced for the gate to meet the CIA agent. A minute later the agent pulled up in the Suburban. He climbed out and took a box containing the sniffers out and set it down, then removed Abraham's Stone—still in the box—off the rear seat.

"I'm Kasim, give me the stone."

The agent hesitated. "I'm a Muslim," Kasim said quickly. "Give me the stone."

The agent handed the box to Kasim.

"Take the sniffers inside and hand them to the first man you see," Kasim said. "Then get the hell out of here. This is not going as smoothly as we'd planned."

"Okay," the agent said.

Kasim, clutching the box to his waist, ran toward the entrance with the CIA agent right behind. Once inside the gate, the agent handed the box of sniffers to a man who raced over, then he stood for a second and watched as Kasim ran across the courtyard toward the curtain that hung over the Kaaba. Kasim was just slipping under the curtain when the agent turned and raced back to the Suburban.

A FEELING OF peace, tranquility and history flooded over Kasim as soon as he was under the curtain. For the briefest of moments he was filled with hope. A single spotlight cast a beam toward the silver frame where the Greenland meteorite was now displayed.

Kasim stepped closer, then set the box down and cut the tape on the seam with his knife. He reached up, wrested the Greenland meteorite from the frame and set it on the ground. Then he carefully lifted Abraham's Stone from the box.

Slowly and reverently he put it back in its rightful place.

Then Kasim stood back, made a quick prayer, and gathered up the Greenland meteorite, which he placed back in the box. Slipping back under the curtain, he carried the box over to the guard's building. The rest of the men were already searching the mosque with the sniffers when he reached for his phone.

SKUTTER SAT IN the passenger seat of the truck. The rest of his team sat in the rear. Just then the telephone rang.

"We're watching you from above," Hanley said. "There has been a slight change in plans—we don't want you to go to Jeddah. We're going to pull you out before that."

"Where do you want us to go?" Skutter asked.

On the *Oregon,* Hanley was watching the infrared satellite image of the truck racing south. "Go six point two miles farther south," Hanley said, "then pull over to the side of the road. There is a ship just offshore there now. They are sending in a shore boat to extract you from the cove there. Just get all your men aboard, Captain Skutter, and we'll take it from there."

"HOW MANY CHARGES had Kasim and his team found when he called?" Stone asked.

"Five," Hanley said.

"Well, sir, I'd order him to leave the rest to the Saudis. I just intercepted a call from one of the guard's wife. She was calling the local police to inquire why her husband was not home yet."

"It's two twenty-one!" Hanley thundered.

"Women," Stone said, "are impossible to live with sometimes."

Hanley reached for the phone.

Kasim was crouched down disabling a C-6 packet when his phone beeped.

"Get out now!" Hanley said.

"We haven't covered the—" Kasim started to say.

"I'm ordering an immediate evac," Hanley said. "This thing is blown. I have a truck in front to take you to your second escape hatch. Do you understand?"

"Got it, boss."

"Now, go."

JUST AS KASIM was placing the telephone back in his pocket, a CIA agent pulled up in front of the Great Mosque in a Ford extended-cab four-wheel-drive pickup truck. He nervously clutched the wheel as the seconds passed.

"That's it," Kasim shouted across the courtyard, "everyone to the gate."

The four fake guards started to sprint across the courtyard as the others that were searching the grounds began to appear from behind buildings and pillars. Kasim raced through the gate and approached the truck.

"We're coming out now," he said to the driver.

"Load them in back," the driver said, "and pull the tarp over them."

Kasim lowered the rear tailgate and the men started climbing inside. Kasim counted them off, ten, eleven, twelve, and thirteen. With him there were fourteen—one man was still inside. He raced for the gate and stared across the courtyard. The last man was sprinting across the distance.

"Sorry," the man said as he ran over, "I was in the middle of a disarm when you shouted."

Kasim grabbed him by the arm and pushed him along. "Get in the back," he yelled when they reached the truck.

Then Kasim pulled the tarp over his team and climbed in front with the driver.

"You know where we're going?" he asked as the driver slid the Ford into gear and hit the gas.

"Oh yeah," the driver said.

U.S. AIR FORCE Major Hamilton Reeves understood both the need for military decorum as well as having a loose hand with his crew. Hanging the radio microphone back in the holder, he turned to his copilot and flight engineer.

"You boys up for penetrating the airspace of a sovereign nation this evening?"

"I've got nothing going on," the copilot offered.

"All pays the same," the flight engineer noted.

"All right then," Reeves said, "let's go visit Saudi Arabia."

SKUTTER AND HIS team climbed out of the truck as Cabrillo ran across the beach.

"Leave the truck and come with us," Cabrillo said to the driver. "If your cover isn't blown, it soon will be."

The driver turned off the truck and climbed down.

Then the sixteen men and Cabrillo made their way to the shore boat. James was waiting and started to help the men aboard. Once they were all crowded into the boat, Cabrillo climbed in as James took his place behind the wheel.

"Mr. C.," he said, "this is very unsafe—I don't have enough life vests for all these men."

"I'll take full responsibility for this," Cabrillo said.

James started the engine and backed away from the beach. "Say it," he said to Cabrillo.

"Home, James," Cabrillo said loudly.

"WE HAD TO use the air force," Hanley said. "It got hairy at the Kaaba."

"Is Abraham's Stone back in place?" Overholt asked.

"That's done," Hanley said, "but they couldn't complete the explosives sweep."

"I'll call the president," Overholt said, "he has a State Department dinner at seven, but I can catch him now."

"If he calls the Saudi king and keeps him from firing on the C-17," Hanley said, "we're out of this clean."

TWO SAUDI POLICE cars, sirens blaring and lights flashing, passed next to the Ford pickup traveling in the opposite direction. They were two miles from the mosque, but Kasim and the driver had no doubt where they were headed.

The driver of the Ford was doing ninety miles an hour, and he stared at the GPS navigation system built into the dashboard. "It says less than a mile," he said. "Watch for a dirt road heading north."

Kasim stared through the gloom. He just caught sight of a road angling off as the driver slowed. "I got it," the driver said.

He stood on the brakes and the Ford slid on the sand atop the pavement. At the last instant, the driver spun the wheel and turned sideways. Then he pushed down on the gas again and raced up the sandy road. Reaching over to the dash, he pushed the button for four-wheel drive. On the left and right of the truck, hills started to grow taller as they raced down the wash. The driver stared down at the navigation system.

"Okay, we're going to do a right up here and tuck behind that hill."

A few minutes later the truck slid to a stop. The driver reached into the compartment between the seats and removed a spotlight and plugged it into the power outlet.

Then he flashed it across the land behind the hill.

There was a large expanse of flat packed sand one mile long and a half mile wide.

"Let me turn this around," the driver said, backing up and twisting the wheel until the cab was pointed to the west.

"You want me to have the men climb out?" Kasim asked.

"Nope," the driver said, "I'm driving right up into the back."

REEVES AND HIS crew flew the C-17A as low as safety would allow. Even so, the plane was picked up by the advanced Saudi radar they had purchased from the United States. Within ten minutes of entering Saudi airspace and just before they were due to land, the Saudi Royal Air Force had a pair of fighter jets off the ground from their base in Dhahran. They headed across the expanse of desert at Mach speed.

Hearing the approaching C-17A, the driver began to flash his lights. Reeves saw the lights, made one pass over, then turned and lined up to land.

"IT'S THE MIDDLE of the night," the aide to King Abdullah said.

"Listen," the president said, "I'm sending the secretary of state over there now—he'll be there by late morning tomorrow to explain what has happened. Right now, I have a United States Air Force plane inside your airspace. If this plane is fired upon, we will have no choice but to retaliate."

"I just don't—"

"Wake the king," the president said, "or there are going to be serious consequences."

A few minutes later a sleepy King Abdullah came on the line. Once the president explained, he reached for another telephone and called the head of his air force.

"Have them escort them out of the country but do not take hostile actions," he said in Arabic.

Returning to the open line with the president, he said, "Mr. President, if your secretary of state does not supply a proper answer to what is happening, your citizens will have a very cold winter."

"Once you hear what happened, I think we'll be good."

"I look forward to the meeting," King Abdullah said and disconnected.

REEVES LANDED THE C-17A, then turned around and faced the opposite direction.

"Drop the door," he said to the flight engineer.

The Ford pickup was already making its way across the sand as the door slowly lowered. When the truck pulled up, the door was fully extended down, making a ramp. Edging forward through the sand, the driver reached the end of the ramp. Then he gave it some gas and drove inside the cargo bay.

Opening the door, the driver ran forward to the cockpit. "We're in, sir," he said.

"Door up," Reeves said.

As the door was rising, Reeves ran the engines up to check the operation. Everything looked good, so as soon as the light on the control panel went green, indicating that the door was locked in place, he pushed the throttles forward and raced down the patch of sand.

Two minutes later they were airborne again.

"Ninety miles to the Red Sea," he shouted back to the rear, "five minutes or so."

"I have two fighter jets inbound," the copilot said.

"Prepare countermeasures," Reeves said.

But the jets never turned on their firing computers. They

just stayed off the wingtips until the C-17A passed over to water. Then they peeled away to head back to their base.

"WE'RE OUT OF Saudi airspace," Reeves yelled to the rear, "two hours to Cutter."

Kasim walked to the rear of the pickup and pulled back the tarp. "Okay, men," he said, "we did it—we're going back to Qatar."

The cheers filled the cargo area of the C-17A.

"Take over," Reeves said to the copilot.

Reeves walked back into the cargo area. "I would have brought you a cooler of beer but I understand you men don't drink. So I had the mess hall prepare a cooler of iced soda and some food in case we did have to come get you. There are some hamburgers, hot dogs, potato salad and such. It's been a few hours, but they packed it in those silver insulated bags so it should still be warm. Enjoy."

Reeves headed back to the cockpit.

"Okay, men," Kasim said, unzipping a silver padded bag, "dig in."

EPILOGUE

THREE HOURS BEFORE sunrise on January 10, U.S. military crews working with Saudi military and intelligence officials finished complete sweeps of all three mosques. Any explosives found were removed and destroyed, and the area was deemed safe for the hajj.

Saud Al-Sheik stared down at the courtyard as the last of the aging prayer rugs were being fitted into place. He wished he'd found the new ones but they'd disappeared into thin air—so he had the old ones dug out from storage and used again this year.

Behind the curtain surrounding the Kaaba, Abraham's Stone awaited the faithful.

At sunrise, a sea of white-robed pilgrims began to fill the holy spots.

The hajj would go off without a hitch.

January 10, 2006, dawned clear with a light wind blowing from the east and temperatures in the low seventies. Nearly a million pilgrims crowded into Medina, where they visited the tomb of Muhammad and then boarded the large open cars on the Hajaz Railway for the 280-mile trip to Mecca.

As the train drew nearer to the sacred city where the Kaaba was located, the pilgrims disrobed and dressed in aprons with pieces of cloth over their left shoulders. Once the train pulled to a stop, the first group climbed off and began walking toward the mosque. Once inside they began the Tawaf, or circumambulation. The pilgrims started to circle the Kaaba seven times in a counterclockwise direction then, when finished, entered the Kaaba to kiss the Sacred Stone of Abraham.

As the first group filtered out, thousands more were already entering the mosque.

During the next few days, the pilgrims would drink from Zamzam Spring, have a ceremony where they stoned the Devil, and take walks to the other sacred places nearby. Hundreds of thousands would do a route from the mosque containing the Kaaba to Mina, the Mount of Mercy, Mount Namira, Muzdalifah, and Arafat.

The areas around Mecca and Medina would swarm with white-robed pilgrims.

The days would be spent with prayer and meditation, contemplation, and the Koran. At the hajj, each person would find a meaning. And all would remember it the rest of their life.

Today was just another day of many, with thousands more to follow.

POSTSCRIPT

IN THE END it had all worked out. The poisoned prayer rugs were taken into the Indian Ocean and the containers dropped into a deep hole and depth-charged. Cabrillo, along with Skutter's and Colgan's teams, continued on the *Akbar* to Qatar, where they were greeted at the base in a lavish ceremony. Each of the thirty-seven men received one grade in rank and pay, with Skutter and Colgan being offered two. Skutter became a lieutenant colonel, but Colgan, offered a chance to become an officer, declined. He was happy with his current rank so he was given two years tacked onto his service time. The next day, Cabrillo, Kasim and Jones flew out in one of the Corporation's jets and met up with the *Oregon* in Barcelona.

The crew from Florida hired to deliver the *Akbar* to the shipyard in the Mediterranean were offered double pay to complete the journey. They arrived home two weeks later than they had planned, but their pockets were bulging with cash.

The only Saudi injured, the guard who had cracked his head when he fell trying to escape, suffered a few months of blurred vision but eventually recovered completely. In reward for his attempted bravery, King Abdullah retired him with a full pension.

Michelle Hunt was returned to California with apologies and instructions to never discuss the matter. She mourned the loss of Halifax Hickman, but in that she was alone.

The meteorite from Greenland was taken to the laboratory at Fort Detrick, where it is currently undergoing continued testing. Woody Campbell made it through his treatment program and has yet to take another drink. Elton John tells his friends about the concert on New Year's Eve, but few believe his account. Lababiti was tried in a secret court and sentenced to life in prison. A few weeks after returning from England with his MG TC, Billy Joe Shea got the largest order for drilling mud in his life.

The order was from a company drilling in Tibet.

And at a crowded shop in England, a man slowly rebuilt a Vincent Black Shadow.

And far out in the Atlantic Ocean, the *Oregon* steamed toward South America.